An Investigation of Local Color

by

Susan Maguire

The contents of this work, including, but not limited to, the accuracy of events, people, and places depicted; opinions expressed; permission to use previously published materials included; and any advice given or actions advocated are solely the responsibility of the author, who assumes all liability for said work and indemnifies the publisher against any claims stemming from publication of the work.

All Rights Reserved
Copyright © 2024 by Susan Maguire

No part of this book may be reproduced or transmitted, downloaded, distributed, reverse engineered, or stored in or introduced into any information storage and retrieval system, in any form or by any means, including photocopying and recording, whether electronic or mechanical, now known or hereinafter invented without permission in writing from the publisher.

Dorrance Publishing Co
585 Alpha Drive
Suite 103
Pittsburgh, PA 15238
Visit our website at www.dorrancebookstore.com

ISBN: 979-8-8912-7863-9
eISBN: 979-8-8912-7361-0

1

Vermont, the idyllic home of maple syrup, brightly colored autumn leaves, and beautiful snow-covered mountain peaks, of tree-lined dirt lanes, picturesque hill farms, and quaint village greens with their quaint village general stores. Vermont, where life's simple pleasures still exist, where hiking, fishing, and horseback riding take precedence over video games, fax machines, and three-story shopping malls. Vermont, where it is possible for even the most jaded New Jersey-ite to rent a bicycle and recapture his innocence by overreacting to the sight of a field of common black-and-white Jersey milk cows or to don a red wool jacket and tramp around in the woods in search of deer to blow away. Vermont, where crime is limited to the odd citizen thumbing his nose at the hunting regulations in order to jack a deer out of season or the infrequent fender-bender after a night of putting away too many Budweisers while telling tall hunting or fishing tales. All in all, Vermont seems an unlikely scene for cold-blooded murder. One tiny town with a population of fewer than six hundred, cows not included, seemed an even less likely place for murder, especially when one murder nearly became two murders, most foul.

Bill Dunfield was presently a very unhappy man. Once he had been a very clever man, but it had been a good eight years now since he had seen the last of that particular state. He had once been a machinist of such exceptional merit that he and a partner had operated a profitable business near a metropolitan area in Southern Connecticut.

Bill drove a Corvette or a Harley Davidson motorcycle in the summer and a Range Rover in the winter. He kept his wife and four children in a nice, if not luxurious, neighborhood, and if the wife was a little dumpy and plain with middle age, well, there was always some gal from one of the bars Bill and his partner frequented on the weekends who was willing to have him back to her apartment in exchange for dinner and a couple of drinks.

But all that was before son number two had brought home a tall, leggy blonde with hungry eyes and big ambitions just when Bill was in the midst of a frenzied midlife crisis and his wife was in the throes of menopause. Before Bill could say change of life, he was divorced, had three children who cast their lots with son number two and would have nothing to do with him, and his successful business belonged to his former partner and his former partner's new spouse, Bill's own menopausal ex-wife. Yet he still considered himself to have come out on top of the deal. He still had, after all, the leggy blonde. She wasn't exactly a beauty, strictly speaking, but Bill fancied that her height gave her elegance, and he admired elegance, especially since he was a short, plain-looking man himself and had never possessed elegance, except in the course of his imaginings. And besides that, she loved him, she really did. She even wanted to marry him, despite the fact that he was fifty-one and she was barely twenty-four. Of course, the idea appealed to him and helped sooth the wounds inflicted by his wife's throwing him over for his partner. And he was clever enough to have learned from the betrayal of his former wife and partner: He had the new Mrs. Bill Dunfield sign a prenuptial agreement, relinquishing her rights to any of his possessions should she ever wish to part company. That she signed, and so willingly, too, proved her love.

When the lovely, leggy Mrs. Dunfield came home from her secretarial job at the state offices six months later and suggested that they leave Connecticut with its horrible memories and stressful lifestyle for a more relaxing environment—"perhaps Vermont. Remember how much you enjoyed hunting up there, honeybun?"—it had seemed like a good idea. He had enjoyed Vermont, but not so much for the hunting as for the people. They were unsophisticated hicks, all of them. The women were frumpy, but fun, easy pickings for a man of his sophisticated background and skill at silver-tongued, if insincere, flattery. The men could be persuaded to buy a round of beer by merely thinking about it, and their farmy, outdoorsy demeanor would limit the amount of competition they would give him. Bill had only to do a lit-

An Investigation of Local Color

tle research in order to choose the place where, with his big-city ways and his elegant wife, he would be king of the hill.

Bill did an excellent job researching his new location. Benton Harbor was considered remote even by Vermont standards. Its population was 99% dairy farmers and their dependents. Bill was clever enough to choose one of the largest farmhouses in town surrounded by sixty acres of choice fields. The house sat high on a hill and had the advantage of being accessible by its own private, though town-maintained, road. It was an exclusive kingdom and easily purchased with cash when he and the blonde Mrs. Dunfield pooled their resources, most of which were his by virtue of the fact that he had been a member of the workforce for a good fifteen years before she was even born.

But the one thing that Bill neglected to research were Vermont's divorce laws. Before he could even utter a good, healthy "Aw, shit, not again!" he found himself divorced and in possession of only half of his kingdom by virtue of the state's 50/50 laws. Not only that, but because he had landed himself a well-paying job, by Vermont standards at least, and the now ex- Mrs. Dunfield had not, Bill found that he owed her money, and no small amount either. He was forced to sell his share of the sixty acres of fields in order to pay. She sold her share but kept the five acres directly across from the farmhouse on which to build herself a tidy little modular ranch house. With the money Bill was forced to pay her, she bought herself one of those cute little Morgan horses for which Vermont is so famous and, in the Vermont tradition, learned how to ride and drive the cute little buggy she bought to go along with it.

It wasn't that Bill specifically minded losing the blonde. It turned out that country life had agreed with her overmuch, and she was no longer the elegant creature for whom he had lost his wife and kids and business and that wonderful Corvette. In fact the span of her backside, or more specifically the span of her backside in relation to the backside of her horse while she was riding it down the road, was the talk of the village when there was nothing more exciting going on, which was most of the time. Bill did so dislike a fat woman. No, what he most minded losing was his little kingdom on the hill and the status he supposed it gave him with the local townsfolk. Now instead of his sixty prime acres of fields, there were three new houses, not counting that annoying modular right outside his front window.

And, as if building a house across from one's ex-husband wasn't perverted enough in itself, the house sat with its rear side toward the road facing Bill's house. No one, Bill included, was sure if the former Mrs. Dunfield had merely mis-instructed the crane operators who erected the modular or if a statement was being made concerning her former married state. In any case, it provided the town with much gossip during that March mud season, traditionally a slow time of year for exciting news in small-town Vermont. But though it might be unpleasant to wake every morning to the backside of someone else's house, Bill found that he at least didn't have to witness the parties that his wife hosted to attract available males, and some that were not too terribly available, throughout the following summer. Hearing them was enough to bring the ex-husband to near violence. That, and having the unsuspecting visitors use his front lawn for overflow parking.

But all that had happened seven years ago. Since then an uneasy truce had been established, due in large part to the arrival of outsiders on the hill and the somewhat vague idea that they must at least give the appearance of living side by side amicably in order not to be considered stupid. No one was terribly fooled, but except for the rare occasion when a newcomer arrived in town and the situation had to be explained all over again, accompanied by the ever-embellished running commentary and rude laughter, the Dunfields were largely considered old gossip.

That is until one night in the late fall, on the eve of the opening of deer-hunting season, to be exact.

Nick Strauss was roused from a sound sleep by the persistent ringing of the phone on his bedside table. With a quick glance at his glowing watch, he picked up the receiver on the fourth ring.

"What?" he snapped while visions of freaked-out drug addicts and mangled auto accident victims vied with each other for his attention.

An Investigation of Local Color

"Sorry to disturb your sleep, Detective Strauss," came the cheerful voice of the night dispatcher at the Fairview State Police Barracks, where Strauss was temporarily assigned. "But there has been a murder."

This last was announced as cheerfully as most Vermonters announce the arrival of the first sign of spring. Strauss shook his head in disbelief.

"This had better not be a joke," he growled into the receiver.

"No joke, Detective Strauss. There's been a murder in Benton Harbor, and the constable up there is asking for help."

"And he's sure it's a murder?" Strauss had heard plenty of stories of hunting eve rifle accidents. Too much beer, too many guns, too much enthusiasm. That sort of thing.

"Well, according to radio reports, they got a guy up there with a big knife sticking out of his chest. Sort of sounds like murder, doesn't it?" the dispatcher replied mildly.

"I'm on my way."

"Good deal, sir," the dispatcher said, sounding more like he wanted to say *Have fun, sir.* "And keep us informed."

"The radio ought to do that well enough, son," Strauss told him. He shook his head as he hung up the phone.

Well, the kid was young. Can't blame him for being enthusiastic. Night dispatchers in Vermont usually sent out calls for assistance for jackknifed trucks on one of the twisting backroads or for help for some farmhand who had too much to drink and took out his neighbor's mailbox. Very routine, very calm, very boring. That, after all, was the point, Strauss reflected as he pulled on his pants.

At age thirty-seven, Nick Strauss had spent the majority of his adult life working his way up through the Boston City Police Department. He had dealt with drug addicts, witnessed murders, and handled accident victims with all the aplomb of youth. But then his wife left him, and a month later his best friend and partner of ten years had been killed while they were making a drug bust. During the year that followed, Strauss went through three different partners. A brilliant police psychiatrist determined that he was suffering from some form of post-traumatic stress syndrome, which to Strauss translated along with the rest of the psycho-babble into the doctor thinking he was crazy. Strauss didn't agree, but he had to admit that roaring his objection to the woman doctor's diagnosis and throwing her notebook containing hefty documentation on him through a window and out into the street three stories below probably gave significant credence to her argument.

He didn't want to lose his job, and he had the good fortune to have a commander who didn't want to lose him. So that good man worked out a solution with the Vermont State Police where he had a cousin in some sort of administrative position. Strauss would take a leave of absence from the Boston PD for a year and work in Vermont, and in exchange the Boston PD would take on a young Vermonter as an apprentice and teach him the ropes of big-city detective work, skills that would surely prove useful later as more and more outsiders started to populate Vermont, bringing their crime statistics with them.

It had seemed like a good idea at the time, especially as the alternative had been returning to uniformed street work, and everyone knows from watching TV that no self-respecting detective wants to go back to directing traffic and checking parking meters after having achieved the status of detective. But two months into his assignment, Strauss was bored to death. He didn't do investigative work, he did policework. He had stopped counting the number of times he had been sent out to inspect the damage inflicted on some out-of-stater's car after they had collided with a deer. (Vermonters never reported such an incident; they merely hiked the deer up on the roof of their car and headed for home and the freezer.) But folks from New Jersey never wanted the deer, which was just as well as they weren't permitted by law to have it anyway. They just wanted a report to file with their insurance companies so that they could have the damage to their BMWs repaired. And they were always angry and offended, as though the poor creature had intentionally sabotaged their vacation plans by leaping out in front of the vehicle and getting itself killed.

Anyway, it wasn't the sort of work Strauss was used to, and he found it much more stifling than relaxing. Because his work had always been his life in Boston, he had very few friends there. But he had

An Investigation of Local Color

even fewer in Vermont. Two fewer, which meant he had none. That wouldn't have been so bad except that coming from the city and a sixty-hour-a-week job, he had never developed the skills necessary to entertain himself in the country. He neither hiked nor biked, nor did he want to. He didn't ski, which was almost a crime in some parts of the state, and he didn't deer hunt, which was practically against the law in the remaining parts of the state. All in all, Nick Strauss was ill equipped to survive in the state of Vermont.

So when he got the dispatcher's call on the eve of the opening of deer season, he found his interest was pricked for the first time since arriving in September. His enthusiasm quickly waned, however, when he got lost twice on the back roads of Benton Harbor. There were few road signs. Many of the roads, including the one Strauss needed, looked suspiciously like driveways or farm tracks. After ending up once at a dead end and another time climbing a steep drive to wind up in someone's barnyard, he managed to flag down a stray vehicle by turning on his flashers and pulling it over.

"Can you possibly tell me where Frampton Hill is?" Strauss growled as he approached the car.

The driver of the dilapidated car grinned up at him, reeking of alcohol. "Is that all you want, Officer?"

"That's all I want," Strauss sighed, completely out of patience. He felt sure that the only way he would get directions would be to ignore the driver's present drunken state.

The driver grinned some more, unable to believe his luck. "It's that second road back the way you just come."

Strauss glanced back into the darkness. He must have driven by it half a dozen times. "Don't you folks ever put up a road sign?"

"Why should we? We know where Frampton Hill is."

"Go on, get out of here before I arrest you," he snapped in reply.

"Thanks, Officer. You have a nice night now."

The driver stepped hard on his accelerator and spun mud all over Strauss' shoes. Strauss made a note, as he had at least ten times since coming to Vermont, to get some new footwear. He got back into his car and headed up the road.

A mile up a steep, rutted road he found his destination. It would have been difficult to miss as there were two ambulances, both with lights flashing, and two four-wheel-drive pickups with large tires and more flashing lights than Strauss had seen on most fire equipment. There were also several other assorted vehicles, most of the four-wheel-drive variety, parked in the yard. Strauss waded through the mud stirred up by the other tires and made his way up to a group of men who were standing around smoking and chatting. They looked up curiously at his arrival.

"Who's in charge here?" he asked.

"Who wants to know?" a burly man dressed in a fireman's coat and boots replied.

Strauss bit back the first retort that came to his lips. Instead, he pulled out his badges, both from the Vermont State Police and from the Boston PD, though he felt that the latter was the only thing that ever really gave him authority.

The big fellow peered at the badges for a moment. Then he whistled and turned to his pals.

"All the way from Boston! This must be really big. Wouldn't old Bill be pleased that he warranted such attention?"

The other men nodded. Most were dressed as if going to a fire, so Strauss deduced that the fire alarm had been sounded somewhere along the line.

"You want Constable Thibault," the helpful one went on. He pointed with his chin toward the upper regions of the house. "Upstairs, with the coroner."

"Thanks."

Strauss pulled open the back door. In the kitchen he passed the ambulance teams sitting at the table, their first-aid boxes, worthless at this point apparently, piled on the floor beside them. Strauss wondered why there were two groups since it would only require one ambulance to transport the body. One of the medics pointed the way to the stairs.

It was considerably less crowded in the upstairs bedroom. An old man stood over the body on the bed while a woman and a man wea-

An Investigation of Local Color

ring a jacket with a medical insignia looked on. Everyone looked up when Strauss tapped on the doorframe and came in.

He glanced quickly at the three and said, "I was told I would find the constable up here."

"That would be me," said the woman. She gave him a few seconds to digest that information, then she put out a hand and added, "Adrian Thibault. And you would be?"

"Nick Strauss." He pulled out his badges.

She looked carefully at both and then at him. He could see the question in her eyes, but she didn't ask. That was okay by him. She must have seen the question in his, too. They would just have to cross-examine each other later.

"This is Dr. Stanton, the medical examiner, and Ellis Smith, the head of emergency services for the area."

Nick recognized Smith from some of the emergency calls he had been on out on the highway. The doctor, on the other hand, was a new character. He was past being elderly and well on his way, Nick thought, to being senile. His gray hair stood on end, giving him a wild appearance that his thick glasses and slightly myopic gaze added to. Beneath his wool hunting coat and trousers, he still wore his pajamas and, beneath those, his long johns. He stuck out a hand for Strauss to shake.

"Yup, your man's dead, all right." The old man grinned as if enormously pleased to have been called from his bed in the middle of the night to make that earthshattering diagnosis.

Strauss noticed that he had forgotten to collect his teeth in his haste to get to the scene of the crime.

"See here, young man," he went on, drawing Strauss closer to the bed where the body lay. "Someone stuck this big knife in right here, and with some force, too. Nicked the aortic artery. That's why all the blood."

That was something of an understatement. Blood was all over the t-shirt of the deceased and on the bedclothes and even sprayed on the floor and the wall over the head of the bed. Strauss had a weakness when it came to the sight of blood. He swallowed hard and glanced up to see how the woman constable was taking it. She stared without expression at the body as if she had seen thousands in such a state, which seemed highly unlikely, all things considered.

"Well, I guess if we have a cause of death, we can let you take the body, Ellis," she commented to the ambulance chief. She glanced at Strauss. "Okay with you?"

"Who else has been in the room?"

"As far as I know, just the three of us."

"What about the crowd downstairs?"

"Nope. I kept everyone out. I don't know much about the handling of this sort of thing, but it seemed the wisest thing to do. You can take it from here. That's why I called the barracks."

"Fill me in on the deceased as much as you can." Strauss pulled a pad of paper and pen from his pocket and began to scribble.

"Bill Dunfield, fifty-nine next month. Moved here from Connecticut seven, eight years ago. Lived here alone. Worked at the tampon factory in Rutland on the 3-11 shift," Constable Thibault reported efficiently.

Strauss looked at the dead man on the bed. In his present state it was hard to tell if he looked his age. He looked to have been a slight man, and that was about as much as Strauss could deduce. He swallowed hard again and noticed the constable watching him closely.

"Who found the body?" he asked brusquely.

"I did."

"Care to elaborate?" Nick urged while he silently cursed the reluctance of the native Vermonter to be forthcoming.

"He didn't show up for work tonight. Apparently that is very unlike him, so when his supervisor couldn't reach him here he phoned a woman Bill sees occasionally, Martha Cutting. She came around to see if she could find him but got uneasy and called me. I roused Franklyn Birch to come along like he sometimes does if I get a big problem. He's the fire chief. He waited out in the yard with his boys while I let myself into the house."

"You have a key to the house?"

An Investigation of Local Color

"It wasn't locked, Mr. Strauss. Most folks around here don't lock their houses at night."

Ellis Smith cleared his throat in a less-than-subtle manner. "Ah...the body. May we take it now? It's getting late, and some of the crew were wanting to go out hunting first thing in the morning."

Constable Thibault looked to Strauss for permission. He nodded slightly.

"Go ahead, Ellis. Send away the Benton Harbor ambulance. There's nothing they can do here. Bring in one of your men and don't touch anything." She turned back to Strauss. "I've already sent for a fingerprint expert, but he has to come from Montpelier and won't be here until tomorrow morning."

Strauss regarded her with growing respect. She was admirably coolheaded and efficient, especially for someone who must surely have been roused in the dead of night to shocking circumstances. Strauss despised hysterical women in any circumstances, regardless of how shocking.

"Any clues at all?" he asked her.

"Someone very strong," Dr. Stanton put in from his position by the bed, where he was still gazing with what seemed like undue fascination at the knife that had been rudely inserted into the dead man's chest. "Had to have been someone with a lot of force behind him—or her—

to have broken through the chest wall like this. It looks as though that person may have had surprise on his side, but nevertheless, there had to have been some strength involved."

"Know this man at all?" Strauss asked the constable.

"All of Benton Harbor at least knows of him," she replied in her disconcertingly unelaborate way.

"Know of any enemies?"

Adrian Thibault nearly smiled. "Half the town. Probably half of his fellow employees as well. Who knows who might be down in Connecticut."

"Unpleasant sort of guy?"

"That's one word for it."

Smith and his partner had arrived back upstairs with their stretcher and, with gloved hands, began the business of wrapping the body into a bag for transport. The constable watched with the same dispassionate gaze she had had during the course of Strauss' involvement. Curious, he thought.

A sudden blood-chilling scream sounded below. Both law enforcers leapt with quick reflexes for the stairs.

"EEEeeeek! Let go of me! I have to see him! AAaaahhh! Bill, Bill! Let me see him!"

Strauss reached the bottom of the stairs first, followed closely by Adrian Thibault. A blonde woman of enormous proportions barged through the door into the kitchen, dragging the burly man in the fireman's boots and one of his fellows with her. She was screaming hysterically.

"Let me by!" she demanded, having shaken off the others and coming face to face with Strauss, who was a sizeable man in his own right.

"Ma'am, I think it would be better if you didn't go up right now."

"I don't give a damn what you think. Who the Hell do you think you are? Let me by, I said."

Strauss was never at his best with screaming women. Behind her, the burly man seemed to be having the same problem. He appeared to want to flatten the large woman and be done with it, but he looked to both Strauss and his constable for direction. Both reacted too slowly. Having already mowed over four men by sheer size alone, the raging blonde tried her hand with the latest human obstacle in her path. She shoved hard but couldn't squeeze past Strauss. She succeeded, however, in tossing him into Constable Thibault, and both of them sat down hard on the stairs, nearly in each other's laps.

"I can see you're in over your head on this one," Adrian said from her place on the floor. "Please, allow me."

She calmly got to her feet, stepped over Nick, drew back her arm, and smacked the big blonde soundly on the cheek.

"Bitch!" the large woman screamed.

An Investigation of Local Color

Strauss thought, upon careful consideration from where he still sat on the floor in utter amazement, that she seemed decidedly less hysterical than he had originally thought.

"How dare you strike me! I'll have your badge for that!"

"Do people really say that?" Strauss asked no one in particular.

"Apparently," the burly man replied.

"Calm down, Gwen," Adrian said firmly.

"Don't tell me what to do, you hick," Gwen answered nastily.

Strauss finally got to his feet and moved between the two women. "Look, ma'am. I don't think you want to do this right now."

The woman eyed him for a moment, assessing his position. Then her expression changed. "I just wanted to see Bill. They said he was dead. I just had to see for myself," she blubbered. Somehow she managed to fall short of sincerity.

"Why don't you tell me your name and we'll talk tomorrow, when you've had a chance to recover from your shock," Strauss said with his best attempt at sympathy.

Gwen gazed up at him with blue eyes that weren't quite tear-filled. She had bigger jowls than any woman he had ever met, Nick thought irrelevantly, and he was glad that he still stood two steps above her.

"I'm Gwenivere Dunfield. Will you really come to see me tomorrow?"

Strauss hid his surprise. "I will really come see you tomorrow."

"Why don't you and as many of your boys as necessary see Ms. Dunfield home, Franklyn," Adrian inserted.

The burly man grinned. He was obviously glad to be able to recover some of the self-esteem lost when he was run over by a woman. Given permission from an authority figure, he happily grabbed one of Gwenivere's arms and nodded for one of his boys to do the same. It was impossible for them to physically lift her off her feet, so they settled for dragging her across the floor.

"Take your hands off me. Bastards! Hicks! Lowlifes! Unhand me!"

Strauss' eyes widened. "Unhand me?" he repeated to his fellow law officer.

She shrugged.

"Dr. Stanton, would you have something in your bag in the way of a sedative?" Constable Thibault asked the ancient medical examiner, who had come to the top of the stairs to watch the excitement.

He rifled through his bag, throwing one or two items out on the floor before drawing out a small vial.

"I believe I have just the thing."

"Wonderful. Would you mind accompanying Ms. Dunfield?"

"It would be my pleasure." The old man grinned.

He took out a syringe that looked like it would be suitable for injecting a draft horse and inserted the contents of the vial. He recapped the needle and followed the others out, grinning in anticipation of his task.

"He certainly seems to be enjoying himself," Strauss commented.

"Old Doc Stanton loves a little excitement," Constable Thibault replied.

"Gwenivere Dunfield? Ex-wife?"

"That's correct." The constable followed the ambulance attendants as they wheeled the body out the back door and through the mud to their vehicle.

"Who called her?"

"No one needed to. She lives right over there."

Strauss followed the direction of Adrian's chin to the house directly across the road from the one they had just come out of. In the darkness all he could really see was the back of the house. He couldn't quite make out the layout of the property.

"Over there? You're kidding? How friendly were the two of them?"

"How friendly would you be with a woman who took you to the bank and then built a house right across the road to remind you every day of your life?"

"That good, huh?"

"That good."

"Would she kill him?"

Adrian shrugged. "I wouldn't really have thought so. They've lived like this for around seven years without doing each other in, so why now?"

"Any other likely suspects?"

An Investigation of Local Color

"I can think of at least a half-dozen people who really hate Bill Dunfield and with good reason, but I can't actually picture any of them killing him either. On the other hand, I have very little experience with murder and its motives. I take it that that is really more up your alley."

Strauss looked for signs that the lady constable was being snide. He couldn't tell. So far she had been as competent and efficient as any fulltime cop he had ever worked with. He liked the no-nonsense manner and look of her. She was tall and sturdy-looking but had none of the masculine affectations that many women trying to do a traditional man's job possessed. Her dark hair was shoulder length, and she had direct dark eyes. She was dressed in the inevitable wool coat that so many of the farmers around her sported and had tucked the bottoms of her jeans into heavy work boots to keep them out of the mud. Strauss made another mental note about his own shoes.

"I've got experience in that area," he agreed. He didn't bother to tell her that his actual area of expertise was vice and not murder.

"That's what they said when I called the State Police barracks. Well, good then. The forensics man will be here about 8, though I would count on 9 since he will probably get lost unless he is very lucky." Adrian glanced at her watch. "I'm due at work at 7 so I'll just leave you to it. Nice to have met you."

She started off in the direction of the parked trucks where Franklyn and his cronies were gathering, having apparently disposed of Ms. Dunfield.

"Wait!" Strauss called. He was torn between his reluctance to ask for help and his fear of letting this one link between him and the natives get away.

"Was there something more?" the constable asked when he didn't speak up.

"Look, I could really use some assistance on this case."

"You could? They said you were an expert. From down country. That usually means you know everything." She smiled slightly, and this time Strauss didn't miss the irony.

"I know almost everything," he corrected her. "But you know all these people. I think we could work together and find the murderer more quickly than either of us could alone. How about it?"

She shrugged. "If you want. But as I said, you are on your own for a while anyway. I'm a nurse at the ER in Rutland. My shift starts at 7, and I need to grab a little sleep before I go. Remember, forensics at 9. Ms. Dunfield is across the road, but she works 8 to 5. Martha Cutting, who originally called me, lives on Horton Road, across town. She doesn't work. Be careful of her, she's a little...different. If you get lost or stuck, stop in at the Hook, Line, and Sinker in the middle of town. Someone there will help you."

Strauss scribbled furiously on his notepad. He'd be damned if he'd ask her to repeat anything. He certainly wouldn't want to keep her from her sleep by bothering her with a murder. Silently he cursed all parttime cops, including self-possessed, sturdy-looking ones.

"Okay?"

"Got it."

"I get home about 4:30. Stop by around then and fill me in."

"Are you going to tell me how to get there or do I have to put my detecting skills to use?"

"Take the Stage Road south out of town to the first lefthand dirt road. Go two miles to the third dirt road. Go half a mile to the crossroads and turn right. My house is the second farmhouse on the right."

"Doesn't anyone around here believe in road signs?" Strauss asked for the second time that night.

"Why put up road signs? We all know where we are."

It seemed a standard Vermont reply.

2

As Constable Thibault had predicted, the forensics man from Montpelier got lost in pretty much the same way that Strauss had the previous night and arrived at the scene of the murder shortly after 9 o'clock. He was clearly not a Vermonter—he wore a vest and a bowtie and impractical shoes—but he had lived in his adopted state long enough to complain bitterly about being dragged out on an assignment on the first day of deer season. He hurried through his work and left, telling Strauss he would have fingerprint and blood test results in about a week.

How specific, Strauss thought silently. He thought about Boston's big-city crime lab and same-day results. No wonder crime didn't run rampant up here. It took too long to solve and presented no challenge to the perpetrator.

After the state man left, Strauss took his first really good look at the house across the road. He had not been mistaken the night before: The house, in fact, sat directly opposite the farmhouse where Bill Dunfield had resided, and it was facing backward to the road. Even the garage was facing backward so that the driveway made a U-turn from the road. Rubbish cans and the fuel tank sat outside the back door as they did at most houses. Strauss was puzzled by the location since there was no particular view in the opposite direction that would have caused a house to be placed in such a way. He walked around to the front door and knocked. After five minutes with no answer, he assumed that the hysterical Gwenivere Dunfield had recovered her wits sufficiently to get herself to work. 8-5, Adrian had said. Twice now she had been right on target.

Strauss consulted his notepad. Martha Cutting, the sometimes girlfriend, no address, and farther down the page, the Hook, Line, and Sinker. He wasn't sure what that was, but Adrian had said he could get help there. He had a fairly good idea where the center of Benton Harbor was, so he got into his state-issued cruiser and headed out.

Benton Harbor was the last Vermont town on Lake Champlain before that body of water turned into a swamp and then became a series of locks leading to the Hudson River. It was a farming community, and no one really remembered how it had gotten its name since the waters there were too murky and dull to harbor anything except a small fleet of rickety wooden fishing boats. There were, however, fish to be caught, although folks didn't come from miles around to do so. Mostly, the lake near Benton Harbor provided residents with fish and recreation when they couldn't indulge in their other favorite pastime, which was deer hunting or, to some of the less law-abiding, deer poaching.

Strauss had never had a reason to go into the town itself. It was inhabited by some six hundred people, mostly all farmers. The few who didn't farm were mostly flatlanders from down country who thought it would be charming to live in Vermont but had neglected to find out if it would be cost-effective as well. They found themselves working in Rutland or Fairview in an effort to pay for the lifestyle to which they had become accustomed in other, flatter parts of the country.

The center of town—a general store, the town clerk's office, a small elementary school, and the Hook, Line, and Sinker—was nowhere near the water, that area being prone to flooding during the spring rains, thereby greatly altering the shoreline and destroying the plans of any farmer who had hoped to sell his acreage as expensive lakefront property. A few had tried, but not many had gotten in on the deal before it had become obvious that there were problems with the idea. Even flatlanders are only so gullible.

Strauss had no problem identifying the Hook, Line, and Sinker. There were so many four-wheel-drive trucks parked outside the door of the town's only eating place that they overflowed into the street and limited driving to one lane only. Then there were the deer. Nearly every pickup bed or rooftop held a freshly killed deer, many of which

An Investigation of Local Color

were still dripping blood. Some of the rooftop variety dripped blood down the windshields of their conveyances. Some stared at him accusingly with their glassy eyes. All had antlers and the smooth coats of once-proud animals. As always when viewing dead bodies, Strauss swallowed hard. He swallowed again when he heard a roar of laughter from within what he now assumed from the smell of frying food and clank of cutlery was a restaurant. He pushed open the door and went in.

One or two men looked up at the sound of his arrival. Gradually, like a wave at a football stadium, silence swept over the room. With the exception of a girl burdened down by at least four plates of eggs, everyone in the room was male, and they were all staring at him with varying degrees of hostility. Strauss didn't wear a uniform, but he had a state trooper's parka and his hat held the state insignia, and it was on these rather than on him that attention focused. He felt as uncomfortable as he ever had investigating a crime in the wrong neighborhood in the city, and as threatened. It hadn't escaped him that every truck outside, besides carrying a deer, also held a clearly visible rifle in the back window. In addition, he caught sight of half a dozen lined up neatly against the bar on the far side of the room. He tried to smile confidently.

"Aww, he's all right, boys. That's the state feller investigating Dunfield's murder," a voice called. "Come on over here and sit." The burly fireman from last night waved to him from a corner table.

Immediately conversation resumed. Strauss heard the words "deer," "murder," and "kill" spoken frequently as he made his way to a long table occupied by Franklyn Birch and a dozen other supposed hunters. A little relaxing breakfast conversation, he guessed.

"Everyone's out hunting today," Birch said. "You caught yours yet?"

"Not yet." Strauss sat down at the end of the table.

"Dear, bring coffee for Mr....?"

"Strauss, Nick Strauss."

"Bring Nick some coffee. Want anything else? Harvey makes great eggs."

"No thanks." Nick watched one of Birch's pals stirring ketchup into his hashbrowns and remembered the deer blood. Quickly he looked up and caught Birch watching him. "Coffee's fine."

"The boys here thought you were the game warden or some feller come around to check on their kill. That's why the cold reception. You look too official."

Birch had a gravelly voice that made his words come out in a growl. That combined with his dark features and a peculiar manner he had of lowering his brow and staring intently gave him a sinister demeanor. Even the man's smile seemed menacing to Strauss and made him wonder if Franklyn Birch intended to be as helpful as he seemed.

"Is this place always so crowded?" Strauss asked in order to generate friendly conversation. "It looks like the whole town is here."

Someone jostled the waitress, a pretty blonde teenager with a few too many curves for her own good, and she slopped Strauss' coffee onto the table with an apologetic smile.

"Naw. This is just the half what caught their deer this morning. The other half is still out in the woods. They'll be in here tonight. They hope."

There was a roar over by the front door. "Yeah, the sucker thought he gotten away from me. Then KABOOM! Right through the heart from three hundred yards, I swear it! Biggest goddamned deer I ever shot. And right under Dalton's nose, too."

The speaker sharply elbowed his companion, causing that man to utter an obscene reply.

"So who killed Bill Dunfield?" asked the man sitting to Strauss' right.

His question immediately drew the attention of the rest of the diners at the table.

"Don't know. Who're you?"

"Donnie Thibault." The speaker stuck out his hand after wiping it on his wool hunting pants.

"The constable's—"

"Second cousin. Or something like that. You got any suspects?"

"One or two. Do you?"

An Investigation of Local Color

Donnie Thibault had an open, honest smile, and he used it often. "Hell, nearly everyone in town has wanted to kill Bill Dunfield at one time or another. I never thought anyone'd ever actually do it, though."

"Nobody liked the man, then?"

The other men at the table guffawed rudely.

"It's not like anyone really hated Dunfield," Birch put in.

"He was just so much smarter than the rest of us could keep up with," another speaker added. "I'm Leo Chandler. These are my brothers, Edmund and Kenyon."

Leo pointed out his brothers with his chin. The three Chandlers all bore a strong family resemblance. All had the ruddy complexion and work-worn, callused hands of men who worked outside, and all three could have been anywhere from forty-five to sixty-five years of age, with it being impossible to tell who was the eldest.

"What do you mean he was smarter?" Strauss asked, not missing the sarcasm in Leo's voice.

This drew laughter. Obviously the dead didn't generate a great deal of respect in this community.

"Bill Dunfield was one of those fellers who come up here from down country and think they're going to show us the best way to go about things. He thought we was all just a bunch of redneck hicks and dumb because of it," the brother who Strauss thought was Edmund explained. "I never could figure how he thought he was going to teach a bunch of farmers how to farm, what with him being a city boy and all, but he sure seemed to think he could."

"We kind of talked him out of that idea when it came time to butcher," Birch added with a laugh.

"What happened?" Strauss asked.

Everyone in hearing range laughed.

"We all try to help each other out at butchering time, so we were going to help Dunfield. 'Course we warn't going to do it for him. He thought he'd oversee, and we'd do the work," Leo Chandler explained. "But we told him the animal's owner does the killing. It's a tradition, see. Well, that feller's hands shook so much when he took aim at that steer that he missed and grazed the beast alongside the head. That bastard goes running around the barnyard mooing like the wounded sucker he is, and poor Dunfield really got to shaking and babbling like an idiot. We was laughing so hard, we could hardly yell at him to shoot the poor steer and put it out of its misery. None of us was going to do it, of course."

More laughter followed.

Birch took up the story. "'Course that crazy Dunfield starts shooting wildly, all panicked like. We all had to jump down off the fence there for fear he'd hit us instead of the steer. By this time that steer had bled itself everywhere, and I ended up shooting it just to get the job done and save the wrong person getting killed. After that Dunfield wasn't so sure he wanted to tell us our jobs. We were always happy to retell that story."

"So he lightened up after that?" Strauss prompted.

"Naw. He just turned his attention in a different direction. Like he give Junior there a shitload of trouble over the road up to his house."

By this time Strauss was learning to follow the inevitable point of the chin in the direction indicated. Junior sat opposite him at the far end of the table. He was an enormous man somewhere near middle age, though it was hard to be sure. The bulk of his midsection had swallowed his neck so it appeared that his head was sitting on his shoulders. Perched atop it all was a tiny hunting cap whose size further accentuated the size of the wearer. His expression as he was brought into the conversation was fierce and unsmiling.

"Junior...?"

"Junior Thibault, sir," he said politely, belying the ferocity of his looks. And before Strauss could ask, "Third cousin. Or something. I'm the road manager for Benton Harbor."

"And Dunfield gave you trouble?"

"Manner of speaking. He'd get to calling after every rainstorm in the spring and want me to bring the grader up to do his road. In the winter he'd call every time a snowflake hit the ground. He'd say he couldn't get out to work. I'd keep on explaining that we had to plow out the milk runs first, you know, roads where the dairy farms are. There ain't no farms up on Frampton Hill," he stopped to explain.

An Investigation of Local Color

"Then, when the ex-missus built her own house, it was like a competition to see which of them could call me first. Regular pains in the ass, they were."

The big man shook his head. He looked angry even at the memory, but then again Junior Thibault was an angry-looking man in general.

"Made you mad, did it?" Strauss asked.

"Not mad enough to kill him. It was a lot easier and more legal to just let him get snowed in." Juniorr. grinned, displaying several gaps in his teeth. "I left him to get snowed on for twenty-four hours once. I just couldn't seem to get up there before then," he said in a tone that clearly indicated that he could have. "'Course now there are other folks up there so I try to do as good a job as I can."

"Was he still calling you?"

"Just last week when we got that spell of freezing rain. He was calling for some sand, but like I said, the milk runs are always the first, and there ain't nothing ever going to change that short of all the cows leaving town."

"Nobody liked the man much, Strauss," Franklyn Birch interrupted. "But warn't nobody here going to kill him neither. That just ain't our way. If you need a suspect, you'd best look to that ex-wife, though I got to admit, if one of them was going to kill the other, I'd a thought it'd be the other way around."

"I'm checking into that," Strauss said. He was fairly sure his new friends would become very tightlipped if they thought that they or, as it was turning out, their relatives, were suspects. "Where would I find a woman named Martha Cutting?"

"Crazy Martha?" Birch grinned. "Nice lady. Just crazy. She lives across the main road...."

Shit, Nick thought, grabbing for his pad and pencil and scribbling rapidly as Birch talked. *Here we go again.*

He stood up, shoved the paper into his pocket, and reached for his change.

"Naw, you hang on to your money. We got your coffee this time," Birch said as he laid some of his own change next to Strauss' empty cup. Clearly, he was the unofficial leader of the group.

"Thanks. And thanks for the help."

"Hey, Strauss!" Birch called when he was halfway to the door. "You hunt?"

Strauss was aware of the deafening silence as every ear of every deer hunter in the room awaited his reply.

"Uh, no. Never have."

"Well, you want to learn, give me a call. I'd be glad to take you out. Best time you'll ever have. Relaxing, too, after working all week," Birch offered politely with his peculiar smile.

"I'll keep that in mind." He tried smiling at all the weathered, outdoorsy faces that had blown away deer that morning and loved it. They all grinned back, but he wasn't really sure he understood why. Outside, he stared back at all the lifeless eyes staring at him. Relaxing?!

He swallowed and got into his cruiser. As he turned the key, he glanced up at the window of the restaurant and saw at least two dozen faces looking back.

Martha was the last of the ten children born to Henry and Edna Cutting, poor farmers even in the better days of farming. Henry's death by drowning while ice fishing on the lake during early April, when the ice was just beginning to break up, had also caused the breakup of the farm, which most of the children had left already since it had always proved unprofitable. The entire family had immigrated to Rutland, Burlington, or the cities in Southern New England where, after years of hardship on the farm, they were all doing reasonably well, if not actually enjoying themselves. The Cuttings had never been the sort of people who enjoyed themselves.

All except Martha. At thirty years old, she was idealistic and eccentric. She lived in a small rundown tenant house within sight of the old farm and, over the years, had come up with several schemes to try to make a fortune to buy back her family heritage, none of which succeeded enough to even pay for themselves. Nevertheless, she refused to lose her optimism or her overall, some would say insane, good humor.

Strauss found Martha's house mainly by chance. Following Birch's instructions got him into the general area, but it was his own idea of

An Investigation of Local Color

a crazy person's domain that told him he had, in fact, reached his destination. He had been about to stop at the next farm to ask again for directions when he came across a shack of weather-worn clapboards. In spite of its general lack of paint, the battered shutters were freshly painted bright purple to match the color on the falling-down picket fence in front of the property. Inside the fence was the remains of last summer's garden and a variety of animal pens, all of which had been vacated by their former tenants. Strauss got out and made his way through the mud in the yard to the front door.

"Martha Cutting?" he asked the woman who answered his knock.

"I'm Martha."

Based on the limited information he had so far, Strauss didn't have any doubts on that point. The woman in the doorway had unruly, flyaway hair that she had unsuccessfully attempted to contain with a rubber band. Both her long wool skirt and heavy sweater had seen better days, and in spite of the cold weather outside and the plain wood floors inside Martha's feet were bare. Yet she was much younger than Strauss had supposed she would be. He hadn't expected her to be pretty either, though her appearance was tempered by the strange look in her eyes. Strauss wouldn't have said it was insanity, but it was definitely strange.

"I'm sorry to bother you, ma'am, but may I come in and talk to you?"

Martha smiled as though she was delighted to have a visitor and opened the door further.

"You're here about the murder," she said when he had shut the door behind him and introduced himself.

The kitchen-living area was cramped and inhabited, not just by Martha but also by an ancient unkempt dog who dozed in front of the stove and didn't bother to look up at his arrival, and a few cats who lounged on the limited counterspace, alongside an assortment of baking utensils.

"Yes. You called Constable Thibault last night," Strauss began with an effort not to sound distracted. "What made you do that?"

"Let's see, whatever did I tell Adrian? I'd better get my story straight, hadn't I?" She smiled engagingly at his wrinkled brow. "Would you like a cup of tea?"

Strauss didn't really think he did, under the circumstances, but Martha hadn't waited for a reply. She turned to the woodstove at the center of the room and took a kettle off and poured water into two prearranged cups. She strained some tea leaves off and handed a cup to Strauss.

"Let's see. Bill's supervisor at the tampon factory called me because Bill hadn't showed for work. I told him I'd go around to his house and see if I could turn him up."

Strauss took a cautious sip of the steaming tea. It wasn't too bad. He peered into the cup, trying to determine its contents.

"Do you like my tea?" Martha asked. "I'm an herbalist, among other things. I've read and practiced extensively with all sorts of medicines and cures and poisons. For varmints, of course."

She laughed delightedly when Strauss took another, more startled look into his cup.

"You needn't worry, Nick," she said familiarly. "I try to make a living with my herbs. I don't generally try to kill people with them, though I suppose it would be a useful skill."

"The tea is very good," Strauss replied. With care he set his cup on the floor beside his chair. "Did you go into the Dunfield house?"

"No, I did not. As I told Adrian, I got nervous. Something seemed sinister, and I left immediately."

"Sinister? What do you mean?"

Martha shrugged. "I can't say exactly. I have a sense about these things. I always have had, and I am rarely, rarely wrong. So I got out of there in a hurry."

Before he could ask her to elaborate on her sixth sense, a prodigious squealing started in the house's only other room. Strauss jumped to his feet. The noise sounded suspiciously like a woman being knifed. Martha gave another delighted laugh and disappeared through the batik curtain separating the two rooms. She came back with a pig in her arms, a pig squealing wildly.

An Investigation of Local Color

"This is Boris. Isn't he beautiful?"

Strauss didn't reply over the din. He merely stared. He had never in his life seen anyone hold a pig and couldn't imagine why anyone would especially want to. Martha set the pig on the floor and it ran, or whatever it is pigs do, to Strauss.

"What is it?" he asked doubtfully, having decided after all that it couldn't possibly be a pig. People didn't carry pigs around, much less set them loose in their homes.

"It's a Vietnamese potbellied pig. They are all the latest rage in pets. I intend to breed them and make a living selling them." She disappeared through the curtain again and emerged with another pig. "This is Esmeralda. She is going to have piglets any day now. I think she must have gotten a trifle testy with Boris just now to make him squeal like that."

Esmeralda considered the police detective through squinted eyes and promptly dumped on the floor. Martha ignored both the mess and the further activities of the pigs as she sat and took another sip of her tea. Strauss struggled to follow suit.

"How long had you been seeing Bill Dunfield?"

"Off and on ever since he divorced Queen Gwenivere. Bill liked to think of himself as a ladies' man, so any time he could pick up a new conquest he did. But women tire easily of him, and he of them."

"But not you?"

Martha shrugged. "Oh, I tired of him all the time."

"But you kept seeing him?"

"Can I be honest with you, Nick? You look like a man I can be honest with."

"I wish you would be." Strauss pulled the toe of his shoes back, as one of the pigs seemed to be overly interested in it.

"You don't much like animals, do you?"

"They're alright."

But Martha wasn't fooled, he knew. She wasn't that crazy.

"You were going to tell you why you were seeing Bill Dunfield," he reminded her.

"Oh, yes. It was the farm."

"The farm? I don't understand."

"No, you wouldn't. No one does who hasn't been a farmer. Bill had that beautiful farmhouse. God, I love that house. I have ever since I was a child. I stayed with Bill for the farm, Nick. Well, it's not much of a farm anymore, but I'd have settled for the house."

Martha smiled at his still-baffled expression. She truly had an unusual beauty.

"If I had hung around long enough, Bill would have ended up with me. He liked a pretty woman, did Bill, and at his age he was running out of women who were very interested in him. Besides, the last two women he slept with got him into a lot of trouble."

"What sort of trouble?"

"Well, they both had husbands, for one thing. Husband number one beat the little rodent black and blue. Husband number two trashed that beautiful house. He went in one night while Bill was at work, plugged the sinks, upstairs and down, and turned on the taps. Water made a mess of everything. It was quite expensive to fix because the insurance company, under the circumstances, didn't want anything to do with it."

A scratching sound distracted Martha. She watched as one of the cats poked through the litter box in search of just the right spot for its purpose. After the animal was done, she went to the counter and took some herbs from a pot and sprinkled them over the box.

"I had this idea for herb-scented litter, all natural, you see, so it wouldn't be in any way harmful to the animals. But when I tried to sell it to the Agricultural Store, they said it had already been done. And very unpleasant they were, as well. They wouldn't even give my litter a try."

"I'm sorry about that," Strauss said. Although he felt more incredulous than sorry, he felt that would be the wrong thing to say. "So you dated Bill because you thought he would eventually marry you, and you could have the house?"

"That is more or less correct."

"And did he ever talk as though that were a possibility?"

Martha shook her head. "Not really. But I know about these things. He was running out of options. And besides that, it would have made Gwenivere furious. Bill would have loved that. He loved dangling me under her nose, especially after she got too fat to attract men anymore. He laughed about how angry she would be if he married again. I often thought he might marry me just to make her mad."

"You don't like her, then?"

"No. She's a very stupid woman. But then, Bill was a very stupid man."

"If you will forgive me for saying so, Ms. Cutting...."

"Oh, please call me Martha. Everyone does. Actually, everyone calls me Crazy Martha, even though I'm not crazy."

"Well, Martha, you don't seem particularly upset by Bill's death."

"I'm not. I'm only sorry that he didn't leave me the house before he got himself knifed," she replied very matter-of-factly.

"But you didn't do it?"

Martha shook her head. "Gwenivere might have. She certainly hated him. You might also talk to Milly Boyce, who lives in the next house up the road. She might have a reason."

"What reason would she have?"

Martha shrugged. "Ask her."

"I'll do that. Thank you for your time, Martha, and for the tea." Strauss got to his feet, stepped over a couple of cats and made his way to the door.

When he had carefully picked his way to the car, having noticed along the way that what he had thought was mud on the way to the house was, in fact, a combination of that and other things as well, Martha called out to him.

"It couldn't have been me, you know. I'd have poisoned him."

She laughed and closed the door before he had a chance to hide his amazement.

Strauss scribbled a couple of notes on his pad as soon as he got into the cruiser.

Glancing at his watch, he saw he had almost two hours before Adrian would be home for their meeting. Just enough time to swing back through Fairview and get some new shoes. The ones he had on were already wet from his trips down muddy walks at both Martha's and the Hook.

Fairview wasn't a large town. Besides the State Police barracks there was only a handful of small stores, a Grand Union, a feed mill and two small restaurant/bars along the lines of the Hook, Line, and Sinker. Strauss had tried these when he had first arrived in Vermont, not being the greatest cook, but he had found that the stares of the locals became disconcerting over the course of the meal, and he learned to either cook, drive to Rutland, or do without.

Strauss drove now to the sporting goods store on the main street of town. Like all the other stores it was small, but as soon as he walked in the door Strauss could see that no inch of space had been wasted. All the sporting goods required by the regional high school, as well as the jerseys and t-shirts worn by fans, were stocked along one wall in an orderly, if crowded, manner. The opposite wall held every manner of fishing items, both for ice fishing and open water and brook fishing. Numerous rods and reels were lined up like so many soldiers. Their inevitable Vermont counterparts—hunting rifles—were lined up similarly along the back wall with all the ammunition and accouterments of the deer and game hunters. Before examining the shoe department, Strauss idly sorted through the weapons. It amazed him that any civilian with relatively no weapons training could be turned loose in the woods with some of the firepower he was now looking at. No wonder he heard stories of men accidently shooting each other, having mistaken their fellow man for a deer. They were, after all, so similar in appearance. He ran his finger over the barrel of a 30.06 with a large scope. It was a beautiful thing, if one didn't think too carefully about the results of its work. Without warning, a picture of the bloody, sightless deer popped into Strauss' head. He turned back to the shoes.

"Pretty fancy rifle, hey, hotshot."

Strauss nearly collided with fellow Vermont trooper Gary Shubert. There were other men at the barracks that he could either take or leave, mostly leave, if he were honest, but Gary Shubert he truly disliked and had immediately on meeting him. Gary was a heavy man about five or six years younger than Strauss. He had small eyes that now reminded Strauss of Martha Cutting's potbellied pigs. Come to think of it, Gary rather had the same stomach as well. One of the younger troopers had told him that Shubert had grown up in Fairview as the school bully, and it was a job he apparently intended to keep as he moved into the ranks of the State Police. He enjoyed the power that the law gave him and wasn't, in fact, a bad patrolman, even if he tended to be a little too strong-armed and a lot stupid. He hated outsiders, outsiders to him being anyone who wasn't born and raised in Vermont. It was a feeling shared by many natives, so it didn't tend to get Shubert into much trouble except when he was forced to deal with those superiors and fellow officers who had the misfortune to be born outside the state.

Shubert had a particular hatred for Nick Strauss. Strauss was a big-city detective with more life experience than the normal cop in Vermont will ever see unless he watches a lot of TV. Because he wasn't privy to the reasons for Nick's temporary assignment to the barracks, Shubert assumed that it was for the purpose of showing Vermont's finest how to do their jobs. It was an idea that particularly grated on him, and it took all of two seconds upon meeting the younger man to understand that Shubert intended to make his life miserable.

"You buying a deer rifle?" Shubert inquired, pointing his chin in the direction of the 30.06.

"No, just looking."

"What do you hunt with now?"

"Don't hunt."

Trooper Shubert grinned. "You don't hunt? You mean a weapons expert such as yourself doesn't know how to hunt?"

"That's right."

Strauss moved off toward the boot section and looked over the choices. Shubert picked up a few boxes of ammunition and rejoined him.

"I guess a city boy such as yourself never would have learned much about the woods," he prodded.

"I guess you're right," Strauss affirmed, picking up a work boot that looked as if it might bear up well in the mud of Benton Harbor's roads.

"Hell, you city boys don't even know what to put on your feet, do you, hotshot?"

Shubert looked down at Strauss' sodden street shoes. Besides being wet and muddy, Strauss was fairly sure they were also bearing something foreign from Martha Cutting's yard. He picked up a foot and examined the bottom of his shoe.

"I guess we don't at that," he agreed. He grinned at the other man. "These didn't work too well last night in Benton Harbor."

Trooper Shubert's eyes narrowed angrily if, that is, they could get narrower. "So you got assigned the big murder, huh? Did you solve it yet?"

"Nope."

Shubert raised his eyebrows in mock surprise. "No kidding? Big-city crime stopper, and you haven't made an arrest yet. What are you waiting for? Isn't that why you came to Vermont? To show us woodchucks how it's done in the big city?"

Strauss grinned at the other man even though he was far from amused. "You watch too much TV, Shubert. You've got the wrong idea. We big-city boys just sit around on our hands and wait for the murderer to confess. It's a little known fact, and one that doesn't make for very dramatic television, but there you have it."

The younger man looked at him uncertainly. His doughy face flushed slightly, though Strauss couldn't tell if it was because he believed what he had just been told or if he resented being made fun of.

Strauss laughed. "Don't think too hard about it, Shubert. Something will short out up there."

Shubert stood and smiled down at Strauss. "You'll find out soon enough that you city dicks don't have all the answers. Then you'll either come running for help or the chief will smarten up and put a real man on it. 'Course you can always get help from that nice lady constable who still hasn't realized that she was voted in as a joke. She could probably be real useful to you. Real useful. Was a time when

An Investigation of Local Color

she was real fond of men from down country. 'Course now even Ms. Constable knows what a joke they are. See you around, hotshot."

"Yeah, later, Shubert. I'll give you a ring if I need your help, but don't wait by the phone."

Strauss saw the other man's shoulders tighten in annoyance, but he kept on his track out the door. He picked up several different boots and shoes in an effort to determine which would be the most suitable, and better yet, which would make him appear least like a city boy. Folks around here seemed to associate the city with incompetence for reasons that Strauss couldn't figure.

"May I help you, sir?"

A small man dressed in pressed khakis and a flannel shirt appeared beside him. Strauss looked down at his shoes, a pair of worn light-colored work boots.

"I want to buy some boots."

"Are you going to be hunting?"

Strauss had the sudden urge to reach out and strangle the man. Didn't anyone around here think of anything else besides wiping out the deer population? As there was nothing convenient to throw through a window, he satisfied himself with answering through clenched teeth.

"I do not hunt. I just want something that will hold up in all the possible conditions Vermont is likely to subject me to in the next six months. I'm doing some work out in the country around Benton Harbor."

"Ah." The little man nodded knowingly. "You're investigating the murder."

"Yes," Strauss admitted. He had no idea how the man deduced that fact from the information he had just been given.

"Well, this is a nice boot." The salesman held up a pair similar to the ones he had on himself. "Comfortable to wear all day, fairly dry in the rain and snow as long as you don't overdo it. Or we have these here, which hold up better in your average barnyard conditions. In other words, cow shit doesn't rot the stitching. I sell a lot of these to farmers. Or I do keep a few pairs of these around." He held up a pair of boots that looked to be straight out of an L.L. Bean catalogue. "The tourists really like these. It makes them feel like real Vermonters. I've never been sure why. I don't recommend them myself because they fall apart more easily, and your feet sweat badly if you wear them for any length of time. I just hate it when that happens."

Strauss wordlessly selected the first pair and tried them on.

"Good choice, sir," the salesman beamed at either his good sense or the fact that he proved not to be a tourist. Sometimes even with cops it was hard to tell.

"I'll wear them now," Strauss told the man.

"Maybe you'd like me to just toss these out?" The sporting goods man held up one of the old shoes with a look of distaste. He didn't appear to be a man who would be bothered by whatever had come in from Martha Cutting's yard, so Strauss had to assume the disgust was accorded the shoes themselves.

"If you would," he agreed. Personally, he thought the shoes had some life in them yet, but he had to face the fact that no one around here was going to let him get away with wearing them. He paid for his new boots and admired the comfort of them as he went out to the cruiser.

A glance at his watch told him he would have just enough time, allowing for the inevitable loss of direction on the back roads, to make it to Adrian's for the appointed time.

Adrian Thibault had lived in Benton Harbor all of her thirty-three years. She was a late-in-life blessing to Harvey and Audrey Thibault, who had tried for nearly twenty-five years to produce a family and had given up all hope when Adrian was finally and unexpectedly conceived. Unfortunately, her birth caused extensive health problems for Audrey, who died two years later, leaving Harvey grief-stricken and in command of a small, willful child. With the help of numerous brothers and sisters and various cousins and other extended family members, all of whom apparently had no trouble reproducing, he managed the task ably and, many would say, produced better results than many younger two-parent families. For Adrian was bright, independent and outspoken without being offensive. She knew how to

An Investigation of Local Color

work hard, both at school and on her father's dairy farm, and could keep up with any of her male cousins in the woods or out in the hay fields. She remained devoted to her father, going against his will only once in her life, until his death three years earlier, and his contemporaries loved her for it since it was a time when fewer and fewer young people were respectful of their elders.

Adrian had only made one miscue in her life. While attending nursing school at nearby Castleton State, she had met and foolishly fallen for a tall, rakish young man from Connecticut who was majoring in some sort of business administration. After a flurry of exciting events, which included ski trips in Northern Vermont and sunny vacations in Florida for spring break, Adrian decided to quit school a year short of graduation and marry this Brian Borden, who was that year receiving his diploma. Everyone assumed that she would, by marriage, become a flatlander, returning to Vermont only to ski and take pictures of the trees from a Volvo during foliage, and for a while things went in just that way. But two years into the marriage, the Bordens reappeared in Benton Harbor, driving a Volvo, in fact, and moved into the old farm. The story was that Adrian had tired of life down country and worried about her father alone in Vermont. For his part, Brian had determined that there was a better life to be had in Vermont away from the perils of big industry run primarily by his family. He was determined to learn to milk Harvey's cows with the idea that the Bordens could take over the farm when that man wanted to retire. The private account, which didn't stay private very long in a town the size of Benton Harbor, was that Brian had just the littlest bit of a drinking problem of which Adrian had been blissfully unaware until after the marriage. It was suggested by his CEO father that Brian take himself away for a couple of years for the purpose of drying out if he wished to have any future with the family business. Cows seemed like just the thing to make him relax and achieve that goal.

Brian Borden, however, hated physical labor. He hated cows. He hated Benton Harbor. Pretty soon he even started to hate his wife. And the only cure for his problem was to drink. Harvey Thibault wanted to throw him out, especially when Adrian appeared at breakfast one morning with a suspicious bruise on her cheek, but she was one to accept her mistakes and try to make the best of them and wouldn't allow it. Mercifully for all involved, Borden was kicked in the head by a cow. No one could quite explain how it happened since he had never done any of the milking or handling of the cows and had been in the barn alone at the time, but no one wanted to question too closely what seemed to the townsfolk to be a blessing for the Harvey Thibaults.

Adrian returned to school to finish her nursing degree and wisely avoided young men from "away." Harvey returned to a quieter life at the farm. And the town, who chalked the whole experience up to one of those things that young people sometimes get themselves into when they go off to college, forgave Adrian for what they considered to be the only unintelligent thing she ever did in her life.

Strauss found the Thibault farm after only two wrong turns. He was getting better at this, he thought. After knocking on the front door, he peeked through the window to see the constable coming down the stairs pulling a sweater over her head.

"You found it," she said as she pulled the door open.

"Drove right to it," Strauss replied. He didn't think she needed to sound so surprised.

"Come into the kitchen, and I'll give you a cup of coffee. Nice shoes, by the way."

Adrian turned away but not before he caught the trace of a smile.

"They come highly recommended."

"Do they? By whom?" Adrian nodded to a chair by the table and put a cup of coffee in front of it.

"The man down at the sporting store in Fairview. He threw my old ones away."

"I shouldn't wonder."

Strauss picked up a foot and examined his new purchase. "I thought they would make me look less conspicuous."

"If you want to look less conspicuous, Mr. Strauss, it might help if you walked around someone's barnyard a time or two."

An Investigation of Local Color

Adrian smiled, but Strauss couldn't tell if her suggestion was meant as advice on breaking in new shoes or breaking in city cops.

"If we are to be partners, you may as well call me Nick."

"I don't know about the partner thing. This particular crime is a bit above my head. But I'll help you where I can. And you can call me Adrian. What did you turn up today?"

Strauss scratched his head. "Fingerprints won't be available for another week. You probably knew that already?"

"Not really. I never had a crime here in Benton Harbor that required fingerprinting beyond what they do at the station."

"I met with the boys down at the Hook, Line, and Sinker for brunch. They bought me coffee and offered to teach me how to hunt."

"Did they give you any useful information?"

He shrugged. "Mostly they told me that Bill Dunfield was not a very likeable fellow and that lots of people would have liked to do him in, but none of them would have actually committed the crime. That, and that you are related to nearly the whole town through a series of second, third, and fourth cousins, no one is quite sure of the number."

"Well, at least they weren't holding back secrets." Adrian smiled.

"Weren't they?"

"People around here are wary of outsiders, Nick. You are a detective investigating a murder, and for all anyone knows they might all be suspects. We don't have murders around here. They will all be very careful for fear that a misplaced word will point a finger at one of their friends or at them. Personally, I don't think your murder suspect is going to be found at the Hook, but the information you need to find that suspect might very well be."

"Meaning?"

"Meaning it's a good place to listen to the people who might know something or have heard something that might be helpful to you. Franklyn Birch is a good man. As the fire chief and selectman, he is the unofficial leader of the group that gathers down there every morning for coffee. Bill Dunfield used to stop in then, too, from time to time. The guys might not have liked him very well, but they did tolerate him and more than one of them must have their suspicions."

Strauss took a sip of coffee. "What about you? Do you have any suspicions?"

Without bothering to answer, Adrian asked, "Did you talk to Martha Cutting?"

"Yes. Interesting woman. Did you know she has pigs in the house?"

Adrian just looked at him. Her face registered no surprise at his revelation, as though everyone had a pig running around in the house.

"Pigs," he repeated in case she hadn't understood. "Two of them, in the house."

The constable nodded her understanding of the subject at hand. "1 didn't realize that," she replied. "But it sounds like something Martha might have. Could she help at all?"

"She seemed to think Gwenivere was the most likely candidate, but Milly Boyce up the road might have a motive. She declined to tell me what that motive might be. She informed me that she didn't mind all that much if someone wanted to do Dunfield in, but it couldn't have been her because she would have chosen to poison the guy."

Adrian laughed at that. "Martha's quite handy with the potions," she said in answer to Strauss' frown.

"So she says. It seems odd that she had a premonition of something being wrong and called you way out there based on just a feeling."

The constable smiled again, and this time Strauss was annoyed to see that she was laughing at him.

"Martha's always had premonitions," she assured him.

Well, that explains just about everything, Strauss thought irritably. He remembered Franklyn Birch insisting in his gruff voice that nobody from here would kill Dunfield. Maybe Adrian had the same opinion.

"The hysterical Ms. Dunfield must have pulled herself together and gone to work," Strauss said with a glance at his watch. "I was planning on going over there now. Anything you can tell me about her?"

An Investigation of Local Color

"She is about twenty-five years younger than her ex-husband. They came here together from Connecticut and shortly afterward got divorced. Then she built the house across the road. Apparently, she doesn't think highly of us locals, judging by her talk last night and by the fact that she has no contact with anyone in town that I know of. Some of the single men chased after her when the divorce was finalized, but it never seemed to be more than a short-term thing. She works at the Holiday Inn in Rutland as a receptionist, I think. Her friends are either in Rutland or she keeps to herself, I don't know which." Adrian frowned.

"What else?" Strauss prompted.

"Nothing. I just never cared much for her."

"That was obvious last night."

"Look, if the woman was truly hysterical, she needed a slap. That is the prescription for hysterically screaming people," Adrian told him with surprising anger. "If she wasn't actually out of her mind, then she shouldn't have picked those particular circumstances to be overdramatic."

Strauss held up a hand. "Don't get all heated up. I wasn't questioning your actions. You certainly saved me."

Adrian looked at him uncertainly.

"Care to come along while I talk to her?"

"You mean so I can protect you from her if she gets wound up again?"

"Something like that."

Adrian shrugged. "Why not?"

She got to her feet and Strauss followed, pulling on his parka. He looked around the tidy kitchen with an investigator's eye to check for signs of other occupants of the house. There were none. Everything was clean, though not obsessively so, and there was nothing in the way of shoes or clothes to indicate anyone besides Adrian lived here. She bent over the table, though, and scratched out a hasty note, which Nick read over her shoulder.

"Lester, Have gone into the village with Det. Strauss. Back later. -A"

"Mr. Thibault?" Nick asked.

She looked at him with unfathomable dark eyes. "There is no Mr. Thibault," she replied abruptly and characteristically, she didn't elaborate.

As Adrian led the way out the back door, she waved to someone standing in the doorway of the barn, but whoever it was disappeared before Strauss could identify him. Since he didn't really figure the constable to be the single-mother type, he figured she must have a live-in interest and certainly there could be little doubt that it had to be a local man.

When they had gotten into the cruiser and Strauss started the engine, Adrian asked, "Do you remember the way?"

"Of course, I was just there this morning."

"Sorry," she said, though Strauss suspected that she was not. "I just thought things might look different from this side of town."

"Why should they?" Strauss asked impatiently.

She shrugged.

But after crossing two different dirt roads, Strauss was forced to admit that he was uncertain of the direction and Adrian didn't miss the opportunity to give him one of those smiles Vermonters are always giving to flatlanders they consider too thick to have survived so long. Generously, she helped him out by pointing the way to the intersection of Frampton Hill. Strauss had to agree, though he did so silently, that he would never have found it on his own.

The house that Gwenivere built, or more accurately the location in which she had had it built, had long been a source of discussion in Benton Harbor. Her share of the split Dunfield lands had consisted of a long narrow strip on the opposite side of the narrow dirt road from that of her ex-husband, so no one quite saw the point in building directly opposite of the house they had once both inhabited. No one quite understood its position facing backward to the road either, but then no one in Benton Harbor ever professed to understand the Dunfields or, for that matter, anyone else who came up to Vermont from the flatlands.

Adrian explained all this to Strauss on their way up the hill. His only reply was a slightly amazed shake of his head.

An Investigation of Local Color

"So do cops who want to question Ms. Dunfield as a potential murder suspect knock at the front door or use the servant's entrance?" he asked.

"Let's go to the front."

Strauss pulled the cruiser into the drive and around to the front of the house, which overlooked the horse pasture where the cute little Morgan horse lived. Adrian followed as he climbed the steps and knocked on the door.

Gwenivere Dunfield answered immediately. Unquestionably, she was in a quieter frame of mind than she had been the previous night. Strauss took note of her carefully applied cosmetics, a subtle shading around her eyes, a muted lipstick, and just a touch too much blush on the full cheeks. She either dressed very well for her job at the Holiday Inn or she had anticipated their coming, for she was attired in an expensive-looking wool skirt and blazer with a silk shirt, all of queen-size proportions, which Strauss imagined must have cost dearly considering the amount of cloth involved.

The large woman smiled brightly when she saw Strauss and, ignoring Adrian completely, said, "Do come in, sir. I was so hoping you would come by to speak with me."

She took the detective's arm and turned her back on Adrian as she guided her visitors into the living room. Adrian remained standing in the doorway and Gwen, who seemed content to let her, nearly physically placed Strauss on a horribly floral couch and plunked down close beside him.

"I've just been beside myself all day," she began and placed a dramatic hand on her sizeable chest. Her lips trembled slightly. "Do you have any idea who could have done such a thing?"

"We're certainly working on it, Ms. Dunfield. That's why we're here. The coroner has put the time of death somewhere between 3 A.M. and 6 A.M. on Thursday. Were you home here at that time?"

Gwen placed her hands on her cheeks in horror. "Surely you don't suspect me, Officer! Why, I could never do such a thing! Never! He was my husband!"

Her tone was quickly taking on a higher, more hysterical note reminiscent of the previous night. In spite of the seriousness of the crime, Strauss saw Adrian suppress a smile. Was she laughing at him? he wondered. At his inability to get a grip on his suspect or at his amazement of that suspect?

"I'm sure you realize that I have to ask you these questions," Strauss told the big woman impatiently.

"Yes, of course I do." Gwen dropped her eyes and did her best to make tears come.

Strauss didn't think she quite got the job done, but he waited a few seconds while she sniffled and made the most of his opportunity to look around.

In spite of having somewhat questionable taste, at least by his bachelor male standards, Gwen appeared to keep a very tidy house. The couch and matching chairs were upholstered in something with large pink flowers in the pattern. The tables at either end of the couch were dressed for some reason in long, frilly pink skirts. On the sparkling white walls were two matching sunhats, one in pink and one in blue, with ribbons and flowers that people often suppose give their decor a crafty appearance. The windowsills were lined with ceramic shepherdesses and their herds of animals, all neatly dusted and arranged in a tableau only Gwen could understand. Near Strauss' end of the couch stood a bookshelf, which easily contained three dozen books with titles like *Restless Highland Rogue* and *Kidnapped Heart and Unchained Innocence,* and which he felt sure had a man and woman in various groping positions on their covers. A glance at the coffee table, which was the only table in the room to be left undressed, proved his suspicions. There on the table were several such books neatly arranged to show off their titles.

"Did you notice anything unusual that night? Any lights from passing cars? Any strange noises?" Strauss went on.

The big woman shook her head. "Nothing unusual happened until I saw all the flashing lights from you people."

"Had you spoken recently with Mr. Dunfield, say in the last week or so?"

An Investigation of Local Color

"Well...," she hesitated as if trying to determine whether or not to go on.

"Please, go on," Nick prompted.

"I had to call him on Monday. Yes, we spoke on Monday."

"And what did you call him about?"

"I had to talk with him about that horrible Martha Cutting coming around so much. I just don't like her at all." Gwen made a face that successfully illustrated her distaste.

"I'm not sure I understand. She was coming around?"

"Yes. Over at the house. She was there nearly every night last week. She would come early in the evening while Bill was at work and stay around until he came home. I'm not sure when she would leave because I retire early," Gwen informed them primly. "When I left for work, her car would be gone."

"So you called your ex-husband to let him know that you didn't like the woman he was seeing?"

Over Gwen's shoulder Strauss saw Adrian smile. This time there was no questioning her reason when she met his eyes. Welcome to Frampton Hill, Mr. Big-City Detective.

"That is correct. I just have to remind him that if he should decide to hook up with someone of whom I disapprove, I will be forced to take action."

Her words hung in the air for a moment until she realized, belatedly, what she had said. Her hands rushed to her cheeks again, and she affected a sob. Reaching for a Kleenex from a box tactfully placed on the nearby prissily attired table, she dabbed at her eyes.

"I didn't mean that I would kill him! I loved that man once. I would never, NEVER, kill him!"

She sobbed noisily into her Kleenex. Strauss looked to Adrian for help. Clearly, as she had said last night, he was in over his head with this woman. Adrian shrugged in return.

"Exactly what action did you threaten to take?" Strauss tried again.

"I just let him know that I would paint my house and barn hot pink if he ever married Martha Cutting. Bill is ... oh, dear!... Bill was very fussy about the farm. Everything had to be just so. I don't think he would like looking across the road at a pink house and barn. I don't think anyone would, do you?"

Strauss admitted that he didn't think so either. "Is that why you built your house backward, to upset Bill?"

"Of course not!" Gwen snapped in outrage. "In spite of what everyone thinks, we got along very well for a divorced couple."

"If you get along so well, why did you get divorced?"

Gwen had lost her cloying, clinging manner and looked angrily at the big detective sitting on her couch.

"I am a young woman, Officer. I needed my independence. I found it rather stifling after a while to be married to an older man. Men my own age still find me attractive, you know."

"I'm sure they do," Strauss replied. He glanced again over Gwen's shoulder to make sure the constable appreciated his efforts at diplomacy.

"Are you seeing anyone special at the moment?" he asked when he failed to draw a response from Adrian.

"Well, I was up until last week."

"What happened?" Strauss asked very gently, all sympathetic ears, causing the big woman to preen once more.

"I had to end it. It turned out that the man in question was just not the man for me."

"Why was that?"

Gwen pursed her lips for a moment while she considered her answer. "It's rather personal."

"Please," Strauss persisted with just the right amount of sympathy in his voice.

"Well, if you must know, he had no flare for romance."

"No flare for romance," Strauss repeated while he tried to determine how badly he wanted that point elaborated on.

Adrian's eyes strayed to the books on the table and back again to meet his. Strauss, too, glanced at the heaving bosoms and loincloth-clad characters portrayed on the covers. Gwen might be setting her expectations a little high.

"A woman needs that sort of thing, you know."

"I see. And he didn't have it?"

An Investigation of Local Color

"No."

"And so you stopped seeing him?"

"That is correct."

"Just last week?"

"That's right."

"And his name?"

Gwen's eyes narrowed fractionally. "I don't really see what that has to do with arresting Bill's murderer," she replied coldly.

"Well, we never know about these things, Ms. Dunfield, and we have to check everything and everyone out. I'm sure you understand that."

Gwen folded her hands on her expansive lap and pressed her lips together as if she didn't intend to give any further information. "I'm afraid I do not understand. I don't think I wish to speak with you anymore."

Adrian stepped away from the door. "Gwen, if you aren't involved in this, how would it hurt you to talk with us?"

Gwen turned to look at Adrian, acknowledging her presence for the first time since their arrival.

"I would thank you not to speak in my home. You were not invited here. My conversation is with this officer here and not with some local woman who likes to think she's better than she is."

She turned back to Strauss and sat up a little taller. No one could call her a local.

"The man's name is Lee Madigan. There is really no need to involve him in any of this because the closest he ever got to Bill was in passing on the road. They never met. Lee lives in Rutland."

"Did he know your ex-husband lived across the road?"

She shrugged. "It never really came up. If he knew, he never mentioned it."

"And Bill knew you were seeing this Madigan?"

"Of course. As I have said, we weren't unfriendly."

"Then you would know if your ex-husband was seeing anyone else besides Martha Cutting?"

Gwen laughed, causing her massive jowls to jiggle in an unsightly manner. "Officer, Bill would see anyone he could talk into seeing him.

Any size, any color, any marital status. Why, just ask your friend there. He asked her several times that I know of."

Unlike a Vermonter, Gwen had no problem indicating direction with her finger, which she pointed directly at Adrian, who stared back impassively. Strauss ignored her remark.

"Do you have any ideas who may have killed your ex-husband?"

Gwen shrugged. "I just don't know who would do such a wretched thing," she answered, lapsing again into the dramatic. "But it wasn't me."

Strauss got to his feet, signaling an end to the interview. "One last thing, Ms. Dunfield. Do you have any idea what is in Mr. Dunfield's will?"

"He told me in a fit of anger once that he had left everything to his four children in Connecticut. But it doesn't matter."

"Why not?"

Gwenivere Dunfield beamed proudly. "I made sure I got most of what he had left in the bank the last time I took him to court."

She saw them to the door and said goodnight to Strauss with a flirtatious smile that made him squirm all the way down to his toes. He ran a hand over his short-cropped hair before replacing his hat and gulped in some of the freezing night air.

"That was nothing short of amazing," he commented.

"She's different, all right," was Adrian's mild reply. "What do you think?"

"I think you might have warned me about her. I did ask, you know," Strauss answered irritably.

"Warn you about what?"

"About the theatrics, the hysteria, the overall…," Strauss searched for a word to describe what he had just witnessed, "…weirdness."

"Didn't you notice that last night? I thought you were a detective. Besides, I thought you handled the interview quite well. That 'please' thing was a nice touch, really showed your sensitive male side."

"Yeah, well, that's not my favorite technique when questioning a murder suspect," Strauss grumbled.

"And what would your favorite be? Screws to the thumbnails?" Adrian smiled. She was still making fun of him.

An Investigation of Local Color

Strauss got into the car and fired the engine. He smiled back across the seat, a not altogether friendly smile. "Maybe you're closer to the truth than you know. That's why I'm stuck out here in the middle of nowhere questioning a fat woman who is trapped in an X-rated book."

"Romance novel."

"What?"

"They're called romance novels," Adrian informed him.

"Well, I wouldn't have any way of knowing that!" Strauss nearly shouted in frustration. "Good God!"

The constable remained unruffled. "Do you think Gwen did it?"

"She's certainly the most likely suspect at this point, but no, I don't think she did it. Somehow I think it suited her to have an ongoing drama with the ex. And by the way, did the ex really ask you out?"

Adrian pushed her hair back. It was her turn to be annoyed. "As Gwen said, he asked out every woman in town. He may have asked me more often because I am not married. My reply was always the same. I always thought the guy was slimy, but that was about all the time I spent thinking about him. Am I a suspect?"

"Everyone is a suspect in a murder investigation, Adrian. Where do the Boyces live?"

"Up there." Adrian pointed to the left with her chin.

Strauss turned the cruiser left. Through the window of the house they had just left he saw Gwen watching them. He saw that Adrian made note of it as well.

"The Boyces came here from Chicago about four years ago. They built their cabin themselves with money they had saved from their city jobs. He is a nurse at the hospital in Middlebury, she does volunteer work with Meals on Wheels and at a nursing home in Rutland. They claim to want a simpler lifestyle than they had before. They both seem very personable, and as far as I know people like them well enough. Tom Boyce is probably the closest thing to a best friend that Dunfield had."

"Martha Cutting said that Milly might have a better reason than most to dislike Dunfield. Would you know about that?"

Adrian shook her head. "No. Tom and Bill palled around some nights, did some guy things, hunting camps, drinking binges, such stuff. Tom is on the rescue squad with me. He has always seemed competent."

Strauss glanced across the cruiser at his new partner. "And that's all you know about them?"

"That's all."

The Boyce house was the last one before the road turned to a dirt track or, more precisely, more of a dirt track than it already was. It looked as though it had been constructed by a first-time housebuilder. Its proportions were not quite pleasing to the eye, and the windows were placed strangely and of too many varying shapes. In addition, there was a cluster of outbuildings that looked as though they had sprung up whenever it had sprung to mind that another shed might be useful for some purpose. It was nearly dark as they climbed the log steps to knock on the door. Through the window Nick could see into the kitchen, where a woman sat alone at a table eating. She rose immediately when she heard the knocking, but before answering Strauss heard her calling someone from the interior of the house.

"Tom? Tom! We have visitors.... I don't know. Could you please just come up?"

The woman who opened the door gave them an anxiety-ridden smile. "Oh, hello, Adrian. What can I do for you? I suppose this is about poor Bill?"

"Yes, it is. Milly, this is Detective Strauss of the Vermont State Police. We need to ask you and Tom a few questions."

"Of course," Milly replied, looking even more anxious. "Come in please and sit down."

She led them into a living room that gave an overwhelming impression of wood, mostly because it was made up entirely of that material. Strauss, who had never been in a log cabin outside of the Plymouth Plantation Museum, where his school classes had toured when he was a boy, felt fairly sure the presence of so much wood would, over time, annoy the Hell out of him. The walls were the same logs as on the outside of the house, the floor's wide planks had been polyurethaned to an unnaturally bright sheen. Even the furniture was mock Adirondack camp style with only bright cushions decorated with Indian prints breaking up their wood features. Overhanging part of the living room was a loft with a log stairway leading up.

As Strauss was checking all this out, a little man about his own age strolled casually into the room.

"Who's here, Milly? Oh, Adrian and...well, this must be about Bill. What a shock for us. We were all pretty close, you may have heard."

Strauss introduced himself and took the uncomfortable chair that Tom indicated. He noticed that, as at Gwen's house, Adrian remained standing in the doorway, where she was slightly removed from the conversation. Tom picked up a poker and stabbed around in a woodstove before adding a log from the pile on the hearth and closing the door of the stove. He stood rubbing his hands together and warming his back while his wife sat on the wood couch in guarded, hunched position.

"It's gotten cold in here," Tom Boyce said in an overly hearty voice. "Well, Detective, how can we help you?"

"You and Mr. Dunfield were good friends?"

"Yeah, we were good friends. In a manner of speaking, of course."

"What do you mean?"

"Well, Bill had his...peculiarities, I guess you would call them. I think I could tolerate them better than most people could."

"What sort of peculiarities are we talking about?"

Boyce shrugged. "He just rubbed people wrong, knew how to get under their skin. Sometimes it almost seemed like he was trying. Like he studied a person to try to understand how best to annoy them."

"And that didn't bother you?"

Boyce gave Strauss a smug, self-satisfied smile. He had a habit of rolling up on his toes and back down again while he talked that the detective found extremely irritating. "I'm not a person who is easily bothered, Detective. It's a real asset, I can assure you. I just seem to be able to roll with things a lot easier than most other people. Anyway, if you could get by some of those quirks of Bill's, he was a great guy to be around, a great guy. We used to go hunting and fishing. We used to go to deer camp with some of the guys in town. Now there's a good time! Yeah, Bill was an all-right guy to drink a beer with. I'll really miss him."

Personally, Strauss thought Boyce seemed awfully cheerful for a man who had lost his best friend, but maybe it just came down to that ability to roll with things easier than most other people. He glanced at Milly, who was looking far more miserable than the conversation warranted.

"What about you, Mrs. Boyce? How did you get along with Mr. Dunfield?"

"Oh...all right, I suppose. Bill wasn't as great of a friend of mine as he was to my husband, of course, but we got along all right." She smiled her strange, unhappy smile. Her voice with its cultured accent surprised him.

Milly Boyce was middle aged and, by all outward appearances, a relic of the hippy era. Her frizzy hair was long and hanging untidily in her eyes. She was tall and somewhat gone to seed, though she had a long way to go before she would reach the proportions of Gwenivere Dunfield and her clothes were oversized and frumpy. There were signs of a once-pretty girl, and having heard her speak Strauss suspected the pretty girl had once been a high-society girl as well.

"Can you think of anyone who might want to kill Mr. Dunfield?" he asked her.

Milly looked startled, overly startled, Strauss thought.

"Why, no, of course, I can't. Bill could be annoying, certainly, but no one would want to kill him for it."

"Mr. Boyce, do you have a theory?"

"Well, he made a couple of husbands angry from time to time. Other than those, you might look to Marlon Kinney or Jack Glenn. They live up in the houses on the hill behind Bill's. Both professional guys. You probably know the type: ultra uptight, workaholic, money obsessed. Missing all the good things in life, if you ask me."

Strauss didn't point out that he hadn't, in fact, asked. "Why would you suggest one of them?"

"Jack Glenn was Bill's supervisor at work. I know Bill didn't care much for Jack, always called him a smart ass. Jack's wife, Sally, is a very intense, overly emotional woman. She really hated Bill, and he got to needling her whenever he could. I don't know if that would make either of them a suspect, but it couldn't hurt to look into it."

"Thank you, I will," Strauss agreed far more politely than he felt. "And Marlon Kinney?"

"There was some question of ownership of that big hayfield between the Kinneys and Bill last summer. Some pretty heated words were exchanged, but I don't really know the details. You'd have to ask Marlon about it. He only comes up here on the weekends. At least," Boyce added with a significant look, "as far as I know, he only comes up on weekends."

"That's a pretty interesting situation between Mr. Dunfield and his ex-wife. Did he ever talk about it with either of you?" Strauss asked abruptly.

The Boyces exchange quick glances, but before he could decide what they meant Tom walked over and sat beside Milly on the couch. He patted her knee while he said, "Yes, it is odd. But despite some rough spots, they seem to have been making a good go of things."

Strauss noticed that he had stopped patting his wife's knee and now sat with his fingers clenched on it. For her part, Milly examined her feet and was silent.

"He never mentioned her being angry, say, over who he was dating?"

Tom made a transparent attempt at thought. Then he shook his head.

"Not really. We came here after they had already been divorced. I think most of the anger was past then, wouldn't you say, Milly?"

Milly nodded without looking up.

"Wait a minute!" Tom exclaimed with sudden, if slow insight. "Do you think Gwen might have been the murderer? That would be creepy."

"Creepier than if it were someone else?"

"No, no, I guess not. Yes, I suppose that would make sense, now that I think about it. I can't quite picture it, though. With her new boyfriend and all, what would be the motive?"

"New boyfriend?" Strauss asked quickly.

"Yeah. Some guy from Rutland, she brought him up here a couple months back. What was his name, Milly?"

"Lee Something, I can't remember," Milly said. "I just remember that he was a Jehovah's Witness. Tall guy, extremely thin. Not terribly attractive, though Gwen certainly seemed to think the world of him."

"That's right, and Gwen was going to convert to the Jehovah's as well. You know, Jehovah's are the ones who go up to people's doors and try to show them the way and give them a handful of religious pamphlets. They were sort of practicing their technique on us that night she introduced him. They didn't convert us, though, did they, hon?" Tom laughed loudly, giving the story far more humor than it deserved.

"You wouldn't happen to know if Gwen and this Lee fellow are still seeing each other?"

Tom shrugged. "I assume so. I saw his van there just last week. Of course, it might have been someone else's van. Gwen likes a man with a van. The last three men she dated all had vans. I think it is a prerequisite with her, if you know what I mean." Again he gave Strauss that significant man-to-man look.

"Yes, I believe I do," Nick answered. "Can you tell me where you were on Thursday morning around 3 A.M. to 4 A.M.?"

Boyce grinned. He had obviously been waiting for this: his alibi, an easy question.

"I was at work. I work nights in the ICU at Middlebury Hospital. I would have been there tonight except that I felt I needed the night off."

There was a pause and Strauss let it drag.

"You know, because of Bill. He was my friend, after all."

"Sure. Do you work with anyone?"

"Not after 11. My shift is from 7 P.M. to 7 A.M. There is some staff overlap, but I'm alone from 11 to about 6. There are other nurses on duty that time of night, and I'm sure someone can vouch for my whereabouts when Bill was killed. I see people on and off all night, Officer, and they see me." He smiled with the knowledge that, of course, he was correct.

"Mrs. Boyce, how about you?"

"I was here at home. I do volunteer workdays. Nights, I sleep. I was alone. But I wouldn't have killed Bill. I had no reason to dislike

An Investigation of Local Color

him," Milly said softly and, if possible, looked even more stressed than she had previously. She even managed what Strauss thought could be termed a convincing wringing of her hands.

"Okay. You've both been very helpful. Thank you. Here's my number if you think of anything else that might be helpful." He looked especially hard at Milly Boyce. "I may be around to ask a few more questions later."

Tom stood up with quick energy and put out a hand. "Anything we can do to help, Detective. We want to get this whole thing cleared up as quickly as possible. It has just been so shocking for us, hasn't it, Milly?"

Dutifully and on cue, Milly nodded. Her husband rewarded her efforts by putting an arm around her shoulder and giving her an affectionate squeeze.

"Adrian?" Strauss asked, just in case she had some query of her own.

"Thanks, both of you," she said and smiled pleasantly. Just as she started for the door, she turned around again and asked, "How long have the two of you been married?"

Clearly, the Boyces were caught off guard. They looked at each other and smiled nervously.

Finally, Tom grinned heartily. "Let see, I have to think. Mmmm. Fifteen years, right, hon? And I hope to make it another fifteen."

He threw his arm around his wife again. She smiled and looked green. Apparently, the thought of another fifteen wasn't quite as appealing to her.

"I hope so, too. Thanks again." Adrian gave a little wave and pulled the front door open.

"You were pretty quiet in there," Strauss commented as soon as the door closed behind them.

"Just letting you do your job, Detective," Adrian replied.

"But something didn't seem quite right to you, did it?"

Adrian shook her head. "I've heard some secondhand stuff, too."

"What kind of stuff? And couldn't you have shared it with me before we went in?"

She shrugged. It maddened him.

"Gossip. It's not always worth repeating."

"It's probably worth repeating that this is a murder investigation, and anything that might or even might not be worth repeating should be until we get this thing solved."

"Okay? Want to get some dinner at the Hook? I'm starved."

"Adrian! How did we get from a discussion of suspects to the state of your stomach?"

"What, it's not relevant? I just might think better with some food in me. Besides, we might get some help there."

"You keep saying that about that place. Just what kind of help do you expect to get there? Do you actually think the gang down there can solve this crime? Based on what? And if they know something, why aren't they coming forward?" Strauss asked with the very last of his patience.

Adrian gave her new partner a patient look. "You just made the wrong turn. You wanted to go straight back there."

"Goddamn," he muttered. He stopped the cruiser and turned it halfway around in the road, backed up, then turned it the rest of the way, managing in the process to barely miss a set of dilapidated mailboxes that looked as though they hadn't always been spared.

"They don't know they know anything, Detective. I told you that. They don't know who killed Bill Dunfield, but I'll bet you dinner that one of them will tell you what the Boyces wouldn't. Bet?"

"You're on." He sent the cruiser flying down the road but had to slow, as three different herds of deer crossed the road in front of them before they reached the center of town.

"You'd think the stupid beasts would know better," he commented.

"They do. They can't be shot after dark. Roadkill can't be always be kept. Who're the smart ones here?"

"Do you hunt, by any chance?"

"Sometimes."

"Figures."

Strauss had to park the cruiser in the drive alongside the firehouse, the Hook's lot overflowing with the inevitable four-by-fours with their cargo.

An Investigation of Local Color

"I will personally shoot the first person who asks me if I hunt," he warned.

"I'll keep that in mind."

The tables were full, and there were plenty of men around who seemed to be there just to socialize. Tonight there were women around as well, a fact Strauss found encouraging. Maybe there would be another topic of discussion besides guns and deer. There would have been no seats for them except that a man he didn't recognize from earlier in the day called to Adrian from the bar and then pushed his companion off his stool to make room.

"Thanks, Herm."

"No problem, Adrian. We got to be getting home anyway. Cows will be close to bursting unless Ethel took it on herself to get started without us."

They climbed onto the stools, and a bartender in a t-shirt stretched tightly over his stomach with suspenders barely holding up his drooping trousers slapped the bar for their drink orders.

"Budweiser," Adrian ordered.

"Sam Adams," Strauss ordered.

"Sam Adams, who the Hell is he? There ain't no Sam Adams around here."

Adrian turned her head away to hide a smile.

"Sam Adams is a...never mind. What do you have on tap?"

"Budweiser."

"How about in bottles?"

"Budweiser and Bud Lite. We also got some of that fancy non-alcoholic stuff for the guys that got to stay out of trouble with their wives, but I don't recommend it. I hear it raises Cain with the bowels and tastes like goat piss besides."

"Just give me a draft," Strauss replied wearily.

Looking down the bar, he saw that every face was turned toward him, every ear unabashedly tuned into his conversation with the bartender. To Adrian's credit, she had managed not to laugh.

"The burgers are good," she told him. "And so are the steaks."

"A burger would be fine."

Seconds later, he heard the bartender shout the order into the kitchen.

Adrian swiveled around in her stool and looked around the room. She waved and a man and woman on the far side of the room got up from a table, dragging their chairs along with them. They squeezed them into the limited space near the bar next to Strauss and Adrian and went back for their beer mugs. Nick recognized the man as one of the group he had spoken with that morning, but he couldn't immediately put a name to him without consulting his notepad. He made the safe assumption that he was in some way related to Adrian.

"This is my cousin Donnie and his wife Jean," Adrian helped him out.

Donnie grinned and offered a hand. His wife had as ready a smile as he did.

"Get your deer, Donnie?" Adrian asked.

"First thing this morning. Right out back the house. Standing there just waiting for me to come out and shoot him."

"He was back in the house before the coffee stopped perking," Jean added proudly. "Do you hunt, Mr. Strauss?"

So much for the feminine point of view, Strauss thought. He glanced at Adrian and admired how easily she kept a straight face.

"No, ma'am. Not deer, anyway."

"You been working on the Dunfield murder, Adrian?" Jean asked. "What a shocking thing that was! Right here in Benton Harbor. Unbelievable!"

"We've been up talking to Gwen and the Boyces." Adrian shrugged to indicate that they had nothing concrete yet.

Strauss was immediately annoyed that she would talk about the case at the bar even if there wasn't really any evidence to relate. Didn't she know that idle chatter could ruin a case?

"The Boyces...now that's a strange thing. Rather sad, I think," Jean said.

Her cheerful features lapsed momentarily into a pained expression that was so honest that Strauss believed she was actually sad for whatever strange thing she was talking about.

"What's that, Jean?" Adrian asked.

An Investigation of Local Color

"You know, that they're splitting up. I rather like both Milly and Tom. They seem like nice folks, as outsiders go."

"They were both at the house when we were there tonight," Strauss commented, trying to push Jean out of the usual slow revelation of the facts.

"It's crazy, really," Donnie offered. "Especially after the Dunfields showed it couldn't be done. Trying to live together while you're in the process of splitting up. It just doesn't work. It goes against human nature, especially when a third party is involved."

"Whoa, whoa! Could you back up a little and fill in a little of the details?" Strauss asked. He avoided looking at Adrian since she was bound to have a smug look, as he was forced to extract information from people he had earlier claimed would be of no help.

"Sorry. I assumed they would have told you." Donnie waved for another Budweiser, which the bartender slid down the bar for him.

At the same time the buxom teenager who had been working that morning set down plates heaped with fries and huge hamburgers next to Strauss and Adrian.

"They are getting divorced, but they have decided to share the house for the winter. Tom says he wants to build again, up there on the hill above the present house. Obviously he can't start that until spring, so he's living in the cellar for the winter, and Milly's got the upstairs."

"You all got to be talking about those crazy folks up on Frampton Hill," Franklyn Birch interrupted. "How're you doing, Adrian, Nick?"

"Good, Franklyn." Adrian smiled.

Apparently she didn't mind the intrusion into the conversation as much as Strauss did. Like Donnie, Birch had his wife in tow. She was a big woman and as tough-looking as her husband. In fact, Nick suspected that a tussle with her might leave Franklyn the loser. Like her husband, too, her smile was guarded, wary where the Thibault cousins were open and honest.

"There is something wrong in the water up there on that hill," Madge Birch commented. "Always has been. Even when we were kids, there were strange folks living in that farmhouse up there. But

I gotta tell you, that lot up there now tops anything that's been in this town before."

Clearly, Strauss had lost control of the conversation or, rather, he had never had control of it in the first place. Irritated, he settled for tucking into his huge meal and hoping talk would come back around to a place where he could ask his own questions.

"Jim, bring the detective another beer, will you?" Birch ordered.

Strauss didn't bother telling the other man the first beer had tasted every bit like the aforementioned goat piss and he didn't really want another one. Somehow he suspected it would have been considered bad form.

"So there's someone else, is there?" Adrian asked casually. She had already made a sizeable dent in her burger.

"Well, now I just heard that from Dunfield. He was in here one morning talking about how screwed up Tom Boyce was to get rid of one woman and get hooked up with another right off. He was always telling Tom that Milly led him around by the balls...sorry, ladies." He grinned, not at all apologetic. "Actually that was what Dunfield told everyone who had a wife. I think it was a case of misery wanting company."

"Yeah, and Misery didn't expect Company to find himself another woman so soon," Madge Birch laughed.

"Who's the lucky other lady?" Adrian asked.

"Don't know," her cousin replied.

"Must not be someone from around here," Jean commented to Strauss with a grin. "Or we would know. My guess would be someone from the hospital there in Middlebury. That's what I would try," she added helpfully.

"What about Gwen's boyfriend?" Adrian asked around a mouthful of hamburger.

"Anybody met him?"

"The Witness fella?" Franklyn's identification of the boyfriend drew loud guffaws from people Strauss hadn't even realized were listening to their conversation.

"He convert any of you?" Adrian asked good-naturedly.

An Investigation of Local Color

"Naw, never met him. You, Donnie?" Franklyn looked around at the eavesdroppers, but if any of them had met the man in question no one was owning up to it.

"Speaking of the ex-Mrs. Dunfield, any of you come up behind her while she was driving around in that little cart recently?" Birch held out widespread hands to indicate the width of the view that could be expected if any of them hadn't yet experienced it for themselves.

This was met with more widespread hands from the audience and a sharp elbow to Franklyn's ribs from his Mrs., who was no flyweight herself.

"You all must be talking about Ms. Dunfield," yet another nameless but familiar face joined in.

This time the face was nameless because Strauss never had been able to ascertain that morning which Chandler brother was which, and this was certainly one of them. He waited for someone to make positive ID.

"More specifically, you're speaking of the ever-charming Gwenivere Dunfield on her fancy little buggy."

More laughter, more widespread hands.

"This certainly isn't a group that spends a lot of time mourning, is it?" Strauss said softly to Adrian, who had nearly cleaned her plate.

"What would be the point?"

"Or for that matter," he went on, ignoring her question, "worrying that there may be a murderer loose among them. One who might very well repeat the crime."

But he hadn't spoken softly enough. A hand was clapped firmly on his shoulder.

"We wouldn't worry about such a thing, Detective. The murderer ain't one of us. And he ain't going to murder one of us."

Strauss met Franklyn Birch's warning stare, then turned his glance to the hand on his shoulder. He disliked being threatened, even in a subtle manner. And he especially disliked being touched. Out of the corner of his eye, he saw Adrian shake her head slightly at Birch. That man unclenched his hand and patted Nick lightly on the shoulder where it had been.

"But you knew that, didn't you?" Birch smiled, but the two big men continued to stare at each other with a hostility that permeated the air.

"Say, Detective, you got yourself some new boots," Donnie said cheerfully into the silence. "Good choice, too."

All heads bent on cue to check out the new footwear. Strauss saw Adrian silently mouth something at Birch, but he couldn't quite catch it. Then that man was laughing at something the Chandler brother had said. Silently, Strauss took a gulp of beer and looked around. It seemed as if the whole of Benton Harbor had joined in on their meal. With the crowd having increased in numbers and appearing to have come under the influence of a not-small amount of Budweiser, he figured that there wasn't much more to be learned here. At least not tonight. He asked for the check.

3

Sally Glenn was a lonely woman. Even at thirty-five years old, she was shy and didn't make friends easily. She counted her husband as her best friend, but he was a hopeless workaholic and though he loved his wife dearly he spent very little time with her. When he had gotten a transfer and a much-coveted promotion from his job as an engineer with the New England Tampon Company, Sally had cried to herself for days over the thought of leaving Massachusetts and moving north to a state she had previously thought of as only a vacation resort. Benton Harbor was the last place in the world she had wanted to live, but Jack had said that land was cheap there and they could build their dream house and still have enough open space that she could take her beloved dogs for long walks without fear they would be run over by speeding motorists. He hadn't exactly convinced her, but it wasn't as though she had a lot of choice short of killing Jack's career so she quit her job as a librarian and packed their household into boxes for the move north.

The reality of Benton Harbor was even worse than she could ever have imagined. Two days after ground was broken on their new house, Sally met Gwenivere Dunfield, who informed her in language that could only have had its origins in a romance novel that she and her espoused were in the process of divorcing, and if that man ever came near her again she would use the tiny derringer that she kept under her pillow to protect her womanhood.

"Yes, ma'am, I intend to shoot first and ask questions later. And I ask you, who could blame me?"

Who, indeed? Sally's eyes had widened in horror. The country was supposed to be so much safer. The newspapers all said so. Jack had promised.

Sally tried the other neighbors on the hill. Mrs. Kinney in the house next door to theirs was twenty years her senior. She and her husband were retired and used their house as a vacation home. Jane Kinney loved Vermont, she just loved it, but as far as Sally could see Jane loved Vermont as long as she didn't have to spend more than forty-eight hours there. After a weekend of splendid views and hiking and breathing the fresh air, the Kinneys quickly beat a path back to the city and its upscale restaurants, theatres, and shopping malls.

Milly Boyce was the closest in age, but Sally had trouble relating to Milly's desire to grow her own food and weave her own clothes. Like Sally, Milly loved to read books but the ones she lent to Sally dealt with *Finding Inner Peace, Spiritual Growth through Herbs and Meditation,* and *Dream Analysis.* Milly lectured frequently on the perils of ambitions, particularly as they related to Jack's job and Sally's resulting lifestyle.

"Sally, you simply have to make time to enjoy life. Stop and smell the flowers, enjoy the view. Things won't give you inner peace."

Sally didn't like to point out that Milly didn't seem particularly peaceful in spite of spending hours in her garden. Maybe there were no flowers in the garden to smell. She also couldn't help noticing Milly's look of envy when Jack had brought home a new red Honda Accord for Sally's birthday. Sally suspected that Milly might be just a touch crazy.

Surrounded by this cast of characters and fearing more than a little for her own sanity, Sally decided to take matters into her own hands and find a way to prevent herself from lapsing into despair. She came up with two things: dogs, which she already had, and exercise. Middle age and library work had thickened her ever so slightly, so she determined that she could both shape up and cure her blues by developing her own exercise program. Being a decisive sort of person, she drove to Rutland immediately and bought a dozen exercise videos by all the beautiful actresses she thought she might enjoy looking like, and she had never looked back. Within six weeks she had a body any twenty-year-old would envy, and she had a purpose in life. Besides that, she had lots of neat leotards. Whenever she found herself feeling

An Investigation of Local Color

upset, she would just don one of her favorites, pop in a video and, surrounded by her canine family, which now numbered four, exercise until she felt better.

And so, two days after Bill Dunfield's unfortunate demise, Sally was attired in her favorite red, yellow, and orange leotard, furiously jumping up and down, going for the burn when Strauss rang the doorbell. The loud music accompanied by someone's shouted but enthusiastic commands was immediately replaced by the barking of what sounded like an entire kennel full of fierce dogs. Then the door opened slightly, and a timid face peered out at him questioningly.

"Mrs. Glenn? I'm Detective Nick Strauss." He showed his two badges and noticed that she looked at them more closely than most people did and still seemed reluctant to open the door further than a crack.

"Quiet, please," she said over her shoulder, and the barking immediately stopped.

"I need to speak to you and your husband concerning your neighbor Bill Dunfield."

"My husband isn't here at the moment."

Sally Glenn continued to hold the door just slightly ajar so Strauss couldn't get a good look at her.

"Well, could I talk to you, then? It's very important, Mrs. Glenn." Strauss abandoned his official voice in favor of his most soothing. He was starting to miss shouting at suspects to get answers.

Sally hesitated a fraction of a second longer, then opened the door to admit him. As she stepped back, Strauss got a better look at her. She was a plain, not unpleasant-looking woman with overly pale features that were accentuated by the splashy colors of the damp leotard that she wore. There was, however, nothing plain about the woman's figure, which was nothing short of fabulous. After a quick assessing glance, Strauss tried not to stare at the firm muscles, narrow waist, and rounded breasts made more evident by the tight fabric of her exercise clothes. He was quick to notice that although the woman appeared at once to be shy, she seemed unconcerned about appearing dressed in only Spandex in front of a total stranger who wanted to question her about a murder. But then she didn't exactly need to be nervous of letting strange men into her house: Lined up in orderly fashion behind her were four large German Shepherds, each with his lips curled in a silent snarl designed to show his teeth to best affect. God, how he hated dogs! He decided to keep his eyes off the delectable Mrs. Glenn in case one of them noticed and went for his throat.

"Perhaps you would like to sit in the living room," Sally said, and when he moved in the direction she indicated with a backward look at the dogs, he heard her whisper, "Stop that!" All four sets of lips snapped shut and all four tails thumped on the floor.

The house that had looked so appealing on the long drive up the hill was even more spectacular from the inside. A huge wall of windows overlooked a view that included both the nearby hills, the farther, steeper mountains, and off to the west, the swampy end of Lake Champlain, which from this distance appeared far more glamorous than it did up close. Unlike the Boyce cabin, with its oppressive wood features, this house was designed to make the most of the light. On top of that its white walls and light-colored furniture and carpeting were modern and spotlessly kept. Everything was in perfect order right down to the four dog beds lined up neatly beneath the windows and the exercise bike and NordicTrack in their respective corners.

"Great view you have," Strauss commented. "You must enjoy it up here."

"My husband, Jack, worked with an architect to get just what he wanted. It's the house he always dreamed of," she replied, going to the window to look out.

She wiped her face on a towel hanging around her neck and smoothed back a strand of pale hair that had escaped its ponytail. She noticed at the same time Nick did, two hunters in red-and-black check traversing the hill not far from the house.

"Sometimes, though, the view is a bit more than one might wish."

Strauss was uncertain whether she meant the hunters or the fact that she also had an excellent view of both the farmhouse and its newer counterpart across the dirt road below.

"You don't care for hunters?"

She shook her head.

"Why don't you post 'No Hunting' signs on your property?"

"They would hunt anyway. I have heard that when a hunter gets on the trail of a deer, nothing will stop him. He will shoot at anything, dogs, cows, people, anything. We were also warned that posting signs was considered very unfriendly. I just stay inside for two and a half weeks and try to ignore it. Would you like some tea?"

"No, thank you." He sat in the plushy white chair she indicated while she pulled up a bare wood chair, which presumably wouldn't be made worse for having a sweaty leotard plunked down on it.

"You know, of course, that Mr. Dunfield has been killed?"

Sally nodded. "Jack heard about it yesterday when he was down at the general store. Do you know who did it?"

"We're still investigating. Do you have any ideas?"

She shook her head, seeming neither surprised nor offended by the question. Neither did she seem concerned that there hadn't been an arrest made.

"He wasn't a very nice man, but I don't know who would want to kill him unless his ex-wife did it."

"How well did you know Mr. Dunfield?"

"Jack was his supervisor at work."

"So your husband works on second shift?"

"No. He works days, but he always stays over a couple of hours or so in order to make sure the lines keep running smoothly. The shifts overlap somewhat so there is always a supervisor there for at least the beginning and end of a shift. As far as I know, there were no problems at work, but Jack could tell you about it better than I could."

"What about you, Mrs. Glenn? Did you have any trouble with Mr. Dunfield?"

Sally looked decidedly more uncomfortable than she had previously, if that were possible. She bent to stroke the heads of the dogs, who had all arranged themselves around her feet. Although they no longer bared their teeth at him, as per their mistress's request, they continued to eye him with what Strauss considered to be hostility. But then, he considered every dog to be potentially hostile.

"I thought Bill Dunfield was a nasty little man," Sally said. "He made very persistent advances when we first came here. It made me so uncomfortable that finally I couldn't even be polite anymore, and I told him he was sleezy and low-class. After that he settled for doing mean things to me. Jack says they were harmless and just meant to bug me."

"What sorts of 'mean things,' Mrs. Glenn?"

"Well, once he called up and said my dogs were down at his place digging up the yard. I had just two then, and I told him they were both with me. He said I was wrong, and not five minutes later he came speeding up the drive with two dogs in the back of his car. He dragged them both up to the door by the scruffs of their necks, poor things, and my boys met him at the door. The dogs he brought up here didn't even look like Shepherds except for being relatively the same color. He never even apologized for calling me a liar, just set the strays loose and took off in a fit of temper. After that, whenever I walk the dogs down in the field anywhere near the property line he fires off his gun. It scares me and it's bad for the dogs' ears. Les was here one day last summer when he did it, so he knows it really happens."

"Who's Les?" Strauss asked, wondering if he should make notes to keep track of the ever-growing cast of characters in this unfolding and increasingly odd case.

"Lester Blake. He lives at Adrian Thibault's. He comes up here to mow in the summer and to plow in the winter. Jack can't really keep up with everything because of his work, so he hires Les. He's a really nice man. Les, I mean."

For the first time since Strauss had met her, Sally smiled. He wondered about this Lester fellow who lived with Adrian, and why Adrian hadn't mentioned him last night, and why he made the sober-faced Sally Glenn smile.

"Les said that he thought Bill was just one of those miserable people who like to stir things up to make other people miserable along

An Investigation of Local Color

with him, but that he would never actually do anything to harm either the dogs or me. He said the one to watch out for was Gwen."

"She's got a gun?" Strauss asked.

Sally nodded.

"And you've actually seen the weapon?"

She nodded again. "Once when I was out jogging, I saw her shoot at her horse."

"She shot at her own horse? Are you sure?"

"Yes, because I screamed and screamed at her to stop. Then she told me that she didn't mean to hit him, just to keep him from rubbing his rump on the wood fence. I said I thought there must be a better way, but she insisted a gun was the most effective. She said a gun was most effective for a lot of things. I didn't ask what things. I just keep the dogs away from her. She's a horrid person. She's just a...well, she's a big fat pig."

"Excuse me?" Strauss couldn't keep the astonishment out of his voice. He didn't figure Sally Glenn for the sort of woman from whom the words "bitch" or even "tramp" would easily slide out. He did, however, find her epithet of choice to be a little surprising.

"Well, personally, I just don't see how one can expect to be happy living across from one's ex-husband, but to become so FAT on top of that. It's just such a prescription for misery, don't you think?"

Strauss had to agree that maybe it was. But did being fat actually make the former Mrs. Dunfield want to kill her ex-husband?

"I don't know about that," Sally said. "I just think if she got some exercise and trimmed down some, she would feel better. People usually do, you know."

Strauss nodded, more because he was starting to hear the tones of the obsessive-compulsiveness in her voice and wanted to change the subject then because he particularly agreed with her. In his mind, nothing made him feel much worse than a brisk foot chase through the streets of Boston in hot pursuit of a petty thief. The huffing and puffing and aching in his chest afterward were enough to make him swear off cigarettes except that smoking made him feel happier than any amount of exercise was ever going to. And besides that, every time he tried quitting he automatically put on ten pounds and coughed incessantly and lost his temper more easily than he already did. But he was fairly sure those things would be unwise to tell Sally Glenn.

Instead he asked, "Where were you on Thursday night, Mrs. Glenn?"

"Home," she replied with none of the offense at the question shown by the others he had interrogated so far.

"And your husband was here with you?"

She nodded.

"When do you expect Mr. Glenn home?"

"I don't know. He's at work right now."

"He's at work? On a Sunday?"

Sally shrugged as if it was a commonplace occurrence. "They called him early this morning. Apparently there was some sort of emergency with one of the lines and production stopped. It happens a lot. They always call Jack."

Strauss was uncertain what exactly would constitute an emergency in the business of making tampons. What could be so important that it couldn't wait until a man's regular shift started? A sudden shortage in the world supply? Somehow it seemed wiser not to ask someone whose livelihood, not to mention very fancy house, depended on the little cotton items.

"I see," he said instead. "Maybe it would be easier if I spoke with him at work."

But Sally shook her head. "Probably not. NET is very big on secrecy. They don't let just anyone in. Even their suppliers and outside contractors have to sign forms guaranteeing that they will not divulge any information pertinent to the business to anyone on the outside."

The outside?

"Sounds more like they're manufacturing nuclear warheads." Strauss laughed.

Sally didn't.

"Sorry. Well, I'll see what I can do. Thanks very much for your time, Mrs. Glenn."

An Investigation of Local Color

Strauss stood and so did four German Shepherds, all panting eagerly as if they would enjoy making him their next meal. As he was shown the door, he caught sight of the house next door. It was an even more massive, showy house than the Glenns', being higher up on the hillside and having an entire front of windows and skylights.

"When are the neighbors usually here? The Kinneys, isn't that right?"

"Yes. They are here most weekends, although I haven't seen them this month at all. They live in Hartford, Connecticut, during the week."

"So they weren't here last weekend or anytime during the week?"

"Not that I noticed, and I probably would have because they have to drive right by the house to get up there, and they often honk the horn on the way by. They also turn on every light they have outside so it's a little hard to miss them."

"Mmmm. Thanks, again. Oh, one more thing, if you don't mind. How do you like living up here?"

The question caught Sally off guard as none of the others had seemed to. For a moment Strauss thought he detected a sudden tear in her eyes, but she quickly looked away and didn't meet his eyes again.

"It's a pretty nice place to live."

Strauss could have sworn she had been about to say something else. Before he took two steps from the door, he could hear the disembodied voice from the video machine shouting instructions to go for the burn accompanied by the thumping of Sally Glenn jumping around in energetic compliance.

4

Although Strauss was very rarely tempted to throw his weight around via his badges, either in the city or even more especially in Vermont, the idea of infiltrating the supersecret infrastructure of the New England Tampon Company was just too amusing to pass up. Besides, he excused himself, it would probably be more useful to talk to Jack Glenn outside the presence of his wife, and he could check into the whereabouts of Dunfield's coworkers the night of the murder at the same time. He called Adrian with his plans, and she told him she would snoop around on her lunch hour and try to come up with some information on the Witness boyfriend. They agreed to meet for dinner after her shift at the hospital. Strictly for the purpose of exchanging information, she insisted. Of course, he agreed.

Strauss tried not to admit to himself that he was somewhat intrigued with the woman. In his mind, being too intrigued by anyone unrelated to an investigation, especially if that person was a woman, constituted a loss of control on his part. At this point in his life he most certainly didn't want relationships of any kind. He had, in fact, been sent here to overcome the effects of the destruction of more than one relationship, and he had no intention of involving himself again.

If he had been honest, he would have had to admit that he admired Adrian Thibault's no-nonsense style. He liked a person who didn't fluster easily and kept a cool head. He also would have had to add that he liked a woman without fluff, a woman who dressed not for appearances but for the occasion and didn't bother with all that hairspray and plaster of Paris crap women smeared on themselves. Besides being overly time-consuming, as Strauss had learned firsthand, it didn't add to beauty as much as women thought it did.

So he convinced himself that he was interested in Adrian Thibault only because she was his best link for information in the investigation of the Dunfield murder, and when Sally Glenn brought up the name of a man who lived, surprisingly, with Adrian, Strauss' only interest in him was in how he might also be linked to information that might be useful in his investigation.

Armed with that conviction, Strauss headed for the Hook, Line, and Sinker first thing Monday morning to see if Lester Blake might be a member of that very useful male coffee club that Adrian had told him about. At 7:30 on what for most people was a working day, there were significantly fewer trucks and only two dead deer in the parking lot. Strauss steeled himself for his task and pushed open the door to be greeted by a waft of fried bacon and eggs, brewing coffee and cigarette smoke.

"Hey, it's the law," someone said as he adjusted his eyes to the dimness of the inside light.

Half a dozen cigarettes were put out on the corners of breakfast plates in deference to Vermont's no-smoking laws. Strauss felt like a high school principal in the boys' bathroom of his former high school, except that he had always been the one flushing the cigarette.

"Mr. Strauss, have a seat." The man Strauss recognized as the hefty town road manager and one of Adrian's many relatives pushed out a chair with his foot. "Great new boots you got there."

"Thanks."

Strauss took the chair and waved for coffee. Franklyn Birch held down the same end of the table he had on Saturday morning. He was surrounded by the Chandler brothers, Donnie Thibault, the road manager, Junior Thibault, and three other men whose names Nick had either forgotten or never learned. He figured to have them all down by this time tomorrow, as long as they didn't switch chairs.

"You're out early," Birch commented.

"Always," Strauss replied, and the two men did their ritual sizing up of each other.

"Hunting?" Donnie commented.

An Investigation of Local Color

Strauss nodded. "In pretty much the same place I have been all along, but with less luck than you seem to have had."

"Aw, Mr. Detective, that ain't luck," big Junior Thibault laughed. "Donnie feeds them deer all summer and fall. He shoots a big buck in the same spot every year."

Donnie grinned at his relative. "You're not supposed to tell an officer of the law."

Junior looked momentarily startled by his faux pas. Then he recovered quickly. "Well, I didn't say it was true, did I?"

Strauss looked from one to the other. He had heard of the practice of taming the deer during the off-season to make hunting them easier, but he honestly couldn't tell whether there was any seriousness to the younger Thibault's claim or not. All eyes around the table were trained on him for his reaction, at any rate. Casually, he took a sip of steaming coffee and, since there was no one else in the restaurant except a heavy man tossing pans around in the kitchen while puffing on the cigarette that hung from his lips, Strauss lit one for himself. Without taking their eyes from him, half a dozen men also lit cigarettes.

"You met the Glenns yet?" Birch asked from the end of the table.

Strauss had the distinct impression that the man already knew he had been up to the Glenn house. Was Adrian keeping her pal informed of every step along the way? His impression was further strengthened when his audience of cow farmers all leaned forward in anticipation of new information, i.e. gossip. Normally, Strauss wouldn't have discussed a case with casual observers who might take the information further, but Adrian had certainly solicited some valuable tidbits the other night while appearing to be merely gossiping.

Pushing aside his misgivings, he replied, "I met Sally Glenn yesterday."

He paused, waiting for a reaction. There was none. Just half a dozen faces waiting for something juicier.

"What? None of you know her?"

"Physically speaking, Mrs. Glenn is the polar opposite of her neighbor, the always charming Gwenivere Dunfield, and obviously suffering not at all from the effects of exogenous obesity. But to answer your question: No, none of us knows her at all."

Strauss choked on the smoke from his cigarette. He wasn't sure if it was his choking or the speech that came out of a lean middle-aged man who, but for his wire-framed glasses, looked every bit the typical Benton Harbor dairy farmer, that caused the laughter around him.

"Don't mind Ira. He's our local veterinarian and he reads way too much" Donnie grinned. "Every one of us needs a dictionary when he talks."

"I'll keep that in mind," Strauss replied. "But you were saying about Mrs. Glenn?"

"Nothing, really. I know nothing about her, except that she brings the dogs to me on a very routine basis. They are more disciplined than any other animals I deal with, as is Mrs. Glenn herself. I'm sure it didn't escape you that Mrs. Glenn is very disciplined?" Ira asked with a smile.

Strauss thought back to the spectacular figure in its sweating orange-and-yellow leotard. "No, I didn't miss that," he admitted.

"Sometimes I come up on her jogging when I'm out with the grader or the snowplow, even in nasty weather," Junior added. "You know, Benton Harbor could really use more scenery like that, but she sure does look like her nose is in the air."

"Never comes to town either. You gotta kind of wonder about that," one of the Chandlers said.

"Nothing to wonder about that, Kenyon," his brother said, and Strauss made a quick note to remember which one was Kenyon. "She don't have friends in this town. Who'd she get in with? All the other ladies are either busy with kids or helping out on the farm or out working. Who's got time to stay home and exercise all day?"

"Your point is well taken, Edmund," the vet said. "You are, however, overlooking Les' theory that Mrs. Glenn is just extremely shy."

"Les?" Strauss picked up on the name immediately. "Would that be Lester Blake?"

"It would be," Ira told him.

"Where could I find him?"

An Investigation of Local Color

There was silence. Strauss was aware of several warning glances being exchanged across the table before all eyes returned to him, every expression blank. They didn't know a thing, their expressions said. They knew all sorts of things, Strauss' experience told him.

"You guys want any more eggs?" the heavyset man shouted from the kitchen. "If ya don't, I'm shutting down the grill."

"Go ahead," Birch told him without taking his eyes, now narrowed in a dark glower, from Strauss' face. "It ain't Les Blake, Strauss."

"What ain't Les Blake?"

"He ain't the murderer."

"No, of course he isn't," Strauss replied, although he didn't especially know that for certain, having never met the man in question or, for that matter, not knowing a single thing about him except that he lived at Adrian's and did some work for Sally Glenn. Oh, and he made that woman smile when nothing else seemed to.

"Then why'd you want to know where to find him?"

"Just some routine questions. He seems to know some of the folks up there on Frampton Hill better than some of you do."

No one appeared convinced by this explanation. Birch looked hostile, the Chandlers, carefully indifferent, Donnie played with the spoon in his coffee, Junior finished eggs that must by now have been cold. No one spoke.

Nick shrugged. "Just looking for some help."

"The thing is, Les is a good man," Ira offered and was rewarded with a warning rumble from Birch, which the vet ignored. "He is the one who looks after the doe with a broken leg or the widow lady with a broken-down furnace in the middle of the night. The idea that he could do harm to anyone is inconceivable."

"I understand."

But he didn't. It was a curious description of a man Nick wanted only to question in order to get his opinion of the climate up on Frampton Hill. He hadn't even considered that Blake could be a suspect. Now it crossed his mind. There was a lot of fidgeting going on at the table. And there was Birch's growled insistence that it wasn't one of them. Maybe it was, in fact, one of their own, and if they didn't exactly know it they suspected it.

"Time to get back to work," Donnie announced with his usual cheerfulness. He got to his feet, stubbing out his cigarette, and his move dispelled the tension in the air instantly as his fellows followed suit. The movement of the men putting out cigarettes filled the air with the scent of smoke and cow dung.

"Good to have met you," the vet said to Strauss.

"Yeah, be sure to come on down again," Birch added, though he appeared less friendly.

Strauss suspected that his offer was less inspired by potential friendliness as a desire to know how the investigation was progressing.

"And if you got yourself a dog, be sure to do business with Ira here. He does a pretty decent spay job, but his specialty is really neutering."

Birch clapped the veterinarian on the back with emphasis.

Ira smiled. "Actually, cows are my specialty, but any way I can be of assistance.... My office is down the Stage Road on my farm. Right near the Benton Harbor-Fairview line. It's not hard to find."

Easy for you to say, Strauss thought. "I'll remember, thanks."

The men pulled on their canvas barn coats, the seeming uniform of the farming profession as were the rubber muck boots most of them wore today in place of the heavy hunting boots they had worn on Saturday. Following them out the door, Strauss marveled at a group of men who could get up before dawn day after day, year after year, and milk cows before they had even had their breakfast. He wondered, too, if they ever really became accustomed to the stench of cow shit, or if perhaps they were just born smelling it and never noticed. Shrugging his shoulders, he decided to pay a visit to Lester Blake and find out why nobody wanted him to talk to that man.

Lester Blake loved his animals. He especially loved his own animals, which consisted of a dozen soft-eyed Guernsey cows, a mixed-breed hound dog, and two long-haired cats of unknown origin. Technically speaking, the animals belonged to Adrian Thibault, but since she was often gone, either to work or serving in her capacity as

An Investigation of Local Color

the local constable, Les thought the animals were really more his than hers. She wouldn't mind that thinking, he knew.

Les was fifty-one years old and had lived in a now-ancient mobile home alongside the Thibault dairy barn ever since he was eighteen, before which time he tried to remember as little as possible. Every event of any significance as far as he was concerned occurred while he was living with the Thibaults, first as a hired hand to Adrian's father and now as a caretaker to Adrian herself. He didn't deceive himself for a moment that Adrian needed him in this capacity. He knew that the reason she kept cows at all was because she knew all of Les' life had been tied to the Thibault farm and without it he would have nothing. He liked to think, too, that she understood that since the day she had been born he had adored her more than anyone in the world and would do anything for her, and it was for this reason as much as any other reason that she kept the farm intact. But, of course, they never discussed it, and rightly so.

Les' other love was women. He loved all women, any shape or size, any variety, with very few exceptions. He had remained unmarried all his life simply because he could never have decided which woman he wanted to spend his life with. He overlooked the fact that there were really no takers who wanted to share a stark life with little pay living in an old drafty trailer alongside the Thibault dairy barn. Women loved Lester Blake in return, mostly because he would do anything for them. It mattered very little that the number of women who loved him these days was pretty much reduced to widow ladies who needed wood chopped and lawns mowed. He still had his life on the farm with Adrian. He had the run of her house and sometimes they ate dinner together. Sometimes she came out to the barn early on a morning when she wasn't working and helped milk the cows.

All in all, with just a few minor bumps in the road, Lester Blake considered his life to have been a good one thus far. Until he looked up from his chores one morning and saw a big state cop, the same one who'd come around several days earlier, get out of his cruiser. This time Adrian wasn't home.

He was busy shoveling dung into the manure spreader, the automatic gutter cleaner having long ago broken down, when Strauss found him.

"Lester Blake?"

"That's me."

"I'm Detective Nick Strauss."

The man glanced up but almost immediately went back to his shoveling without a word.

"I'd like to ask you some questions, if you don't mind."

The silence was accompanied by the scraping of the shovel on cement. Obviously, the silent type. Silent and apparently not in possession of anything resembling olfactory nerves, Strauss thought, almost completely overcome by the up-close ammonium smell of cow dung. Secondhand dung such as that experienced down at the Hook was one thing. This fresh stuff was quite another, and obviously more than he could handle. A minute more and he might very well expire without ever learning what Blake knew.

"Would you mind if we stepped outside?"

Les Blake pointed with his chin in the direction of the door, and Strauss thought he saw a glimmer of amusement in his eyes, which otherwise looked distant and unfriendly.

"What is it you want?" he asked as soon as they were out in the fresh air and Strauss had had a chance to gulp some into his lungs in a manner he hoped was less conspicuous than it felt.

"I'm investigating Bill Dunfield's murder. In talking with Sally Glenn, your name came up. She said that you helped out around her place."

"That's right," Blake answered in the clipped manner Strauss was becoming accustomed to when dealing with locals.

Les was a man of medium height with the strong build of one who had worked long and hard all his life. Like the farmers at the Hook, he wore the same sort of flannel shirt with long underwear beneath, the sleeves of both pushed up against the warmth of the cowbarn, and workpants and rubber boots. His hairline was receding, but he was a pleasant-looking man aside from his scowl.

An Investigation of Local Color

"Do you know anything about an incident when Mr. Dunfield shot off his rifle while Mrs. Glenn was out in the field with her dogs?"

"I was there once when it happened."

Strauss saw at once that this wasn't to be an easy conversation. "Could you tell me about it?"

"Sally was out walking the dogs, and Bill shot off his rifle."

"Was he shooting at her?"

"Don't think so."

"What was he doing, then?"

Les' scowl deepened. "I can't see what's inside a man's mind."

Strauss sighed inwardly. "I know that, Mr. Blake. You know both Mrs. Glenn and the now deceased Mr. Dunfield, and I don't know either one of them. I just want to get a handle on what was going on up on that hill. I'm not accusing you of anything. I only want to figure out if any of Mr. Dunfield's actions could have gotten him killed. Can you help me?"

"Probably not."

Strauss considered him for a moment. He knew virtually nothing about the man or his circumstances, but he made a wild guess anyway.

"Adrian's working on this problem, too. I guess you'd be helping her as well."

"You didn't say that right off," Les commented. His face lost some of its stubborn belligerence but none of its wariness.

"I'm sorry about that. I just assumed you would know."

"Well, I didn't."

"Anyway, I was wondering if there was any particular reason Bill Dunfield would shoot off his rifle at the same time Mrs. Glenn was walking her dogs."

The other man shrugged his shoulders. "Dunfield was a mean son of a bitch. He didn't like Sally very much, said she was stuck up."

"You seem to be the only one who knows Sally very well," Strauss remarked carefully. "Do you think she's stuck up?"

Les' face brightened unexpectedly. "Oh, no, not at all. She's a very nice lady, very kindhearted. She is just very shy, too shy to be living out here among strangers. Her husband should take her back to wherever her friends are. He never should have brought her here in the first place."

That seemed to be quite a speech for Lester Blake, at least based on what Strauss had seen of him thus far.

"Was Sally angry over the incident?"

"Not as much as she was scared. She gets scared pretty easy, I would say. I told her that I didn't really think Bill would shoot her or the dogs. I don't neither. He was a mean bastard, but I don't think he was no killer."

"What about his ex-wife? Gwen?"

Les made an unquestionably derisive huffing noise. "There ain't nothing that woman wouldn't do to get something she wanted. Nothing at all good about that woman."

"Why do you say that?"

"There just ain't, that's all. I told Sally to stay well clear of her."

"Why?" Strauss persisted.

"She's just no good. And that's all I'm going to say on the subject."

Les set his jaw stubbornly, and Strauss could see there would be no more forthcoming, at least on that subject.

"What about the other folks up there on Frampton Hill? Do you know any of them?"

He shrugged. "Tom and Milly. They seemed nice enough when they first came out here, though Tom always had some smart-ass remark to make to everyone. But now I guess they're having troubles of their own. I ain't seen them around much lately. The Kinneys up there above Sally's, I met them once or twice. Sally got me some work mowing up there, but they were never around. Paid me real good, though. Rich folks, seems like, the kind that like to live here for a half-hour, then run back to the city. Say, you like that yourself?"

Strauss was taken aback, but he managed to smile. "I'm not sure, Les. I haven't spent much time in the country. It's not something a man gets used to all at once."

"Would you like to come back in the barn and see my cows?"

The last thing Strauss wanted was to go back into the potentially lethal air of the dairy barn, but he assumed from the abrupt change

An Investigation of Local Color

of subject that the man either didn't know anything more or wasn't going to divulge any more information. In an effort to keep Blake on his side, he said he would enjoy seeing the cows.

"These are Guernsey cows, give off some of the best milk there is. These girls here are relatives of the original herd that was here when I first come." Les patted one between the eyes with genuine fondness.

Strauss was surprised at the man's gentleness but even more surprised at the look of the cows. Unlike their black-and-white relatives that were often seen in the area, their coats smeared with the mud and slop that November brings to Vermont, these cows had smooth fawn-colored coats without even a trace of dirt on them. They chewed thoughtfully and gazed back at Strauss with wide brown eyes. He wondered how anything so well kept could smell so foul. Tentatively, he put a hand out to see if their coats were as soft and velvety as they appeared.

Suddenly, without warning, he was under attack. Something or someone dropped out of the sky or, more specifically, out of the rafters onto his head with the most unholy, terrifying screech Strauss could ever recall hearing in the short second he had to think about it before his instincts compelled him to defend himself. Something was tearing at his scalp even through the cloth of his hat. With a yell of his own he slapped at it furiously, and when that neither dislodged the thing nor kept it from screeching Strauss tried shaking his head, yelling louder. The cows, unnerved by this sight, started mooing and fidgeting in distress, adding still further to the fray.

"Damn you, hold still, I said."

Through the din Strauss heard Les' voice, though he was a little uncertain just who the man was damning.

"Let go, Elizabeth!"

And with that, the screaming demon on his head released its hold and was removed.

"I don't know what gets into her sometimes," Les commented calmly.

In his arms he cradled an angry-eyed longhaired yellow-and-white cat, presumably Elizabeth. As he gently stroked her head, her expression changed and she purred loudly, but not before she very decidedly licked her lips in Strauss' direction. God, he hated cats! Worse yet, all the scrambling around had made him suck in all sorts of poisonous air, and he felt very close to losing what little breakfast he had had.

"You got yourself cut up pretty good, Detective. We'll have to do something about it."

Strauss wanted to point out that he hadn't gotten himself cut up, but as Les already seemed unduly amused by the whole situation it seemed as though he had better bear up with as much good nature as he could muster. Meanwhile his cheek dripped blood from the self-satisfied feline's claws. Les set the tiny cat on the floor and motioned Strauss to follow him. With a backward glance, he saw the creature shake her head and arch her back arrogantly. He half turned with the idea of giving it a better look at his new boots. Instead of running, the banshee sat down and began to lick her paws.

"Adrian loves that cat," Les commented at his shoulder.

"What the Hell for? Her charm?" Strauss muttered.

"They're a lot alike. Here, smear some of this on those cuts." He handed Strauss a green tin.

Bag Balm. "You want me to put this on my face? Isn't this for...?"

"Yup. Cow teats. But it works good on other things, like cat scratches."

"I'll pass." It was beginning to feel like one of those eternal mornings when nothing goes right.

"Suit yourself."

This time Strauss could see for certain that Lester Blake was laughing at him.

"Thanks for all your help."

"Glad to help," Les returned, looking more cheerful than he had at any time in the interview. He had apparently failed to notice the irony in Strauss' voice.

Before he was even out of the driveway, Strauss discovered the number-one rule of dairy farming: Never go into the barn in clothes you intend wearing out in public later in the day. The smell was so powerful, he felt the urge to glance over the seat to assure himself that none of the fawn beauties had hidden themselves in the back. In spite of the damp cold outside, he rolled down all the windows and drove

An Investigation of Local Color

quickly to his apartment in Fairview, thankfully avoiding the landlady on his way around the back. Steam from the shower sent cow fumes wafting over him, and he washed his hair twice just to be sure. He donned fresh khakis before considering the rank heap of discarded clothes on the floor. He considered burning them, but since he wasn't sure where he would do it without arousing his landlady's ever-present curiosity he settled for stuffing them in the bottom of his clothes hamper.

A cautious sniff at his new boots told him that he was going to continue to bear signs of his visit to the Thibault farm, but he put them on again anyway and headed out the door for the State Police barracks. As Strauss rounded the corner of the house, he saw the curtain in the front window move and he quickened his pace in order to avoid a questioning-and-answering confrontation on the front porch in which he would have to admit to his failure to collar the murderer, and Mrs. Hutchins would wring her hands in distress and then go back into the house and call her friends with her inside information.

It was quiet at the barracks with the bulk of the staff being out on Route 4 catching speeders or assisting the game wardens in their search for illegally obtained deer. There was a message in his box to see the chief. Strauss found that man in the hall outside his office, having just returned from a high-fat, cholesterol-laden lunch at the Tin Soldier, Fairview's equivalent of the Hook, Line, and Sinker. Chief Peterman was a native of that part of Vermont that made Fairview seem like a teeming city. The son of generations of Vermont farmers, he had adopted the low-key, brief-and-to-the-point manner of so many of the locals. He wasn't possessed of an enormous amount of gray matter, but he did his job well and was fair-minded and blessed with the respect of the locals as well as the ability to understand them. That was an important asset in an area that was gradually being taken over by the monies and ideas of people from out of state.

Strauss liked the chief as well as he ever liked any of his supervisors, but even given that man's renowned fairness he thought he could detect the slightest resentment at having a city cop thrust on him, however short the term might be. It seemed to Strauss that like so many other natives, Chief Peterman held the belief that anything an outsider could do a Vermonter could do equally well or, more likely, better. So he approached his chief cautiously, knowing he had nothing substantial to report on his latest case.

"Come in, Detective," the chief said without taking his eyes off the mail he was sorting through in his hand. As soon as he shut the door and tossed the mail on his desk. he continued. "What is the latest on the Dunfield murder?'

"I've interviewed several potential suspects, some with alibis, some without. Until forensics gets back to me, I've really got nothing to make an arrest with."

"You mean no motives, no suspicions anywhere?"

"That's part of the problem. It seems as if the deceased gave everyone in town a reason to wish him dead. Everyone I've talked with had a problem with the man, and apparently there are a few I've not gotten to who have motive as well. But I can't very well make an arrest based on motive and opportunity or I'll have all of Benton Harbor locked up."

"Well, this is unexpected."

"I beg your pardon?" The chief was a man of few words, and Strauss often found himself needing a clarification of a comment. At the moment, however, he had a feeling he knew well where this was going.

"I was assuming with your experience and expertise that this would be a fairly routine assignment," Peterman said mildly.

Strauss was tempted to point out that murder was hardly his area of expertise even when working in the city, but he didn't want to appear to be incompetent or to be making excuses for his failure to arrest a suspect. More importantly, he didn't want to be removed from the case, so he said instead, "I'm not sure a murder is ever very routine, Chief. I'm certainly doing everything I can at this time. The forensics report should help."

"I think it would be a good idea for you to have someone working with you."

An Investigation of Local Color

Strauss thought quickly through the list of possible candidates for that assignment and rejected each immediately. He definitely did not want a partner who at best would be bumbling and at worse would be Gary Shubert.

"I don't think it's necessary for you to take anyone off their regular assignment right now. Constable Thibault in Benton Harbor is giving me quite a lot of help, and since she is familiar with the area she is probably more useful than a man from here in Fairview."

Chief Peterman raised an eyebrow as if he didn't quite buy that argument. He considered Strauss carefully for a long moment before saying, "Okay. For the time being, carry on. But I'm sure that I don't need to remind you that the longer you go without making an arrest, the slighter your chances become. The last time there was a questionable death up in Benton Harbor, it ended up being ruled an accident, though there were certainly suspicious overtones. I do not want another accidental death ruling coming out of that town. Between little old ladies falling down their stairs and hunters shooting each other in the woods and idiots driving their cars through Lake Champlain in the winter, there are enough accidents up there."

"This is definitely not an accidental death, Chief."

"I understand that, son. Just try to wrap it up promptly so that some bigwig from state doesn't come around here thinking someone doesn't know how to do his job. Okay?"

"Yes, sir." Strauss got to his feet. "This questionable death you mentioned, when was that?"

"About six years ago. Before I came on here. One of the troopers was reminding me about it this morning. Fella by the name of Brian Borden supposedly got kicked in the head by a cow."

Since that didn't sound particularly suspicious to him Strauss waited for the punchline, but the chief had turned again to his mail. He sighed. Was it ever going to be possible for someone with a Vermont pedigree to give him a detailed account of a story?

"Excuse me, Chief, but why was that even considered a possible murder?"

"Because a lady friend of the victim, who was married but not to her, called the barracks with information that caused suspicion," Chief Peterman explained patiently as if this were information Strauss should have been able to ascertain without bothering him.

"But there was never an arrest?"

Peterman shook his head. "The only suspect had an alibi."

"I see."

Strauss made a mental note to make a trip to the local paper and look up the story for specifics on the off chance that some of his new friends' names cropped up. He opened the door and came face to face with Trooper Shubert. The younger man had either been listening in or had been about to knock.

"Anything worth hearing, Shubert?"

"You tell me, hotshot."

Strauss turned his back and continued down the hallway, but not before he heard the trooper ask ingratiatingly if the chief had a moment in which he could speak to him.

Strauss went back out to the car and headed for Rutland.

The New England Tampon Company was one of the larger employers in the city of Rutland. A plant had been established there in the early seventies, when the workforce in the Southern New England states had become sufficiently impressed with their skills to form a union that demanded higher wages and greater benefits. The United Tampon Workers had taken fifteen years to discover that there were major injustices being done to their colleagues up North in Vermont, so for that time the company had operated with the great advantage of a sizable workforce that had rarely known anything above minimum wage. With the advent of the union, NET had used its accumulated profits to research new and better technology that would allow them to manufacture their little cotton products at the same profitable rate but with fewer workers.

That was where the manufacturing engineers such as Jack Glenn came in. Jack was a mechanical genius. Along with his team of similarly endowed colleagues, he was responsible for developing auto-

An Investigation of Local Color

mated lines that could manufacture the product as efficiently as people had in the past. He was in the midst of developing and being responsible when a girl from the front office with a big man bearing a visitor's badge following in tow interrupted him. The girl looked familiar, but he couldn't place her and didn't bother to try. The man he had never seen before. He assumed it was one of many salesmen he saw in a week who made an effort to sell him on the newest in automation and technology.

"I'm sorry to bother you, Mr. Glenn," the girl spoke loudly over the humming of the machines bearing little wrapped packages tidily down rows of conveyor belts to their eventual destination in forty-count boxes. "This is a police detective, and he says he needs to talk to you."

"That's fine. I can talk to him."

Strauss watched as the girl hightailed it back to the office. He thought she was probably glad to get out of the stiflingly dry environment of the factory floor. In addition to the dry heat and the constant hum of machines, there was a strange, oppressive odor in the air that he could not readily identify.

"Detective Nick Strauss," he said and showed his badges before offering his hand. He glanced at the man's ID badge to make sure the girl had brought him to the correct person.

"Jack Glenn." The other man shook his hand with an enthusiastic grin. Then he flipped up his ID badge for Strauss' closer examination. "John Glenn, actually. My parents were big fans of the aerospace industry when I was born. They wanted me to become a rocket scientist." Jack's grin widened. "And in a way, that's exactly what I am."

To Strauss' surprise, Glenn drew an unwrapped tampon from his pocket and demonstrated the properties that made it similar to a space rocket. Then as casually as most men stick a pen back in their pocket, he stuck the tampon in his shirt pocket, its little string tail trailing out to reveal its presence. Strauss wondered about a man who was able to walk around with a tampon hanging out of his pocket. Then again, he wondered why he, as a man of the world, felt vaguely embarrassed in the presence of so many feminine products.

"I take it you want to talk about Bill Dunfield. Sally said you stopped by the house yesterday."

"Yes. I understand that your shifts overlapped sometimes."

"Daily, in fact. I always stay late to be sure things run smoothly on second shift."

"Any problems between the two of you?"

Glenn shook his head. "None. I wish he could have been nicer to Sally. She gets lonely up there on Frampton Hill, and he picked on her. But as far as an employee goes, he was one of the best. Always arrived early for work and ready to get on with it. His lines nearly always ran smoothly, production from his machines was always high."

The entire time he talked, Glenn's eyes followed the little overhead conveyors bearing thousands of white cotton products. Now and then he stopped to make an adjustment to a nearby machine.

"So you liked him?"

Glenn shrugged. "Yes, I liked him well enough. As I said, he was a good worker, and as far as I know he never made any trouble."

"What sort of trouble do you have in a tampon factory?"

"More than you might imagine. We have very high standards in here because of the type of product we make, and sometimes it is difficult to get employees to comply. But Bill always wore the proper safety and sanitary attire, and he never stole the product."

"Stole the product?"

Glenn looked away from his lines to fix a deadly serious expression on Strauss. "Yes. We have a lot of trouble with employees stealing the tampons. Putting a few in their pockets every night and taking them home. As far as I know, Bill didn't do that."

"Right," Strauss said for lack of anything more appropriate. Why, for example, would Bill Dunfield steal a handful of tampons anyway?

Just as that thought cleared his mind, there was a sharp crack overhead and he looked up just in time to see dozens of tampons raining down on his head as they broke free from their conveyors. They rained down on Jack Glenn's head as well, and he laughed merrily as he scooped them up and dropped them in a nearby white plastic bucket marked "seconds."

An Investigation of Local Color

"I've been waiting for that to happen," he informed Strauss cheerfully. "I just wasn't sure where it would be." He turned and called to a man hovering over a nearby machine. "It's the number-two line we want to tighten down, Joe. Do that, then set the speed again. They can be such tricky little buggers," Glenn said to Strauss, though Strauss wasn't sure whether he meant the tampons or the machines.

Clearly, though, the man enjoyed the challenges of the tampon industry. It was rather beyond Strauss to imagine how. The lacerations Elizabeth had inflicted on him smarted even more after having been pummeled by three dozen or so tampons, and whatever the smell in the air was it was seriously threatening to overcome him as surely as had Les Blake's cow dung.

"So you were home with your wife on Thursday morning around 3 A.M.?" he asked, trying to draw the conversation back to the murder.

"No, actually, I think I was here."

"You were here? At 3 a.m.? Sally said you were home."

Glenn continued to pick his product off the factory floor. Strauss wondered what became of tampons thrown in the "seconds" bucket.

"She probably thought I was. I get called in so often to fix problems just like this," Glenn held up a fistful of tampons, "she probably just lost track of which night I was here. I happen to remember because it was an odd circumstance. I got this call in the night—it would have been during the third shift—and they said one of the overhead conveyors broke and the product was flying off in all directions. So I jumped in my car and got here as soon as I could, that would be about forty-five minutes later. When I arrived, the problem had been fixed. And let me tell you, that is a memorable event. It's very rare that anyone except one of us engineers can fix a problem of the magnitude of the one described to me on the phone, but apparently someone did, though nobody was able to tell me who. This was about 4:30 in the A.M. I remember that particularly because I debated whether to drive home and come back at 7:00 or just stay on."

"And what did you decide?"

"I stayed on. There didn't seem much point in driving all the way home just to turn around and come back an hour later. I just let myself into the offices and slept for an hour on one of the sofas in there before coming back onto the floor, probably about 6:30."

Leaving both Glenns without alibi for at least part of the time in question, Strauss thought to himself.

"Tell me, Mr. Glenn, did it bother you at all that Bill Dunfield 'picked on' your wife?"

"It bothered me that he upset Sally, sure, but it was basically harmless stuff, just teasing. I told her not to let it bother her. Sally's a great girl," Glenn smiled, "but she is very sensitive. I think it made her a target for a great big tease like Bill."

"A 'great big tease'?"

Glenn nodded, his eyes on the overhead conveyor, which was now running its cargo again in the appropriate direction. Nick glanced up and just as quickly down again, not wanting to risk any further damage to his face.

"You know about his firing off his rifle?"

"Of course I do. I talk to my wife, you know. But he wasn't shooting it AT her, he was shooting it into the air. You know, like they do in the movies."

In the movies? Glenn scurried over to a control panel and made some sort of adjustment before looking up at his precious travelers again.

"One more thing, could you tell me where I might find Bill Dunfield's coworkers?"

"Sure. His station is right around that corner there to the right. The shift changed right before you got here so his group should be all there."

"Thanks."

"Glad to be of help," Jack Glenn replied without taking his eyes off his machines.

Glancing back, Strauss saw him rub his hands together enthusiastically, like a man about to tuck into a thick, juicy steak or an overhead conveyor line with thousands of tampons enroute to God only knew where. Or was it that he had just tucked it to a State Police detective?

An Investigation of Local Color

Strauss followed the path Glenn had indicated and found a group of machine control panels manned by two women and a man. There was also an empty stool. He introduced himself and waited for the usual disparaging remarks about Bill Dunfield. To his surprise one of the women, a large, youngish girl whose proportions could rival Dunfield's ex, burst into tears at the mention of his name.

"I just can't believe it," she said, wiping her eyes.

"You don't know why someone would want to hurt Mr. Dunfield, then?"

"Oh, no. He was so kind," she wailed.

Strauss turned questioning eyes to the other woman. This lady was middle aged, stern-looking, and unlikely to sugarcoat an issue. She also shook her head.

"He was always very good to work with. When my husband was sick with cancer last year, he often took my work for me. Bless him, I don't know how he did it because this place has got us spread so thin we can hardly do all the work one of us's got, let alone take on someone else's. He did, though."

Strauss saw that the male worker felt the same distress at the loss of his coworker as did the women. This couldn't possibly be an act.

"Do you have any idea how Mr. Dunfield got along with Jack Glenn?" he asked the man whose name, according to his starched white coverall, was Harold.

"Bill hated Glenn. Only person I ever heard him badmouth besides that ex-wife of his."

"Any idea why?"

"He just said Glenn was a spoiled, snotty-nosed kid who didn't know his ass from...well, you know."

"Do you share that opinion of Mr. Glenn?"

Strauss glanced at all three workers, who shook their heads in a vague, uncommitted way. No one spoke immediately, as if uncertain what to say. Into the silence came a whooshing sound, and Strauss glanced up quickly to see if anything was about to come down on his head. There was nothing.

"Mr. Glenn ain't a bad man, as supervisors go," the stern-faced woman said. "'Course, he's mainly responsible for these machines replacing all the people who used to work here, but I don't think he knows that. He's just weird."

"Weird? How do you mean?"

The three workers looked at each other, searching for a way to express Jack Glenn's weirdness. The whooshing noise sounded again and apparently lent inspiration, because Harold offered, "It's like all he ever thinks about is this company. All he understands is how to make this factory run better, and he gets so excited about tampons, for God's sake, like...like...." Harold ran out of words.

"Like he's a cheerleader for the tampon business," the youngish woman clarified.

The other two nodded their heads in agreement.

"He's so caught up in the running of the machines that I don't think he ever noticed that Bill didn't like him. He'd come over here before going home for the night and slap Bill on the back and give him a big thumbs-up, and even though Bill'd be snarling practically in his face I don't think he ever really noticed."

"We could give that man the finger," the stern-faced lady went on, demonstrating as she spoke, "and he'd just look up thinking we were pointing at the overheads."

"And that's why Bill didn't like Mr. Glenn?" Strauss asked and was answered not just by three nodding heads but by yet another strong whooshing sound. The smell in the air had become even more overpowering as they spoke. "What is that smell?"

"That is what, in the tampon business, is known as feminine protection," one of the women informed him as easily as if she were describing the weather. "Our shift manufactures the deodorized tampons."

"I see," Strauss replied. He was sorry he had asked, and he decided that now was as good a time as any to make an exit.

As he was leaving, he heard the cheerful voice of Jack Glenn above the hum of the conveyors.

An Investigation of Local Color

"Turn down that sprayer to level three, Harold! Atta boy, good job!"

Well, you had to admire a man who enjoyed his work. Strauss found his way to the personnel desk, where he had been asked to stop and leave his visitor's badge on his way out.

"One more thing, sir," the secretary stopped him before he could leave. "We need you to sign this. Company policy for all visitors."

Strauss quickly read the statement attached to a clipboard. "The undersigned agrees not to divulge any information concerning the manufacturing processes and procedures witnessed while inside the New England Tampon Company. Any violation of this agreement will result in probable prosecution. I,_ _____fully understand the above terms. Date:_____."

Strauss glanced up at the secretary, who stared back impassively.

"Did I miss something in there?" he asked.

"Excuse me, sir?" she replied politely.

"I thought maybe there were state secrets being manufactured in there."

"Oh, no, sir. We manufacture tampons," the girl replied without cracking a smile or even appearing to want to.

"I see. Very secret ones, too, I understand." He signed his name.

"Yes, sir."

She took the clipboard from him, examined his signature and, obviously believing she now possessed the required sworn secrecy, or if not the means to prosecute the Vermont State Police, she finally smiled.

"Have a nice day."

"It's already been so terrific," he grumbled.

Out in the cruiser, he quickly reviewed his information and jotted some notes. He was already slightly late for his meeting with Adrian, but he hoped that she, as a law enforcer herself, would understand and wait for him. So wrapped up was he in that thought that it took a few moments longer than it normally would have for him to notice that a new smell had permeated the air inside the car. On the drive to Rutland the smell of the barnyard had vied with Nick's cigarette smoke for seniority. Now there was a heavy, sickeningly sweet smell that overpowered both. Putting a nose to his jacket, Strauss detected the cloying scent of what Dunfield's coworkers had termed feminine protection. Perfect! He finally had an opportunity for what he had expected to be a pleasant business dinner with a reasonably intelligent coworker, and he smelled like a damned tampon. What little he knew of Adrian Thibault left him wishing he had opted for eau de cow shit.

He smoked a quick cigarette as he navigated the street between NET and the Rutland hospital but had little hope that the smoke that nonsmokers were forever complaining about would overpower his newest body odor. He parked the cruiser in the lot and found his way to the visitors' entrance, where Adrian had agreed to meet him.

When he didn't see her immediately Strauss inquired at the desk, which was manned by a sweet-faced elderly lady of the sort that every hospital should try to employ. She glowed happily at the very idea of being helpful, then smiled even more brightly at the mention of Adrian's name.

"Adrian phoned down nearly forty-five minutes ago to say that an emergency had come in at the very end of her shift. If it's not too much trouble, could you wait? She said she wouldn't be too long."

Strauss smiled and said he wouldn't mind waiting.

"Adrian is such a nice girl, don't you think?" said the little lady whose nametag read "Welcome to Rutland Hospital. My name is Doris."

Strauss agreed that Adrian was, indeed, a nice girl and made another attempt at a getaway.

"The doctors all just love her. They all fight to have her on their shift because she is such a good nurse, very cool, which is what you need down there in the ER, you know."

Strauss agreed again that a cool head was just the thing for a busy ER. He had been around enough little old ladies to recognize the attempt at less-than-subtle matchmaking.

"Oh, here she comes now," Doris said, then lowering her voice so only Nick could hear, "maybe she can fix up those lacerations on your face, dear. They look terribly inflamed. You just ask her."

An Investigation of Local Color

Strauss wasn't terribly surprised when she patted his hand gently and beamed some more.

Unlike him, Adrian had had a chance to change out of her working clothes, and she looked fresher than anyone had a right to look after a full shift of nursing. She had pulled a heavy sweater and parka over her jeans and the inevitable boots, and she carried a shoulder bag, presumably packed with her uniform. Normally Strauss would have admired her, but her fresh good looks reminded him how battered and smelly he himself must be. She looked at once at his face but, in spite of her medical background, didn't comment.

"Thank you for delivering my message, Doris. I see you have met Detective Strauss." Adrian smiled at the receptionist.

"I have met Mr. Strauss. A very nice man," the little lady whispered conspiratorially, as if Mr. Strauss couldn't hear.

"Yes, I'm sure," Adrian commented with just a touch of irony. "Sorry to have kept you waiting."

"Part of the job. Tough day at work?"

She shook her head. "Obviously not as tough as your day." Then she was striding off down the hall in the direction of the parking lot. "I'm parked over in the staff lot. Want to follow me downtown? I know a place that won't be crowded and serves good food."

Strauss nodded. He was glad they didn't have to drive together.

Adrian drove with familiarity through the streets to a small downtown restaurant, away from the more trendy places frequented by tourists and skiers. It was the sort of establishment where you seated yourself where you wanted to sit instead of being shown to a table. Predictably, the menu was already on the table and didn't list quiche and wine coolers as possible choices. The room was, however, nicely lit for quiet conversation and, as Adrian had promised, not crowded.

Adrian picked a table with a stunning view of the downtown shopping center, which was now mostly empty, having been vacated for the economically more promising new mall on the far side of town. She hung her parka on a nearby hook on the wall and sat down. Strauss had barely seated himself opposite when she said, "So, you've met Elizabeth. What were you doing at my farm?"

Strauss considered his answer carefully. He wondered if she was making an educated guess based on the scratches on his face, in which case Elizabeth must be a frequent offender, or if she had been informed directly.

"I've met Elizabeth," he affirmed.

"And the answer to my question?"

She wasn't hostile, exactly, but Strauss definitely had the impression that she was quietly angry.

"I was talking to Lester Blake." He looked at his menu, adopting the "less is better" form of conversing that Vermonters like Adrian found so effective.

"You might have let me in on that, you know." Now there was no question that Adrian was angry. Her dark eyes sparked at him over the table.

Strauss smiled mildly even though he knew it would annoy her further. "I might have, Adrian, but you sort of forgot to mention that Les was such a friend of Sally Glenn."

"What's that got to do with anything? Les loves every nearly every woman he's ever met."

"With one fairly notable exception. He doesn't think much of Gwenivere Dunfield."

That shut her up. She looked at her own menu.

"Sort of forgot to mention that, too, didn't you?"

She looked at him irritably. "No, I didn't forget. So Les can't stand Gwen Dunfield. So he does some work for Sally Glenn and likes her a lot. I'm not sure that warrants questioning him in a murder investigation."

"Adrian, in a murder investigation a good cop questions everyone, no matter how irrelevant they may seem," Strauss explained patiently. "Just because these people are your friends and neighbors doesn't mean you can decide who gets questioned and who is above suspicion. I don't need to tell you that."

For a moment Strauss thought that Adrian might throw the menu at him. But she was basically a sensible girl—a very nice girl, accord-

An Investigation of Local Color

ing to Doris, the receptionist—and she changed her mind, settling instead for merely slamming it firmly on the placemat in front of her.

"God, you're arrogant!"

"Maybe it takes some arrogance to do this job. Look, do we have to argue about this? Could we be on the same side for just a few minutes?"

His question went unanswered because a waiter arrived at their table at that precise moment. He went through a list of specials: special soup, special appetizer, special entree, special dessert, none of which Strauss paid the least bit of attention to, and he suspected that Adrian didn't either. She ordered the special and a beer.

All the while the waiter had been reciting, Strauss noticed that he had been sniffing, as if trying to identify some unknown smell in the air. In order to be rid of him quickly, he quoted Adrian's order, though he had no idea what the special was or how he would cope with yet another Budweiser from the tap.

"As I was saying...."

"You were saying that we should be on the same side. And, in fact, I thought we were, but I stupidly assumed that that meant you would keep me informed and not go around questioning my friends and family behind my back."

This was going badly, Strauss thought. Maybe he should have accepted the chief's offer of a state-issued partner instead of this spitting-angry female constable, but he just had this sneaking intuition that the only way to crack this case was with some sort of inside information that only someone inside Benton Harbor had. Adrian was his best source. What he didn't know, having had only limited success with women and, so far anyway, no success at all with Vermonters, was how to get her working with him. He rubbed his scratched face with both hands and tried to keep his temper.

"You're as bad tempered as that cat," he grumbled.

Adrian's eyes narrowed, but she said nothing. Strauss had little doubt, though, that she had the same lethal tendencies, at least in thought, as did the screeching Elizabeth.

"Let's back up," Strauss suggested. He found himself gritting his teeth when the waiter interrupted him to set two glasses of ice water in front of them, giving a large sniff as he did so. "I only spoke to Lester Blake because Sally mentioned that he had witnessed Dunfield shooting off his rifle while she was out walking her dogs. According to Sally, he had given her assurance that he felt Dunfield was safe enough, but that she should beware of the former Mrs. Dunfield. I thought it was a possibility that since Blake seemed to know all three people, one of whom is now dead and the other two without alibis for the time of that murder, he might be able to shed some light on the subject.

"And you couldn't have told me about that last night when you phoned?" Adrian asked.

Damn, this woman was persistent when she wanted an explanation.

"I would have except that...."

The waiter appeared again, this time with their beer. He sniffed repeatedly, like a dog on a scent, as he set down the glasses. This time Strauss had had enough.

"It's feminine protection, all right? Quit with the sniffing, will you?"

The waiter, who couldn't have been much more than twenty or so, blushed furiously and backed away. For her part, Adrian stared openmouthed, then burst into laughter.

"It's what?"

"You heard me. From over at the tampon plant. Apparently it's one of the hazards of this investigation."

"I thought you had a decidedly unmasculine sort of cologne on," she laughed.

Personally, he thought she was laughing more than the situation actually warranted.

"Yeah, well, I'm not too crazy about it myself."

Strauss sniffed at his sleeve and grimaced. Suddenly, he felt tired and battered, not to mention smelly and in bad need of a shower. He

An Investigation of Local Color

most definitely didn't feel like wooing a woman, even in so much as it took to be able to work amicably together.

"I don't suppose there is any way we can just get on with this business?" he asked.

Adrian's laughter faded. She regarded him evenly, calculatingly.

"Let's get on with it, then. But in the future, unless you want to call on someone else to take over in my place I want to be informed when someone is going to be questioned. I will do the same for you. Deal?"

Her look more than her tone or words left no room for negotiating. In another mood, in another place, outside of Vermont, Strauss might have argued the point just to achieve victory. Now he realized he was outmatched.

"Deal."

"Okay. What's the story on Jack Glenn?"

Strauss filled her in on his conversation with both Glenn and Dunfield's coworkers, ending with the news that now neither Jack nor Sally had alibis.

On that disheartening note the waiter reappeared and, casting a wary glance at Nick, he tossed their plates on the table and made a hasty retreat. Strauss looked down at the special of the day. Meatloaf. Shit!

"What's wrong?" Adrian asked. Let it never be said she didn't have excellent intuitions when it came to those all-important facial expressions. "Isn't that what you ordered?"

"No, I ordered it. It's fine. Really."

She couldn't possibly know, at least he didn't think she could, that every single or newly divorced man gets inundated with meatloaves either from single or newly divorced women or well-intentioned little old ladies. On top of that, it was one of the few things Strauss himself could make, though granted he made it badly. He really, really hated meatloaf. But he saw Adrian watching him. She was already proving more perceptive than he would have given her credit for, so he smiled and picked up his fork. After watching him for a few more moments, she did the same.

"I wasn't even that lucky," she informed him. "I checked out the local Jehovah's Witness church. There is one in Rutland and one in Fairview. I went to the church office here in Rutland, and they never heard of anyone named Lee Madigan. Without a picture or description, I couldn't ask for more. I called the church office in Fairview. Same story."

"It sounded like the Boyces were pretty sure of the Jehovah's Witness angle. Are there any other churches in practical driving distance?"

"Not really. I tried the phone book as well. Three Madigans, none of them Lee, but I called them all, just for kicks. Two were single mothers, sisters living within two blocks of each other. The other sounded like an old man. No one had ever heard of Lee Madigan, or said they hadn't. I could do more follow-up, but I think it would be a dead end."

"You're thinking Gwen gave us the wrong name?"

"That's what I'm thinking. Do you want to go back to her?"

Strauss thought a minute, then shook his head. "Not just yet. I'm still waiting for that forensics report, and in the meantime I think I want to chat with Milly Boyce without the mouthy husband. She might be able to give us some help with the boyfriend thing as well."

They ate in silence for a time. Nick could only manage half of the meatloaf, but Adrian put all of hers away, then eyed him critically, as one might a fickle eater who is wasting a good meal.

"Do you want to know what Blake had to say?"

Adrian downed the last of her beer and shook her head. "No."

Strauss raised a surprised eyebrow and waited for her to elaborate. This time he didn't need to ask.

"Les Blake has lived on my family's farm since before I was born. Anything he might have said to you, I already know about. He is a very, very good man."

"Funny, that seems to be what everyone says, and with about the same amount of defensive emphasis that you just used. I'm curious about that."

"Well, don't be. Take it at face value because that is what it is. Les loves Benton Harbor, and nearly everyone there loves him. He's uncomplicated and should be left alone. He can't help with this murder."

"And does his goodness extend to outsiders?"

"Detective Strauss, these days almost all of us have trouble extending our generosity to outsiders. People from down country come up here, and they want paved roads and new laws and better school buildings and faster-paced lifestyles. None of us wants to change much to accommodate people from the outside. Les is no different."

"It's safe to assume then that he set the attack cat on me?"

Adrian smiled slightly. "Probably. But he probably offered you some Bag Balm to make it all better, didn't he?"

Strauss wondered again if she knew that for a fact or was guessing, but he didn't ask. He nodded instead. "Yes, but I have a philosophical problem with smearing something on my face that belongs on the female parts of a cow."

She shrugged. "Your loss. It's served generations of cows and Thibaults very well."

The waiter tossed their check on the table and ran off. Adrian looked at it and put half on the table along with a tip. Strauss paid his half and added a bigger tip to make up for scaring the waiter. Normally, he was chivalrous enough to either pay for both meals or at the very least, since this was supposed to be a business dinner, have the state pick up the tab, but Adrian seemed like the type of woman who was better left with her own check.

"I have to work an extra half-shift tomorrow to cover for someone so I won't be home until almost 9. You can call or stop by if you're in town. If there is anything I can do here in Rutland, give me a call at the hospital," Adrian said as they left the restaurant and walked to their cars.

"I'll do that. In the meantime I'll see what Milly has to say when she is by herself. And I'll try for a better description of the boyfriend," Strauss told her.

He was trying, as he thought she must be, for a conciliatory tone. After all, it wasn't just Strauss who needed her. She was definitely lacking in experience with this sort of thing.

"Do you mind if I ask just how you happened to be elected constable? Just out of curiosity."

Adrian stop searching through her bag for her keys and searched his expression instead. She surely was one who thought out all her answers carefully, Strauss noted.

"I just wondered. Benton Harbor seems to have something of a male-dominated society, and I just wondered how they happened to elect a female constable." Strauss was beginning to feel sorry he had asked the longer she stared at him, as if measuring the sincerity of his question. He shrugged. "It was just idle curiosity. I didn't mean to imply that you weren't suited to the job."

"I sort of inherited it, you might say," Adrian replied and returned again to the search through her purse. "Generally it isn't a much-sought-after position since it usually involves run-over mailboxes and escaped cows running rampant through some flatlanders' dead herb garden. My father was constable for thirty years simply because he was asked to be. When he died, I was asked. It seemed only right to say yes."

"Oh." Strauss could think of nothing else to say. He remembered Trooper Shubert saying that Adrian had been voted in as a joke and didn't realize it. Which of them was right? It didn't seem politically correct to inquire, so he kept the thought to himself and resolved to sort it out through his new breakfast friends at the Hook, Line, and Sinker.

"Well, then, thanks for having dinner with me. Under the circumstances, it was probably more of a treat for me than it was for you." Strauss smiled, indicating his fragrant state and lacerated face.

"Here, take this," Adrian said. She handed him something but it had become too dark to read whatever was printed on the tiny tin she had given him.

"What is it?"

An Investigation of Local Color

"Peace offering. For your face. Nurse's orders. You can buy it at all the local pharmacies, but this is on Elizabeth and me."

"Thanks."

"Sure thing. See you." She climbed in her truck and drove away.

Strauss got into the cruiser and switched on the overhead light to look at the peace offering she had given him. It was a small green pocket-sized tin of Bag Balm.

5

It was snowing the next morning when Strauss got up. The TV, which picked up only one station, reported that there was a brisk wind blowing and at least four more inches could be expected by nightfall, making this the first significant snowfall of the season. Deer throughout the state groaned, and the men who tracked them cheered. Strauss resolved to buy himself a warmer parka than the one the state issued. If the temperature of his drafty apartment was anything to go by, he would be needing that and much more to get through his first winter in the country.

The mood at the Hook was almost festive due to the snow. It wasn't that anyone particularly loved snow—Benton Harbor could hardly be called one of Vermont's winter resorts—but like Vermonters throughout the state, the citizens of Benton Harbor thrived on any sign that one season was ending and another beginning. Not to mention that snow made deer hunting easier and ice fishing not too far off in the future.

"Hey, Constable," Donnie Thibault called as soon as he stepped through the door. Cigarettes were stubbed out on breakfast plates. "It looks like you tangled with a wildcat."

This comment was followed by enough laughter to let Strauss know that the story of his quarrel with Elizabeth was a matter of public record. He smiled with as much good nature as he could manage while wishing a similar go-'round with the vicious feline on each one of the men at the table. He pulled up a chair.

A young girl who could have easily been the sister of the Saturday waitress set a cup of coffee in front of him before he even asked. She was very pretty and looked as though she should be on her way to junior high school instead of working.

Through the door to the kitchen, Strauss could see Harvey scrubbing down the grill, still in his stretched-too-tight t-shirt. The pretty young girl, having taken care of her customers, puffed delicately on a cigarette nearby.

Strauss sipped his coffee and looked around the table. Franklyn Birch sat at his usual place at the far end of the table opposite Strauss. Beside him to one side were the Chandlers, just as they had been yesterday—Strauss hoped—and on the other side Donnie Thibault and his cousin, or something, Junior. Everyone was in just the same place as yesterday with the exception of Ira, the vet, who wasn't there, though there was an empty chair where he had been the previous day. All eyes watched him until he gradually became aware of Birch tapping his pack of cigarettes on the table and beside him, Kenyon—Strauss hoped—flicking his disposable lighter up and down.

Hint taken, he thought. He glanced around the restaurant. The only other patrons were a couple at the farthest table. The man was sitting with his back to Nick, but he was hunched over and blowing his own cigarette smoke discreetly into his coffee cup in order to hide the smoke rather than give up even one illegal puff.

"Ought to arrest that man," Strauss muttered and lit a cigarette of his own.

His new friends all smiled and lit up with relief. Chatting, gossiping, assisting in a murder investigation, it was all so much easier to do over a cigarette.

"So what's the news?" Birch asked.

"Not so good," Strauss admitted. "Jack Glenn thought Dunfield was a great employee. Dunfield hated him for being a smart, though somewhat dimwitted, boss. Fellow employees loved Dunfield. Said he'd do anything for them."

That statement elicited the surprised looks Strauss was expecting.

"Dunfield?"

"No shit! Can't be."

"Always found some way to be too busy to help me."

An Investigation of Local Color

At his end of the table, Birch smirked as though Strauss had stupidly fallen for bad information. "You must have talked to someone he was sleeping with, Detective."

"Maybe," Strauss granted. "But I talked to two women and a man. He couldn't have been sleeping with them all at once. I don't think this area is all that enlightened."

"And we don't want to be neither," one of the Chandlers commented. "How about that? Who'da thought Dunfield woulda had a generous bone in him?"

"What about Glenn?" Birch asked. "They don't like him down at the tampon place?"

This isn't helpful, Strauss thought. *I'm supposed to drop the clues, and these guys are supposed to fill in the blanks, not ask the questions.*

"He's odd, they say. What do you guys say?"

Shrugs all around.

"We hardly see him," Donnie said. "Once in a while at the store or down at the dump. Nice fella, seems like, but not the type you ask to go fishing or butcher a beef."

"You never know, though," Birch continued. "He certainly's got the right size to have done it."

That made Strauss sit up. How did Birch know that the murder was done by someone with a significant amount of strength? According to Adrian, no one had been allowed into the room where Dunfield had been murdered.

"What makes you say that?" he asked and watched as Birch became instantly wary.

"He's a tall fella, got a bit of bulk to him."

"No, I mean, what makes you think it took someone with size to murder Dunfield?"

Birch shrugged. "Just makes sense."

"The only problem," Junior reminded them, "is that just about everyone who might have wanted to kill the man has some size to him. Or her."

Strauss frowned.

"It weren't me, though," Junior added quickly just in case Strauss was tempted to remember that Dunfield had given him motive along with most of the rest of the town.

The door opened with a whoosh of wind and snow and Martha Cutting. She smiled cheerfully at the male gathering.

"You roosters still here gossiping? News must be juicy today. Hi there, Mr. Nick."

"Hi, Martha."

She stood for a moment with her hands on her hips looking at the men. They grinned back foolishly. Another woman might have been intimidated by the very masculine congregation, but clearly here Martha was the more intimidating. She had on her long wool skirt with a red-and-black-checked hunting jacket pulled over it. On her feet she wore enormous winter pacs with bright red wool socks showing over the tops. Strauss thought she really was a very pretty woman, despite her attire and the fact that something looked not quite right in her eyes. A man couldn't quite help liking her.

"You men ought to be ashamed of yourselves. Those good lawmakers in Montpelier take the trouble to pass that no-smoking law to save you from yourselves, and here you sit smoking wantonly away. If you must indulge, I wish you'd come by the house and get some of my herbs. Much, much better for you."

Strauss put out his almost-finished cigarette and six others suffered the same fate all along the table.

"Oh, don't look so shocked, Mr. Lawman. You're the one sitting here breaking the law. What's one more illegality?"

Laughing, Martha continued on into the kitchen. Clearly she was on a mission of some sort.

"Martha's just the tiniest bit different," Donnie whispered with a grin.

"I don't know about the different part," said Leo Chandler, "but she sure is crazy."

A moment later Martha reappeared, dragging a plastic garbage can across the dining room floor in the direction of the door.

An Investigation of Local Color

"You there, Mr. Nick, mind opening the door for me? And Junior, mind lifting this into the back of my truck?"

Strauss regretted his curiosity at once when Martha pulled the lid of the can and revealed a spectacular assortment of leftovers and unrecognizable plate scrapings with an aroma to rival his encounters of the previous day.

"For my pigs," Martha beamed.

"Lucky pigs."

"No need for sarcasm, Detective. Nothing wrong with a few good leftovers." She poked him in the general vicinity of his ribs as he held the door for her. "You look as though you've turned your nose up at your share of good food. Few leftovers might do you some good as well."

"Here's a clean plate if you want to dig in, Mr. Strauss," Harvey called from the kitchen. He laughed uproariously at his own comment and was joined by the other men.

Martha smiled at Strauss. He didn't really think he had the right appreciation for the moment at hand, but he saw the value in being a good sport.

"Maybe next time. I've had a big breakfast already."

"You're a liar," she whispered so that only Strauss could hear her above the laughter. "But you are a very smart man."

Then she was out the door and supervising Junior as he loaded her truck.

"Too bad she's so crazy," Junior commented as he came back inside. He wiped his hands unceremoniously on the coveralls he wore. "She sure is a nice lady otherwise. Don't you think, Detective?"

Strauss agreed that Martha was indeed a nice lady. What he didn't say aloud was that he was no longer so sure Martha was all that crazy.

After breakfast Strauss decided to pay a visit to the local paper to investigate the story of the former murder that had gone unsolved. Most everyone subscribed to the *Rutland Herald* since it was a daily and covered the important events both nationally and statewide. But there was also a weekly county paper put out in Fairview that would more than likely give him the details of the crime as well as the dates. It might be easier for a local paper to take the time to find the story than it would be for a larger, busier paper to have such a request made in the middle of their working day. As soon as Strauss walked through the door of the *Rutland County Enquirer,* though, he began to have second thoughts.

The office was staffed by two women, neither of whom made any attempt to appear busy. If there were any other employees of the *Enquirer* they weren't visible, and there were few places in which they could have concealed themselves. One woman looked up from reading something on her desk, gave him a friendly smile, then returned to her reading without a word. The other was a young girl who looked as though she should have joined his waitress on her way to the junior high school. She wore an oversized sweater with her jeans and sported two varieties of long dangling earrings in each ear. She chewed gum in the bored fashion that reminded Strauss of her urban counterparts, but she came to the edge of the counter and asked if she could help him. He showed her his badge and told her his name.

"One of you guys gave me a speeding ticket last week out on 4," she commented.

"Were you speeding?"

"Well, yeah."

"That explains it, then."

"I had a good reason. I was late for work."

Strauss had difficulty envisioning the youngster in front of him pushing the petal to the metal in an effort to get to work on time. In fact, he had trouble picturing her ever moving faster than a crawl. He hoped he was wrong.

"I'm not sure being late for work is an excusable reason in some law enforcers' minds," he smiled. "I'm sorry, you forgot to tell me your name."

The teenager chewed her gum sullenly. "Tammy."

"Well, Tammy, I need some help. I'm looking into a murder, both an old one and a more recent one. Want to help?'

An Investigation of Local Color

Her eyes brightened. "Oooo, cool! You must be talking about that stabbing up in Benton Harbor. How can I help?"

"Does the newspaper save back issues on microfiche or on computer discs?"

She shook her head. "Nothing like that. Come on back here."

Strauss followed her behind the counter to a door at the far side of the office.

Tammy pulled open the door to reveal shelf upon shelf of old yellowing newspapers. If there was a system of order it wasn't instantly recognizable to Strauss, and he estimated, judging from the paper's weekly status and the number of copies on the shelf, that this closet must represent the entire history of Western Rutland County since the mid-1800s.

"I don't suppose you know how to find anything easily in here, do you, Tammy?"

"Sure I do. That's part of my job," she informed him with more competency and enthusiasm than he would have credited her with possessing. "Just tell me what you're looking for."

"Six years ago, or so," Strauss muttered, looking at the notes he had made in his car shortly after his talk with Chief Peterman. "A man named Brian Borden was kicked by a cow and died. Unfortunately, I don't know when it happened exactly, only that it was about six years ago in Benton Harbor."

"I thought you said it was a murder," Tammy complained.

"Well, it was suspicious, but no murderer ever turned up. That's part of the reason I'm looking into it now," Strauss explained more patiently than he felt. "Do you think you could find the story for me?"

"Oh, definitely. Something like that would be front page, even if it wasn't a murder." She pulled down a stack of papers from an unmarked shelf. Strauss had little hope of any results in the next hour and had started to entertain thoughts of going outside for a cigarette when she said, "Here it is."

He looked at the newspaper she handed him. "'Benton Harbor Man Killed by Cow.'"

"Look, here's the following week's edition." Tammy handed him another copy.

"'Death by Cow Ruled an Accident.'" He glanced at Tammy and started to laugh.

Despite his initial impression that she was a lazy, indifferent teen, she laughed with him until they were both out of breath.

"Why don't you take those out to my desk? I'll look around to make sure there's nothing more, though I'm not sure what could possibly top that."

Still laughing, Strauss went out front, shrugged off his coat, and helped himself to Tammy's cluttered desk. But as soon as he began reading, he sobered up at once.

"'Fairview and Benton Harbor Rescue Squads raced to the Harvey Thibault farm in Benton Harbor Tuesday morning when that man phoned to say that there had been an accident in his barn. Brian Borden, 26, Thibault's son-in-law and employee, was apparently kicked in the head by one of the herd of Guernsey cows following morning milking. Despite heroic efforts on the part of both rescue squads, as well as Thibault, who is the constable of Benton Harbor, Borden was unable to be revived. According to Thibault, he was out spreading a load of manure and on returning to the barn he discovered his son-in-law prone on the cement floor near the rear of one of the cows. There were no witnesses to the accident, but medical examiner Dr. Edward Stanton said that the death was caused by a blow to the right side of the head. Due to the location of the deceased, it was assumed that the blow was delivered by a cow. A puzzled Thibault claims to have had no trouble with his cows but did admit that Borden was not that experienced with the herd. Borden is survived by his wife, Adrian Thibault Borden, who was not at home at the time of the accident.'"

There followed facts about Borden's parents, who were from Darien, Connecticut, and who had the numeral II after their name as well as two other children, both daughters. But Strauss was stuck on the name of Borden's wife. Quickly, he took up the following week's paper.

An Investigation of Local Color

"'Following a tip from an informant who wished to remain anonymous, State Police have been following up further on the death of Brian Borden of Benton Harbor. On Tuesday, April 26, Borden was found dead, presumably kicked in the head by a cow, on the farm of Harvey Thibault, where he was an employee. A tip was phoned into the State Police barracks in Fairview on April 28 with new information suggesting that Borden's death might not have been accidental. Extensive investigation and questioning failed to turn up a suspect, and the death has been ruled by medical examiner Edward Stanton to have been accidental.

"'Neither Adrian Borden, wife of the deceased, nor her father, Harvey, who employed Borden, know of anyone who would have wanted to kill him. Mrs. Borden was angered by the anonymous information, which she said made a very sad situation all the more difficult for her family and her.'"

Strauss leaned back in his chair. He was uncertain why he should feel so unhappy and deceived. Adrain had very definitely told him she was not married. Technically, he supposed, that was correct. But somehow he couldn't escape the irony of the fact that she was assisting him in a murder investigation but had omitted the fact that she herself was, at least for a brief period, embroiled in Benton Harbor's last suspicious death. Not that Borden's death initially sounded suspicious. But certainly a call to the State Police barracks indicated that at least one person suspected foul play. There were no names, of course, since nothing had ever been proved. There was, however, a picture of Brian Borden, Adrian's deceased husband. Nick looked closely at the handsome, smiling man in the picture, the type of man who quarterbacked successful college football teams and charmed women in his spare time. The sort of man who was born into the laps of wealth and indulgence—his parents had a numeral following their names, after all. Men who inherited numerals became presidents and CEOs. What was a man like that doing milking cows and married to a determined, self-sufficient Vermont girl?

"Did you find any clues?" Tammy asked, dragging him out of his thoughts.

"Not really. Anything else on the cow murder?"

She shook her head. "I pulled this on the stabbing last week. You may have already seen it."

Distracted, Strauss nodded vaguely. Something was puzzling him, but he couldn't quite put his finger on it.

"Is there anything else I can get for you?" Tammy asked.

"No. You've been a great help." Strauss missed the smile she flashed him at his praise. He got up and put on his parka.

"Will you let me know if you turn anything up?" she asked. "I'd really like to know how this turns out."

"Sure thing," Strauss agreed even though he really didn't have plans to do it.

Outside it was still snowing, not hard but just enough to make the trip from the newspaper office to the barracks slick, and just enough to cause sufficient trouble out on Route 4 to keep the other troopers out on their lunch hours. It was an absence Strauss welcomed. He stopped at the dispatcher/secretary and asked for her to pull the file on the Borden investigation while he poured some hours-old coffee into a Styrofoam cup.

The name of the investigating officer was David Ray, a name Strauss didn't recognize, but he had had tagging along a younger trooper, one Gary Shubert. A check with the secretary's computer revealed that the Borden investigation had been one of Ray's last before retiring. He could be found somewhere up North near the Canadian border, enjoying his retirement where Vermont was still owned by Vermonters. Strauss knew where to find Shubert. Quickly, he skimmed through the preliminaries of the initial call when Borden's body had been discovered and the death immediately ruled an accident. Borden had been alone in the barn. Time of death, immediately on receiving the blow, estimated to have been about 8:30 A.M., about a half-hour after milking. Harvey Thibault, owner and employer, had been out spreading manure. Adrian Thibault Borden, wife of deceased, had been on her way down to the veterinarian's office to get some syringes. Medical examiner Edward Stanton pronounced, ruled death accidental. Suddenly, the bell went off in Strauss' head. There had been no

An Investigation of Local Color

mention of Lester Blake. Where had he been at the time of the accident? As one of the farm's employees, shouldn't he have been mentioned somewhere in the report? Strauss went on to the report dated April 28, the day of the anonymous tip.

Of course, what is anonymous in the paper isn't necessarily anonymous to the police. The tipster was Gwenivere Dunfield. And she had pointed the finger at Lester Blake. She agreed to talk to police only if they promised to withhold her identity as long as they possibly could. She was, after all, in somewhat of a delicate situation, you see, small towns being what they are. Strauss could almost hear her. According to her story, she and the deceased had been having an affair during the months prior to his death. She had been noticing that the dumpheap Lester Blake drove passed by her house with alarming frequency while the two were keeping company, and she suspected that the farmhand had followed Borden on several occasions. Borden had informed her that Blake hated him, based, according to Gwenivere, on that man's own love for Adrian Borden. Gwenivere had formed the opinion, apparently without any substantial evidence, that Lester Blake had killed Brian Borden.

Officer Ray interviewed Ms. Dunfield, Adrian, Harvey Thibault, and finally Lester Blake, and came to the conclusion that Gwen's theory was just that—a theory. Everyone appeared to be where they said they were, and no one was without an alibi. In spite of, or maybe because of, Ray's decision to close the case, a young Gary Shubert, fresh out of the police academy and all too full of himself and his uniform, continued to investigate. He reinterviewed everyone beginning with Adrian.

She had been on her way to the veterinarian to pick up some syringes. Lester Blake had been with her.

Why hadn't she told the police that initially?

No one had asked. No one felt an accidental death required an accounting of everyone's whereabouts. (The woman was excessively defensive!) Shubert had written in the margin of his report.

Why would Blake have ridden along on a five-mile trip to pick up such a small item?

He often went along when she did errands.

Did she consider Blake to be obsessively devoted to her?

No, she didn't.

Then how could she explain the fact that he was so often in her presence?

A. Blake had lived on the farm since before she was born. B. They were both employed by her father. C. They considered each other family. Did Officer Shubert want more reasons?

At the end of the interview, Shubert had made a note that Adrian Borden had appeared surly and less than cooperative, as though she might have something to hide.

But if Shubert had found Adrian less than cooperative, he must have considered Blake to be nothing short of hostile based solely on the fact that he wouldn't talk to the trooper.

Where were you during the time in question?

With Adrian.

Can anyone else verify that?

Don't know.

How did you feel about Brian Borden?

He didn't have an opinion.

He didn't dislike Mr. Borden?

Blake never gave it much thought.

What was he doing so often up on Frampton Hill?

He worked sometimes for Mrs. Glenn.

How often?

A shrug.

Did he know about the affair between Mr. Borden and Gwenivere Dunfield?

He did now.

It went on and on in a similar vein with no conclusions. Finally, then Constable Harvey Thibault had complained to Trooper Ray that his family was being senselessly harassed during what should have been a mourning period for them, and the investigation was hastily terminated. Not, however, without Trooper Shubert adding that he

An Investigation of Local Color

felt there were still numerous loose ends, though he was forced to add as well that he had absolutely no substantial evidence.

As far as Strauss could see, there was no sign that the information in the file had ever been made public other than the bit he had seen in the paper earlier. He leaned back in his chair and rubbed his eyes in an effort to think more clearly. Was anything truly suspicious here or was this a case of a young, overzealous trooper and a grieving lover creating suspicion out of an accident? Strauss was disinclined to reason along the same lines as Shubert, but he wondered why Gwen Dunfield would make an accusation of that kind without at least some suspicion. And he had to wonder why, out of all the people he had spoken with during the course of his present investigation, no one, certainly not Adrian herself, had ever mentioned Brian Borden and his suspicious demise. Because nobody considered it all that suspicious? Or because the townsfolk of Benton Harbor were so obviously fond of their constable and her farmhand that they would cover up for them? But an entire town? he wondered. *Hell*, he thought, *we're talking Vermont here. The possibilities are endless.*

"Detective Strauss? There is a call for you on line two," the receptionist interrupted his thoughts. "Use the desk right here if you want."

"Detective? Adrian Thibault here. I think I've found the Witness boyfriend."

Strauss glanced at his watch. Adrian must be calling from work. He could hear something in her voice—excitement or victory.

"Nice going, Constable. Did you talk to him?"

"Not yet. I got his name from the local church. It's different from the one Gwen gave us, but I'm pretty sure it's the same guy, and guess where he works? New England Tampon."

Strauss didn't care to point out that NET was one of Rutland's largest employers and the fact that a boyfriend and an ex, now deceased spouse, both worked there might not be all that significant.

"I thought you might like to question him, so I waited. He's at work now on first shift. It ends at 3:30."

"Did you get a home address for him?"

"Yes."

117

"Good work. I'll pick you up at the end of your shift, and we'll see if we can be converted to Jehovah's Witnesses."

"I know I'm looking forward to it."

Though he hadn't seen it often, Strauss thought he could hear a smile in her voice.

Even though it wasn't snowing hard and most of it was melting as it came down, the winding road up Frampton Hill was slick. The heavy cruiser slid on the first curve in spite of being well equipped with good snow tires. Strauss realized quickly that winter driving on the backroads of Vermont was an entirely different experience than negotiating the snow-laden streets of Boston which were, for the most part, plowed off as quickly as it snowed. Even when the crews couldn't keep up, at least the streets were relatively flat and straight. Strauss thought of the brawny Benton Harbor road manager of Thibault descent. He didn't even know if Junior had a crew or if the big man was it.

Using most of his driving skills, Strauss made it to the top of the hill where the Boyces lived. He pulled into the driveway, deciding as he did so that he would have to develop better skills if he was to survive the winter here. Surely there was going to be more snow by January, and though a trip into a ditch might not kill him he felt fairly sure the ribbing, either at the barracks or, more particularly, at the Hook, would.

He found Milly Boyce, of all places, in her garden. She waved for him to come over while indicating with silent gestures that Tom was asleep in the house.

"He works nights," she said when Strauss was close enough to hear her hushed voice.

The whispering was made pointless when the air filled with the sound of gunshots as a nearby hunter did his best to reduce the population of the deer herd. Milly winced at the sound. Her expression was as pained as it had been on Saturday evening. She continued her work, shoveling something foul that Strauss took to be cow manure from the back of a rusted pickup truck.

An Investigation of Local Color

"I have to do this before there is snow on the ground," she informed him as she scooped purposefully. "The snow is supposed to mix in and act like fertilizer. It's an old Vermont thing."

"And did you have a good garden last year?" Strauss asked. Looking around at the fenced plot that was slowly being covered by dung and snow, he thought he saw more dead weed stalks than deceased vegetable vines, but he was a city boy after all and his plant-identification skills were less than limited.

"Well, it could have been better." Milly's brow furled and she looked sad. "I don't suppose you came all the way up here to talk about gardening, did you?"

"Not really," Strauss admitted.

"Shall I wake Tom?"

"No. It's you I wanted to speak with."

"Oh, dear," Milly sighed.

Her shoulders drooped inside her oversized coat, and the snow coating her frizzy hair made it sag forlornly in her face. Strauss wondered if she was either about to cry or confess to murder. He waited. She shoveled.

"I understand that you and Tom aren't quite as happily married as Tom would have had us believe the other night."

"No, we aren't. We've filed for divorce, in fact. But I guess you already know that."

Strauss nodded. "I've heard. Why the charade?"

"It was my idea. I feel very embarrassed about the break, particularly when Tom announced that he intended to build another house on his share of our land. Bill and Gwen were the town joke for years when they split up. Now Tom and I are about to take their place in the local gossip. I was just hoping to hold it off until the divorce is final."

"Mrs. Boyce, do you hold Bill Dunfield responsible for the breakup?"

Milly threw a shovelful of manure with enough force to clear the garden plot and splatter on the brown grass beyond. Though she was a woman of some heft, Strauss wouldn't have thought her capable of such a physical effort. Somehow she didn't give the impression of being agriculturally competent.

"He was such a hateful, wretched man!" she replied with force as she ungracefully threw another load that almost landed on Strauss. "He always had to stir things up, always had to put his nose in where it didn't belong, always gave advice that wasn't needed. But I didn't kill him. I abhor violence. We saw so much of that in Chicago. We came here to get away from all that and have a peaceful life."

"I gather you didn't exactly get what you bargained for?"

She shook her head, her eyes filled with disappointment. Strauss wondered if disappointment was a permanent state of mind with Milly Boyce.

"We saved everything we made in Chicago. We were going to settle here, build a house, grow vegetables, hunt for our meat, learn some crafts. Tom would do enough nursing to buy whatever we needed, but we would basically be self-sufficient."

"Sounds like a good plan," Strauss said, although it didn't exactly. "What went wrong?"

"Everything! I just hate this place!" Milly wailed. "I hate it!"

She wandered a ways into the garden and kicked viciously at a clump of cow dung. When she turned around in only slightly better control of herself, she was so bedraggled by the snow-dampened, oversized clothes and the almost pouty expression that Strauss didn't know whether to laugh or feel sorry for her.

"There is nothing here for me. All the women are farmwives with kids. They don't know anything about books or theatre. They've hardly been outside the bounds of Rutland County. A big night on the town is dinner at the Hook, Line, and Sinker! I've got a Master's degree, for God's sake! We came here to escape the hassles of city life, but we also gave up fulfilling careers and stimulating friendships. We gave up a social life!"

Her voice rose and tears streamed down her face. She wiped at them, leaving a smear of what Strauss hoped, for her sake, was merely dirt from the garden.

An Investigation of Local Color

"I hate gardening!" she wept. "And I'm so damned sick of the smell of cow shit! It's...it's everywhere. And now it turns out that we haven't even been able to escape the violence."

Milly made another swipe at her face. She was going to have to stop doing that, Strauss decided or, given her present state, she would suffer a mental breakdown when she next came in contact with a mirror. He was really going to have to get into the habit of carrying a handkerchief.

"Did you talk about all this with your husband?"

She nodded. "He doesn't understand. He loves it here. Every time the subject came up, he would just run down to Bill for support. 'Don't let Milly tell you what to do,' he would say. 'Be a man. If she doesn't like it, tell her to take a hike.' Who was I supposed to run to? Gwen? She's trapped in a romance novel. That crazy exercise queen on the hill? She'd set the dogs on me. It's all so unbearable!"

Strauss was silent for a moment in order to give her a chance to catch her breath. Then he continued, "If I may ask, why didn't you return to Chicago when you and Tom decided to divorce?"

"Officer, Tom is leaving me for another woman. I will be damned if I will turn this house over to her after all this suffering. Let him suffer for a change."

"Do you know who she is?"

"No. Donna Something. She works at the hospital with him. She has a career, something Tom always felt turned a woman poisonous. Apparently that doesn't hold true for dear Donna."

"Did Dunfield know about the relationship?"

Milly shrugged. "I suppose. Tom never seemed to hold back from telling him all about us."

"And you were alone in the early hours of Friday morning?"

She nodded. She was calmer now, resigned and disappointed once again. "I was probably asleep. I admit, I hated Bill Dunfield. But I didn't kill him. I swear I didn't."

Strauss wished he had a dollar for every suspect who had ever sworn they hadn't committed the crime. He surely wouldn't be out in the backwoods of Vermont sniffing wet cow shit, talking to suspects who at this point were looking crazier than anyone he had ever encountered in city work. No, he'd be sitting on a tropical beach sipping margaritas and staring at bronzed women who didn't wear oversized clothes.

The cabin door slammed, and Tom Boyce chose that moment to join them. He was dressed in camouflage pants, heavy boots and the red-and-black-checked hunting coat that was the season's fashion in Benton Harbor. He immediately put a supportive arm around his wife's waist.

"I thought I heard shouting. Is everything all right, darling?"

"Oh, can it, darling! I've told the officer all about our little charade. If he is at all professional, he won't run the information to all the neighbors or down to the Hook, the way some people would." Milly shrugged away from her husband's arm. "If you would please excuse me."

Tom looked so taken aback that Strauss was forced to believe that he was more used to Milly whining and sobbing than being actively hostile. He rolled up and down on the balls of his feet and puffed out his chest in what Strauss assumed was an attempt to regain his bruised masculinity.

"Well!" he said. "Well!"

Strauss waited.

"Well!" He puffed his chest up farther still, reminding Strauss of a little rooster. "I see she has just a touch of PMS today."

Strauss didn't reply immediately. Boyce continued to roll up and down. It was something of a feat considering the heavy, stiff-looking boots.

"Could you tell me again where you were Friday morning, say between 3:00 and 6:00?" Strauss asked when he had decided that he had gotten the most out of his pregnant pause.

"As I told you, I was at work at the hospital in Middlebury."

"In the Intensive Care Unit?"

"Yes."

"Alone?"

"Well, sometimes I am alone. But a coworker can vouch for me that night."

An Investigation of Local Color

"Does the coworker have a name?"

Boyce smiled smugly. He wasn't one to be trapped without an alibi. "Donna Pentski. She works the same hours I do."

Strauss wrote the name down and confirmed the spelling. "Thanks for your time, Mr. Boyce. Sorry to have awakened you."

Boyce smiled expansively. "It's no problem, Officer. Milly can sometimes be hysterical that way. It's a little hard to sleep through," he added in a lowered conspiratorial tone. "I'm just glad to have helped."

Strauss was unclear on the helping part, but he said nothing. Boyce headed for the house, the basement part, Strauss assumed.

"This Donna Pentski," he called. "Would that be the same Donna you are leaving your wife for?"

Boyce looked over his shoulder as if hoping the wife in question hadn't heard. "We do have something of a relationship, but I really don't see how it is relative to your case."

"It probably isn't," Strauss told him. "I was just kind of curious. You know, witness credibility and all that stuff. Thanks again."

When he got into the cruiser, he noticed that Tom Boyce was once again rolling up and down on the balls of his feet. For some reason it made Strauss smile. He put the car in gear and backed out of the drive. The snow was sticking now, he noticed, as he idled carefully down the hill.

He had gone about halfway down the road when he came upon Sally Glenn jogging through the slush with her four German Shepherds trotting along on either side of her. She wore a hot pink running suit and high-tech, expensive-looking sneakers that didn't look as though they were bearing up well under the present conditions. Her blonde ponytail bobbed merrily with each of her steps. As soon as she heard the car behind her, she stopped and waved. The dogs immediately sat in unison beside her. Strauss rolled down the window. He kept an eye on the four salivating canines. They appeared to be smiling at him, but he knew better. Dogs never smiled at him.

"Hi, Sally. Not a great day for a run."

"Oh, well...." She smiled uncertainly.

Strauss noticed that she was barely out of breath even though she had been running right along.

"I'm glad I ran into you," she said. "Jack told me that I gave you the wrong information the other day when you were asking me questions. I forgot that he had been called out that night and wasn't home. I didn't mean to lie. It's just that he gets called out so often that I can't keep track of the days. I'm sure that Jack is right. He keeps track of those things better than I do."

"So he was called to work early on Friday morning?"

"That's right. I'm not sure of the time, but whatever he told you is correct. He is very honest."

Obviously, this couple wasn't having the same sorts of trouble that the Boyces were having, Strauss thought. Either that, or they were much better at playing the game than the Boyces were.

"And you were alone?"

"Well, not alone. I had the dogs with me."

Strauss cast another wary glance at the dogs. Four sets of teeth dared him to contradict their mistress.

"I'm sure they would be happy to vouch for you," he commented.

Sally smiled hesitantly. She wasn't sure if he was making a joke or being sarcastic.

"I'd better be going before I cool off. Sorry about the lie."

She ran off, a blur of hot pink against the snow, protected by her four bodyguards. Either the Glenns were delightfully naive and honest, or they were working overtime at appearing to be, he thought.

He rolled the window back up and mulled over the morning's information as he headed for Rutland.

Adrian was waiting for him this time when he arrived to pick her up. Strauss couldn't help noticing that Doris, the "Welcome to Rutland Hospital" lady, smiled knowingly at them as they left together, but if Adrian noticed she didn't comment.

"Did you have a good day?" she asked politely when they were out of earshot of all the sweet little old ladies.

"It was very interesting, to say the least. And you?"

An Investigation of Local Color

"Slow. But that's how I got the idea on this guy. I was thinking that maybe Gwen gave us the wrong name. Remember how she seemed reluctant to reveal it? Why are you staring at me like that?"

Strauss hadn't realized that he had been staring as he tried to imagine her not only married but involved in a murder coverup. He shook himself mentally. They could go into all that later.

"I'm sorry. So Gwen gave us the wrong name?"

Adrian gave him a doubtful look, but she continued on. "Yes. Remember how she didn't want to give us the name of her boyfriend? Finally, she said it was Lee Madigan. That's who I went looking for yesterday. But I got to thinking, what if she gave us the wrong name for some reason, like maybe she didn't want us to find him? So I went back to the church—nice folks there, by the way—and I asked again, only I used the description Tom and Milly gave us. Tall, very thin, early to mid-thirties, drives a van. Both the preacher and the church secretary came up with a name right away. His name is Lee, but his last name is Stout. Lives over on Union Street. That's north of the center of town, up Route 7."

They had reached the state car by the time Adrian finished with this information. Strauss paused before getting in and leaned his elbows on the roof of the cruiser.

"That's really good detective work, Constable. Are you sure you've never done anything like this before?"

"I never needed to before. I know everyone in Benton Harbor." But she looked pleased at the compliment and smiled at him through the wet snow coming down between them.

Strauss thought she looked much more pleasant dripping snow than Milly Boyce had.

"Have any idea why Gwen lied about the name?" he asked as they got into the car.

"I have a good idea: The guy's married. According to the minister, this Lee fellow is an outstanding member of his flock. From my limited knowledge of the Jehovah's Witnesses, all of which comes, by the way, from two conversations with the minister and his secretary, I gather that means Lee is a devoted family man, an active churchgoer and a zealous recruiter for the faith."

Strauss chuckled. "Interesting recruiting technique, wouldn't you say?"

"Turn up at the next corner," Adrian directed. "I wonder if the wife knows."

Strauss saw the older-model van parked curbside at the same time Adrian pointed out the house belonging to Stout. He wrote down the license before getting out. Someone had already been out to shovel the slush from the front walk, an act of diligence since it was still snowing and appeared as if it would continue for some time yet. He rang the bell three times before the door was answered by a man roughly fitting the description Milly had given them.

"Lee Stout?"

The man nodded, an expression of pure misery on his face as if he already knew who they were and why they had come. He kept glancing around, perhaps in anticipation of the arrival of someone else, but when Strauss identified himself and Adrian the man invited them into his living room and asked them to sit down.

The name Stout was an unfortunate misnomer. Strauss didn't believe he had ever seen a man as thin and emaciated-looking as the one in front of him now. A poster man for anorexia, he gave the appearance of being nothing but height and bones, all of which he folded into an armchair. Strauss almost expected to hear a clatter as he did so. His face, while not unpleasant exactly, was hollow-cheeked and lightly scarred by a teenaged confrontation with acne. His best feature was a thick head of dark brown hair. He was dressed in what were probably his afterwork clothes. By all appearances he was a tidy man who kept a tidy, comfortable middle-class home. But at the moment, the tidy, comfortable man was looking decidedly uncomfortable.

"We're investigating the stabbing death of Bill Dunfield over in Benton Harbor," Strauss began. "And your name has come up."

Stout stared openmouthed at him for a moment. "Oh my, oh my," he muttered softly, or something to that effect. "This is even worse than I thought. You think I killed Bill Dunfield? Oh my, no!"

An Investigation of Local Color

He buried his head in his shaking hands. Given his words and his ungainly appearance, it was almost comical. Strauss glanced at Adrian, who gave him a wide-eyed shrug. He was about to start asking more questions of Stout when that man saved him the trouble.

"This is what I get for my sin," he said with a shake of his head. "I didn't kill Dunfield, honestly I didn't. I never even met the man. But I did have an affair with his ex-wife."

"In order to convert her to your religion?"

"Oh, my, no! No, no, that's not how it's done!" Stout couldn't rouse himself from his guilt and misery to muster any outrage at the question. "I bring people to our religion through knowledge and prayer. I take it very seriously, I'm very committed to my faith. But I've suffered this terrible lapse with Gwenivere. Detective Strauss, you must believe me, I've never had an affair before. But when I met Gwenivere, it was just...just...well, it was magic, and I was briefly tempted by the magic into sin."

Out of the corner of his eye, Strauss saw Adrian's hand fly to her face. Ordinarily he wouldn't have thought of practical, controlled Adrian to have been someone easily overcome by the giggles, but under the circumstances he thought he understood. The idea of very large, overdramatic Gwen and anorexic, miserable Lee creating magic stressed the imagination a little bit.

Stout continued on unasked, much to Strauss' relief. "I met Gwenivere at the Holiday Inn. All the Jehovah's Witnesses were having a two-day conference there, and she was in charge of the hospitality."

Adrian coughed. Strauss felt sorry for her.

"One thing just led to another, I'm afraid, and by the end of the second day we slipped into one of the hospitality rooms at Gwenivere's disposal, and we began our affair."

"Mr. Stout, aren't you married?"

"Oh, my! Yes, yes, I'm married, and I know what you're thinking. I know I sinned against my wife. I knew it then, but I just couldn't stop myself."

Strauss cleared his throat. "Actually, I was wondering where your wife was. Isn't she a Jehovah's Witness as well?"

"She is. But her work hours didn't permit her to attend the conference."

"And she works where?"

"New England Tampon, same as me, but she works the second shift. It leaves her out of a lot of late-afternoon and early evening activities. We were hoping to have a family, you see, and so we took opposite shifts so that one of us would always be home for the children. Unfortunately, the kids never came along, though we are still hopeful."

It was on the tip of Strauss' tongue to point out that Stout's chances would be greatly improved if he stayed home and boffed his wife instead of another woman, but he refrained in the interest of good taste.

"Does your wife know about the affair?" Adrian asked.

Stout looked over his shoulder as if he feared the sudden appearance of said wife. Then he shook his head in the negative. "I don't think so. But I became so consumed with guilt that I believe she was beginning to be suspicious. That's why I finally ended it with Gwenivere."

"You ended it? She said she did."

The skinny man shook his head. "I'm afraid that isn't true. But I can't blame her. She was distraught, just so, so upset when I told her. You see...we had talked...we had thought about...well, we had thought about leaving Vermont and going somewhere together to start over. We'd sort of even made a plan. We were thinking of Iowa, maybe. There is an excellent Witness community out there. I visited it on a retreat one summer years ago and was quite taken with the possibilities."

"But in the end you changed your mind?"

"I had to. I was becoming so obsessed with my own sin. Besides..." His voice trailed off.

"Besides?" Strauss prompted.

"Lily would have taken me to the cleaners in a divorce. I know her, and she would go after everything I had if I left her. Gwenivere insisted that Vermont has excellent divorce laws, but I just couldn't risk it. I begged Gwenivere for her understanding but, as I said, she was so undone. And then this thing with her ex-husband happened. I

An Investigation of Local Color

read about it in the papers, but I just haven't dared to get in touch with her."

"Why is that, Mr. Stout? If you two were so intimate, wouldn't it have made sense to show her some sign of your sympathy? Gwen claims that she and Mr. Dunfield were on friendly terms."

For a moment Stout stared at Strauss with a puzzled expression. Then he shook his head. "They weren't on friendly terms, Detective. Gwenivere hated Bill. She told me numerous stories of his cruelty to her. She said he was absolutely obsessed with possessing her and had made her life a virtual Hell on earth while they were married. Once he even beat her and dragged her around the house by her hair."

Strauss exchanged an amazed look with Adrian.

"Mr. Stout, you said you'd never met Mr. Dunfield. Have you ever seen him? Face to face, I mean?" she asked.

Again, he shook his head. "No. I know he worked at NET, but he was in another part of the plant. Once I passed him on Frampton Hill, but I didn't realize it until after I was by so I didn't notice him, really. Frankly, after hearing about Gwenivere's nightmarish treatments at the hands of that man, I thought it better to limit my visits to times when he would be at work."

"And fortunately, your wife was working then as well."

Stout had the grace to show remorse. "That is correct. It all seemed so easy when we started up together, but it has ended so badly. The price of sin is very high."

"Do you have any idea if your wife was acquainted with Mr. Dunfield?"

"I wouldn't have any way of knowing. I couldn't ask her, of course. She never mentioned him by name, but then we don't really talk about work when we are home." Stout's voice was taking on a steadily more frustrated note. "Officers, if there was any way we could keep this from her...I mean, I know I made a very big mistake, but I'm desperately trying to correct it. The last week has just been Hell for me, the worst days of my entire life."

"I understand," Strauss said, though he didn't really. "I don't think last Friday morning was a banner day for Bill Dunfield either. By the way, where were you Friday morning, say 3:00 A.M.?"

"Thursday evening was the last night Gwenivere and I had together. That's when I ended it. But I was home by 11:00. I was always home by then because Lily gets home at 11:30."

"So Lily can vouch for you that night?"

Stout frowned. "No, she can't. There was some sort of a backup on her shift that night, and she was asked to work over."

There it was again, Strauss thought. That problem on the second/third shift that Jack Glenn had mentioned and that had mysteriously been resolved before the engineer arrived.

"But Gwenivere knows when I left. It was the same time I always leave. She can vouch for me unless...." His face fell as a thought occurred to him.

"Unless she has a reason not to provide you with an alibi." Strauss put the thought to words.

"Oh, my," Stout said. "When I read about the stabbing in the paper, I thought it possible Gwenivere might have done it. I had left her so distraught and what, with Bill making her so miserable over the years, I thought she might finally have snapped. But she wouldn't let me take the blame. Of course she wouldn't. She loves me."

"Mr. Stout, you just told her you loved your wife more."

"Oh, yeah," he said, as if the thought had just occurred. He dropped his head again into his hands. "Oh, God! I just should have paid for sex!"

It was Strauss' turn to cover his face with his hand.

"Do I need a lawyer?" Stout asked plaintively, his head still in his hands. "I look really guilty, don't I?"

"I don't know that you need a lawyer just yet, Mr. Stout, although you are certainly free to talk with one if you want. We're not arresting you, but I would ask you not to be making that trip to Iowa just now," Strauss said. "We might have a few more questions later."

He stood and Adrian followed suit. Lee Stout unfolded his bones and stood up to tower over the two of them. Strauss noticed the appalling lack of flesh on the bones that stuck out beneath the short sleeves of his casual shirt.

"About my wife...?"

"We'll be as discreet as we can, but this is a murder investigation. We can't promise that your indiscretions won't be brought into the open."

He nodded. "You know, in a strange way it was good to talk about it. I've been carrying this guilt around since I met Gwenivere last April. You are the first people I told about it."

Stout showed them to the door. They made it to the car and out of sight of the house before bursting into uncontrollable, unprofessional laughter.

"Magic?!" Adrian giggled. "Somehow I just can't see it."

"Constable, this is a murder investigation. Control yourself, can't you?" But he had a hard time getting the reprimand out around his own laughter.

He turned the cruiser back onto Route 7. It had stopped snowing, but enough had settled on the road to make what passed for rush hour in Rutland trickier than usual.

"Sorry," Adrian said. "Do you think he did it?"

"Why would he? If you believe him, he never even met Dunfield. Of course, if you don't believe him he could still be involved with the magical Ms. Dunfield, and that would certainly give him more of a motive. Maybe he was righting the wrongs Dunfield perpetrated on his ex-wife. Do Jehovahs do the eye-for-an-eye thing?"

"I've no idea. But I tend to believe him. I think a man would have to be made of sterner stuff than our Mr. Stout appears to be if he were to be able to deal with Gwen long term. I think he would have to be made of heftier stuff as well."

Strauss chuckled. "You noticed our man was no Schwarzenegger?"

"Mmmm. And he wouldn't need the bulk just for coping with Gwen. Bill wasn't a big man, but I can't see him being overpowered by Stout."

Strauss stopped at the stop sign near the hospital intersection, and an impatient driver blew his horn to move him along.

"Driving one of these things really generates the respect, doesn't it?" Adrian commented.

"Always." He pulled up alongside Adrian's car. "Either Ms. Dunfield or Mr. Stout is lying to us, maybe both. I think another trip to the charming Gwenivere's house is in order. Want to come along?"

"Maybe not. I seemed to set her off last time. You'll do better on your own."

Strauss watched Adrian carefully. After her earlier enthusiasm for the case, why the sudden reluctance? Was she afraid her presence would provoke an untimely outburst from the overdramatic Gwen? Something perhaps that she didn't want Strauss to discover? She became noticeably uncomfortable under his gaze.

"Excuse me, but didn't you just ask me if I wanted to go along?"

"Yes, but I expected you to say yes. Couldn't you tell?"

"You know, you have this really rude habit of staring at people? Okay. I would love to come along and grill Ms. Dunfield. Follow me home. We'll take the official car the rest of the way if you think you can manage with the snow."

"I already practiced earlier today so I wouldn't shame myself."

Strauss followed Adrian home and waited while she checked in with Lester Blake. He wondered how she had worked all day and then just run into the cow barn and still smelled nice when she got into his car. He decided that he was imagining her earlier reluctance to continue the investigation with him, but seeing her talk to Blake had reminded him that it was certainly a subject they needed to discuss. The drive back tonight would be a good time.

Strauss negotiated Frampton Hill with a decided lack of skill, but he got them there— barely—and with Adrian vowing to do the driving next trip. He left the cruiser at the back of the house rather than slush through the mess of Gwen's drive, and they got out and made their way to the back door this time.

"What I really want to hear about is how Bill dragged Gwen around by her hair," Adrian whispered as they approached the door. "But you ask, okay?"

"Ask your own questions, Constable," he whispered back.

An Investigation of Local Color

The light came on at the sound of their knock and the door opened.

"Detective Strauss," Gwen said. Clearly, she was caught off guard. Unlike their last visit, she didn't seemed at all pleased to see them.

"Ms. Dunfield, we need to ask you a few more questions."

Gwen forced her massive jowls into the semblance of a smile. Her eyes, however, were wary, calculating. It wasn't the prettiest picture Strauss had ever seen.

"Detective, maybe another time. I'm afraid you've caught me right in the act of eating my supper."

Another time? Didn't anyone respect the law anymore? Strauss was tempted to return the favor by suggesting that Ms. Dunfield could probably go a week without participating in the act of eating her supper and not feel the difference, but he refrained.

"I really think this is important, Ms. Dunfield," he told her sternly. "This is a murder investigation, and I have to admit that you are a suspect at this time. It would really be helpful to you and me both if you were cooperative."

The big woman's eyes narrowed. Then she forced another smile. "Come in, then, if you must. I certainly don't want it to be said that I have been uncooperative with your investigation, though I don't see how you could possibly have come to that conclusion. Come in, come in," she urged impatiently.

She shoved the door at them and turned to lead the way through the kitchen with none of the hospitality for which Lee Stout had given her acclaim.

"I do wish you would phone ahead before you just arrive on my doorstep," she muttered in something considerably louder than a stage whisper.

Behind her back Adrian shrugged at Strauss.

As they passed through the kitchen, Strauss saw what he took to be the reason for Gwen's irritation. On the table was a piping-hot spaghetti and meatball dinner, the proportions of which could have easily fed a family in a third-world country. A loaf of garlic bread and a half-consumed bottle of red wine forced a demanding growl from his stomach.

As on their previous visit, Gwen sat on the flowery sofa close to Strauss and ignored Adrian's presence entirely.

"What can I do for you this time?" Her smile was less strained now as she turned toward him and folded her hands primly in her ample lap.

Tonight she was clad more casually in a bright pink jogging suit very similar to the one Sally Glenn had been wearing earlier that afternoon, except that Gwen's suit had splashy flowers on the shoulders and hips. Strauss sincerely doubted that Gwen's suit had ever seen speeds faster than that of a slow waddle. On her feet she wore fuzzy pink slippers.

"We questioned your former boyfriend earlier today, and we found some inconsistencies in the story you told us last Saturday."

Gwen's eyes widened and she placed a hand on her chest dramatically. "I'm sure I don't know what you mean. Inconsistencies? I told you the truth about everything."

"Well, for starters, you gave us the wrong name. We couldn't find a Lee Madigan, but with some work Constable Thibault came up with Lee Stout who, it happens, turns out to be the man in question."

"Of course Constable Thibault would discover that. Too bad she isn't as skillful a detective in matters that involve her," Gwen said pettishly. Then she turned to Strauss and said sweetly, "But Officer, you misunderstood me. Madigan is Lee's middle name. Stout is such an unpleasant last name, don't you think? I rarely ever used it. Who would? I'm so sorry you didn't understand that the first time around," she informed him with a breathy little laugh. "It was not my intention to mislead you, of course it wasn't."

"And I suppose you didn't mean to mislead me when you said that you had broken off with Mr. Stout because of his lack of romance. According to him, he wanted to stop seeing you, and you were terribly upset."

Gwen's eyes flashed angrily. "Well, I guess he would say that, but it isn't true. I told him to go back to his horrid wife, and he is the one who went to pieces. I'm sorry, Officer, but I just cannot imagine what this has to do with Bill's murder."

An Investigation of Local Color

"Let me run this by you then, Ms. Dunfield: You told us earlier that your boyfriend didn't know your ex-husband lived across the street."

"Road," Adrian said from the doorway where she stood.

"What?"

"Road. In Vermont it's a road."

"Oh. Whatever. The same boyfriend tells us that not only did he know, but you had told him some stories about abusive treatment at your ex-husband's hands. Now neither you nor your ex-boyfriend seem to have a good alibi for the time of Mr. Dunfield's murder, and I'm starting to wonder if maybe the two of you never really split up and if just maybe one of you is the killer."

Glancing at the upper arms that strained the pink fabric of Gwen's jacket, Strauss was tempted to remind her that she had more of the substance it probably took to drive the knife home. He let the silence drag on and hoped that at the end of it Gwen would give him a clue to the murder. He wondered if he had enough reason to make an arrest right now but doubted if he had substantial evidence to hold up under the scrutiny of a clever lawyer. Were there clever lawyers in Vermont? He didn't know, but from what he was beginning to discover about Vermonters he decided against putting it to the test. He looked up at Adrian standing in the doorway. Her face was expressionless even when their eyes met.

"Are you accusing me, Detective Strauss?" Gwen finally whispered. It was impossible to tell if she was sincerely scared finally or if she was doing more acting.

"Ms. Dunfield," Strauss began with all the patience he could muster after a long, eventful day, "your story doesn't match Mr. Stout's account of your relationship. On top of that, neither of you have an alibi and both of you have what appears to be a good motive for killing your ex-husband. I need to know the truth, or I will keep coming back to the two of you until one of you comes up with it."

Gwen began to cry. She wiped at tears, which this time were very real. "But I have told you the truth," she sniffled. "I told Lee I didn't want to see him anymore. I felt horrible that he had a wife at home. I just couldn't get past the fact in the end."

As she blew her nose into a pink Kleenex, a loud honking sound, Strauss watched Adrian for a reaction. She met his gaze squarely, with the same unreadable expression she had had since they arrived.

"I may have told Lee about Bill. I...I just don't remember doing so." Gwen blew her swiftly reddening nose again.

"So after seeing Lee for all these months, you just suddenly felt sorry about the fact that he had a wife and told him to take a hike?"

Gwen's tear-filled eyes widened. "Oh, not suddenly, Officer. He wasn't all that forthcoming about his wife or their relationship. I didn't even know he was married in the beginning."

"So when you found out, you broke it off?"

"That's right." Gwen smiled tearfully. Things were easier when the answers were supplied to you.

"And he was upset about it?"

"Yes. He was very upset, in fact."

"Tell me, Ms. Dunfield, is Mr. Stout an angry or violent person?"

She appeared to give the question careful consideration. "I never thought about it. I suppose he could be."

"Do you think he could have killed your ex-husband either to frame you..."

Here Gwen gasped and covered her mouth with her hand...

"...or to show you that he could get even with Bill for his bad treatment of you? Maybe he was showing you that he was your champion?"

Gwen smiled at the idea. Her eyes, no longer tear-filled, were again calculating and shrewd. Strauss wondered how she was making the switch so swiftly.

"I never thought of that, but yes. Yes, Lee might have done that for me. He told me on that last night that he would never be able to get over me. Yes, he might have killed Bill."

Strauss got to his feet to end the interview. He stared coldly down at the fat woman who wiped at her now-dry eyes and didn't meet his

An Investigation of Local Color

gaze. He had no more information than he had the first time he had visited this odd, compulsively pink house.

"I suppose we can let you get back to your supper now, Ms. Dunfield."

"Thank you, Officer. This whole affair has been so trying, so hard on the nerves."

"Which affair are you referring to, Gwen?" Adrian asked, speaking for the first time since entering the house.

"You know very well what I am referring to, Constable Thibault," Gwen snapped back, putting a heavy emphasis on Adrian's title. "A murder right next door," Gwen explained in a sweeter tone to Strauss.

She heaved herself to her feet and laid a hand on his arm. To his amazement she rubbed his arm in a too-familiar gesture.

"It's all sooo horrifying."

"Yes," Strauss agreed abruptly. "I'm sure it is. We'll be on our way now. Constable?"

Adrian nodded. They made their way back through the kitchen, where the spaghetti dinner didn't look quite so appealing. In fact, Strauss found that he had quite lost his appetite. Outside the clouds had cleared, and the air was decidedly colder than it had been. He inhaled deeply to rid himself of the mood inside the house. When Adrian looked at him, he shrugged and got into the cruiser.

"You believe her?" he asked as they started back down the hill.

"Not a word."

"Why not?"

"It sounds to me as though she isn't above framing someone else."

Strauss glanced quickly at Adrian, but she was staring out the side window into the darkness so he couldn't see her expression. When he waited for her to elaborate, she didn't.

"But is she casting doubt on the boyfriend in order to divert suspicion from herself or to get revenge for being dumped?"

"Hard to say. Do you think she murdered Bill?"

"It doesn't matter whether I think so or not. I can't arrest her without some sort of proof that will hold up. She has means and motive, but so do several other people."

This was the time, Strauss told himself, to ask her about he own deceased husband and about Lester Blake. But he let the silence go on too long, and Adrian finally asked, "So what now?"

"Keep digging. We're still waiting for forensics. Those results might help us out. We can check into Dunfield's will. I think it might be helpful if you were to question the Jehovah's Witness minister again and see if our Mr. Stout has a history of recruiting young women to the faith. Let's see if we can determine which of this magical couple is the more likely to be telling the truth. Find out anything you can about the wife as well."

"Okay. I'll work on it tomorrow."

"Another thing," Strauss said and took a deep breath.

"What's that?" She turned toward him.

In the glow of the dash lights, he could see the steadiness of her dark eyes piercing into him, and he nearly missed the turn onto the main road.

"I'm really hungry. Aren't you?"

She gave him an odd look. "I suppose I am."

"Stop at the Hook?"

Adrian shook her head. "I've got some food at home. It's only fair, but we won't have to talk about murder if we eat there. Deal?"

Strauss nodded. It seemed a low blow to let her give him supper and then question her about a subject that was sure to be a painful one, but he supposed it was as good an opportunity as he would get.

The yard lights were on at Adrian's farm even though he hadn't noticed that she turned them on earlier. Over by the barn Strauss could make out lights coming from Lester Blake's battered trailer as well, and he wondered if that man was watching them go into the house together.

Adrian shed her coat and boots in the mudroom. Strauss did the same. He followed her into the kitchen in his socks, glad that he had managed to put on a pair without holes in the toes.

"You're going to have to get heavy socks to go with your new boots or you'll have frostbite before the end of the month," Adrian

An Investigation of Local Color

said over her shoulder as she rummaged around in the refrigerator. For some reason the comment made him feel self-conscious, and he looked around for something to do to be useful.

"You can throw a couple logs in the stove," she said as if reading his mind.

Strauss glanced from her turned back to the woodstove against the outside wall of the kitchen. It was surrounded by a brick hearth and a sizeable wood box, which was full of logs cut to the perfect size for the stove. He picked up a log and reached for the handle on the glass door behind which a small flame produced a warm glow.

"Use a glove or you'll burn yourself," Adrian warned without turning around.

Properly armed in the heavy gloves that had been draped over the side of the wood box, Strauss finally managed to complete the task given him, all the while wondering about the appeal of feeding a fire when one could simply turn up a thermostat.

"Is this your only heat?"

"There's another stove in the living room. I don't use it much, though."

"Doesn't it get cold in here when you're at work all day?"

"The fire would go down, yes, but Les usually feeds it a couple of hours before I get home, so it's warm by the time I get here."

"He takes pretty good care of the place, I take it?"

Adrian looked up from putting some salad together. Her dark eyes met his. "Yes, he is a very good man and a very good friend."

Did she say it more forcefully than necessary, Strauss wondered? This was the time to find out. But she had turned back to her salads. He remained silent as she sliced some bread and popped it into the microwave. He liked a woman who knew how to use a microwave. Somehow it restored the faith he lost in her on discovering that she didn't know how to use a thermostat.

"Maybe a furnace would be easier," she continued the earlier thought. "I don't know, because I've never had one. But then, you can't do this with a furnace."

She pulled a small table near the stove and between a large rocking chair and one of the kitchen chairs. Then she set their supper, stew and bread, freshly warmed in the microwaved, and large salads and glasses of milk on the table. Offering him the larger, more comfortable rocker, Adrian settled herself into a hard-looking wooden chair and propped her feet up near the heat of the stove with the familiarity of one who often ate in that position.

Adrian's stew was thick with gravy and vegetables. Strauss realized that he had become hungry again.

"You're a good cook," he said when he thought the silence was becoming awkward.

She shook her head. "Not really, at least not by farm standards. My mother would have made stew the same day she served it and would have baked her own bread. I freeze and microwave everything and buy bread. So much for the intrusion of modern life."

Strauss smiled. "Being a heavy consumer of frozen Morton and Banquet dinners, I can assure you with some degree of expertise that this is much better."

"Thanks. I still think my mother would be horrified. The milk, however, is fresh right out of the barn," she added around a mouthful of stew.

Strauss had just taken a gulp of the frothy white stuff when images of the inside of the Thibault dairy barn as well as an uncanny memory of the smell therein invaded with such force that he nearly sprayed his mouthful of milk all over the front of the comfortably glowing stove. To her credit Adrian didn't laugh, although she did stare at him in such a way that he swallowed the rest of the milk quickly and prayed he wouldn't gag.

"You don't have to finish it if you don't want," she said mildly.

"No, it's great, really." To himself, Strauss added that there were a whole lot of things he was far better off not knowing. Where his food came from was definitely one of them.

"You're having a lot of trouble with country life, aren't you?"

"No, I'm not," he lied defensively. But he could see she didn't believe him, so he added, "Yes, a little. Maybe. A little."

An Investigation of Local Color

She gave him a questioning look, which somehow forced him to go on.

"The truth is, I've hardly ever been to the country, and I'm not at all sure I like it."

Adrian smiled as if she had just yanked his darkest secret from him and, given his usual reserve, he felt resentful that it had been so easy for her.

"Why are you here, then?"

"As in, why don't you go back to Boston where you belong and let us Vermonters get on with our work?"

"No. As in, why are you here? Period."

Strauss sat back in his chair and stared at the fire glowing behind the glass door of the woodstove. "It's a very long story."

"I don't have to work tomorrow, so I get to stay up late."

"This story, besides being long, is ugly as well."

"Aren't they all?"

"Is yours?" Strauss looked over at her.

She returned his gaze steadily. "Sort of."

He turned back to the fire. He decided that he liked it after all, the warmth, the glow of the flame, the heat on the bottoms of his feet.

"I'm on what is called *a* temporary leave of absence from the Boston Police Department. Temporary to them means one year."

Strauss waited for Adrian to ask why. When she didn't, he went on.

"For post-traumatic stress. That's the technical term. I take it that the Department thinks I'm crazy but they don't mind waiting a year to find out for sure. I don't know why anyone in their right minds would send a city cop to Vermont to unwind. When I get done with my stint here, I'm liable to go back nuttier than when I left."

Adrian smiled slightly. "You hate it here, then?"

"Well, I certainly did at first. I'm a vice cop in Boston. There's a lot of vice there, in case you didn't know, so I was always very busy, always in the middle of whatever action was going on. It took some real work on my part to make detective. Then I got sent here and started giving a lot of speeding tickets out on Route 4. It didn't exactly have the desired relaxing effect."

141

She was watching him, but he couldn't read her expression. She just waited for him to go on, as sure that he would as he was himself.

"It sounds like I'm stressed out by a lack of crime, doesn't it? That in itself sounds crazy, doesn't it?"

Adrian shook her head. "Do you think you're crazy?"

Strauss was becoming mesmerized by the flames, remembering the city, unable to look away from the light or forget the past.

"No, I don't think so." He didn't add that there were a few times when he wasn't so sure. "But I have to admit that I gave the wrong people a few reasons to think so. There was a handful of cops who thought being my partner could become a fatal endeavor, and not because of the bad guys, and there is this lady police shrink who is probably still searching the city for all the pages of notes that she took on me. Somehow they fell out a third-story window and blew away. Still want to be partners?"

Adrian nodded. She had continued to watch him steadily the whole time he talked, seemingly unalarmed or unsurprised by anything he said.

"And were you always dangerous to know?"

He shook his head. "No."

But he couldn't tell her what had caused the change or what he had been like before the anger because he could barely remember. Adrian didn't say anything, but the silence wasn't uncomfortable. Usually he wasn't a man given to a lot of introspection, and he always despised talking or even thinking too much about past events in his life, but at the moment, anyway, he didn't feel the usual irritation. He wondered tomorrow if he would wake up in horror that he had told his secrets to a near total stranger.

"So you will be happy to go back to Boston?" Adrian asked finally.

"You know, I think I am catching on to things here, although I'm not sure I could ever adjust to drinking milk right from the cow. But yes, I will be glad to go to Boston."

Adrian nodded as if he had just confirmed what she already knew. It occurred to him that he should be asking her about her past life

An Investigation of Local Color

and about her very devoted hired man, but somehow he couldn't seem to form the thought. There was always tomorrow.

"I think I'd better get on home. It's been a long day."

Strauss got to his feet. Adrian did as well and turned to stir the fire and throw another log in the stove.

"Thanks for the dinner," he said as he laced his boots and shrugged into his parka.

"No problem. There's usually something in the freezer that makes up pretty quickly. I guess I'll see you tomorrow, then."

She had followed him to the door but kept a distance between them. There was a distance in her gaze now, too, that Strauss could have sworn wasn't there while they sat talking by the fire.

He started to open the back door, then paused. "That was good work today," he said. "It's nice to have a good partner again."

Adrian smiled slightly, but her eyes remained remote. He stared at her for a moment longer than was good for him, then put his cap on. "Well, goodnight, then."

As he reached the cruiser, he noticed the light in Lester Blake's trailer go off. When he looked back at the house, he saw that Adrian was still watching him.. Had they both been watching him? Strauss got in and fired the engine. He kicked himself for poor policework. He had to ask Adrian the questions that were on his mind. It was his job, and he had always prided himself on being a good cop and on doing good work, even when it was tough work. He tried to form the questions he would ask her, but another thought kept intruding: He had wanted to kiss her. In the worst way he had wanted to kiss her. By the warmth of the fire, and then again by the door. It was an urge he had very nearly forgotten, and now that he had remembered he couldn't get rid of it. He rolled the window down and let the frigid night air in.

By the time he pulled into the driveway of Mrs. Hutchin's house, it was 11:30 and the entire house was dark. Strauss fumbled with his keys and let himself in, climbing the wooden stairs quietly so he wouldn't awaken his landlady in her half of the house. His own half was cold and cheerless. The radiator clanked but didn't send its warmth very far into the room where Strauss had left the past two days' clothes draped over the backs of his garage sale chairs. The overhead light cast a cold glow over the cheerless living room. After the warmth of Adrian's farmhouse, even if it had even been in the only room she heated, his own miserable bachelor quarters depressed him. Maybe he should think about moving into a more comfortable place. He still had a long time to go in this assignment. It was the first time he had given any thought to being comfortable rather than just waiting out his sentence in the easiest, cheapest way possible.

The sink in the bathroom dripped as it always did. Sometimes it kept him awake at night until he thought he would go crazy, and it crossed his mind to wonder if his superiors in the BPD had been right to send him away. Now he ignored it and looked into the mirror. He was nearly surprised at the face that stared back because other than when he shaved, a quick and often haphazard act at best, he never looked into mirrors. He hadn't known that his eyes had become so hard, so glittering with intensity. At least he hoped it was intensity. He hadn't realized that his face had become so chiseled-looking with a loss of flesh or that there was a sprinkling of gray hairs in among the sandy-colored ones near his temples.

He pulled off his shirt and looked at the body he had come to think of as thickened by middle age. Once, long ago, it had been a joke between his partner and him that they had become thick in the waist due to middle age and the donuts that people always assumed cops ate. He was surprised that he wasn't thick but rather that he needed flesh in an area he had always considered stocky. Looking again at his face, he wondered what a woman would think. Probably not much. And that made him think again of Adrian or, more specifically, how much he had wanted to kiss Adrian. He didn't particularly want to have that thought, though it was far more preferable than the ensuing one: that Adrian was extremely clever, adept at keeping his attention focused away from her past and the very questionable past of her hired man.

Strauss turned on the shower. Water burst out of the nozzle with the usual symphony from the pipes, which clanked all through the

An Investigation of Local Color

building, no doubt delighting Mrs. Hutchins. Well, she would be able to tell her friends at what ungodly hour the state detective showered last night. He left more cold water on than he normally did, but it didn't help much. When he crawled beneath his blankets clad in gym shorts and a sweatshirt for the cold, he was still thinking of Adrian. When he woke up several times in the night, as he often did, she was the first thing on his mind.

6

Adrian was the first thing on his mind in the morning, too, but after a restless night Strauss now made plans for discovering whether he could rule out Lester Blake as a potential suspect in the Dunfield murder. Time to get back to real policework. He ignored the fact that he shaved more carefully than he had in a long time or that he tied his tie in the mirror, something he never did. He also took the time to pick up his discarded clothes and deposit them in the hamper while reminding himself to go to the laundromat soon before he ran out of fresh underwear.

On his way to the car he waved to Mrs. Hutchins, who had obviously been watching for him but who moved too slowly to divert him from his course. Yes, he was getting better at things.

He turned the cruiser toward Benton Harbor and the Hook, Line, and Sinker. Unlike yesterday, today was bright and crisp, with a view toward everywhere. The distant, most elevated peaks were solid white with the November snowfall, and Strauss imagined there would be many happy deer hunters in the woods following tracks today.

When he pulled into the lot at the Hook, Strauss was surprised to see the usual order of the day had been disrupted. All his friends sat outside on the narrow porch, or what was more aptly the proprietor's halfhearted attempt to comply with the state's handicap laws demanding that every public place be wheelchair accessible. The Hook was accessible but only if the wheelchair operator was extremely daring. The ramp was steep enough to warrant the possibility of a rollover accident, and the wooden porch was uneven and so narrow that the use of hands to propel wheels would be severely discouraged. The porch was wide enough, however, for Strauss' new cronies to set their chairs and prop their legs up on the railing if they scrunched up the legs tightly. Everyone appeared to be there as usual, only this morning they drank their coffee while rocking their chairs back on two legs against the wall of the restaurant. No one concerned himself with dousing his cigarette at Strauss' appearance.

"Hey, Mr. Strauss," Donnie called out with his usual infectious smile. "Grab a chair in there and have a seat."

"Why are you all out here?" Strauss asked. The sun felt warm, but not warm enough to offset the crisp air.

Birch dragged a chair out for him. "Harvey's in a terror this morning. Had a fight with his wife first off, then the morning girl didn't show for work. Now he's gone and burnt some eggs. Damn near caught the place on fire. Smoke everywhere."

"Happens about once a month," one of the Chandlers informed Strauss in a lowered voice, leaning across one of his brothers as he spoke.

"We all tread very lightly when it does," Birch said, much to Strauss' amazement. Birch didn't seem like a man who would tread lightly for anyone.

As if on cue, a loud roar came from the kitchen.

"He'll be fine tomorrow," Donnie said. "At least it isn't raining like it was last month. I had to go home and change after sitting out here that time. Usually it isn't too bad, though."

"No, it ain't too bad," a Chandler agreed. "And we can smoke out here."

"You smoke in there," Strauss reminded him.

"Oh, yeah," the Chandler said, "but out here it's legal."

A pan crashed to the floor within, followed quickly by the sound of breaking glass.

"Care for some coffee?" Ira, the vet, asked from his place at the end of the chairs.

"I think I'll just wait on that."

"No need. I'll just sneak in there while Harvey's throwing things. He'll never see me." Ira ducked through the door.

"Saw you and Adrian go upstreet last night," Birch commented. He stared out across the parking area in a semblance of casual attitude. He didn't ask, but clearly he expected to be told where Strauss and the constable had gone.

An Investigation of Local Color

"Upstreet?"

"Yeah, upstreet."

"What's that mean?"

Six pairs of eyes fastened themselves on him, the fellows at the end of the row leaning over to see Strauss better since he was sitting in the middle, next to their leader. Was he pulling their collective legs?

"Upstreet, you know, upstreet." Birch gestured with his chin in the direction of the passing road opposite the Hook.

"I thought it was a road. The constable said in Vermont it's a road," Strauss protested.

The lights came on.

"It is a road," Junior Thibault, Benton Harbor's main road man, agreed, "unless you're going upstreet. You know, up there somewhere."

"Oh. I get it," Strauss said, although he didn't.

"Here you go." Ira saved him by handing him a cup of coffee and a creamer. "I hope you don't use sugar. Something flew by my head just as I was reaching for it, and I was forced to beat a hasty retreat without it."

"Thanks." Strauss peered into the creamer, remembering Adrian's fresh-from-the-barn milk from last night. In spite of the fact that this was the same creamer he had used every morning since coming to the Hook, he decided that it was time to give up dairy products. Cold turkey would probably be the best way. Certainly it would be the least painless.

He sipped his coffee and lit a cigarette but couldn't further ignore Birch's silent expectation of a reply.

"We went back to Gwen Dunfield's to ask some more questions," Strauss said finally.

"Got anything on her?"

Birch asked the questions, but he asked for everyone present. All ears were tuned to the state detective and the Benton Harbor fire chief.

Strauss shook his head. "Nothing. On the surface she looks like she could be our stabber, but if I arrested her with no more evidence than I have now even an average lawyer could have her out in half a day. Besides, I don't think she did it."

That comment brought no response even though Strauss would have bet money that Gwenivere Dunfield was the favorite suspect for those in Benton Harbor who were keeping up with the murder investigation. They smoked and thought and waited for someone else to ask the question which, finally, Junior did.

"Then who did do it?"

Strauss shrugged. "I'm open to suggestions. Anyone got any ideas?"

Obviously that was a question that had been given a lot of thought and, probably while Strauss was off investigating, a lot of active speculation. If the suspect du jour didn't do it, choose another. Jack Glenn was now the favorite choice with Milly Boyce in close second. Even Marlon Kinney's name came up, though no one seemed to know exactly why or even, for that matter, exactly who he was other than he lived beside the Glenns and had had some sort of boundary dispute with the deceased last summer. As they offered up opinions, the smoke thickened and then blew away in the wind. The noise from the kitchen died down, and Strauss noticed Harvey standing just inside the open doorway listening to the talk. None of the names offered as potential suspects were natives of Benton Harbor or even Vermont. Strauss just sat and listened. Beside him Franklyn Birch was doing the same.

"I didn't know Constable Thibault had been married," he remarked casually in a low voice.

He would have sworn that only Birch could have possibly heard him and that no one else was even particularly listening to him or to each other, but his comment met with sudden and total silence. Birch's heavily lidded stare turned to a dark scowl.

"It was a long time ago," he replied in a voice that didn't invite further conversation on the subject.

"What happened to him?" Strauss persisted.

Birch turned his dark gaze on Strauss. "I believe you know what happened to him."

"Story was that he got kicked in the head by a cow."

"And that's what happened."

It was a draw. Both men sucked on their cigarettes, one deciding how to pursue the issue, the other trying to figure out how to fend off such a pursuit. The silence was deafening. Strauss wished Harvey would go back to throwing the pans.

"There were some rumors that the blow might have been delivered by a man instead of a cow. Say a man like Lester Blake."

"That's all it was, a rumor," Birch insisted angrily. "Someone too cowardly to even give a name calls the cops and points a finger based on nothing. They never found nothing, did they? No, and that's because Les was with Adrian. He couldn't possibly have killed that bastard Borden."

"Les is no killer, Nick," Donnie added. "It just isn't in him."

Heads nodded in silent agreement all down the row of chairs. No one leaned back casually against the wall to smoke or drink their coffee. All six chairs were planted firmly on the porch floor, the camaraderie gone. At the end of the row, Ira caught Strauss' eye and shook his head in an imperceptible warning as he lit another cigarette.

"Are you a good shot, Nick?" Birch asked, surprising him with the sudden change of subject.

Strauss was, in fact, a very good shot, not because he had ever really had to be but because he had taken to practicing diligently on the police target range following the death of his partner. He never again wanted to find himself in a position where he was not the best gun. Even though he never expected to have to draw a weapon in Vermont, he had been equally disciplined in practicing at the State Police range in spite of the hour's drive over the mountains to get to the range in Pittsford.

"I'm good enough, I suppose," he replied.

"Ever wonder how Adrian got to be our constable?"

"She said something about inheriting the job from her father."

"That's partly true. But she is the best person for the job even if not for that. And you know why?"

"I imagine you are about to tell me."

Birch took an angry pull on his nearly finished cigarette and tossed it out into the parking area. "You're damn right I am. Adrian comes from a family of good people." This declaration was followed by unbiased nods from the Thibaults present. "She is honest and fair," Birch laid heavy emphasis on the words. "And...."

"There's more?"

"And she is the best shot this town has ever seen."

Strauss nodded. Now that he knew where this conversation was leading, he had to decide what the point was and whether or not to rise to the bait. Ira Thibault saved him.

"You'd better not go down this road, Franklyn. You know how irate Adrian got last time you did."

But Birch was staring at Strauss with his heavy-lidded scowl. His reply was directed at both Strauss and the vet. "Adrian understands that it's part of her job."

Everyone except Ira nodded in agreement. So much for being saved.

"What do you say, Strauss, think you can outshoot the lady?"

The Chandlers, Thibaults, and Birch all leaned forward waiting for his answer.

"For what purpose? Would it help us find Dunfield's murderer?"

"To my way of thinking, it just might help you to get back to looking where you should be looking."

Strauss said nothing. He had very little doubt that he could outshoot Adrian, but he disliked the implied threat he was feeling. And it wasn't just coming from Birch. He was merely the spokesman for what felt to Strauss to be the entire town.

"What do you say, gentlemen? This afternoon before evening chores while there is still good light?"

The plan, unfortunately, drew a hearty response.

"Adrian doesn't get home from work until after 4:00," Strauss pointed out.

"She isn't working today," Donnie informed him with his cheerful smile. Was it cheerful or smug? "I ran into her mailing some stuff at the store before I came over here. She said she had the day off."

"Okay then. Two-thirty, down at the rifle club range. Know it, Strauss?"

An Investigation of Local Color

To that man's dismay he didn't know it, and the directions were yet another series of mysteries involving unmarked dirt roads and numerous turns. As if things weren't bad enough.

"I hope you're going to take it upon your shoulders to inform Adrian since you have set her up without warning," Ira commented to Birch. His expression was unreadable, making it impossible for Strauss to tell if he was as enthusiastic about the match as his friends and relatives seemed to be.

"I'll talk to Adrian," Birch agreed. He got up and walked his chair back inside. On his way out, he commented to Harvey on the fineness of the weather outside.

Strauss didn't believe he had ever seen the man so lighthearted. He headed on foot for his house two doors down from the Hook, presumably on his way to talk to Adrian.

He had no sooner left when Martha Cutting pulled up in her battered pickup with a roar of equally battered muffler and a skid of loose gravel. When she got out, it was immediately obvious that she was excited about something. As before, she managed to silence even the excited talk that had broken out over the shooting match.

"I had piglets in the night!" she announced.

"Do we congratulate you, Martha?" Donnie asked.

"Did you by any chance bring Cee-gars?" one of the Chandlers asked.

"You all ought to go to Hell," she said cheerfully. "Either there or back to your barns. Same difference. Ooooh, Mr. Nick, you're looking a little green this morning."

Strauss smiled at her perception. He wondered if that was really how he looked. It certainly was how he felt. He wasn't afraid of being bested by Adrian. He was afraid that he had stumbled onto the key to the murder, and it was a key that neither he nor the people of Benton Harbor wanted him to have.

"The detective here is going to have a little shooting match with Adrian this afternoon," Junior explained.

Martha put her hands on her hips. The inevitable wool skirt billowed around her legs in the wind.

"Bad move, Mr. Lawman. Does Adrian know?"

"I take it she's about to," Strauss told her. "Apparently, it is a part of her job. Franklyn's on his way to inform her of that fact."

"You men are so damn stupid. Always pissing on the trees. You'll never get it." With that prediction she proceeded into the restaurant, presumably for the leftovers for her newly enlarged pig population.

Those left in her wake had the grace to look shamefaced as they dragged their chairs back inside and began to leave.

"Wait a moment," Ira said in a low voice as he went by.

So Strauss waited and was enlisted to assist Martha with the task of getting the slops into the back of her truck.

"You are a good sport," she informed him again, and he wondered if it were a standard phrase with her. "I hope it will get you something in the end."

"I hope it will, too, Martha. Like maybe an end to this Dunfield case."

"If you're looking for that, you're wasting your time in a shooting match with Adrian. Go back up and look on the Hill."

Was it a warning? She smiled cryptically and left Strauss to wonder.

Ira motioned him over to his car as soon as Martha had driven away.

"I assume I stepped on toes this morning?"

"You assume correctly. You've obviously heard by now that Les was fingered anonymously in Brian Borden's death? That prompted your line of questioning?"

Strauss nodded.

"No one knows who put the suspicion on Les, but he got leaned on really hard, and to bad effect by some young cop from down at the barracks. The guy was convinced Les murdered Borden even though all evidence truly did point to the cow. He kept coming back to question him, even though Les had a solid alibi from Adrian and Les started to get so shook up, he probably seemed to be hiding something."

"Was he?"

"He said he was with Adrian. She confirmed it. Other than the suspicion cast by the anonymous caller, there has never been a reason

An Investigation of Local Color

to doubt their story. Les is a simple man who can be made nervous, maybe even angry in some situations, but I can't see him killing anyone. Not back then and not now. He would do anything for his friends in this town, and the town, in turn, takes care of him for it. That's why you're meeting with hostility."

Strauss thought about that for a moment. "You say you can't see Blake killing anyone. Let's speak hypothetically for the sake of argument. What if Les thought he was protecting someone he cared about? Might he be prompted into an act of violence then?"

Ira looked decidedly uncomfortable with the question. "I think it's hard to determine what any of us might do in that situation," he hedged.

Strauss persisted. "Did Borden, for example, ever give Les a reason to think Adrian needed to be protected?"

The veterinarian stared back at Strauss, and the detective knew in that instant that this was an honest man who would not lie to him. Finally, Ira said, "You would have to ask Adrian about that."

It wasn't an answer and yet it was, and both men knew it.

"I have just one more question, Ira. I'm truly not trying to intrude on your lives here, but everyone needs to know if there is someone capable of killing in their midst."

"I understand that, Nick. I know it's your job."

"According to the police report, Adrian and Blake were at your office to get some supplies at the time Borden was killed. Do you remember seeing them?"

Ira sighed in a resigned manner that gave Strauss his answer. "I saw Adrian that morning. She says Les was with her but waited in the truck. I had no reason not to believe her."

"No, I guess you wouldn't have. Thanks for your honesty, Ira."

"Keep looking, Nick. I know where you're going with this, but you may be wrong."

"I truly hope I am."

Ira nodded and then, because there was nothing more to say, he got into his car. Before pulling out, he rolled down the window.

"Good luck with your shooting match this afternoon."

"I'm going to need it, aren't I?"
The vet nodded.

Strauss headed the cruiser back to Fairview and the newspaper office. With the help of his young gum-chewing friend Tammy, he copied the articles on Brian Borden's death. He also asked her to be sure she hadn't previously overlooked any more information written about it. When she couldn't find any, she happily phoned the *Rutland Herald* and asked that office to fax similar stories. The *Herald* had printed two more stories than the weekly *Enquirer*. With Tammy hovering nearby out of curiosity, Strauss read them without finding anything new. Nevertheless, a picture was beginning to paint itself in his mind. It was just the sort of turnaround he had been waiting to discover, but he was discouraged by the discovery.

"Is this cow thing related to the murder in Benton Harbor?" Tammy asked. She was reading over his shoulder, trying to see what Strauss saw.

"I doubt it," he replied, though he was beginning to doubt it less and less. But it wouldn't do for Tammy to gossip about his theories around town. "I'm just getting a feel for the life and news up there."

The theory had planted itself in his mind that Blake might have killed Borden for Adrian's sake if he knew about Borden's affair with Gwenivere Dunfield. There was no question that the man was devoted to Adrian. And he appeared to be similarly attached to Sally Glenn. Might he also, then, have killed Dunfield for his merciless harassment of Sally? Strauss didn't want to think so, but it certainly was a possibility. He could see that Ira Thibault was too honest for the thought not to have crossed his mind as well. Did the whole town or at least that part of it with which he was acquainted have the same idea? Were they covering for one of their own while hoping one of the less-liked outsiders would get the blame? No one seemed to be mourning the loss of Bill Dunfield, and no one seemed at all shy about speculating as to possible suspects as long as those suspects didn't include one of them.

An Investigation of Local Color

Strauss carefully folded the copies Tammy had made for him and put them in the pocket of his parka.

"You're a prize, Tammy," he told her. "I'm going to recommend you for a raise."

"I would settle for you fixing my speeding tickets."

"Tickets? Did you get another?"

She nodded with a grin. "Just this morning."

"Get out of bed earlier. I don't have much pull with the traffic guys."

Tammy snapped her gum. "I'll think about it."

Strauss doubted if she would. He went out to the car and radioed the barracks to find out if the forensics report had come in. It hadn't. He cursed the slow speed, wanting desperately for something to change his suspicions, then headed back to his apartment to check on his firearms and have some lunch.

For once Strauss was able to follow the directions given to him without difficulty, and he arrived at the rifle club range early. He had never been to the range or any of the many around the area where hunters could often be heard, especially as the opening of deer season drew near and rifles that had sat idle throughout the summer needed to be sighted in for accuracy. He felt outside of the brotherhood of deer hunters and more comfortable and far more welcome at the police firing range. If it was a farther drive it was too bad.

In spite of being early, Strauss had plenty of company. Franklyn Birch greeted him with far more cheer than he had shown him that morning, and the Chandlers and Donnie Thibault were as cheerful as if Strauss had never brought up the uncomfortable subject of Adrian's unfortunate husband. In addition, Madge Birch and Jean Thibault had come along with their husbands, an act Strauss assumed meant that the match was a main event in Benton Harbor that no one wanted to be left out of. His theory was further confirmed when Jean introduced the three Chandler wives, whom he had not met before and who looked as startlingly like each other as their husbands did. All three women had the look of self-sufficient wives who could hold their own whether it be in their own kitchens or helping out with the butchering in the barnyard. Strauss dearly hoped he would never be held accountable for their names, as he was as lost in that area as he was with their husbands.

Still the cars and pickups kept coming. The grapevine in Benton Harbor worked both fast and well.

"The only folks missing from an event like this are those few who haven't shot their deer yet," Birch commented. He had sidled up to Strauss as that man watched in astonished silence the line of vehicles that would soon need to be directed if it continued. "Why, looky there, Strauss, even old man Howe came along with his boys."

Strauss looked in the direction Birch indicated and saw a truck that was battered and rusted through, even by Benton Harbor standards. But it was four-wheel drive, as were most of the trucks in town, and crawled to a spot near where the two men stood. On the front of the hood was a brand-new bug catcher with the bold words "B. B. Howe and Sons, Tit Pullers." Strauss felt his eyes widen in surprise even though he tried not to react.

Birch elbowed him in the ribs. "Ain't that something? Oldest dairy farmers in Benton Harbor, the Howes, and the way they keep breeding sons it's likely there will always be Howes pulling tits."

"Obviously."

Strauss watched as four strapping young men who looked simpler than the day they were born leaped over the sides of the truck. They were dressed in overalls that looked like they had gone dangerously far past the last laundry day and high rubber barn boots. In spite of the cold wind, each wore only a flannel shirt and long johns beneath his overalls, and none looked cold.

The old man jumped out of the cab with a roar. "I'm here for the show, Birch! Get the goddamned thing on the road! S'cuse me, ladies. I got cows to milk!"

B. B. Howe looked like a cross between Yosemite Sam and something that had just been aroused from hibernation. His legs were bowed in their dungarees. Unlike his sons he wore a wool hunting jacket but both elbows were blown out, allowing the cold in anyway. He sported a beard that was thick and mostly gray, though some other suspicious colors could be seen as well, and it could easily be assumed

An Investigation of Local Color

that there were living things that crawled within. Strauss wondered what Mrs. B. B. was like. The fact that she didn't appear to be here must mean that she was one of the few in Benton Harbor who hadn't yet bagged her deer.

"Birch!!" the old man roared again to the accompaniment of his sons' laughter, though why they were laughing was anyone's guess. He left no doubt as to whom he held responsible for the day's festivities or, as it seemed at the moment, lack thereof.

"In a minute, you old bastard! We got to wait for Adrian."

As if on cue, Strauss saw Adrian's truck pull in behind the line of cars assembled on the rifle club grass and spilling out onto the dirt road beyond. She made her way toward them while her friends and neighbors urged her to shoot well and wished her luck. She wore jeans and hunting boots and a dark wool jacket. Her dark hair was tied back in a ponytail and the wind had blown a reddish color into her cheeks. When her eyes moved from the crowd to Birch and, finally, to Strauss, he saw that they were very angry.

Beyond anger, actually. Adrian, he saw, was furious. She carried a holstered handgun in one hand and an older 30.06 rifle in the crook of her other arm.

"Get on with it, Franklyn," she said coldly while casting an equally cold eye on Strauss.

"Detective Strauss," Birch began formally, "handgun or rifle?"

Both Strauss' weapons were state issue, and he was equally good on each one. He could see that, though well cared for, both Adrian's firearms were old and the rifle must give her one Hell of a kick in the shoulder. Still, he figured that she must be better with the rifle since as a Vermonter her shooting activities would be limited to deer hunting.

"Rifle would be good with me. Adrian?"

"Fine."

"Would you prefer to stand or use the bench?" Birch asked him, indicating the frame where marksmen could kneel down and lean their rifles to better steady them.

"Adrian?" Strauss asked since Birch hadn't asked her preference yet.

"Doesn't matter," she replied abruptly.

Strauss shrugged at her indifference. "I'll stand."

Now Birch very definitely turned to Adrian. "First or second. Constable?"

"I'll shoot second," Adrian replied firmly, looking straight at Strauss.

Strauss' rifle was the standard .222 issued to all patrolmen. It had very little kick, nothing at all that a man of his size couldn't easily absorb, and it was as familiar as a comfortable old pair of shoes. He set his feet and took aim through the high-powered scope at the target 150 yards away. Carefully he fired, then re-aimed slowly and fired again until he had fired the four shots prescribed earlier by Birch. His turn was followed by silence. He had been good. He knew it without looking at the target.

"You there, young Howe, go fetch that target over here. Rifles down, you two," Birch warned as the youngest Howe ran out to bring the target in for marking.

Both Strauss and Adrian pointed their rifles with the safeties on at the ground.

"Look at that!"

A low whistle.

"Wow, ain't that something?"

"That might be hard to beat."

"Adrian's got her work cut out!"

Birch snatched up the paper target and, with a scowl, held it up for Adrian and Strauss to see. There were four neat holes near the center of the bull's eye. They were in the shape of a perfect square and no further than three-fourths of an inch apart. Adrian looked briefly, then began putting shells in her rifle. Birch drew circles around Strauss' marks with a red pen, then sent young Howe back out with the target.

Adrian stepped up to the spot Strauss had just vacated. She set her feet and put the rifle to her shoulder in what looked like a very feminine stance. Already her face cringed in anticipation of the rifle's kick against her shoulder. She fired a walloping shot that made everyone grab for their ears and very nearly knocked her off her feet. But

An Investigation of Local Color

before Strauss could even begin breathing again, she had re-set her feet and fired a second shot. Before she appeared to even have a chance to aim, she had powered off her four shots, flipped the safety back on and lowered the rifle. To her credit, she never once rubbed her shoulder, though Strauss had seen the gun kick against her. While another youngster ran for the target in the ensuing silence, she stooped to pick up the empty shell casings and shoved them in her pockets.

"Look at this!" the kid who had collected the target crowed.

The crowd quickly surrounded him, chattering loudly.

"I hope we're done proving whatever it is we had to prove to each other," Adrian said flatly, "or to anyone else who needed it."

"Strauss, you'd better go look at that," Birch said.

He took Strauss' rifle and pushed him toward the knot of people clustered around the target. There were his four holes marked carefully with red ink, and inside the square made by his shells were four holes very nearly one inside the other, they were so close. He stared in amazement. The citizens of Benton Harbor stared at him as he stared, though they were far less amazed than he. When he looked up, they smiled. Were they merely pleased with the outcome of a good day's sport, though they had been sure of the results? Or were they satisfied that he had been duly warned against asking the wrong questions?

He looked over the tops of heads for Adrian. But she had walked to her truck without even bothering to look at the target.

Birch shoved his rifle roughly back at him. The smile he gave was equally rough. "It ain't one of us, Strauss. Go looking somewhere else."

Strauss shouldered his way past the man. His now-frozen fingers were numb against the stock of the rifle, and his mind felt pretty well numb as well. He almost didn't see Trooper Gary Shubert standing just beyond the townsfolk, a knowing smile on his doughy face, his porcine eyes watching the scene slyly.

Just as Strauss reached the car, the radio crackled, the dispatcher's voice paged him.

"Strauss here."

"Detective Strauss, the forensics report you were looking for earlier has just come over the line. I thought you'd want to know."

"That's great." Strauss looked around. He was hopelessly parked in and would be unable to move until some of his new friends moved their vehicles first. "I'm a little tied up at the moment, but I'll be back at the barracks in about forty-five minutes."

"It'll keep," the dispatcher assured him with the typical Vermonter's lack of urgency for anything not directly related to milking time.

Strauss switched off the radio with a heavy sigh. Someone tapped loudly on the window right next to his left ear. Mr. B. B. Howe. Strauss rolled down the window. The day just couldn't get any better.

"Tricky shooting there, Sheriff." The old man grinned. He had watery red eyes and a bulbous red nose that made Strauss think he tipped a bottle or two from time to time. Probably from morning milking time to evening milking time.

"But ain't nobody ever goin' to outshoot that little Thibault gal. Ain't she somethin'?"

"She's something," Strauss agreed.

"Yessir, it really eats at those of us who still got a male ego, but them are the facts and what ya ever goin to do about 'em? How is your ol' male ego feelin' right now, Sheriff?"

"It's feeling just fine, thank you, Mr. Howe."

Strauss peered out at the old man. He had to look into the sun that framed the wild hair that Howe's cap couldn't hold down. Between that and the overgrown beard with its inhabitants and the wild grin, it was easy to believe B. B. was another form of Beelzebub. Surprisingly, though, he had the most perfect set of teeth Strauss had ever seen.

Apparently finished with his torment of the little Thibault gal's latest victim, Howe turned and shouted, "Come on, you worthless sons of bitches! Them cows is calling!"

And Strauss was forced to wonder again about Mrs. Howe and whether the old man's words might not, in fact, be taken literally.

The four boys scrambled over the sides of the rotted-out pickup, all loose-limbed and grinning. All four, Strauss now saw, had perfect sets of pearly whites, which they flashed in his direction for no particular reason Strauss could see.

An Investigation of Local Color

"See ya around, Sheriff!" the father roared above the groan of the engine and the spray of mud and yesterday's slush.

Let's hope so, Strauss thought.

Finally, enough cars and trucks cleared out for Strauss to back up onto the road. The citizens of Benton Harbor had all waved cheerfully on their way by, but somehow it didn't cheer him. He felt even less cheered when he got to the barracks and couldn't locate the forensics report either in his box or on the fax machine.

"The forensics report you called me about?" he asked the dispatcher/secretary.

"I believe Mr. Shubert has it," she said.

"Why does Shubert have it?" he growled.

The dispatcher shrugged indifferently. She had none of the good-natured high spirits of the night kid.

"Oh, and the boss wants to see you as soon as you get here, so I guess you're already late."

Did he hear hostility in her voice? Maybe it was just his own sour mood.

He found Shubert sitting behind a desk with his feet propped up in a cocky manner. In his hand was the forensics report.

"Since that's not your desk, I suppose you don't mind that you're dripping mud all over it?" Strauss commented.

"My, aren't we a little testy? It's hard being outdone by a woman, isn't it, hotshot?" Shubert grinned in obvious enjoyment of the moment. He dangled the report between his fingers. "Looking for this?"

"As a matter of fact, I was."

"Chief's looking for you. Better see him first."

"I don't take my orders from you, son." Strauss put both his hands flat down on the desk and leaned toward Shubert. His voice was low and dangerous. "If you expect to continue enjoying good health, you'll pass that paper over here now."

Shubert didn't need to be asked again. He had just seen the side of Nick Strauss that had lost him several partners in the past.

"It doesn't matter anyway," he blundered on. "There's nothing there. No identifiable prints, no blood that isn't the victim's type."

Shit! Strauss thought.

"Detective Strauss!" a voice called from the office down the hall. "Could you please grace me with your presence?"

Shubert gave him a snide grin, and Strauss wished the barracks was a third-story building with large windows.

"Yes, Chief."

"Come in, Strauss, and shut the door."

Strauss did as he was told and sat down in the chair opposite the desk Chief Peterman sat behind.

"It has come to my attention that you are having some trouble with the Benton Harbor murder." He held up a hand in order to prevent Strauss from defending himself. "I know that things are done a little differently around here than you are used to, and I know of your reputation for being something of a lone wolf. But here in Vermont we like to get our crimes solved quickly and neatly with as little undue glamour as possible. The vice squad in Boston may have the luxury of indulging in public shooting matches while on the clock, but around here we don't do that sort of thing," Peterman said mildly.

"It wasn't a public shooting match," Strauss protested. "Constable Thibault and I were merely—"

"Yes, Detective?"

"Practicing and sighting in our firearms in case we need them in the future. How was I supposed to know that half the town would show up to watch? Not much exciting happens up there, I guess." Even to him, it sounded weak.

"I have just recently been informed that Constable Thibault has developed something of a reputation for 'sighting in her firearms.'"

"She's very good at it," Strauss said, trying to ignore the sarcasm in his chief's voice.

"Apparently. At any rate, Detective, we need to make an arrest on this case, as I told you before. I think that it would be helpful to you if I put someone else on it with you, someone who knows the area and the residents better than you do. Someone, perhaps, who could have clued you into the Constable's 'sighting' skills before you embarrassed yourself."

An Investigation of Local Color

"I'm not embarrassed," Strauss said.

"You're not? You should be. Any red-blooded male would be. But that isn't the issue. I'm assigning Trooper Shubert to the case along with you. You may continue to make use of Constable Thibault's services if you wish, but I want an arrest made and soon."

"Not Shubert, sir. The man's a first-rate ass."

For the first time in their professional acquaintance, Strauss saw Peterman's eyes light with anger.

"According to your supervisor at the Boston PD, you think anyone partnered with you is a first-rate ass, Strauss. It matters not in the least to me what you think of Shubert. He is now your partner, and you are to work with him to get this case closed. You are the lead on this case, but Shubert will be your partner. I don't want to hear that he has flown out of any windows, been dropped into any bodies of water, or left out on any back roads in the middle of the night or you will find yourself emptying parking meters back on your old stomping grounds. Do I make myself clear?"

Apparently Peterman had been talking to someone important. Strauss scowled.

"Are you clear on this, Detective?" the chief persisted.

"Crystal, sir. Is Trooper Shubert clear as well?"

"Shubert knows what he has to do."

Strauss got to his feet. "Okay, then."

As he went out the door his mind was already working in overdrive, all his big-city instincts intruding with the simple gift of a new partner. Why was this always happening to him?

Shubert was still sitting in the same place with his feet up. Judging by the look on his face, he knew pretty much what had transpired in the chief's office. Strauss was fairly sure, too, that Shubert had been the one who had instigated the change in Strauss' solo status, which meant that the young man had been listening at doors and spying through keyholes. It was not a habit Strauss found endearing in a partner, especially when he was the one being spied on.

"So, hotshot, what's the plan?"

165

Strauss stared at his new partner. Windows, water and back roads being out of his repertoire as per the chief's orders, he considered some of his more drastic options. If ever there was a partner who warranted it, it was Shubert. He smiled at the thought.

"You've obviously had your mind on this case all along, what would you suggest, Mr. Shubert?"

"I think we need to go after Lester Blake. He's been trouble in the past," Shubert replied confidently.

"Has he been trouble?"

"I know Blake has ties to Frampton Hill and didn't like the victim. I know, too, that he was involved in the questionable death of the man who used to be married to Adrian Thibault. I bet you never even knew about that, did you?"

"As a matter of fact, I did know that Blake was under suspicion in that investigation, but unlike you I can't say for a fact that he was involved since it was never proved."

"But don't you think it's an amazing coincidence that Blake is involved with both women who have trouble with certain men, and then suddenly those men turn up dead?" Shubert persisted stubbornly.

Strauss was more than a little irritated that Shubert had zoomed in on the very idea that had been nagging at him for the past two days. Although he knew the tough questions had to be asked, regardless of the message Benton Harbor seemed to be sending him, Strauss would have liked to choose his time and place, not to mention his tactics, which he knew would be different from the blustering accusations this buffoon was likely to make.

"We may be talking about more than a coincidence here," he conceded grudgingly. "What else have you considered?"

Shubert shrugged. "Well, there is the possibility of the ex-wife, but I don't think she did it."

"Why not? Isn't she the most likely suspect? Motive, not to mention a better opportunity than anyone else."

"I've met her. Really nice lady. I can't picture her doing it."

"Are you talking about Gwenivere Dunfield?" Strauss asked in amazement.

An Investigation of Local Color

"Yes. You've questioned her, of course?"

Strauss ignored his sarcastic question. "And just because you can't picture her doing it, you've ruled her out as a suspect?" He kept his voice calm, one partner asking another his opinion.

"Well, not entirely. But she is very sensitive. It's hard to imagine her sticking a knife in anyone."

"But you can imagine Lester Blake knifing someone?"

"Definitely."

"So he's our man?"

"I think he is the most likely suspect. And let me tell you something else: You won't get any help from Adrian Thibault. She has covered for him before, and she'll do it again." Shubert's voice was bitter now, thick with distain as soon as he mentioned Adrian's name.

"And you know that for a fact?"

"Look, hotshot, there are a few things I'm more aware of than you are because I have been here all my life. I grew up around here, and I've put in my time. Adrian Thibault has been a snotty little bitch with her nose in the air ever since she was a little kid. She thinks she can do anything she wants because she is from one of the founding families. If you lean on Lester Blake, she will pull the same thing old Harvey did when we tried to question Blake on the Borden murder."

"So what do you suggest?"

"I suggest you bring Blake in and question him here and keep Thibault away."

Strauss nodded while appearing to consider the idea. Then he turned and walked away.

"Hey, where are you going?"

"Home. There's nothing more to be done today."

"But we haven't decided on a plan for tomorrow," Shubert protested.

"Actually, I have, but we'll discuss it in the morning. Oh, and one other thing, Shubert," Strauss lowered his voice to its most dangerous level, "if you ever call me hotshot again, I will do something to your male ego that will make you wish you were the one who had faced off against Constable Thibault this afternoon. I hope I'm speaking bluntly enough for you."

Shubert, who had been confident of himself while he thought he had the upper hand and the chief's ear, immediately deflated. Strauss saw a flicker of fear creep into his eyes.

"Good," Strauss said. "I'll see you tomorrow."

He smiled on his way out but only for purposes of show. Inside, he was snarling.

His landlady must have been able to read his face because even though she was standing on the porch with her broom as she was most nights when he pulled in, this time she didn't try to engage him in conversation about his investigation. He was free to let himself into his gloomy apartment just in time to hear his phone ring. There had been maybe two calls since he had arrived in Vermont, so he had gotten out of the habit of hearing it and it surprised him now.

"What?" he growled into the receiver.

"Charming as always, Nick. Isn't country life agreeing with you?" It was the voice of Lowell Petrosky, his supervisor in Boston, his mentor, and one of his few good friends.

"Hey, Lowell. I'm surprised to hear from you. Tell me you want me to come back to Boston."

It was Petrosky, by way of his cousin with the Vermont State Police, who had gotten Strauss this assignment instead of the discharge for mental instability that the furious lady shrink, among others in the department, had recommended. Strauss assumed that meant he could also pull him back to Boston if he wanted, but now Petrosky only laughed.

"You don't like it in Vermont, Nick?"

"This is definitely the weirdest place I've ever been, Lowell. I got a whole cast of characters up here with everything from a fat lady with romance on her mind, to an exercise fanatic with a pack of mad dogs, to a tampon maker, to three middle-aged triplet farmers and their triplet wives. That's leaving out the nurse packing a 30.06 who shoots better than I do and just proved it in front of the entire town. If that's not enough, I've just been assigned a partner who is dumber than dirt."

An Investigation of Local Color

There was a silence on the other end of the phone while Petrosky processed that information. Belatedly, it occurred to Strauss that he may have sounded just a little off the deep end and given his friend cause to think he was even crazier than when he had left Boston.

"Nick, you think every partner since Hawkins is dumber than dirt."

"That's because they all have been."

Strauss heard clearly the exasperated sigh on the other end of the line.

"That's part of the reason I'm calling. Your chief up there, Peterman, called today asking about you."

"Why?"

"I don't know. You can probably answer that better than I can, but I know you won't. Anyway, he was asking about your qualifications and why you happened to be assigned up there, etc. I kept the explanation to the strictest need-to-know facts, but the bottom line here, Nick, is that you have to get along up there. If you rock the boat at all it's all over, and not just in Vermont. You know that, right?"

"Yeah."

"I've done all I can for you, pal. You've got to help yourself now. Can't you just relax and enjoy the country?"

"Have you ever been in the country, Lowell? It's cold up here, the roads are all snow and mush already, and I'm always lost. On top of that the only thing to drink is Budweiser, and there are dead deer everywhere, and the locals make fun of my shoes. I can't even understand them when they talk."

"Obviously you can understand that they are making fun of your shoes."

"They point and laugh, Petrosky. It's hard to misinterpret. Can't I come back to the city where a murderer is a murderer and a dealer is a dealer? I understand that sort of shithead. These folks smile happily while they tie dead bodies onto the roofs of their cars. Did you know they still make fires up here to heat their houses? And I never even knew there were such things as attack cats. I'm really not well equipped to live in the country, Lowell. I've had no training in it. I don't like it."

Petrosky laughed at him. "It sounds interesting. My cousin loves Vermont, wouldn't leave it for double his pay."

"Shows the quality of breeding in your family," Strauss replied irritably.

"Stop being so irascible. If I were in your position, I'd have some fun, learn some new things."

"Easy for you to say from your nice cozy stationhouse in the city. I've just been outshot by a nurse, for God's sake."

"That's the second time you've mentioned the nurse. Maybe life in Vermont isn't so bad?"

"You're a bastard."

"And you aren't? Seriously, I want the old, clear-thinking, fair-minded Nick Strauss back on my force. But Internal Affairs won't even consider it until next August, Nick, and it's not for lack of trying on my part. Put your time up there to good use. If you consider it a punishment and let it fester for a year, you're going to come back to Boston with a bigger chip on your shoulder than when you left, and they aren't even going to let you be a beat cop. Understood?"

"Yeah."

"Good. Hey, learn to ski, milk cows, date the nurse. It might be fun. Then come back to the city the way you used to be. Okay?"

"Yeah," Strauss replied absently.

"Really," Petrosky caught his distracted tone, "you're okay?"

"Yeah. Call me if you hear any more complaints, will you?"

Petrosky agreed and Strauss cut his only link to the city and home.

He thought for a moment. His mind felt like it was working faster and better than it had since he had been in Vermont. Was it the contact with the city? Or maybe having Shubert forced on him felt so much like the way things had always been done, he felt less out of the loop than he had before, more in touch with his job here? It certainly couldn't be that he had just been humbled in front of an entire town by a woman.

On a whim, he picked up his heretofore unused phone directory and searched through the T's. Finding what he wanted, he dialed.

"Hello," said a flat, very irritable male voice on the other end.

An Investigation of Local Color

Strauss was surprised enough not to notice how much the voice sounded like his own when he answered a phone.

"Detective Strauss calling for Adrian," he said shortly.

The phone was set down without a reply, so Strauss couldn't tell if it had been Blake who answered. The connection wasn't broken, however, so he waited and listened to the background noise.

"Yes," Adrian answered after a lengthy wait.

Strauss heard the click of another line as it was hung up, or at least given the impression of having been hung up.

"Hello. Nick Strauss."

There was silence, then, "What was it you wanted, Detective?"

"Dinner. Would you join me?"

Clearly she hadn't expected that and didn't reply.

"In Rutland. You pick the place, I'll pay."

"Why?"

"I'm hungry, for one thing. Something has come up, too, that I wanted to talk with you about."

"You can't do that on the phone?"

"I'd rather not. Besides, I owe you one after today." As always, Strauss had the feeling he was falling far short in the charm department. He was never going to be smooth. It must be something some men were born with.

"You don't."

"So you're saying no?" Strauss tried to keep the disappointment out of his voice. "I could subpoena you."

"No, you couldn't." He didn't know her well enough to tell if she smiled or not. "Okay, I'll go, but I'll pay for my own meal."

"Suit yourself. But you're missing an unusual opportunity. I hardly ever buy a lady dinner."

"In this case I would say I'm a coworker before I'm a lady," Adrian replied in a cool voice.

"You've made your point. I'll pick you up in forty minutes."

"Fine." And she hung up without saying goodbye.

Strauss looked at the humming receiver in his hand. Was there any truth to Shubert's claim that Adrian possessed some attitude? he wondered. Perhaps tonight was as good a time as any to find out.

After another session with his clanking shower, he donned his last pair of clean khakis and a heavy sweater and ran a damp rag over his boots to get rid of the mud from earlier in the day. Then he got his own car out of its place in Mrs. Hutchins' otherwise unused garage. It was an older-model Buick Skylark, a remnant from his married days that he hadn't bothered replacing since he told himself he couldn't really afford to, and he rarely used it anyway. Now he wished he had something a little more suitable. Something, say, in four-wheel drive with considerably less rust and, more importantly in Vermont, something that didn't have bald tires.

At the Thibault farm, Strauss got out and started to the door for Adrian. He had that much charm, after all. But she obviously didn't want to consider this a date and was out the back door and down the steps before he got very far. He shrugged to himself, assuming as he did that he probably shouldn't try opening the car door for her either.

She had, after all, just bested him with a rifle. Maybe she should be opening the door for him, he thought irritably. He found himself further irritated when he saw Lester Blake standing in the doorway of the milkhouse watching them, the vicious Elizabeth stretching herself up to her full height beside him. Strauss assumed neither of them were watching him with particular favor. Adrian waved. Blake waved back. But Strauss was sure that as soon as his back was turned, both Blake and his feline friend looked daggers at him.

"This isn't an official dinner?" Adrian asked over the top of his battered car. She didn't get in immediately. Was she really going to make an issue of their means of transportation?

"It's official, Constable. I just haven't driven my car for a while, and as you can see if I don't exercise it from time to time, it won't be worth driving. If the state emblem and flashing lights are more your style, we can make a switch."

An Investigation of Local Color

She eyed him unsmilingly as if trying to determine if he was kidding, then she got in. Strauss had forgotten how bad the springs were in the passenger seat. He was used to it on his side, but it occurred to him to wonder if Adrian was getting poked by stray springs in places she would probably just as soon not have been poked.

"You're smart to drive this now," she commented as they started out of the drive. "We're supposed to get a huge snowstorm late tomorrow, and you won't be able to get around in this thing much longer."

"I really hope you're not insulting my car, because it is my most prized possession," Strauss said sternly. He didn't feel obligated to mention that it was one of his only possessions.

Adrian raised a questioning eyebrow at him, then said seriously, "I didn't mean to be insulting, but you have bald tires. I'm just being honest."

Strauss shrugged. "That's okay, I'm not insulted. And I'm not attached to this car. It's about the only thing my ex-wife didn't want when she left me."

"Oh. Sorry."

"Don't be. I probably got the good end of the deal."

She didn't look at him or ask any questions, which didn't really surprise him. Finally, she said, "I have business, too. I went back to the Jehovah's Witness minister today to ask about Lee Stout. According to that man both Stout and his wife, Lily, are great supporters of the faith. I think that means they are regular churchgoers and spend a significant amount of time going door to door in order to spread their message to unsuspecting citizens who are unfortunate enough to answer their doorbells. The minister says the Stouts have both been employed by New England Tampon for as long as they have been parishioners. They appear to be happily married. He was more than a little annoyed when my line of questioning made it seem as though I was suspicious of Lee's faithfulness."

"So if we can believe a minister, Lee Stout is just what he said he was—a good husband and devout Jehovah's Witness who was temporarily mesmerized by the charms of Gwenivere Dunfield?"

"It seems so."

"And are we also to assume that Mr. Stout has come to his senses?"

Adrian shrugged. "It's hard to say. The minister never noticed any change in Stout's behavior. Nothing to make him think the man might have been considering any major changes in lifestyle, that sort of thing. I asked him if he ever thought Stout might pack up and leave the area, but he said nothing would be more surprising. All of Stout's family is in the area. They are all Witnesses and all very close."

"So we're left either believing Gwen's story that she dumped him. Or, more likely, Stout was just indulging in some form of midlife crisis and never intended to have a long-term relationship with the lovely Gwenivere."

"That was my conclusion. I don't think there is any real reason connecting him to Dunfield's murder. Do you?"

Strauss shook his head. *Unfortunately,* he said to himself, and thought he saw Adrian feeling the same discouragement. They still had no clear suspect. At least no one they would both agree on.

"Well, that's what you went there to find out for us, so you got valuable information. Where am I going here?"

Adrian directed him to a small Italian restaurant on the near side of Rutland where she said they could order good spaghetti and meatballs and, Strauss would be pleased to know, a variety of different beer. He was also pleased to see that it was only crowded enough to appear to serve good food.

As he moved to help Adrian with her coat, he saw her flinch slightly in pain and he couldn't hide a smile.

"That .06 has a bit of a kick, doesn't it?"

She nodded. "Always has."

"How does that happen to be your weapon of choice, if I might ask?"

"After my father taught me how to shoot, I had to have the biggest and the best in order to keep up with the boys, my cousins mostly."

"It looks to me as if you did a fair job of keeping up. Have you always been so good?"

An Investigation of Local Color

Adrian nodded. She neither apologized nor seemed especially proud of the skill that must have brought a few good men to their knees.

"It's a natural thing, I think. God's way of making it up to my father for giving him such a late-in-life kid who also turned out to be a girl. It used to make the boys mad, still does sometimes, I think, but as you can see they use my skills for their own purposes when it suits them."

"I see. And what were their purposes today?"

Adrian took a drink from her beer and appeared to consider an answer. "What do you think, Detective?" There was a slight edge to her question.

"I would say they were trying to show me whose town it is and where their support lies. I'm not sure why they couldn't just have been satisfied with telling me you could make a fool out of me with a firearm. I'd have believed them."

"No, you wouldn't have."

"You don't think so?"

"No, I don't. You people from down country never think we can do anything up here as well as you can."

With the memory of his recent conversation with Lowell Petrosky concerning Vermonters in his head, Strauss didn't bother contradicting her. "If I was in fact thinking that, I now stand corrected. And I also consider myself warned."

"Warned?" Adrian asked warily.

"Mmm. I think I was being not-so-subtly warned off a certain line of questioning."

Their food arrived. Adrian took a lot of time buttering a piece of bread and winding her spaghetti around her fork while he watched her. But there was no readable expression on her face.

"Maybe you should heed the advice, then," she said finally.

"Now that brings me right around to another problem."

"What's that, Detective?"

"What are the chances of you calling me Nick, at least until dinner is over?"

"Depends on what you're about to tell me."

"We got ourselves a new partner today. Name's Gary Shubert. I guess you know him from way back."

Adrian stopped chewing long enough to show an uncharacteristically hostile expression. "Oh, shit!" she said equally uncharacteristically.

"Yeah, he's not so crazy about you either. Is there any chance you might tell me why?"

"There's nothing to tell. We were in school at the same time. He is from Fairview and those kids go to their own elementary school so I never really knew Gary well. He was a year behind me, and he was sort of fat and a bully when he could get away with it. He was big so he got away with beating up some of the smaller boys from Benton Harbor. Then one day he turns up on the Vermont State Police. My father had some dealings with him when he was constable. I've had some of my own. Neither of us ever saw things quite the same way Gary did."

She shrugged as if she had explained everything. Strauss waited.

When she went back to eating with an end-of-story expression, he asked, "There's nothing more?"

Adrian stared at him as if wondering how much he knew or how much to tell him.

"Gary was also one of the officers on the scene when my husband was killed in an accident on our farm. But you knew that already, didn't you?" Her voice was without expression, making it impossible for Strauss to know how she felt about the past incident.

"Yes, I knew, but I wondered if you were ever going to get around to telling me about it."

Adrian's eyes lit with anger. "And just why do you think you needed to be told about it? Because we're working on a case together, at your request, I might add. And I might also point out that you only just happened to mention on the way over here that you were married before. Do you hear me complaining at the lack of personal information?"

"That's a little different."

"What makes it different? Just because you're some pro from a big-city police department? You get to have all the answers just because you want them?"

An Investigation of Local Color

"Adrian, your husband's death was considered by some, Gary Shubert among them, to be suspicious. You know that. He wants to look at Les for this Dunfield murder, too."

"Oh, of course he does," Adrian replied. Strauss didn't think she seemed surprised. "And so do you, I suppose?"

"It's part of my job. I have to look at all the possibilities, and so do you."

"I looked into that possibility already. Les didn't murder Dunfield. And just so you know for certain, he didn't murder my husband either."

"Okay. Let's say you and I drop that point for the moment. But history must be telling you that Shubert won't."

"Tell your boss you don't need another partner. You must have some pull down at the barracks."

"That's just it, Adrian, I don't. I'm crazy, remember, and I've been given Shubert because the big boss thinks I need some local help with this one. I also have a bad history with partners, and I've been warned in no uncertain terms to make this relationship with Shubert look as if we've been happily joined at the hip or it's the end of my career."

Adrian rubbed her eyes. "Just how bad is your history with your partners?"

"I left one in an alley on Boston's Eastside. He talked too much and got on my nerves. The one after that got thrown into Boston Harbor because he blew our cover on an assignment we were working on with the DEA. He nearly got us killed and that sort of got on my nerves. I threw the last guy out of a window—it was on the first floor. He gave over the name of my best snitch on the streets, a petty thief on his worst day. So the guy gets arrested for some niggling crime, and I lose the best source of information I got. It really bugged me."

"Jesum, Detective! And you talk about me withholding information. Don't you think you might have told me all this before you asked me to work with you?"

"You didn't seem like the type who would be bothered by it."

"No, of course not. I'm really used to being thrown through windows. We do it all the time around here. And what is the lake for if not to throw our partners in when they get on our nerves?"

But Strauss didn't get the impression that he scared her or even that she was particularly angry. "Look, the point is—"

"I know what the point is, Nick. The point is that we have to work with Shubert, and if the man wants to be an ass there is nothing we can do about it. Right?"

"Well, not exactly nothing. I just have to use more refined tactics than I have used in the past."

For some reason that made her smile. "Why do I think that might be a stretch for you?"

"Because I have never been a refined type of guy. I'm much better suited to windows and lakes. But we can put Shubert in those places where he will do the least amount of blundering around. Did you get around to Dunfield's will today?"

"No. I got the name of his attorney, but the office closed at noon today so I didn't get a chance to speak with him."

"Okay, we'll send Shubert there tomorrow. We'll see how our boy deals with legal jargon."

"And you will be working on...?"

"Adrian, whether you like it or not, I've got to ask Les some questions. He knows and likes Sally Glenn. He didn't care for Dunfield." Strauss left out some of his other suspicions when he saw the stubborn set of Adrian's face.

"Ask him anything you want," she dared. "He didn't do it."

Strauss nodded to placate her. "The more questions I ask, the more likely the chance that someone will say something that will give me an idea. You know we have to operate that way because at this point we have nothing else to go on."

"Fine." She swallowed the last of her beer and asked the waitress for the check. "I'm on until 3:30 tomorrow, so you're on your own."

Strauss moved to help her with her coat, but she shrugged into it before he had the chance with no sign of her earlier discomfort. Anger and irritation, apparently, were fast-acting pain relievers.

An Investigation of Local Color

Outside the wind was picking up as quickly as the temperature was dropping. Strauss turned up the collar of his jacket and reminded himself to buy a heavier parka as well as some long underwear at the first opportunity.

"You said something about a storm tomorrow?"

"A big one supposedly with a good Nor'east wind. That usually brings us the heaviest snowfalls. The Vermont weathercaster said it's supposed to start as icy rain and turn to snow by afternoon and snow all night."

"Isn't it kind of early for this sort of thing?" It never blizzarded in Boston in November. In fact, the big complaint around Christmastime was that it rarely turned out to be the promised white holiday.

"It usually snows up here for the first time sometime during hunting season. It's not that rare to get a big storm this time of year. The hunters will be unhappy if it snows enough to require snowshoes in the woods."

"Snowshoes?" Weren't snowshoes the things of pioneers and early trappers and Indians? Hadn't they been relegated to museum pieces at least two hundred years ago?

"Yeah, you know, wood frames with rawhide mesh strung with deer gut. Strap them on your feet, walk on top of the snow when you go out to shoot dinner for your cooking pot?"

Strauss nodded as if familiar with the items in question. Adrian laughed at him.

"Actually, these days they are high-tech affairs made out of some sort of metal alloy, and they are used more for recreation than for real work, just like skis are. When we had a bigger herd, I used snowshoes sometimes between pastures. Now I just use them to play out in the snow."

"You play in the snow?" He couldn't quite picture it.

"Sure, we all do once the lake freezes. Most everyone in Benton Harbor has an ice house for fishing. There is a whole community out there on the weekends. We have fishing contest, snowmobile races, a community picnic every year. Last year the school kids had a snow-sculpting contest that the wives of the firemen judged. It's a lot of fun and makes the cold weather go by faster. Maybe you'll have to come out to the lake and see for yourself."

Come out and see how wonderful our town is, how well we get along, how unlikely it is that any of us could be murderers. Was that what Adrian was saying with her sudden burst of community spirit? Or was she sincerely inviting him for a peek at the joys of rural winter life? He really had become jaded, he thought, when he didn't even know the difference anymore.

"I think I'm going to have to make some changes in both my wardrobe and my wheels if I'm going to enjoy the winter up here."

"Good idea. Even that big state cruiser isn't going to help you much if we get that storm tomorrow, so get your work done early or you'll get stuck somewhere."

"Nice show of confidence, Constable."

"It wasn't a commentary on your skills or lack thereof, Detective. It was just a warning. You just drove past my road, by the way."

Strauss groaned inwardly. He would never get used to the unlit, unmarked dirt paths that passed for roads up here. How could anyone be expected to find his way without a landmark?

"It would really be helpful if you natives would stick a McDonald's on your corners, or at least a nice little streetlight."

"Why should we? We know where we're going."

Strauss turned the car around in what was either someone's driveway or yet another road. Of course, the townsfolk knew where they were going. It wasn't necessary for outsiders to know, too.

But when he gave voice to that opinion, Adrian only smiled mildly and said, "I don't really think we're as unfriendly as all that, Nick."

Her use of his name instead of his title warmed him, and perhaps it was because of that that he got out of the car to walk her to the door. He normally didn't walk his partners to their doors. They had all been male, for one thing, but even if he had had a female partner he knew better than to ever try to walk her to the door or even open it for her. It wasn't exactly the done thing in the tight, well-defined society of male/female cops. But Adrian was different. Or so he thought until he noticed that she walked briskly to her back door,

An Investigation of Local Color

hardly giving him a chance to catch up with her. He followed her into the unheated mudroom and waited for her to find her keys and turn on a light. Instead she pushed open the door to the kitchen.

"You ought to lock your door," he reminded her.

"I've never locked the door. I don't even know where the key is." She turned on the light in the kitchen, obviously unconcerned with his opinion. She didn't invite him in.

"I probably don't need to remind you that there is a murderer running loose around here, do I?"

"No, Nick, you don't. But I don't think I have to worry about it here."

"That's obviously what Dunfield thought, too."

Adrian smiled tolerantly. "Thanks for the dinner company," she said, ending his conversation on the subject of murderers and disarming him at the same time.

He considered closing the distance between them and kissing her. It was dark in the mudroom and she had called him Nick, and she had even smiled a little. That meant it was okay, didn't it? Of course, he had been in similar situations with other men and women and he didn't go off kissing them and creating what was popularly termed "issues."

Before he could decide, Elizabeth moved through the gap in the kitchen door and hopped up on the mudroom bench. She purred noisily and rubbed against Adrian's leg. Then she turned to Strauss with narrowed eyes and arched her back to the very limits of her not-too-considerable size. She licked her lips hungrily. Strauss backed up before she could launch herself at him.

"That animal isn't normal," he commented. The still-healing scratches on his face and scalp ached in warning.

Adrian laughed at him and picked up the fuzzy yellow-and-white banshee, who purred happily and nuzzled her. "Yes, she is. She just isn't used to strangers."

"Obviously not." *And neither are the rest of you people up here.* "Goodnight, Adrian." He backed down the steps while keeping a watchful eye on Elizabeth.

"Goodnight."

"Oh, and Constable?"

"Yes."

"Good shooting today."

Adrian smiled. Standing there holding the preening yellow cat with the dim light behind her, she looked as delightfully feminine as she had earlier that afternoon. But then she had awkwardly shouldered a big 30.06 and preceded to fire like the leader of a SWAT team, so who ever really knew?

7

"Here you are, Shubert," Strauss said early the next morning.

"What is this?" the younger man asked, looking at an address on the piece of paper that he had just been handed.

"That is the name of Dunfield's lawyer in Rutland. You are to go and have a chat with him and see what you can discover about the terms of his will. According to the lovely ex-Mrs. Dunfield, everything has been left to Dunfield's children. Check it out. See if you can come up with anything that might be helpful to us."

"Like what, exactly?" Shubert asked. His annoyance was clear.

"Like whether any of the kids had any reason to hasten their father along. Big sums of money, bad family relations, that sort of thing."

"You're just sending me on a wild goose chase, Strauss," Shubert complained. "You know where we should be looking."

"I don't know anything for certain, Shubert. That is why we are checking into all our leads. If, however, this assignment is beyond you, Constable Thibault can undertake it when she gets done working at the hospital today and you can go back to writing tickets out on the highway. It's your call."

"And what are you going to be doing, if I am permitted to ask?"

"I'm going to be talking with Mr. Blake this morning. After you're done in Rutland, I want you to meet me at the Hook, Line, and Sinker around 1:30 to go over our information. Then I want to go back up to the Dunfield house to see if there is any possibility we missed something the first time."

"Don't you mean you missed the first time? I wasn't in on that scene, so don't blame any oversight on me."

Strauss shrugged with apparent unconcern. "Whatever. One-thirty at the Hook. Got it?"

"I think I can manage it, Strauss."

Shubert picked up his trooper's hat and shoved it onto his head angrily, accidently flattening his ears down in the process. Strauss smiled to himself. Just seeing the other man's ill humor made his own act of patience worth it. He followed his new partner outside to the parking lot. As Adrian had warned it was beginning to rain, an icy sleet that would soon make driving hazardous.

"Better be careful, Detective," Shubert called from his cruiser. "Flatlanders don't usually handle winter driving very well up here. You don't want to have to get towed out of a ditch up there in Benton Harbor."

Strauss smiled and waved his hands vaguely to indicate that he couldn't hear. Privately, he hoped Shubert would find a ditch of his own and solve the problem of dealing with an unwanted partner.

Strauss got into his own cruiser and headed for Benton Harbor. His rendezvous with Shubert had made him too late to have coffee with his friends at the Hook, so he headed for the Thibault farm instead. He tried to form in his mind the questions he intended to ask Lester Blake, but what really came to mind was the memory of the smell in the barn and the fear that the interrogation might include Elizabeth and a herd of Guernsey cows. Who knew what else might live in that barn? He really, really hated animals!

You didn't kiss a good-looking woman because you were afraid of her cat, he reminded himself.

She probably wouldn't have let me anyway, he argued back.

Probably not. What woman would want to kiss a man she had just humiliated in front of the whole town?

It has a lot more to do with suspecting her beloved hired man of murder, not once but twice, and her of covering it up.

It's more likely she can't respect a man who's afraid of the cat.

This and similar arguments had been running through his head most of the night, making his sleep disturbed and limited. So it had to be said that his mood was not the best when he pulled into the driveway at the Thibault farm. He got out and knocked on the back

An Investigation of Local Color

door in the happy event that Blake was not in the barn crooning over his charges, but no one answered.

The barn was everything he remembered, spotlessly clean, snuggly warm, suffocatingly rank. Blake, in an act of admirable courage, stood in the middle of the aisle with his face buried in the fluffy coat of the fierce Elizabeth, who lay upside down in his arm, a look of grave contentment on her face. His precious Guernseys looked on, chewing contentedly, and a previously unintroduced mutt sat at his feet. On seeing Strauss intruding on the scene, the dog leaped to his feet and howled threateningly. He dashed at Strauss with his back up and teeth showing. Blake looked up without concern or welcome. Elizabeth's look of adoration became a sneer of distaste. When set down on the floor, she promptly arched her back and stalked in Strauss' direction. Thus protected, Blake felt confident enough to fold his arms and lean back casually against the stanchions holding the cows in place.

"Morning, Detective. You're not down at the Hook looking for murder suspects."

"I had a couple things to do this morning, and it got a little late."

Blake nodded knowingly. It really bugged Strauss sometimes that he was such a lousy liar. Even as he spoke with Blake, the boys at the Hook were probably sitting on delaying their morning chores in hopes that Strauss would put in his usual appearance so they could rib him over yesterday's performance. He could well imagine the suggestions flying that he was off somewhere licking the wounds inflicted on his male pride and big-city-cop ego. And they wouldn't have been far from incorrect. Making excuses would only make things worse, so he ignored Blake's smile. He knew how quickly he could get rid of it, anyway.

Ignoring the animals was harder, though. The hound was sniffing around Strauss' backside in the rude manner typical of their species, and he hoped fervently that the mutt didn't decide to take a chunk out of something that he himself valued. Elizabeth, not to be outdone in the tactics of intimidation, had made her way to Strauss' feet and sat staring up at him with an expression he couldn't read. He didn't know much about cats but felt fairly certain that she could be on his head again with a simple leap.

Blake's eyes traveled from his pets to Strauss' face and back. He seemed to be amused. Strauss swallowed, cursed everything that was alive but not human, and crossed his own arms defensively. He hoped the gesture would deter any super-feline efforts Elizabeth was currently considering, because he would be damned if he would show his fear to Blake or ask to talk outside. He took a deep breath to begin interrogating his suspect. Big mistake. The steamy, dung-infested air seeped into his throat, making him cough so hard he nearly gagged. The dog kept sniffing. Elizabeth kept staring. Blake kept smiling.

"I got a new partner assigned to this case I'm working on," Strauss began when he had gotten himself under control. "An old acquaintance of yours, I understand."

Instantly, Blake's eyes became wary.

"Gary Shubert," Strauss went on. "Remember him?"

Blake shook his head. But he looked unhappy.

"He remembers you. He questioned you about Brian Borden's death. Remember now?"

Blake looked at the barn floor and stubbed the toe of his boot against the cement floor. Strauss hadn't meant to be quite so direct. He hadn't meant to sound so accusing. He was handling himself in just the way he had imagined Shubert would have, and it was for that very reason that he had sent Shubert off in another direction.

"I was with Adrian. I told him that. Adrian told him that," Blake muttered in a voice Strauss could barely hear.

"Les, why would someone have thought you killed Borden?" he asked, trying to sound less intimidating.

"I hated the man. But I didn't kill him. The cows killed him, and weren't no one sorry neither. He was a mean son of a bitch."

Something prickled at the back of Strauss' memory. He was about to ask Blake to elaborate when the other man said, "I told all this before. That young fella you mentioned made me go over and over it until Mr. Thibault made him quit. I ain't got any more to say on it."

His expression was closed and stubborn, so Strauss merely nodded.

An Investigation of Local Color

"Okay. Let me just ask you a couple more questions, Les, then you can get back to work. Where were you last Thursday night and early Friday morning?"

Blake stared at him as he tried to sort out where the trap was before he replied, "I didn't kill Dunfield."

"I didn't say you did. I just wanted to know where you were when he was getting himself killed."

Blake's fists clenched and unclenched either in concentration or in frustration. "I was here, in my house, all night." He indicated the direction of his trailer with his chin.

"Did you talk to anyone? Did anyone see you?"

"Only...." He stopped.

"Yes? Only?"

Blake looked at Strauss helplessly, his frustration now clear. "Only Adrian."

So it all came down to Adrian again. She was his alibi now as she had been when Borden had died. Strauss could read in Blake's worn features that he understood the implication, too. It was an honest, hardworking face, even if it turned suspicious toward Strass. Ordinarily, it was a face he would have trusted. This wasn't a man who would murder anyone unless maybe he thought some mean son of a bitch was abusing someone Blake thought highly of. Mean son of a bitch he had called Borden, just as he had described Dunfield two days ago.

"Well, thanks, Les. You've been a big help."

Blake appeared startled by Strauss' comment. If he had helped, it wasn't because he had meant to. Possibly to hide his confusion he bent to scoop up Elizabeth, who had stopped staring at Strauss and made her way back to him. The cat skittered away, then came to a stop and looked over her shoulder with a flip of her tail. With another flip of her tail, she marched off. Blake frowned.

Strauss started to go, needing both fresh air and a cigarette. Then he thought of something else.

"Did you get your deer yet, Les?"

"I don't hunt." Blake uttered the words Strauss thought never to hear from anyone in Benton Harbor.

"I thought everyone hunted."

Blake rubbed a cow in the wide space between her eyes, causing her to make contented snuffling noises. "I don't. I don't like the thought of shooting anything."

Strauss smiled. "Me either." It made him feel more kindly toward this man, whom he didn't dislike anyway. He was obviously hard-working, unflaggingly devoted to Adrian, kind to little old ladies and, best of all, he didn't throw bullet-riddled bodies in the back of his pickup. Strauss gave him a departing nod and went out to his car, pulling his cigarettes from his pocket as he went.

It wasn't possible to enjoy the fresh air outside because the icy rain was coming down heavier and mixing with snow. He shivered as a cold-wind-bearing sleet blew out his second match before he could get his cigarette lit. He was forced to get in and light up, something he wasn't supposed to do in theory just in case the cruiser was subsequently assigned to some poor trooper who didn't smoke and whose rights were thereby being trampled on. But because he was a big-city cop with an ego to match, Strauss didn't worry about it right then. Instead he was lost in thought, oblivious to the smoke fogging his windshield or the ice caking up on the wipers, trying to figure out who could have killed Bill Dunfield if it wasn't Lester Blake. When he got to Fairview, he bought himself the heaviest down parka he could buy at the sporting goods store and drove back through the snow to his meeting with Shubert without coming up with an answer.

Shubert was waiting for him when he arrived. His trip to Rutland and back and the lack of exciting information he gained from it had caused him to become more irritable than he had been earlier in the day. He sat at a table by himself, which would have been unusual in a restaurant that was so small and so busy that patrons were usually required to share at least part of the long tables in the dining room. Today's weather kept most of the lunchtime business away.

Shubert nodded to Strauss as he sat down across the table. His mouth was full, but he washed his food down with a hearty gulp of his chocolate milkshake.

An Investigation of Local Color

"How can you drink that on a day like today?" Strauss asked with a grimace. "It's like swallowing the weather outside."

"Better get used to it, Detective. There's plenty more days like today to come."

"So I've been told." He asked the waitress for coffee and a bowl of soup. "What did you come up with at the lawyer's?"

"Like I told you, it was a wild goose chase. Ms. Dunfield was well informed. Dunfield's four children inherit his fortune, which amounts to about $9,000 in the bank, his house, and whatever treasures are inside it. The lawyer spoke to the two that showed up for the old man's services. None of the four were on very good terms with their father, something to do with the second marriage, but there doesn't seem to have been any reason for foul play. The entire estate split four ways doesn't amount to much, according to the attorney, and he seemed to think all four kids were established comfortably in Connecticut." Shubert paused to stuff some more hamburger in his mouth. "So you see, not much gained there. What did you find out?"

"Nothing I didn't already know."

"Do you think Blake did it?"

"I think he could have done it. But I think several other people could have as well."

"It was him, I know it."

Strauss ignored him and ate his soup.

"Well, does he have an alibi?"

"Yup."

"Let me guess, it's Adrian, right?"

"That's right."

Shubert huffed in annoyance. "Can't you see through that, Strauss? This is exactly what happened last time, when Brian Borden was murdered. She is covering for a man who is killing people in this town."

"And you know this for a fact?"

"Look, Strauss, the Borden case was one of my first really big cases. I worked hard on it, and I've given it a lot of thought ever since. I think I'm right on this."

"Let's say just for the sake of argument that you are right, what would be Blake's motive in killing Borden and Dunfield? And why would Constable Thibault cover it up?"

"This is how I see it: Both Dunfield and Borden were outsiders in Benton Harbor. Neither was especially well liked. Blake and Adrian are both known to be very resentful of outsiders. Adrian's marriage to Borden was said to be in trouble. I think it is likely that Blake killed Borden probably because he was jealous or because he thought it would help Adrian. When a man like that kills once it is easy to do it again, especially if he thinks he can get away with it. Dunfield may have just pissed him off over something, and because Dunfield wasn't a local and wasn't much liked Blake knocked him off."

Strauss kept eating his soup. He heard the enthusiasm in the younger man's voice for his own theory. In fact, his idea wasn't without its merits, but there was too much speculation in it.

"You don't appear to like flatlanders much yourself, Shubert. Should I be suspicious of you?"

"Of course not," he snorted indignantly. "I wouldn't kill anyone."

"Maybe Blake wouldn't either. The man doesn't even hunt, Gary, because he doesn't like to shoot animals."

"That's easy enough to say."

"True. But it's also pretty easy to check out in a town this size," Strauss pointed out.

"Are you finished?"

He paid the bill for both lunches and slid into his new parka. "Let's see if we can find anything up at the Dunfield house."

"Better let me drive," Shubert suggested. "I'm a lot more used to this than you are."

Strauss shrugged and got into the passenger side of Shubert's cruiser. He had put his skills to the test yesterday. He didn't especially feel the urge to flex his muscles again today.

Shubert was mindful of the smoking ban in his car, but whatever need Strauss fulfilled with his cigarettes Shubert filled with candy bars. Wrappers littered the floor of the car on the passenger side. The man

An Investigation of Local Color

was an indiscriminate chocolate lover. It was small wonder he hadn't outgrown his adolescent complexion and doughy middle.

Strauss kicked aside the rubbish and fastened his seatbelt as Shubert backed out onto the road.

Driving on the dirt roads was even more hazardous than on the main road, where the plow and sander had at least been making a bihourly attack. Strauss made a note as they went by that the little school had released its students early, a sure sign of worse things to come. The locals were inordinately proud of the fact that they could move around in all but the most extreme conditions. Halfway up the road to Frampton Hill, they passed Junior Thibault making his way back to town with the snowplow. The big man waved cheerfully, passing them so closely on the narrow, crowned road that he nearly drove them off the road. The cloud of snow following the plow enveloped their car and temporarily obscured any view of the road.

"Idiot!" Shubert snarled as he stepped heavily on the brakes.

Unfortunately, Junior wasn't laying down sand at the same time, so the car had only ice and snow underfoot and went into an immediate spin. Shubert's foot stayed glued to the brake. His arms were braced straight in front of him on the wheel. Strauss grabbed for the armrest on the door to hold himself upright.

"Get off the brake!" he shouted too late.

The cruiser skidded around in a circle and came to rest off the side of the road with his nose in a ditch, its back wheels in the air. The snowplow continued blissfully unaware down the road to Benton Harbor.

"You all right?" Strauss asked his new partner. His own shoulder belt was nearly strangling him, but it had kept him from falling into the dash when the car reached its final, steeply angled destination.

"Yes," Shubert gulped.

Cautiously, Strauss pushed open the door and hooked his leg outside before releasing his belt. He fell with a tumble into the snow. He congratulated himself on his foresight in buying his new jacket before trekking off with Shubert in a blizzard.

Unsympathetically, he waited for Shubert to extricate himself from the car on the opposite side. The younger man fell with even less grace than his partner face first into a drift and came up sputtering snow. Strauss surveyed the wreck. There was probably minimal damage since they hadn't been going fast and the impact had been a soft one, but they certainly weren't going to get the car out of the ditch without help.

"Mmmm. I wasn't sure how to drive in a Vermont snowstorm," he commented wryly. "So this is how it's done."

"That bastard in the snowplow drove me right off the road! You saw him!"

"Mmmm." Had Junior crowded the middle of the road just a little? Strauss wondered. It was within the man's capabilities.

He looked around. He had mostly been up this stretch of road in the dark, and the way it was snowing didn't make much of an improvement in the daylight hours. Up ahead he thought he could make out the shape of mailboxes.

"Come on," he called to Shubert.

"Where are we going? Shouldn't we call for some help on the radio?"

"What good would that do in this weather? We'll get help from one of the farmers along here. Someone will have a truck or tractor." He hoped. He also hoped he wasn't about to walk in on one of his new friends who would quickly turn the incident into fodder for local gossip tomorrow morning at the Hook.

They trudged uphill with Shubert muttering about the wind and the snow in his shoes and the incline of the hill and the lack of respect plow drivers had for men in uniforms. For a Vermonter he sure was unprepared for weather, and Strauss was beginning to feel annoyed. He eyed Shubert thoughtfully.

There were lights on in the barn even though it was short of milking time, so he headed there. The warm, suffocating aroma with which he was becoming more familiar than he wanted to be enveloped them at once. Shubert wrinkled his nose in distaste. A man looked up, startled at their sudden windblown appearance. He was dressed in rolled-up sleeves in the warmth of the barn, but he wore hunting boots and his red-checked wool pants were wet from snow. He crouched over the corpse of a deer brandishing an enormous knife similar to the one that had been stuck in Bill Dunfield. The deer's coat was also wet from

An Investigation of Local Color

the snow. There was a long incision in his gut and part of his innards were on the floor beside him. Strauss swallowed hard and suffered an unpleasant memory of his lunchtime soup. Thank God he hadn't ordered a hamburger.

"Are you game wardens?" the man asked in alarm, mistaking Shubert's state patrol uniform pants and parka. "I got my license right over there in my coat." He held up bloodied hands to show them that he couldn't fetch it for them.

"No. State Police," Strauss said. "We were making our way up to Frampton Hill and had a bit of a problem with the ice on the road. We wondered if you'd be able to help us out."

The farmer, who looked to be middle aged, had the rugged features and hands of the hardworking. Like many of the men Strauss had met in Benton Harbor, he spoke slowly and appeared to think slowly as well, though Strauss was beginning to realize in some cases it was an affectation rather than actual slow thought processes.

The farmer stared at his visitors a moment, then smiled as comprehension dawned. "You mean you're stuck?"

"That's right. Do you have a tractor you can pull us out of a ditch with?"

"Yup." He went back to working on the insides of his victim. "Isn't this feller a beauty? I just saw him out the back door on my way to the woodshed, just standing there in the snow, pretty as a picture."

"Eight-pointer, real nice," Shubert threw in hastily. "Can you help us?"

The farmer focused his gaze on Strauss. He squinted one eye as if it would help him see better. "You sure you're stuck?"

"I'm sure," Strauss said.

"'Cause I don't really want to fire the tractor up if I can just give your car a little extra gas and rock it out." He pulled something else out of the deer and tossed it on top of the other innards.

"I'm sure we're stuck."

"Bastard with the snowplow ran us off the road," Shubert added.

"Junior done that? I can't picture it," the farmer said mildly. "Huh."

"I think it was more a case of poor visibility," Strauss commented. He wanted to shoot a dirty look at Shubert, but he found he couldn't take his eyes off the carcass on the floor. It sure was hot in the barn, he thought, as he wiped a bead of sweat off his forehead.

"More'n likely. That ought to do it."

The farmer gave the dead deer a fond slap like one might give a particularly good milk producer. Then he got to his feet and rubbed his hands briskly under a nearby spigot. Drying them on his wet wool pants, he rolled down the sleeves of his long underwear and layers of flannel shirts.

"I'm Harold Thibault, by the by." He stuck out a hand to shake.

Strauss tried not to think about the moisture and slightly red color of it, tried to smile the smile of a grateful man in need of a favor and not to cringe the cringe of one who can't stand the sight of blood.

"Pleased to meet you, sir. I'm Detective Strauss, and this is Trooper Shubert."

"You're the feller working on the murder with my niece," he said as if another light had just come on. "Nice piece of shooting you done yesterday. Can't no one top Adrian, though."

"No, sir."

"Quite the little Annie Oakley," Shubert said in annoyance.

He was wet and dripping and, no doubt by this time, smelly as well. It didn't improve his already bad nature. But if Harold Thibault understood the reference, he ignored it. In fact, other than a polite nod of the head when introduced he ignored Shubert altogether, speaking only to Strauss.

"Okay then, if you're sure you're stuck...?"

"I'm sure," Strauss confirmed patiently for the third time. "Down the hill a ways and on the other side of the road."

Thibault grabbed up his coat and put on his red-checked hunting cap and followed them into the barnyard. The buildings, including the house, all looked slightly dilapidated and in need of a coat of paint. At least they appeared that way with the snow driving down. But the tractor that Thibault backed out of its bay was a brand-new John Deere with the heavy-treaded front tires of the four-wheel drive models. The big diesel engine snorted as Thibault gave it the gas and waved for the two policemen to follow him on foot. This brought more grumbling from Shubert.

"You didn't think he was going to let you ride in the back seat, did you?" Strauss asked. Now that he was out of sight of the bloody guts and out of range of toxic vapors, he found himself in surprisingly good spirits, all things considered. He was probably just enjoying Shubert's discomfort.

When they reached the accident scene, Thibault was already off the tractor surveying the wreckage with his hands on his hips.

"Yup, you're stuck." He nodded.

He made no further move, leaving Strauss to wonder if he was thinking or just stuck in place. Beside him Shubert huffed. He was definitely going to have to get rid of that habit if he hoped to remain Strauss' partner.

"What do you suggest?" Strauss asked diplomatically.

"There is only one thing to do." Thibault stared at the tilted cruiser for another full minute, then nodded his head sagely. He walked around to the back of the tractor and unwound a chain heavy enough to anchor an ocean liner. He held up one hooked end proudly. "Use a chain." He handed it to Strauss. "You want to hook on to the frame so as not to pull anything off the car. This ol' tractor's going to give a mighty big yank."

With that piece of advice, Harold Thibault climbed back onto the high seat of the John Deere, threw it into gear, and yanked on the chain with such force that the cruiser flew out of the snowbank and briefly became airborne before it landed with a crash on all four wheels in the middle of the road. Whatever hadn't been killed by Shubert's driving most certainly expired at the hands of the green tractor. The cruiser definitely sported a new, lower-slung look than it had earlier in the afternoon. Strauss unhooked the chain and dragged it back to the tractor.

"Easy enough when you got the right equipment for the job," Thibault said. He was obviously well pleased with himself and his machine's performance.

"Thank you, Mr. Thibault. Can I pay you for your trouble?"

"No, no, Detective Strauss. I consider it my duty to help the law." Then he lowered his voice conspiratorially. "Besides, this was just damn fun. I've been wanting to see what she could do." He gave the rear tire the same fond slap he had given his slaughtered deer.

Strauss shook his hand, and they parted company with his newest Thibault acquaintance warning him about winter driving.

"They ain't got such good equipment up there on Frampton Hill, son."

"Get in, Shubert," he called as he got behind the wheel. "Time's wasting!"

The younger man climbed into the passenger seat with a grumble. His state-issued parka was soaked with snow and fragrant with the essence of the dairy barn. His chubby knees were outlined clearly through the wet clinging uniform pants that stuck to them. The top of his trooper's cap was covered with freshly fallen snow.

Strauss rolled down the window and shook the snow off his own cap. He felt warm and toasty in his new parka. His feet were dry in his new boots. Other than being slightly wet on his legs where the parka didn't reach and a trifle smelly, which was unpreventable, he felt he had survived the incident pretty well.

"I'm going to write up the bastard on the snowplow just as soon as we get back to the barracks," Shubert sputtered. "He's another one of those Thibaults. Too much damned inbreeding up here, if you ask me."

"No one did, Shubert, and you won't be writing the man up. He was just doing his job."

"He didn't even stop!" Shubert protested.

"So he doesn't use his mirrors. Last I knew that wasn't against the law. Personally, I think you'll be damned lucky if I don't advise the chief that you need additional foul-weather behind-the-wheel training. He's not going to be delighted with the damage to this cruiser as it is.

"Like that's my fault. That idiot with the tractor didn't have to use that much force to get it out of the ditch."

"Obviously, he thought he did." Strauss smiled to himself.

An Investigation of Local Color

"It's just another clearcut case of the lack of respect for the law in Benton Harbor."

"I sure wish I saw things as clearly as you do, Shubert." He gave the car extra gas and fought the wheel to clear the first rise on Frampton Hill. So far, so good. Only three more rises and they would be there. "Just remember that you are the one who was anxious to be assigned to this case."

Shubert huffed a response. The car fishtailed violently as they continued uphill, but Strauss kept control. He could barely see the road ahead of him, but on Frampton Hill there was little question of where it was. It was the only place that wasn't either a ledge wall or a sheer drop into the adjoining swamp. A few minutes later he delivered them safely in the deceased Dunfield's driveway, with an enormous, though mainly silent, sigh of relief. Mentally he gave himself a hearty pat on the back, glad he hadn't further embarrassed himself. He felt even happier that he had passed what he had thought of in his mind as a test of skill.

Strauss kicked away the snow that had piled in front of the kitchen door and let them in with the key that he had brought along from the barracks. The police tape that had been placed on the door to seal the scene was still there, so the grieving Dunfield children must not have come by the house yet. The temperature inside the house had dropped to the minimal needed to keep the pipes from freezing, and in spite of the tidy kitchen there was a lonely, harsh feeling to the place that wasn't helped much by the cold gray light coming in from the snowy weather outside. It was strange how easy it was to feel that no one was living in a house. Strauss had had a similar feeling on many occasions on coming into an abandoned building. You always knew.

"Better wipe your feet," he advised as Shubert started across the clean floor, tracking slush with him.

"Why?"

"The guy obviously kept a clean house."

"The guy's also dead, Strauss. Remember?"

"In that case show some respect, huh?"

Shubert went back to the rug by the door and made a show of wiping his feet. "What exactly are we looking for?"

What, indeed? Strauss had no idea. It was so easy in Vice. You looked for drugs. You looked for stolen articles, you looked for perpetrators. What did you look for in the backwoods of Vermont in the murder of a man no one liked but who was in no way linked to any previous crimes? Strauss wasn't used to crimes of passion. He needed some hints, hints he hoped he would recognize when he saw them.

"Just look around. I went through the obvious things the first time I was here. Address and bank books, so forth. Nothing seemed significant. See what you come up with."

"Okay."

Shubert had shed his soaked jacket and seemed in better spirits. Poking through someone's belongings apparently made him happier than questioning lawyers or getting stuck in ditches. He started right in on the drawers of the writing desk in the living room. Strauss went upstairs.

The bedroom where Dunfield had been stabbed was just as it had been except that the forensics expert had thrown a heavy quilt over the bed after removing the bloodstained sheets. The drawers Strauss pulled open were filled with neatly folded clothes, as they had been when he had looked before, and there wasn't anything hidden amongst the underwear any more than there had been the first time. The man's shoes were neatly lined up in the closet, along with his hanging clothes. No clues surfaced on the shelves overhead. Bill Dunfield was an obsessively tidy man, and whereas it was helpful in searching a crime scene Strauss found such fussiness disconcerting, more because it made clues hard to come by than because he himself was a slob as a single man.

Even the bathroom was spotless, as if someone had just cleaned. Dunfield was a healthy man, judging by his medicine cabinet, which contained only vitamin C, aspirin, shaving cream and a razor, all lined up neatly on their respective shelves. The towels in the linen closet were folded and stacked according to size. The half-dozen rolls of toilet paper were lined up neatly alongside.

An Investigation of Local Color

Then he noticed it. As he turned from his inspection of the closet, Strauss caught sight of something beneath the clawfoot bathtub, something he hadn't noticed before.

He got down on his hands and knees and peered under the tub. There on the floor, which had a distinct lack of dust bunnies and the other scum people usually found in such out-of-the-way places, was a book. Strauss pulled it out.

On first glance he thought it was an account book, but when he opened it expecting to find numbers he saw words instead, lots of them. It was the sort of blank book that people kept track of their lives in, a kind of diary, judging from the dates and the personal scrawls. Did men actually keep diaries? In their bathrooms? Strauss had an unpleasant vision of Dunfield sitting naked in his bath writing down what went on during his day at the New England Tampon Company. The water marks on some of the pages suggested that his vision was not entirely out of the realm of possibility.

Strauss flipped to the beginning. It was dated seven years previously, right about the time the Dunfields had been divorced. Sure enough there was an annoyed scrawl making note of the incident.

"Divorce final today. Gave her what she wanted, easier that way."

Dunfield failed to mention, Strauss noted, that he hadn't had a choice, Vermont's laws being what they were.

"Thought she could give me a big kiss on the cheek as she walked away with what was mine. I put the bitch in her place."

The next few dates were random, and for the most part in the same vein, expressing his anger at losing his land and money to Gwenivere, whom he always referred to as "she" or "the bitch." Strauss turned toward the back of the book. The most recent date was during the week of his death.

"L. hopping mad today. Very, very funny!! Ha, ha! Didn't break my heart one little bit."

L.? Strauss bit his lip in consideration. Lester? Lee? The next-to-last entry made no reference to L. Neither did the five previous ones.

"Hey, Strauss, come down here! I think I have something." Shubert's voice was excited.

"Be right there." Strauss carefully folded the book into his parka. It wasn't great policework, he knew, to suppress evidence, but it was only until he could read the diary himself and determine what evidence, if any, was within. Besides, it was only Shubert.

He clattered down the stairs to find Shubert on his knees next to the drawers that were built into the window seat in the living room. They were old-style built-ins with glass knobs. Strauss hadn't bothered with them when he had been there earlier, mostly because the first one he had tried hadn't opened beyond an inch or so and hadn't contained anything anyway. More bad policework, he thought to himself.

"What have you got there?"

"Take a look at this!"

The younger man heaved himself to his feet with effort and handed over a photo album. Strauss opened it to what appeared to be a wedding scene. Except that the face of the bride had unceremoniously been cut from the picture.

Judging from the ragged edges of the hole, the head had been removed with a razor or some similar tool. Though he had only seen the man dead, Strauss recognized the grinning wiry figure of Bill Dunfield. He was wearing a white tuxedo, ruffled shirt and white shoes. His faceless bride wore a short white dress, and if her head had been in the picture it would have been at least six inches higher than her groom's. Her legs were long and spectacular as was the line of her figure.

Strauss flipped the page to a family portrait. The bride was faceless in this picture as well, but there were other grinning relations or family members, some in formal dress. All of them were either blond or in some graying form of blond, and to a one they were all obese. They resembled, Strauss thought, the present Gwenivere Dunfield, though whether he actually deduced that from their features or from their size he couldn't have fairly said. He flipped through some more pages. More family shots, another of the bride and groom and a flower girl, one of the groom proudly carrying his bride, who appeared to be all legs. Certainly she had no face, not in any of the photos.

"What do you make of that?" Shubert asked.

An Investigation of Local Color

Strauss shrugged. "It's interesting. I'm assuming these are pictures of the happy Dunfields at their wedding. By the look of it, things had changed a great deal for them. It would be my guess that Mr. Dunfield didn't lug Mrs. Dunfield around much anymore."

"Do you think he cut the faces out of the pictures?"

"Probably. If she had been the one to be stabbed, I think I would be more troubled by it. But as it is, I'm not sure this is anything more significant than a pissed-off ex-husband getting what little vengeance is available to him legally. It's sort of like everything else about this case."

"What do you mean?" Shubert asked, puzzled.

"Every time something turns up, it points to a good reason to kill Mrs. Dunfield rather than Mr. A lot of people hated him, but no one exactly had a reason to kill him. She, on the other hand, seems to have given several people rather passionate reasons to go after her."

"Gwenivere Dunfield? I'm sorry, but I just don't see it. She seemed like such a nice woman when I had dealings with her in the past."

Strauss raised a questioning eyebrow in Shubert's direction.

"I had reason to question her in the case of the Borden murder."

"The Borden accident," Strauss corrected.

But Shubert went on as if he hadn't heard, obviously intent on his topic. "She was very helpful, very warmhearted."

"Yes, well, that may very well be open to question."

"You don't think she did it, do you?"

"You've already asked me that, Shubert. Unfortunately the answer is the same. We don't have enough evidence to suspect anyone enough to make an arrest. Did you come across anything else while you were poking around?"

"No, nothing. This guy was a freak for cleanliness. He doesn't have any clutter or junk. There wasn't even anything in his trash, unless...!" Shubert's eyes grew large as his brain switched into high gear. "Unless someone was here before us. Or maybe Dunfield got rid of all the evidence himself!"

Strauss gave his partner a patient look. "Why would he do that? We have to assume that he didn't know someone was going to kill him. The medical examiner agreed that the position of the body and the blow itself seemed to indicate that Dunfield was surprised when he entered his bedroom by someone who possessed a fair amount of strength. If you intend to kill someone with a knife, I would think you would need the element of surprise on your side, wouldn't you?"

"Not necessarily. Not if you are really strong," Shubert argued.

Strauss rolled his eyes. "That covers just about all of our potential suspects, Shubert. Everyone in this town has size or strength or both. Even you. Should I be suspicious?"

"Cut that out, will you? You know I have nothing to do with this."

"Do I?" Strauss asked just to bug him. "Come on, the weather isn't getting any better. Let's get off this hill while we still can."

"Should I take this?" Shubert hefted the wedding album.

"No. We know it's here, if we need it later."

Strauss carefully zipped the diary into his parka. Then he locked the door behind them before going out to the cruiser. It had snowed and blown so hard while they were inside that they could barely see the tracks they had made going in. He tossed the ice scraper to Shubert and while that man scraped the windshield, Strauss carefully slipped the diary from his parka and put it under the driver's seat. Glancing at his watch he saw it was 4:30, but the gathering darkness from the storm made it seem later. If the driving wasn't too bad, he could stop by Adrian's and show her the diary.

Junior still hadn't been up Frampton Hill, but Strauss could make out the tracks of other vehicles that had made a run at the hill and apparently made it, as there were no signs of cars in the ditches or smashed on the ledges along the way down. Visibility was worse than limited, but he was pretty sure they were nearly to town when a truck passed him going the opposite way and moving along faster than the slow crawl the weather demanded.

"Every idiot with four-wheel drive thinks he's invulnerable," Shubert muttered.

Strauss didn't answer. He was thinking that the truck was similar to Adrian's.

No sooner was the thought out of his mind when the car's radio crackled, and the dispatcher's voice asked for Shubert.

An Investigation of Local Color

"Is Detective Strauss with you, Shubert?"

Strauss snatched the mike from his partner. Suddenly he felt overcome with misgiving.

"Strauss here."

"Constable Thibault from Benton Harbor called in for you, Detective. She got a call about some shots being fired at the Dunfield residence. She's on her way up there now. The weather's so bad, we've got every available car out on the highway with stranded motorists. Any chance you can get up there?"

"We're in the area right now."

"Very good. Say, when you get done there, we could really use one of you out on Route 4 with a cruiser."

"I'll keep it in mind, son."

"Kid's a real smartass," Shubert commented.

Strauss dropped the mike and spun the car around in the road so he could head back in the direction they had just come. That had been Adrian's truck. With four-wheel drive she would be well ahead of them, no matter how much skill he could summon in a pinch to get them back up the unplowed hill—if, in fact, he even could. He switched on the cruiser's flashing lights in hopes that anyone else foolish enough to be out on a night like this would see them coming and get out the way. He very much doubted if he had the control to do it.

"How well do you know these roads, Shubert?"

"Well enough."

"We didn't pass anyone on the way down except that one truck. Is there another way to Frampton Hill besides this one?"

"Yes. You can get there on Route 22. It's longer than coming through town, but on a night like this it's probably a better bet since the state plows it."

"What about Frampton Hill itself? Is it a through road?"

Shubert shook his head. "It didn't used to be. It used to end at Dunfield's farmhouse. But that was before all the building up there. I can't say for certain where it ends now. I don't think you can go through in a car, though."

Strauss wrestled with the wheel. He pressed the gas as hard as he dared but found he had to back off as much as he sped forward. What could Adrian possibly think she could do alone up there? They cleared the first rise and then, with too much gas, the car spun around in the road and stopped facing the other way. Strauss swore and backed around and surged forward once more. He could hear the snow up under the bottom of the newly lowered police car. The engine grumbled stubbornly as it pressed ahead in the deep drifts, trying to cut a path in the same place as the vehicle ahead of it, but Adrian's truck had left icy tracks and Strauss was forced to move the cruiser to an unbroken course in order to plow ahead without spinning the tires.

"There it is!" Shubert shouted, pointing through the blinding snow at the flashing light on the dash of Adrian's truck parked at the front of Gwenivere's house. Eagerly he drew his service revolver from its holster as Strauss pulled the car up close to the back of the house.

"Look, be careful with that thing," he growled. He ducked as Shubert waved the gun around the car in his excitement. "Adrian is out there somewhere. Don't go shooting at anything that moves."

Strauss turned off the ignition but left the lights flashing. Then he drew Shubert's state-issued rifle from its rack and reached for ammunition.

"Why are you taking that?" Shubert protested.

"Because I'm unarmed, you ass!" More bad policework, he chided himself. He hadn't worn a gun since coming to Vermont unless he was assigned highway duty, and even then he felt it was just for uniform purposes. It hadn't seemed necessary to wear a weapon into the Hook or when he questioned Lester Blake or Sally Glenn. In spite of the bad judgment, though, he felt his colder instincts kick in as soon as he had gotten the dispatcher's call. He felt short-tempered and on edge, a sure sign that he was thinking clearly.

It was a good thing, too, because a shot cut through the darkness.

"Shit!" Shubert gasped.

"What's the matter, Shubert? Isn't it fun anymore?"

The shot had come from the front of the house. Strauss opened the car door and crouched down in the snow, willing himself to see into the blinding snow and darkness. But there was nothing, not even a light in the house.

"Come with me!" he said in a low voice. "And stay down!" Cautiously, he climbed up the back steps. He opened the door a crack and called loudly. "Adrian! It's Nick! Kitchen door!"

"Over here, Nick," came the calm reply.

Without waiting for his eyes to become accustomed to the darkness, he grabbed Shubert by his collar and dragged him through the door and into the kitchen.

"The shots have all come from out front," Adrian's voice informed him softly.

When he located her, he very nearly burst out laughing. In what was possibly the safest corner of the room, she had flattened Gwenevere up against the wall and had a hand firmly planted over the large woman's mouth, in her other hand she held her 30.06, though as a weapon it would have been useless unless she had found the need to club Gwen with it. Gwen's eyes were huge with tears and horror. How Adrian was finding the strength to keep her pinned against the wall was anyone's guess.

"You guys are just in time. Not much I could do in this position."

"Shooter hit anything?"

"He shot my front window! All my china shepherdesses!" Gwen managed to get in hysterically before Adrian slapped a hand to her mouth again.

"Good idea, Constable."

"I thought so."

"HELP!" said Gwen in a voice muffled by Adrian's hand.

"What should we do, Strauss?" Shubert asked in a shaky voice.

As if in answer to his question, a shot splintered through the front window. Shubert hit the floor and covered his head with his hands. Strauss ran in a crouch to the front of the house and peered out a different window. Without lights, he could be fairly certain he wouldn't be seen. If he got shot now it would be sheer luck, and he didn't really believe in luck, no matter which side a shooter was on. In the gloom, he saw a dark form moving across the front lawn in the direction of the road. Somewhere out of sight there had to be a vehicle. He hadn't seen one when they arrived, but then he hadn't really looked carefully. The shooter was headed there now, he was sure. He ran back to the kitchen.

"Come on, Shubert!" he called quietly as went out the back door.

"Are you kidding?" the younger man gulped.

Adrian dropped her hold on Gwen and held a forefinger in front of her face. "Stay!" she said forcefully. Then she followed Strauss.

"Don't leave me!" Gwen shrieked immediately.

Shubert, left with the option of following Strauss or listening to her screams, moved for the door, albeit slowly.

Strauss moved to the corner of the house closest to the road. When he turned and saw Adrian instead of Shubert, he motioned her to the opposite corner, farthest from where he anticipated the shooter appearing.

"He must have a car around here somewhere. He was heading for the road. Cover that end of the house." Adrian moved obediently to the far side of the house and peeked around the corner, her rifle at the ready.

"Good of you to join us, Shubert," Strauss commented over his shoulder as his partner made his way through the snow..

"I had to be sure Gwen would be all right on her own."

"Not a bad idea," Strauss replied, though he didn't believe him. "Go back in and watch the front to make sure he doesn't come back around that way. Keep your head down."

"You want me to go back inside?" Shubert squeaked. "Alone?"

"You won't be alone, Shubert. Gwen's in there. Get going, we're supposed to be protecting her."

Strauss turned back to look around the corner without waiting to see if his orders were followed. He figured the shooter must have left his car either in the Glenns' driveway or somewhere nearby. In his haste, and with so much snow, he must have driven right by it. Based on the direction he had seen him moving from inside the house, the shooter would have to come onto the road on Strauss' side of the house. Adrian should be fairly safe, but it didn't hurt to have her watching as well.

An Investigation of Local Color

He waited but nothing happened. No sound, no movement. He glanced over his shoulder at the other end of the house. Adrian suddenly stood up with a shout and shouldered her rifle at the same time as Strauss saw a shadow moving across the lawn in the opposite direction than he had anticipated. It was too far for him to take aim, so he ran through the heavy snow toward Adrian. Shubert took that opportunity to blunder through the back door and crash into him, sending him to his knees. He disentangled himself from the heavier man in time to hear Adrian shout to the shooter to stop. Clearly, she was following him through her scope, and he was within her considerable range. But follow him was all she did.

When Strauss got to her side, she lowered the rifle, her victim by then out of range, heading up the hill toward the end of the road.

"Come on! The car!" He grabbed her coat sleeve.

"No, use my truck!"

Together they turned and both ran into Shubert, who had come trudging up behind them. As one, they shoved him to one side and ran for the truck at the front of the house. Adrian climbed behind the wheel and Strauss rolled down his window to see better. But as soon as she put the truck in gear, it was apparent that something wasn't right. There was a clunk, and they didn't seem to be moving smoothly.

"Damn it!" Adrian swore, getting out. The front tire was decidedly flattened, probably by one of the shots they had heard earlier.

"We can still use the car."

Together they floundered through the snow to the police car. Both were aware that they were losing precious seconds. This time Strauss drove, but when he stopped to think about it later he didn't really think it would have mattered. There was finally too much snow. Even the cruiser with its weight and snow tires couldn't crest the last hill that would have brought them to Tom and Milly's house, the last on the road. Once again Strauss switched off the ignition, left the lights flashing, and went out to check the road for tracks. There were no tire tracks, but there was a set of rapidly disappearing footprints headed up the road. Quickly he stepped out of the headlights to consider his next move.

"Looks like he's heading for the Boyces'," Adrian said.

"Could it be one of the Boyces?"

Adrian shrugged.

"I'd better go on. If it isn't one of them, whoever it is could be about to take shelter in their house."

"I'm coming along."

Strauss was on the verge of saying no, but he could tell by the way she set off in front of him that it would have done little good. Besides, he felt a little safer knowing where she was.

"Look," Adrian said suddenly as they reached the top of the hill just before the Boyces' driveway.

At first Strauss couldn't see what she was pointing at, and he wondered if he might have missed it entirely if he had been alone. A fresh set of tire tracks began at a point where the shooter must have parked his car. It must have been parked there for some time, because the tracks only left the scene.

"Damn," Adrian swore softly as she followed the prints.

They moved past the Boyces' driveway, which was at the very top of Frampton Hill, and then started down.

"I thought the road ended here," Strauss said.

"It does, but if you know where you're going and have four-wheel drive you can go through." Adrian wiped the snow from her face and pushed back her icy hair. She hadn't taken the time for either mittens or a hat, but she looked more dismayed than cold.

"Where does it end?"

"Down on the Dump Road, which doesn't have many houses on it. From that point there are any number of choices, a whole network of dirt roads."

"But you'd have to know where you were going?"

Adrian nodded. "Especially on a night like this."

That narrowed the field somewhat, Strauss thought. "Let's go up to the Boyces' and see if they noticed any activity on the road tonight."

There were lights on in the Boyce cabin, making it appear welcoming through the swirling snow. Strauss decided he would amend his opinion of their craftsmanship and wood obsession if Tom and

An Investigation of Local Color

Milly let him stand for five minutes next to their woodstove. He pounded on the door and immediately roused Milly with all her anxieties.

"Oh, dear, what's happened?" she gasped as she held open the door for them to come in. Her eyes went at once to the rifles her visitors carried. "Tom! Tom! Please come up!"

They could hear Tom's feet stomping up the steps from the cellar, where a radio or TV was playing loudly.

"What now? Oh, Strauss, Adrian. Little late at night to be hunting, wouldn't you say?" Tom chuckled at his little attempt to be witty. He was dressed in sweatpants and what appeared to be three or four various layers of sweaters. It must be cold downstairs.

"There's been some trouble down at Gwen's, and we wondered if you saw any unusual activity any time today. Any strange cars, maybe someone parked where they shouldn't have been?"

"What sort of trouble?" Milly asked, ignoring the question.

"Someone fired some shots into Gwen's house."

"At her? Were they firing at her?"

"We don't really know at this point, Milly. It's all just happened and we're trying—"

"God, I just can't believe it!" Milly cried out before Adrian could finish. "God, Tom, we were safer in Chicago. This Godforsaken place has ruined our lives!"

Her voice ended in a sob. She moved away in the direction of the woodstove and stood alternately warming her hands and clasping her arms around herself as if to ward off some supposed evil lurking in the vicinity of this Godforsaken place. Strauss would have liked to follow her in order to lend her comfort in the form of his proximity to her and, thereby, the stove, but Adrian stayed put on the rug by the door. Manners apparently dictated that they either remain dripping on the rug or remove their boots, unless they had been invited to slosh across the polyurethaned floors. Since neither was inclined to unlace only to lace up again in a few minutes, they stood together on the rug while Tom seemed torn between finding out more and going himself to the stove either to comfort his soon-to-be ex-wife or to grab a quick warmup before being forced to retreat again to the cold cellar.

"Did you notice anything unusual today?" Strauss asked again.

"Just that it is only November and it has been snowing as though it's the middle of January," Milly said.

"Ditto," Tom threw in. "I worked last night, so I slept until about 4 or so. With all the snow, I really didn't see the point in going out. Obviously, I'm not working tonight. So is Gwen all right?"

While Adrian assured him that Gwen was fine, Strauss took note of the assorted boots on the floor near the door. None of them appeared dripping with fresh snow, nor did any of the coats hanging on hooks. Similarly, neither Tom nor Milly had wet hair or freshly wind-whipped faces to indicate they had just come from the outside. If they said they had been inside all day Strauss was inclined to believe them, though how they could manage together in their present state of hostility was beyond him.

"Okay then, we won't bother you further. Thanks for your help," he told them.

"Can't we give you a cup of coffee or tea?" Tom urged with something that went beyond mere politeness. Longingly, he cast an eye toward the glowing woodstove.

"No, but thanks," Adrian said before Strauss could speak. "We'd better get off the hill ourselves."

"But what about poor Gwen?" Milly asked in renewed alarm. "You're not just going to leave her alone so someone can come back and finish the job, are you?"

"We'll take care of Gwen. Try not to worry."

"And please call either Adrian or the State Police barracks if you see anything suspicious," Strauss added. "Better keep your doors locked, too."

"We've always locked the doors, Strauss," Tom said as he puffed himself up to his full height. "I've never thought much of this backwoods idea that no one will bother anyone else's home. That just isn't human nature, if you ask me."

An Investigation of Local Color

Strauss didn't bother to point out that no one had asked. He pulled the door open and followed Adrian back out into the night. It was easier making their way back down to the cruiser than it had been coming up, but harder to know what to do once they got back to Gwenivere's. They knocked noisily on the kitchen door and identified themselves. Apparently feeling the danger was past, Shubert had turned on the lights and begun cleaning up the broken glass from the front window. He had even managed to fit some tape and cardboard over the holes left in the window by the shells from the shooter's rifle but admitted that he hadn't thought to look for signs of the bullets.

"Did you find him? Did you catch the man who ruined my beautiful, beautiful house?" Gwen asked, jumping up from her place on the couch, where she had apparently been supervising Shubert's work.

"I'm afraid not, Ms. Dunfield," Strauss told her. "He got away by driving down over the hill. We couldn't follow in the car."

"Oh, God, he'll come back! I know it! He'll come back and kill me!" Her voice rose to hysterical levels.

Shubert moved across the room to comfort her with more speed than Strauss had yet seen the man generate.

"Has she been like this the whole time?" Strauss asked. He noticed that, for all his size, Shubert couldn't quite get his arms all the way around the woman.

"She was fine until you got here," the younger partner snapped. He turned angrily toward Adrian. "Why didn't you shoot, Constable? You had the shot." Without waiting for her to answer, Shubert turned to Strauss and said, "I hope this clears up the question in your mind of who our murderer is. Now we know it's someone local because who else would know there's a back way down this hill? It's someone with four-wheel drive."

"Well, that really narrows it down," Adrian said calmly.

Shubert shot her a dirty look and then went on speaking to Strauss. "And maybe you should ask yourself why your friend there didn't shoot. Maybe it's because she knows who the murderer is, too. If you bothered to check, Strauss, you would know that Lester Blake drives a four-wheel drive truck, and with Adrian here I would warrant a guess that this time he doesn't have an alibi."

"It's Les Blake! I knew it! He's always hated me, and now he's trying to kill me, just like he killed Bill," Gwen sobbed hysterically. Then she shot a surprisingly sly look at Adrian. "And just like he killed Brian."

That caused Adrian to blink. "Les didn't kill anyone," she said impatiently.

"He did, he did! And now he's trying to kill me!" the big woman screeched.

Her heavy jowls trembled mightily with the strength of her emotion. This time even Shubert's comforting touch didn't calm her.

"You must arrest him, Mr. Strauss, or he will mow me down as he did all my lovely shepherdesses!" She waddled to pink-clad side table and picked up one of the china figurines that had lined the windowsills of her living room. She held the pieces up for Strauss' inspection. "Don't let him do this to me! Please, I beg you."

Never at his best with screeching women, Strauss felt totally out of his element with hysterically sobbing obese women bearing broken glass shepherdesses. They didn't prepare you for this sort of thing in Vice, he thought.

Shubert, however, had found his niche. "Come now, Gwen. Don't upset yourself. A little glue will put these ladies back together just like new. Come on, sit back down. Here's a Kleenex."

He patted her massive shoulder gently and earned himself a tearfully grateful smile. He smiled right back. Then he angrily turned on Adrian again.

"Why didn't you just shoot, Constable?" He laid unnecessary emphasis on Adrian's title as he often did.

"I couldn't see what I was shooting at, Trooper," she responded in kind. "For all I know I could have been aiming at a horse."

"Oh, God, not my horse. You would shoot my horse?" And Gwen was off again.

While Shubert set about calming her again, Adrian rubbed her face with both hands. She looked very tired. Her hair was dripping

An Investigation of Local Color

with thawed snow and her jeans were wet all the way to her parka. Strauss doubted that she had been home from work a half-hour before getting the call to come up here.

"None of this is helpful right now," he said with what he hoped was a warning look at Shubert. "I don't think there's much more we can do here tonight. We've lost the shooter for now, and he's not too likely to come back here tonight in this weather."

"You can't just leave me here alone!" Gwen protested.

At this point that was just what Strauss wanted to do, though he stifled the urge to say so.

"Of course we won't leave you alone," Shubert assured her. "I'll stay here tonight just in case that maniac comes back."

Shubert spoke bravely in the manner of one who had just offered to throw himself on a live grenade to save his beloved from certain death. Too bravely, Strauss thought, for a man who had very nearly wet his pants at the mere sound of gunfire. On the other hand, there was very little chance the shooter would return, so there was no harm in leaving Shubert to protect his damsel. His offer seemed to please her at any rate. She nodded her assent to Strauss.

"We'll have to take the car back to town because Adrian's front tire has been shot out. You'll be okay without transportation until I can back up here in the morning?"

"Of course." Shubert appeared to be bearing up well under the stress of sacrifice.

"I'll see if Junior can't run the plow up here first off," Adrian added.

"I'm sure anything is possible if you know the right strings to pull, Constable."

She ignored him.

"Ms. Dunfield, it might be a good idea if you went and stayed with family or friends for a few days until we can sort all this out."

"How long is it going to take to arrest Les Blake?"

"We can't just arrest someone without proof. I'm sure you understand that."

"How much proof do you need, Mr. Strauss? I don't know of anyone else who would want to kill me."

Something clicked in Strauss' brain but he stored it away for the moment and called on his reserves of patience. Patience had never been something he had great reserves of in the best of times, so he was really reaching now.

"I'll certainly keep that in mind, Ms. Dunfield. In the meantime, why don't you try to get some rest tonight?"

"I don't know how you expect me to get some rest when there is a madman out there trying to kill me, and the closest law enforcement officer would rather shoot my horse than the man who murdered her own husband," her voice rose yet again.

"Now, now, Gwen," soothed Shubert.

"Ms. Dunfield!" growled Strauss.

"Good God!" snorted Adrian.

And finally, there was silence as they all stared at each other.

"I think we'll be going. I'll call first thing in the morning," Strauss told his partner. He turned and nearly pushed a stony-eyed Adrian into the kitchen and out the back door.

He turned the car out into the snow and hoped for what seemed to be the hundredth time that day that he could manage to get where he was going. If he ended up in a ditch between here and Adrian's house, he doubted if he could be responsible for his actions, particularly if he ended up knocking on Harold Thibault's door again. He radioed the situation to the dispatcher.

"I suppose this means neither of those cruisers is going to make it out to the highway tonight, Detective?" the dispatcher asked.

"No, son, they are not," Strauss answered with the last of his patience.

"I didn't think so," came the cheerful reply, "but it never hurts to ask. You have a nice night, Detective."

He hung up the radio thinking that the kid should take a few less No-Doze, amphetamines or whatever caused him to be so goddamned cheerful in the middle of a blizzard.

"So why didn't you shoot?"

"I thought I answered that already," Adrian replied irritably.

"Would you mind giving me an answer now, while I don't have the benefit of a running commentary from Dudley DoRight?"

An Investigation of Local Color

She turned toward him and he could feel her eyes boring into him, daring him to doubt her. "I didn't have a shot," she said very slowly, as if explaining to a moron.

"You didn't? It looked like you did from where I was standing."

"Look, Detective, I don't know how you do things in the big city, but I like to be able to identify what I'm shooting at. All I saw was a blur running across the field. If I'm going to shoot someone, and it's something I'm not currently in the habit of doing, I would like to know who I am shooting at and why. We don't even know if the person up there tonight was trying to kill Gwen or just scare her. Did you really want me to kill someone who was just trying to scare the beast?"

"Are we talking tonight or in general?"

"That's not funny."

"Did it cross your mind at all that it might have been Les Blake?"

"It wasn't Les," she replied firmly.

"How do you know? You said you couldn't see who it was."

"Well, it wasn't Les," she snapped stubbornly. "He wouldn't do that."

"And you're sure?"

"I am sure."

Strauss wondered if Adrian was as sure in her own mind as she sounded, but he didn't have time to wonder long because the car hit an enormous drift and fishtailed wildly before he could bring it under control again.

"Do you think Junior gave up and went home?" he asked. He tried not to sound annoyed, but he could hear it in his voice.

"No. But there is just him, and on a night like tonight anyone with a pickup and a plow who will help him. It takes a long time with one snowplow and four or five pickups. This isn't a rich town, Detective. We do the best we can."

"I didn't mean to imply otherwise."

"Yes, you did," Adrian insisted argumentatively. "I know Benton Harbor needs to join the twenty first century but it isn't as easy as just wanting to. It takes more money than desire, and, if you don't mind my saying so it takes fewer dissatisfied, know-it-all outsiders."

"I stand corrected." He could be just as irritable as she.

He grew careless with the gas pedal and the car spun around in the road. He swore silently. Adrian wisely withheld comment until he had righted it and started down the road again.

"You'd better plan on staying the night. It's only going to get worse, and you have to be back first thing in the morning anyway."

Her voice was carefully neutral, but Strauss had the feeling that, at the moment at least, she would just as soon have been offering shelter to Gwen's rifle-bearing friend. Maybe she would at that, he thought, considering the possibility that the shooter might very well be living in her barnyard anyway.

"That won't be. . ."

The tires grabbed the snowbank at the edge of the road and hung on as if given sudden life. Strauss lifted his foot off the gas with no effect. He twisted the wheel and went further toward the edge of the road. Just as he was certain he was headed for yet another trip into the ditch, the tires released their hold and the car leaped back onto the road.

"That's an excellent idea, Constable," he said when he caught his breath. "I'd love to sleep on your couch."

"Okay. Did you know you just drove by my driveway?"

He swore silently again, and yet again, though this time not silently, when his sudden braking caused the car to slide some more. Carefully, he backed into the drive until he had the cruiser just off the road.

"This is as far as we go. We'll walk to the house before I get into any more trouble."

There were lights on in the farmhouse, he noticed, as they approached from the front. Then he noticed something else: tire tracks leading from the road to the side of the barn where Les Blake lived. They were fresh enough to be seen, though they were filling and drifting over quickly. He didn't point them out to Adrian because he knew she would have seen them and was now asking herself the same question as he was. If she wasn't, she should be.

Inside the house was warm and cozy—for about two seconds. Les was putting more wood on the stove. He straightened as they came

An Investigation of Local Color

in carrying their wet rifles and stomping the snow off their feet. He was obviously not pleased, judging by his scowl, to see Strauss.

"Where have you been?" he asked Adrian angrily.

It was definitely not the tone of voice one normally expected from the hired hand. Strauss sensed that Adrian, too, was taken back, but he couldn't have said if it was by Blake's anger or by the fact that Les' boots were dripping all over her floor and his clothing was wet from head to toe.

"I was out on a call," she replied slowly. Her eyes crawled over Blake. "Where were you?"

"When I come in to put the wood on, I heard 'em talking on the scanner about shots fired somewhere in Benton Harbor. You didn't come and didn't come, so I went out to look. I didn't see nothing, so I went over to Franklyn's. He didn't know nothing about any shots. Where'd they come from?"

"Up on Frampton Hill." Adrian's reply sounded cautious.

Strauss looked from one to the other. She was staring steadily at her hired man. He was fidgeting under her stern gaze.

"How come you didn't call Franklyn to go with you? Or me? I'da gone."

"I called the State Police."

Blake looked from Adrian to Strauss. *He's hiding something,* Strauss thought. He looked as though he would have said more if Strauss hadn't been there. Instead, he settled for patting Elizabeth, who had just jumped out of the wood box to wind herself around his legs while staring at her company inhospitably.

"Are you done with the fire, Les?"

"Yeah."

"You'd better get out of those wet clothes before you get a chill, then," Adrian said in a gentler tone.

Blake moved to obey, but he was clearly unhappy about something. He stopped in the door.

"I brought some of my hamburger casserole in."

"Thanks, Les. Did you eat already?"

He shook his head. "I ain't too hungry tonight. I'll just go turn in now." His eyes moved once more from Adrian to Strauss.

Adrian's gaze followed him out the door. She didn't look any happier than her hired man.

"Adrian, does Les—"

"I'm going up and get out of these wet clothes," she interrupted. "Bathroom's through that door. Help yourself to the towels and go stand close to the stove because I don't have any dry clothes to fit you."

Strauss did as he was told. When he came out of the bathroom, he thought he could hear Adrian talking. He tried to move to a place where he could hear better, but she was speaking softly, presumably on the phone, and he could only hear the murmur of her voice. Who would she call at this hour in the middle of a storm? Any number of people, he assured himself. Life didn't stand still just because snow fell. Especially not here in Vermont. Wasn't someone always telling him that?

A few minutes later she came down the steps in dry jeans and a sweater and sock feet.

"Who were you talking to?" he asked without preface.

Adrian looked more than just a little annoyed. Her cheeks blazed angrily in competition with her red sweater. "I'm not sure you have the right to question whom I call on my private line. You're a guest in my home, after all."

"I haven't lost sight of that fact. You can throw me out in the snow now if you choose, but you'd leave me wondering why you wouldn't answer me. And I'm already wondering what your handyman was doing wandering around on a night like tonight."

She gave him a look with daggers in it and went into the kitchen, where she shoved a casserole dish angrily into the microwave and punched the timer. Strauss followed her as far as the kitchen door. Elizabeth was napping on the hearth, so he didn't see much point in trying to make use of the stove. Her mistress didn't make entering the kitchen any more inviting, so he stuck to the doorway.

"If you must know, for the record, I was talking to Franklyn Birch. Since he heard part of the story from Les, I thought I'd fill him in on

An Investigation of Local Color

the rest. By the way, he said Les was really there and, surprisingly, he really was looking for me."

"Quit with the indignation bit, will you? You'd be lying either to me or to yourself or both of us if you told me you didn't wonder about Les. Isn't it time to get the story out in the open?"

"What story? There is no story. There is just a lot of suspicion brought on by a lot of innuendo that Ms. Dunfield created years ago. She hooked Shubert with it then, and now she's got him again. And obviously, she's hooked you as well."

"Okay, how about this? I'll believe you and drop the subject forever if you can assure me of one thing."

"What?"

"When we walked through the door and you saw Les standing there dripping snow, it never crossed your mind that he could have been the shooter up on Frampton Hill."

Strauss had a dubious feeling of satisfaction when she looked away and started getting out plates and silverware for dinner.

"Adrian?" he asked softly.

Her dark eyes met his, but he couldn't read the expression there. "It occurred to me," she admitted flatly. "But Les doesn't even own a gun."

"Are you sure?"

"Pretty sure. He doesn't hunt."

"Do you have any besides the one you had with you?"

"A handgun and one other rifle. All of them were my father's."

"Where?"

"In a gun case, in the living room," she indicated the direction with her chin. "It's unlocked."

Strauss went into the living room and switched on a light. It was colder in here. The woodstove that would normally have heated it wasn't lit, and in spite of some nice furniture, including the couch he assumed was to be his bed for the night, it didn't look to be a room Adrian much used. The gun cabinet was in the corner. As Adrian had said it wasn't locked and looked as though it never had been. There were several boxes of shells for each rifle and the handgun in the single drawer. The shots at Gwen's house had come from a rifle, so he lifted the only one there from the rack. It was clean. There was no possible way Blake could have used it up on Frampton Hill, stopped to talk to Birch, and had time to clean the rifle before Strauss and Adrian had gotten back.

"I don't think Les even knows how to load a weapon of any kind," Adrian said from the doorway. Strauss hadn't even heard her come in. "Food's hot, if you want some."

He put the gun back in the rack and closed the door. Adrian spooned some casserole onto two plates and handed him some bread and salad.

"Take it over to the stove, where it's warmer," she told him. "Push Elizabeth out of the way."

I can do that, Strauss thought. But when he sat down in the big rocker by the stove and Elizabeth opened one eye, he decided she wasn't really in the way and left her alone.

"What happened with Les when your husband was killed?"

"I told you, nothing happened."

"If nothing happened, why does everyone immediately become hostile when the subject comes up? If it's truly nothing, wouldn't it make sense to tell me about it, so I can rule him out as a suspect in this case?"

Adrian looked at him as if she'd rather eat nails. She settled for casserole instead.

He tried again. "Shubert was suspicious before. He's never forgotten that he couldn't prove Les killed your husband, so naturally he's pushing the same theory on this case. I've got to tell you he's got the chief's ear. That's how he got assigned to this Dunfield thing in the first place. I've still got one or two ideas of my own, but I've got to admit that his suspicions are looking more and more plausible at the moment, and besides that, I've got a boss who is clamoring loudly for an arrest. If you can tell me anything that could help us rule out Les as a suspect, I would be as happy as you. I hate partners. Do you think I want this one to be right? Adrian?"

But Adrian, on her side of the stove, with her face in the shadows, ate her dinner and said nothing. When she was finished, she got up and got a beer from the refrigerator and brought one to him. Before sitting down to drink it, she took away Strauss' glass of fresh-from-the-cow milk, which she knew he couldn't stomach but was too polite to refuse.

"I married Brian Borden when I was very young and more than a little foolish," she said as she washed the milk down the drain. "I thought staying in Vermont for the rest of my life would bore me to death. I thought I deserved a little adventure after being a good little farmgirl all my life. I wanted to go where I wasn't related to everyone in sight and do all the things people in Benton Harbor only dream of doing. Brian was handsome and exciting and rich. He just forgot to tell me he was a drunk. It took me a long time to notice because in college we went to parties every weekend and all our friends drank. After we were married, I thought we were being sophisticated having cocktails in the afternoon and then before dinner and during dinner and after dinner and before bed."

"How did you finally know?"

"He stopped going to work and every now and then he hit me."

Strauss wasn't sure how to reply, so he swallowed some beer. Adrian came back and sat by the stove. Her arms were folded across her chest in a defensive posture.

"Brian worked for his father, who finally threw him out, so we came back here. My father was getting older and not feeling well, and the idea was that we would take over the chores and, when he was ready to give it up, the entire farm. It was just another dream, though, because dairy herds the size of ours can't sustain a family of four anymore. Besides that, Brian hated the physical labor. He kept drinking. My father hated him, but he wouldn't throw him out. And then one day he got kicked in the head by one of the cows."

"But no one actually saw it?"

"No. Dad came in from spreading the manure and found him lying on the floor next to one of the cows. He was already dead." Adrian's voice was without emotion. She stared at the glow in the window of the stove. "Doc Stanton came and said the death was due being kicked by a cow, and that was that. We had a funeral, no one cried, and everyone decided that it would be best to get on with our lives as quickly as possible.

"I had no idea Brian was having an affair with Gwen. Besides helping Les with the cows, I had picked up a couple of courses at the college to try to finish my nursing degree. I suppose while I was doing that my husband was doing Gwen. She was much prettier back then, and right after her divorce she let all the men know she was very available. If she could have gotten Brian to dump me, she would have had herself a prize, I suppose. Obviously, she knows how to work a divorce, and as I said Brian's family has money. I don't know how heartbroken she was that her drunken boyfriend was dead, but I bet, judging from the way she treats me, that she was pretty angry to have lost out on the money angle."

"Who else knew about Brian and Gwen?"

Adrian looked embarrassed. "Probably the whole town. There aren't many secrets in Benton Harbor."

"I've noticed that."

"I might have known, too, if I'd really wanted to."

"Gwen gave the police a not-so-anonymous tip. Did you know that?"

"The former chief shared the news with my father because they were old friends. I suspect that's another one of those secrets everyone in Benton Harbor knows but doesn't mention, at least not to me."

"Any idea why she'd finger Les? Why not someone else?"

"I don't know. Les didn't like Brian, but neither did my father. In fact, Brian didn't really have any friends in town. He thought we were all hicks and rednecks and inbred idiots."

"But Les was with you when Brian was killed."

There was silence.

"Wasn't he?" Strauss didn't know why he had asked. He had known all along that Adrian had lied for Les.

The fire crackled in the stove, but tonight it didn't feel as cozy as it had the first time. Strauss wondered if he really wanted to hear any more, and what he would do if he heard the wrong thing? He half hoped Adrian would end the story there. But she didn't.

An Investigation of Local Color

"When Doc said Brian died from a kick, there were no more questions asked. Suddenly the state cops came back and zeroed right in on Les. Shubert was going at him pretty hard, and Les was very unhappy. Dad didn't know what to think, so I said he was with me. I didn't know then about Gwen's tip. I thought they were going at Les for another reason and so did Dad."

"What other reason?"

Adrian got up and went to the window. She cleared a place on the frosty glass and peered outside. "It's still snowing," she commented irrelevantly.

Strauss pulled his chair closer to the stove and put his feet nearly on it for warmth. His movement made Adrian come back to the fire and poke the burning logs before adding another.

"Les came from the worst possible family," she said as she worked the poker. "They were dirt poor mostly because his father sat around drinking instead of working. When he got drunk enough, he beat his wife and kids. Les' older brothers were just like the old man. They've been in and out of jail for petty stuff most of their lives. I've no idea where they are now or even if they're still living. Mom was no prize either. A hard-talking woman who needed a good lesson in housecleaning and child rearing. But she was Les' mom. And one night when Mom and Dad got to screaming at each other, then Dad got to beating Mom, Les picked up a shotgun and shot his father."

"Killed him?"

Adrian nodded. "Les was seventeen, so the courts went easy on him. It was clear from his mother's bruises that she had been beaten, and anyone in town could have told that old man Blake had a history of beating his family. The judge agreed to release Les on a sort of probation thing if some family would foster him, give him a job, a place to live, basically a new start on life. Because my parents were older and hadn't been able to have kids, they agreed to take him. If he could stick to the terms until he was twenty-one, he could have his juvenile record cleared. Dad said it was the best decision he ever made. Les became totally devoted to my father for giving him a new start. He worked hard, he kept his trailer and the barns tidy, he loved my folks."

"What happened to his mother?"

Adrian gave a humorless laugh. "You know, the funny thing is, in spite of old man Blake's abuse and his drinking she didn't seem to be able to live without him. She died shortly after Les came here. She just sat in a chair in their filthy shack and drank all day. Les would go down to see her and she would scream obscenities at him, until Dad stopped him from going. In the end no one could really help her.

"This is a good town, but there is a lot more of that sort of thing around than any of us want to admit. When I was younger, I thought it was a result of low income and hopelessness and the long winters. I thought you got rid of that sort of thing when you moved to a more upscale area, but the Bordens certainly disproved that theory. Upscale areas just drink fancier drinks and have a high-income hopelessness."

Strauss had never thought about it, but she was right. He thought of the number of three-piece-suited drunks he had arrested along with their prostitute du jour. He didn't know if they exactly outnumbered the guys he saw sleeping alongside dumpsters, but it was a significant number, nevertheless.

"Les has never had a drink. He's never shot a gun. The Blakes were never well thought of in Benton Harbor, but he has tried very hard to make something of himself when the others did not. That's probably why you run into hostility when you ask the wrong questions about him. The town takes care of its own when it thinks they're worth taking care of. No one who knows Les could possibly imagine him killing anyone."

But as much as he would have liked to have had a similar faith in Blake, Strauss was thinking of that very devoted man watching a young woman he must have loved being hit by her drunken husband. Could Blake have frantically been watching the downward spiral of Adrian's marriage and seeing the parallels to his own parents' union? Could he, as a result, have sought to remedy the situation? And Borden had been killed by a blow to the head. Maybe Blake had seen him in the barn and on sudden impulse had whacked him over the head before the situation could deteriorate further.

An Investigation of Local Color

"He wouldn't kill anyone, Nick," Adrian insisted. She seemed uncomfortable with his silence. This was an area she didn't want him thinking about too much.

"Adrian, isn't it just possible that he might have been trying to protect you the same way he was trying to protect his mother?"

She sighed heavily. "It's possible, but he said he didn't do it."

"And you believe him?"

"I have to believe him, Nick. Les has never lied to me. In spite of being related to half the town, I consider him to be my closest family. If I start doubting what he tells me, where will I be? If he said he didn't do it, in my mind he didn't do it."

But Strauss could hear the doubt in her voice, in spite of her words. He knew she resented him for making her voice the very thing she had probably been thinking for years.

"What could all this have to do with the Dunfield murder?"

Strauss shrugged. "What do you think? What would you be thinking if you were me?"

She thought about that for a moment. Maybe she wanted to know after all because she surprised Strauss by saying, "I would be wondering if Les killed Dunfield because he was indirectly threatening Sally. Les really likes Sally. He likes anyone who needs his help. Sally was scared of Dunfield, ergo Les knifed him to help her out. And you would be reminding yourself that the weapon of choice was a knife, not a gun."

"You're reading my mind fairly accurately," Strauss admitted.

"Did you ask him if he killed Dunfield?"

"He's says he didn't. He says he was here all night."

Adrian gave him a "there you have it" look, as though that was the end of the story.

"Did you by any chance happen to notice, say between 3 and 5 in the morning, if he was, in fact, here at home?"

She looked away. She scooped Elizabeth from the hearth and settled the feline into her arms. "I didn't notice," she said softly. "I have never had much reason to check up on Les. He never goes out late at night."

There seemed no more to be said. Adrian was clever enough to see the predicament. Even Shubert was smart enough to make the connection between Les and his only alibi for two different deaths. Besides, when they had come through the door that night, he had sensed the horrible doubt in Adrian as she watched her hired hand dripping snow on the floor. A man who rarely goes out at night goes out on the worst possible weather night of the year?

"You could have told me all this before," Strauss said finally.

"Why? It's hardly made the picture clearer, has it? It's only done what I thought it would do all along: It's made Les look like the most likely suspect."

For some unexplained reason known only to her little cat brain, Elizabeth chose that moment to jump off Adrian's lap and onto Strauss'. She stared, close-range, at him, and he stared back fearing for his face, the murder investigation temporarily forgotten except in that he wondered why, when the subject of Blake came up, someone in Benton Harbor saw fit to threaten him in some way. He looked out of the corner of his eye at Adrian, hoping she would rescue him. If she noticed his discomfort, she ignored it. So Strauss stared at Elizabeth, and she stared back for nearly five minutes while the wind blew noisily outside and the fire with its new logs crackled warmly in the grate.

"Uhmmm, Adrian," Strauss cleared his throat when he could take it no longer.

"Tell me you're not afraid of the cat," she said in a voice that suggested no one could possibly be so stupid.

"Not really." This wasn't the best possible moment to assert his masculinity, he assumed, as Elizabeth slowly ran a pink tongue over her nose. "I'm just not all that used to animals."

Adrian finally looked up from her contemplation of the glowing stove. She actually laughed at Strauss sitting rigid in his chair while the tiny cat stared at him.

"I'm a city boy, Adrian," he said in a voice that begged to be rescued.

"You are that, Strauss." She still made no effort to remove Elizabeth.

"Have mercy, will you? I'm out of Bag Balm."

An Investigation of Local Color

"I'm sure that's a lie." But she reached over and snatched the cat off his lap. Immediately the cat settled happily into her lap, purring and licking its paws.

Suddenly, Strauss leaped to his feet. The diary! He had forgotten all about it after the dispatcher's call sent them back up to Frampton Hill.

"What is it? Where are you going?" Adrian, too, got to her feet.

"I just remembered something. I'll be right back."

Hurriedly, he shoved his feet into his wet boots and pulled on his parka. It had nearly stopped snowing, but he still had to wade through what was on the ground to get to the car, causing him to wish he had been more daring and pulled right up to the back door. He fished around under the seat and had a moment of panic when he didn't find the book, but it had merely slipped from its original position with all the spinning and fishtailing they had done up and down Frampton Hill.

As he slammed the car door and started back to the house, he noticed Les Blake standing on the steps of his trailer, snow shovel in hand, watching him. Odd hour to be shoveling, he thought.

"Does Les usually turn in early, Adrian?" he asked as he pulled off his boots.

"Yes. He gets up around 4:30 to milk the cows, so he goes to bed early. Why?"

"Just wondered."

She looked at him suspiciously but then saw the book he carried. "What's that?"

"Shubert and I went back to Dunfield's this afternoon. I found this underneath the bathtub. It seems to be sort of a diary."

"You mean you've had this all along, and you're just now remembering? I might have just gone through this whole thing about Les for nothing?" Adrian seemed unduly irritated, he thought.

"I'm sorry, Adrian, but what, with getting shot at and all it just sort of slipped my mind."

"Oh. I didn't realize you were the one getting shot at. Where did you say you found it?"

"In Dunfield's bathroom, under the tub."

"Under the tub? That's a strange place to put a diary unless you were sitting in the tub while you...." Adrian's voice trailed off as her mind painted the picture. "Yick! That's using more imagination than I needed. What's in it?"

Strauss sat down and opened the book. "I haven't had much of a chance to read it. I kept it hidden from Shubert until I could check it out for myself. It looks as though Dunfield just started scribbling down things that came to him, beginning right around the time of his divorce from Gwen. The last entry is from the day before he was killed."

He held up the last page for Adrian to read. She read the entry that the dead man had written about L. being hopping mad, but her face showed no expression.

"What else is there? Go to the beginning."

She pulled her chair closer to his and leaned over the arm of his chair in order to see. Briefly, Strauss wished they could stop talking murder.

They examined the diary carefully for over an hour, but if there were any clues to the murder neither Strauss nor his partner could easily find them. Dunfield's sentences were mostly angry, but not overtly threatening. In the beginning there were several angry entries concerning Gwen and her new lovers, no specific names, the occasional initial, including a "B." at around the time of Brian Borden's involvement. *"A well-suited couple, if there was one,"* he wrote of Gwen and B. Then, *"Maybe it's time to see if A. would be amusing."*

Strauss glanced at Adrian, but she said nothing. She did, however, flip the page quickly.

"This one's good," she commented, pointing to an early entry.

"Butchered the steer today. Yokels came from town to help. Said they were pros. Made a goddamned mess all over my barnyard. Real pros."

Adrian laughed. "Not quite the version I heard."

"No, me either."

"The bitch took me back to court. She won and for what? She wants to buy herself a goddamned horse! A horse! Sweat all day stuffing tampons, and she takes the money for a horse! Rate she's eating, she'll be a horse herself and I'll be stuck with two feed bills!! Can't these damned hick judges see she's sucking me dry?"

An Investigation of Local Color

There were several similar entries as well as the mention of taking on extra work when a coworker's husband died. The woman he had met at NET, Strauss assumed.

"Look, this must be Jack Glenn," Adrian said.

"*'What G. knows about this business could fit into one of the tampon covers. Man's an ass!'*" No specifics. Three pages later, there was a reference to "G." sitting behind a desk picking his nose while the real people did all the work and he took the credit.

"Suppose there's any truth to that?" Strauss asked.

"I can't say for certain, but Jack has a reputation for being a real worker and a go-getter. I know his hours at NET are very long. Les says when he's home he's always working on some project around their place. They've cleared a lot of brush off the hilltop to improve their view. If I had to guess, I'd say Bill's resentment of him comes from the fact that Jack now owns a piece of the hill that once belonged to Bill. I doubt very much that Jack is either lazy or incompetent."

Strauss nodded. "That was sort of the impression I got when I went over to the factory. He didn't seem to be a behind-the-desk sort of guy."

The only other entry of significance was the reference to "L." Since there was no other L. in the book, they were left wondering to whom Dunfield was referring.

"Other than Glenn, Dunfield seems to have no hostility toward his coworkers, which would seem to confirm what they said when I visited NET. Most of his anger is spent on Gwen, which would make sense, and on local people."

"You're right. But even if he had words with some of them, I doubt if his accusations of Sally's dogs doing their number on his lawn or Milly's 'constant bawling' about her boredom would cause one of them to stick a knife in him. Even Gwen would appear better off with him alive. If she were the victim, I think we would have a suspect in Dunfield, but the other way around...?" Adrian stared at the book in Strauss' hands as if she could will it to give them the answer.

"That's the same conclusion I keep coming to," Strauss admitted. He didn't add that he reached the conclusion every time he eliminated

Les from the formula. "There seems to be a better reason for someone wanting Gwen dead than the other way around. Dunfield seems, at worst, to be an irritating little bastard. No one seems to have hated him enough to kill him, even the ex-wife."

"And you didn't find anything else in the house?" Adrian asked, but she didn't sound particularly hopeful.

Strauss shook his head. "Nothing. Except...a wedding album. The bride's face in all of the photos had been cut out."

Adrian looked at him in surprise. "You don't seem to think that's unusual. Under the circumstances, don't you think that it's significant?"

"No. Just the opposite, in fact."

"Why?"

"It was obviously a messy divorce. I might have done the same thing, except that my wedding album was part of my ex-wife's share of the divorce settlement. Come to think of it, she might have done some very interesting things with the pictures. At any rate I don't think many divorcees take out their wedding albums for fond memories. I bet more than one of them has seen the bottom of a dumpster."

"I suppose you're right," Adrian conceded. After a pause she asked, "What happened? To you, I mean."

"Nothing quite as dramatic as with the Dunfields, though I think there was probably a time when Denise would have been delighted to have heard someone stuck a knife in me. I think the demands of my job might have left her alone too much."

Adrian looked as though she didn't quite believe him. Normally, Strauss didn't think she would have pressed for more of an explanation, but since he had pressed her on Les Blake she seemed determined to even the score somehow.

"We were having problems, you know, the kind the police shrinks are always saying that cops have, but as it turns out everyone else has, too. We got married too young because we thought we were madly in love. Then reality set in. She was bored, unfulfilled. I was busy. That sort of thing. So she wants to go to a marriage counsellor. I said no."

"So she left you?"

An Investigation of Local Color

"No. She sort of wore me down," Strauss explained sheepishly. He always hated to admit he had been anywhere near a shrink's office, not once but several times. At least the second shrink hadn't been his idea. "We went twice a week for a couple of months and this guy, who actually wore a bowtie every day, told me that Denise was the sort of woman who needed attention and commitment. I had to find a way to spend more quality time with her and reduce the stress in her life. It was a little hard to do with my schedule being what it was, but I tried and she seemed happier. And at the end of our sessions, she ran off with the marriage counsellor."

Adrian looked at him in disbelief.

"Really," Strauss assured her.

"Really?"

"I'm afraid so. Apparently the shrink fellow had a better handle on the quality-time part. They have two little kids."

"And he's a marriage counsellor?"

"Obviously you're having trouble with this concept, Adrian. I'm glad I'm not the only one. Apparently, my ex-wife wanted someone less exciting than a cop. The man wears a bowtie on a daily basis. I think that about says it all on the issue of excitement, don't you? How did we get on this subject, anyway?"

"The wedding album." Adrian was laughing.

"Oh, yeah, the wedding album. I was always in the dark about why she wanted ours, but maybe today I got my first clue. Now I wish it had been part of my share. It probably would have been more therapeutic than a worn-out car with bald tires. And, no doubt, it would have made the lady police shrink even more excited about me than she already was."

Adrian laughed again. Up until tonight, Strauss had seen very little humor in the end of his marriage. He thought it quite possible that he had unknowingly stopped loving his wife long before she left him, but it still rankled him to have her choose another man over him, especially an effeminate little shrink who was supposed to be sorting out their problems, not contributing to them. He still missed having a warm body to come home to and at least the pretense that someone loved him. He had never failed to see the irony, he had just never seen the humor in it, as several of his unfortunate partners had discovered. But he laughed now, for the first time, and he thought it was probably far better for him than all the psycho-analyzing the cop shrink had tried to do on him.

Adrian sobered first. "I've got to get some sleep. I'm on at 7 tomorrow." She stood up, dumping Elizabeth off her lap with far less ceremony than Strauss would have dared. "Come on, I'll show you where you can sleep."

Because he had thought he would have to squeeze himself onto a too-short couch, Strauss was surprised when she led the way upstairs. She opened a door to reveal what appeared to be a long unused bedroom. It felt cold, but it was tidy and the bed was made up.

Adrian went to the closet and got out an extra blanket. "It's cold in here. If you want, you can make a fire in the stove below and it will warm it up in here. I like to sleep in the cold myself, but you don't have to if you don't want."

"No, this is fine. Just like home."

It was even colder than his apartment. But Strauss wasn't about to admit that Adrian was tougher than he was any more than he was going to confess that he hadn't the faintest idea how to build a fire, though he had a sneaking suspicion that she probably knew. It was easier to be cold.

"Okay then. There's just the one bathroom downstairs. I'll be getting up early, so just make yourself at home." She started to go, then turned to him again. "Now that we've told each other the worst, where does that leave us, Nick?"

He wasn't sure he understood. "Leave us? You mean with the case?"

She stared at him a moment, her eyes dark in the dim light. He thought she looked pretty in red. He also thought he'd like to kiss her and wondered if she would be agreeable.

"Of course, with the case," Adrian replied shortly, leaving no doubt as to her agreeableness.

"I'll talk to Jack Glenn again tomorrow. Let's see if he knows of a coworker who might be 'L.' There's also that strange problem on the second and third shift the night Dunfield died. It might be worth telling Gwen about Dunfield's diary to see if it shakes any previously hidden secrets from her."

"What about Les?"

"Adrian, you know I've got to ask him where he was earlier tonight."

She gazed steadily at him so that he lost some of his resolve. He hoped she didn't notice.

"Let me do it."

"Adrian, that's not such—"

"Please, Nick?" She spoke softly and laid a hand lightly on his arm.

"*Objection!*" his brain screamed. But like most men, his flesh overrode it.

"Okay." He started to warn her that that would not likely be an end to it but found that he couldn't.

"I'll talk to him before I go to work in the morning." Adrian smiled warmly at him, and Strauss couldn't escape the feeling that he had been manipulated somehow.

Even though it was nearly 2 A.M., Strauss was sure he would be unable to sleep. He had nothing warmer than his underwear to sleep in, and he lay curled under the blankets listening to Adrian's creaking floorboards and wondering what she was doing. He wondered, too, if Adrian was just as ruthless as she was practical. But she did make him laugh. And in the end he fell asleep feeling warmer than he thought he would.

8

He awoke as he had fallen asleep several hours earlier, to the sounds of Adrian moving around on the creaking floorboards. It was still dark outside. His eyes didn't adjust to the darkness of the room since he was unaccustomed to a room unlit by streetlamps, but he knew immediately where he was. The cop in him rarely allowed him to sleep soundly, especially since he had been sleeping alone. It had been a long time since he had awakened to the sound of someone else moving around in the same house, if he discounted Mrs. Hutchins, who seemed to be constantly dropping pans in her kitchen below his bedroom, or any of the dozen or so tenants who shared the low-rent apartment building with him in the city. He thought he should get up if only to show Adrian that he wasn't lounging around in bed while she hustled off to work on the same limited amount of sleep as he had had. But maybe she wouldn't appreciate the intrusion. There was, after all, only one bathroom. Besides, he didn't have anything more suitable than his day-old clothes to put on. It occurred to him that things were considerably more difficult than they used to be. He never used to consider what his next move should be, at work and certainly never at play. If he wanted to kiss a woman, he just did it. When he felt like getting out of bed in the morning, he didn't worry about what he put on, or even if he put anything on. He didn't worry about who else was around either. But here he was middle-aged, out of shape, apparently out of courage, cowering under the covers in his underwear hoping Adrian would hurry up and leave so he could go downstairs and use the bathroom. Life was definitely not getting better. He dozed off again.

When he woke up again an hour later, it was with a heaviness on his chest. He cleared the fog in his head with effort and opened his eyes to see Elizabeth sitting on his chest staring into his face. With a startled yell he threw all the blankets, the cat and himself off the bed, then braced himself for what would surely be her revenge. And him with nothing more than his shorts on. But Elizabeth merely shook herself indignantly, gave him a reproachful stare and sat down in the doorway to wash her paws.

God, he hated animals! Strauss thought as his heart gradually slowed. Adrian must have left because she hadn't come running at his shout. Maybe it would have been better if she had, he thought, as he pulled on his pants, the freezing air in the room cutting into his bare chest, because now he was faced with the problem of getting out past the cat in the doorway. As soon as he moved in that direction, she stopped her grooming and stared. When he tried to slip around her, she stood up. Adrian hadn't handled her gently, maybe he shouldn't either. He reached a hand out to her to test the waters but she only continued to stare indifferently, neither moving toward or away from the proffered hand. She gave him no more clue about whether she would appreciate a kind pat than her mistress had about whether she would enjoy a kind kiss. They were well suited, Strauss thought, as he made a sudden dash for the door, whisking it open, sweeping back Elizabeth with it. He covered his head and ran down the stairs and nearly into Les Blake, who stood at the bottom.

Blake raised an eyebrow questioningly. Strauss was suddenly aware that he was barefoot and bare-chested and unarmed. He was also face to face with a man who might have killed for the very woman Strauss had been lusting for only an hour ago. He was never one to feel fear, but the present state of affairs did have a way of emasculating even a tough city cop.

"Ah...ah...the cat," he felt compelled to explain, making things even worse. "Excuse me, I gotta pee."

He hustled himself off to the bathroom. Since it didn't have a lock, he kept his eye on the door while wondering if Adrian had talked to Les before leaving for work. What had he been doing in the house, anyway? Had he been about to come upstairs, and if so, why?

He flushed, zipped, and splashed some water on his face. He found Blake in the kitchen feeding the stove.

An Investigation of Local Color

"I come in to keep the stove going," Blake said without looking up.

"Oh," Strauss said for lack of anything better.

There was some coffee in the Mr. Coffee on the counter, so he helped himself to a cup, black so he wouldn't have to poke around looking for cream and hoping it didn't come right out of the cow that morning.

"I didn't kill Dunfield," Blake said suddenly. He caught Strauss off-guard with his blunt statement. "I weren't up on Frampton Hill last night neither. I was upstreet looking for Adrian. I mighta gone to Frampton Hill if I knew she'd gone there, but I didn't."

Adrian's hired man stood up suddenly and faced him. His jaw was set stubbornly, but he didn't seem threatening.

"Did you tell this to Adrian before she went to work this morning?" Strauss asked.

"Yup. Now I'm telling you."

Strauss wondered if Adrian had suggested to Blake that he repeat his statement to the cop in charge, but he didn't ask. Les wasn't an especially big man, but he was strong-looking in the way of men who have always worked hard. Strauss had little doubt that in a good fight, all that mucking out and chopping wood and tossing hay would amount to something. All that loyalty would probably be a good motivating factor too. He wanted to believe the man had nothing to do with the murders, though he suspected he wanted it more for Adrian's sake than Les'.

"We're following up on some other leads, Les."

"I know. Adrian told me."

He moved to the counter and fixed himself a cup of coffee, but Strauss noticed that Blake kept an eye on him as if he were just as suspicious of him as Strauss was of Blake. He also noticed that Blake added thick white cream from a noncommercial container to his coffee before taking a big gulp. Strauss' stomach turned with a sickening desire for city life and all its additives and preservatives.

"You going to be coming around here often?" Blake asked. The man certainly didn't lack for subtlety.

237

Strauss was getting cold standing around with no shirt on and trying to look as if he didn't notice. He also thought he had a sliver in his foot from the wood floors in spite of their smooth, well-worn look. Somehow the whole experience, starting with last week and moving forward, was one he didn't want to repeat.

"It's not really in the plans, Les," he said. "We're just trying to get this case solved. The going was a little tough last night."

"Yup." Blake took another gulp of cream-ridden coffee. "Snowplow buried your car out by the road.

"Is that right?" he asked mildly. *"Oh, shit!"* his brain screamed.

"Yup. You get ready to leave, let me know. I'll give you a hand."

Blake finished the rest of his coffee and rinsed the cup. Then he went out into the cold. Strauss went to the window. Yup, the cruiser was sitting in a pile of snow, compliments of Junior and the town truck, only its flashers and the green-and-yellow state emblem on the driver's door were visible. Good thing it was Shubert's car because the chief was bound to squawk at what was left of it after a day's cruising in Benton Harbor.

He remembered that Shubert was stranded at Gwen's, a fate Strauss would have considered even more miserable than waking up with Elizabeth on his chest, but one that Shubert curiously hadn't seemed to mind volunteering for. He picked up the phone.

"Shubert? How are things up there?"

"Fine. Quiet all night. Gwen's just now leaving for work."

"She's calm?"

"Of course. Are you on the way?"

"As soon as I can dig your cruiser out of a snowbank."

"How'd you manage that?"

"I didn't. It happened in the night. Give me an hour, and I'll have you out of there."

"Okay. No hurry."

Strauss hung up. Shubert sounded strangely lighthearted this morning. Must be Gwen didn't have cats and kept her stove lit at night. Or was there something more? The thought was a little more

An Investigation of Local Color

than he could bear at the moment, so he went back upstairs and finished dressing.

Adrian didn't have anything as mighty as her Uncle Thibault's John Deere, but the tractor Les brought out was, nevertheless, a decent-sized farm tractor. Strauss dug through the snow to hook a chain to the frame of the car. He was getting pretty skilled at this end of the process, at any rate. Les might have had the lesser tractor, but he took no less pleasure in yanking the car from the snowbank and with similar results. The cruiser hit the ground this time with a rattle of loosened parts Strauss could only guess at, and when he handed the chain back Les was grinning from ear to ear

"There you are, Mr. Strauss."

The car must have sat a good six inches lower than it had at this time yesterday, Strauss thought. He was tempted to smile himself.

"Thanks, Mr. Blake."

He drove off to rescue his partner, hoping he wouldn't come across any deep snow or ruts in the road. He doubted the car could recover from much more abuse.

Shubert climbed into the car in a downright cheerful mood. He prattled on about what a remarkable woman Gwen was, how tough in the face of danger. Personally, Strauss couldn't see it, but he appreciated the change in his partner's demeanor even if it meant he was romanticizing about a woman who began to bellow when the shooting started and had to be restrained by someone a third her size.

As they were headed down the hill, they came across a couple walking down the drive the Glenns shared with their neighbors, the Kinneys. The weather had calmed, leaving the air crystal clear and bright with sun even if it was still cold. Strauss had passed several hunters going into and coming out of the woods on his way up the hill, but these two were obviously not of that variety, and since they were also not the Glenns he surmised that they must be the Glenns' sometime neighbors, the Kinneys. They were in their mid-fifties and were alike in their long, lanky physiques, though the woman had salon-platinum hair while Mr. had real gray. Both could have stepped right from the pages of the L.L. Bean catalogue. They wore boots of the variety that the sporting goods salesman had informed Strauss only the flatlanders wore and tucked into those were the sort of pants the catalogue specifically labeled hiking pants, though what made them hiking pants specifically was anyone's guess. Add to that colorful parkas with matching fleece hats and designer walking sticks and the picture was complete.

Strauss pulled off the road as far as he dared without the risk of getting stuck. Praying Junior wouldn't come along to finish the car off, he got out and introduced himself to the Kinneys.

"Yes, yes, a bit of excitement last night, eh?" Marlon Kinney said. He talked in clipped words, as if he was in a hurry to end the conversation before it even got started.

"Yes, there was. Did either of you happen to see anything unusual yesterday, either during the day or at night? Any strange cars on the road, maybe?"

Jane Kinney shook her platinum head. Strauss had always wondered how that color was achieved or why, for that matter, anyone would want it.

"We usually aren't here during the week at all, so any car would be strange to us unless it was the Glenns'. Besides, there are so many hunters up here now."

"How did you happen to be here during the week, if I might ask?"

"We came up for Dunfield's funeral," Marlon said.

"You did?" Strauss returned. He was surprised. "You were close then?"

"Not at all. I didn't care much for the man, personally. We came up to discuss the possibility of buying his property from his children."

Kinney spoke in a no-nonsense, frank manner. If he was sorry to see Dunfield dead, it didn't show.

"Have you been interested in his property for a while, then?"

"No, no," Jane put in. "We just got the idea when we heard he had died. We thought maybe it would be a good idea to buy it so that our children would have more room when they come to visit us. You know, they could stay in the farmhouse."

"Yes, yes," her husband echoed. "More comfortable all around."

An Investigation of Local Color

"I'm sure," Strauss agreed, though he wondered at their haste to put their neighbor's demise to such good use, not to mention their desire to house their children in a room where he had been brutally stabbed. Perhaps they didn't think in those terms.

"Mr. Kinney, did you have any problems with Mr. Dunfield?"

"No, no. Well, there was that little matter last summer when he sold my hayfield. You've heard about that from the neighbors, I take it?"

"Why don't you tell me about it?"

"Not much to tell. The man sold my hayfield to a farmer who came and mowed it, baled the hay, and then paid Dunfield for the use. I confronted him, but he said that the farmer had just gotten confused about the boundaries since Bill had used to own all the land at one time. That wasn't the story I got from the farmer. He said he had made an agreement with Dunfield to bale the entire area for the same price he always had. Dunfield told him he was acting as agent for all the property owners and would pay each his share. You can talk to Jack Glenn about it. Some of his land was involved, too."

"Were you angry about it?"

"Sure. We both were. It's the principle, you know. We own the land, pay taxes on it. We didn't exactly expect someone else to lease it out for profit."

"But it's not something people kill each other for, Officer," Jane added. "At least it isn't here in Vermont. That's one of the reasons we come here. It's so lovely. None of that kind of thinking. No violence."

It was on the tip of Strauss' tongue to remind her that having her neighbor stabbed with a hunting knife was a fairly violent act, when Shubert did it for him.

"Well, it's not like that happens all the time," Jane said as if once was perhaps excusable as long as another murder didn't mar the countryside. "Statistics show that Vermont is one of the least-violent states in the country."

That certainly makes it safe, Strauss thought. Too bad someone didn't inform Dunfield's murderer.

"I keep trying to tell poor Sally that, but she insists on being undone by all this commotion," Jane continued. "I assured her that it has nothing to do with us, but there is no convincing her. Why, her husband had to take the day off today because of the shooting last night. She was afraid...."

"Jane, Jane," her husband interrupted. Then he turned to Strauss. "We like to avoid that sort of thing when we come here to Vermont. After all, we come here to relax, don't we, dear?"

"Yes, we do," she agreed with a firm nod.

"And now, Detective, if there is nothing more, we need to be on our way. We've got to get back to town."

And they strode off taking the long, arm-swinging strides of people who have been taught how to walk properly for purposes of exercising. Their steps had the same hypertension that their words did. Strauss wondered what they were like when they were not benefiting from the effects of relaxation in Vermont.

Strauss had a couple of questions for Jack Glenn, but mindful of his rumpled clothes and day-old beard he decided it might be better if he headed back to Fairview and cleaned up first. He also wouldn't mind ditching Shubert in the process. That man, it turned out, didn't mind being ditched. He agreed that he needed some sleep after standing guard all night, and he headed back to the barracks in his sadly battered cruiser without even seeming to notice.

After retrieving his own car from the Hook, Line, and Sinker—because the Hook turned out to be the best plowed out place in town, he thankfully had spared the cruiser from the help of the locals—he headed back to his apartment. The sun was already starting to melt the November snow piled up on the streets of Fairview, but he had a little trouble finding a clear place to park anyway and in the process of sneaking between snowbanks he drew the attention of Mrs. Hutchins.

"Detective! I heard on the scanner that there were shots fired up in Benton Harbor. Are you okay?" she asked breathlessly. *Please, please give me some juicy news to tell my girlfriends,* she was really asking.

"I'm just fine, Mrs. Hutchins. Just a little excitement. It's all under control."

Mrs. Hutchins had a scanner?

An Investigation of Local Color

"But you were gone all night! It must have been very frightening. Whatever happened?"

"We're still investigating, ma'am." He dropped his voice to a conspiratorial tone. "Talking to suspects and such, I can't say too much right now. I'm sure you understand. I'll tell you all about it when I can."

"Of course," she whispered back.

He smiled his thanks and climbed his stairs with a wave. By the time he could tell her anything, it would all be in the newspapers anyway. In the meantime he avoided the issue, and she had just the right sort of secret to tell over the phone.

Strauss stood under his clanking shower until the hot water started to run out, then he dressed and reread the end of the Dunfield diary just in case he had missed something last night. Still, nothing jumped out at him. He tucked it away in one of his drawers and drove over to the barracks.

"Chief wants to see you right away. He's not a happy man this morning," the day dispatcher told him in a bored voice while she worked her chewing gum around her mouth in an unattractive manner.

Strauss thought the night dispatcher was about due for a promotion to the day shift. He tapped lightly on the chief's door.

"What's the story on Shubert's cruiser?" the boss asked mildly enough, though Strauss could see he wasn't feeling in a mild kind of mood.

"Didn't he tell you?"

"I'd like to hear it from you, Detective, since you're in charge on this case."

"Shubert had a little trouble with a snowbank, and a willing farmer with a very large tractor helped us out. Then I had a little snowbank problem of my own, and another willing farmer with another large tractor came along and helped with just about the same results."

"Are you being a smartass, Strauss?" The chief looked like he was about to let loose with a first-rate roar at any second.

"No, sir. I'm just telling you what happened."

"What happened is that the suspension and the springs and God only knows what else is totally gone on that cruiser. I have to file a report with Montpelier and try to explain why two of my men wrecked a perfectly good state car. I hate that kind of thing, Strauss. The taxpayers of this state expect and deserve a better performance."

Strauss digested that for a moment so that he would at least give the appearance of thinking before he spoke, but he said the first thing that came to his mind anyway.

"It seems to me, sir, that the taxpayers of this state, most specifically the taxpayers of Benton Harbor, assisted the cruiser into its present state. And I can assure you, sir, they didn't mind at all."

Chief Peterman got red in the face, but he didn't explode. He was a smart man and usually a rational man as well, when all was said and done. It just irked him to have a unsolved murder on his watch. The thought of some state official watching the clock tick while his men tried to find a suspect to arrest made him feel itchy and inept. Every time he answered a reporter's call asking for more information, he felt irritated that there was nothing new to offer, and he transferred that irritation to the man he held most responsible for the problem. Weren't these big-city boys supposed to be able to solve crimes the same day? Peterman knew Vermont troopers who made an arrest quicker than Strauss could get himself to Benton Harbor, although he had to admit that most of the arrests made by local boys were the results of incidents that had been witnessed by half a town. It was a little hard to avoid arrest if five neighbors saw the perpetrator drag his eighth deer of the season out of the woods or drive his oversized four-wheel drive across the village green in the middle of mud season while on a weekend drunk.

So Chief Peterman sighed and asked as patiently as he could, "Are you anywhere close to wrapping up this case?"

"You know, I think we are," Strauss said, although he didn't really think that at all. "We found a diary yesterday at the Dunfield residence, which has provided some new information that I'm just on my way to follow up."

"Any idea who fired the shots last night?"

"We have a likely suspect, but no weapon. The weather presented some unfortunate problems, but we're trying to work through them."

An Investigation of Local Color

"*We?* Can I take that to mean that you and Shubert are getting along?"

"Sir, Shubert proved himself invaluable last night. I was very glad to have had him along."

The chief looked for signs of sarcasm on Strauss' face. Strauss surprised himself by being at least partially serious. Certainly he wouldn't have wanted to guard Gwen all night.

"Well, then…Peterman seemed at a loss with Strauss' change of heart. "Well…carry on then, Detective. But try to close this thing, please. And Strauss?"

"Yes, sir?"

"No more damage to state vehicles. Understood?"

"Yes, sir. I'll do my best."

"No, do better than that. Take care of your cruiser. It is your own personal property since at the present time you are a Vermonter yourself."

"Now there's a frightening thought," Strauss muttered.

"Excuse me, Detective?"

"I said, 'Will do, sir.'"

On his way out, he stopped to inform the dispatcher that he was on his way back to Benton Harbor.

"Try to have a nice day," he added and was rewarded with the sneer that his sarcasm probably deserved.

He climbed into what was now his own personal cruiser, backed out of his parking space, and headed over the now-familiar road toward Frampton Hill. He found that although he was now master of the Hill itself, he had neither the courage nor very likely the skill to manage the steep, snow-covered Glenn driveway, so he backed the car into the entrance and left it. Hopefully, no one would come flying down the drive and plow into it. He would hate for that to happen to his personal property.

To his surprise, Strauss found the Glenns happily stomping through the snow, dragging brush to a huge burning pile. Jack waved to him with the same eager enthusiasm he had displayed while at his job.

"How are you, Detective Strauss?"

"I'm fine, Jack, thanks. I'm surprised to find you home today."

"You know, with all the excitement around here lately, and with those gunshots last night, I thought it might be a good day to stay home and just unwind. Spend some time with my wife."

The wife, for her part, gazed gratefully up at him, and he gave her head beneath its brightly colored wool cap an affectionate pat.

"You heard the shots, then?"

"No, we didn't. Milly Boyce called last night and told us. She was quite upset. Said you hadn't caught whoever it was. Of course, that gave us a nervous night, so I called in well at work. Get it? Called in well?"

Sally smiled as if her husband was the cleverest man on earth, and who knew? Maybe with a tampon he was. Strauss smiled tolerantly.

"I've been wanting to get this brush burned anyway. Les Blake helped me cut it earlier this fall, but he said I should wait for a good snow to burn it. All around, it seemed like the perfect day," Jack said enthusiastically.

"Honey, maybe Detective Strauss would like to come in for some coffee," Sally suggested, giving his sleeve a tug.

"Detective? I don't think this pile is going anywhere, ha, ha."

Strauss nodded, glad to step out of the deep snow, and then instantly regretted his decision. As they stepped out from around the fire pile, all four dogs surrounded them. All four tongues lolled out happily as they frisked around, but Strauss was certain they were watching him carefully for any perceived wrong move from him. To his dismay, Sally let them into the house and they hovered while the boots were removed.

There was already coffee made, and because Sally didn't look like the type to keep cream straight from the cow he felt safe in asking for it in his cup. Jack prattled on about the latest in the tampon business as if they were old pals. Sally didn't seem to mind the somewhat limited, social conversation. She just seemed happy to have her husband and her dogs around. The anxious, worried look she had worn on his previous visit was gone, as was her brightly colored exercise leotard. Strauss had to admit that he missed that part just a little. Now she was dressed in jeans and a sweater and, Strauss assumed due to the

An Investigation of Local Color

presence of her husband, she smiled and looked very nearly pretty, rather than compulsively fanatic.

"Actually, Jack, the business is what I came here to ask you about," Strauss began when he could get a word in. He sipped his coffee and savored the familiar taste of Cremora.

"Really? How can I help?"

"Remember the night last week when you were called in because of a problem, and it was fixed by the time you got there?"

"Yes, of course. It was rare that someone fixed it."

"Is there any chance that there never was a problem?"

"I'm not sure I understand you. Do you think I made it up?" Jack asked carefully.

For once his smile faded.

"Oh, no, Detective!" Sally interrupted. "There was really a problem. The phone is on my side of the bed, and I answered it."

Strauss remembered that Sally had initially told him that her husband was with her at the time of Dunfield's murder. Were they covering for each other now? His gaze went back and forth between the two. He couldn't believe it.

"Did the caller identify himself, Sally?"

She shook her head. "They never do. They always just ask for Jack."

Jack nodded in agreement. "Sometimes I know who it is, but just as often it's just one of the foremen who says he has a problem he can't fix."

"So you don't know who it was that night?"

"I'm afraid not. He might have said, but I didn't catch it."

"But definitely a male caller?"

The Glenns looked doubtfully at each other.

"I don't wake up easily, Detective," Jack admitted. "I assumed it was a male, but the truth is that at 3 in the morning, usually all I hear is that they need me in there. Sally?"

"It was a deep voice, and I guess I assumed it was a man, too. Now that you ask, it could have been a woman's voice as well. I'm sorry."

"Does it matter?" Jack asked.

"I'm not sure. But it is possible that anyone might have called you and got you to come in?"

"Yeah, I guess it's possible. I never had a false alarm before, but I guess it could happen. What would be the point, though?" For a mechanical genius, the man could be a little thick, Strauss thought. "You have no alibi, Jack, for the time of the murder. Unless you're guilty, and I'm guessing you're not, I think someone was hoping to leave you unprotected by placing you on the road at the time someone was killing Dunfield."

Sally's face paled. "Why would anyone do that? Jack doesn't have any enemies, do you, honey?"

"Not that I know of." He looked baffled and more than a little hurt.

"It might not be that someone dislikes Jack, it might be that someone was protecting himself by using Jack. I found a diary in Dunfield's house that refers to someone called L. The entry says that L. was mad on the day before Dunfield was killed. Can either of you help me out with that?"

They both thought a minute. Jack shook his head.

"The only L. I can think of is Les Blake. I haven't seen him for a while, but he wouldn't have killed Bill."

Get in line with that opinion, Strauss thought to himself. "Do you know Lee Stout, Jack? Works for your company, first shift."

"No. I know Lily Stout, though. You must have met her the other day when you were in. She works in Dunfield's area."

The bell in Strauss' head went off. He reached for his notebook and flipped to his notes on Lee Stout. Wife—Lily, second shift, NET.

"Youngish woman, fairly heavy?"

"That sounds like Lily. But as far as I know, she got along well with Dunfield. That particular group always worked well together with no complaints, at least not on the overlap. They are all very productive."

"I need you to do a little policework for me, Jack. Get on the phone with whoever would have been in charge of the second shift last Thursday night, and see if any of the four workers in Dunfield's area were held over into the third shift. Can you do that?"

An Investigation of Local Color

Jack nodded. "Sure. It might take some time, though, because the second-shift foremen won't be there now. I'd have to go into Personnel or maybe Accounting."

"That's okay. See what you can do."

Jack jumped to his feet, always at his best with something to do. Sally poured Strauss another cup of coffee while they waited and added a liberal dose of Cremora.

"Sally, this is about the best coffee I've ever had," he told her honestly.

She beamed, her worry over her husband temporarily forgotten, but just as quickly revived when they heard Jack's voice on the phone.

"I wish this would end," she said quietly. "I'm afraid I made him stay home today because I was so scared. But I can't ask him to do it again. It kills him not to go to work. Jack's work is his life."

A picture of Jack on the floor of the New England Tampon Company, rubbing his hands together eagerly, a white string dangling from his shirt pocket, flashed through Strauss' mind. He wondered if Sally had ever visited her husband's place of business.

Jack came back into the living room. "According to last week's timesheets, no one was held over from second shift except a foreman who was covering for a friend whose wife was in labor, and a maintenance man who works on the overheads. Neither one was in our section of the plant. Usually, no holdovers means that things were running smoothly all week. That was certainly my impression, except for that one incident we talked about."

Strauss stood up. "Good. Thanks, Jack."

Jack frowned. "Do you know who killed Bill, Detective?"

"I'm not sure, but you've certainly helped me narrow the field. If you think of anything else, give me a call."

"We'll do that. Thanks for coming by, Detective. We feel a lot better just talking to you."

Jack smiled. He saw Strauss to the door and kept his arm protectively around his wife. Sally looked worried but overall had a much more pleasant outlook than on his previous meetings with her. Strauss thought the Glenns were either the only happily married couple on Frampton Hill or their acting abilities were far superior to those of their neighbors. Whatever the case, it didn't rule them out as murder suspects—motive and opportunity, after all—but Strauss believed they were as sincere as they seemed. Mostly that was what he wanted to believe because someone had to be what they appeared to be in this place.

He walked down the driveway to the place where he had abandoned his car. The sun was rapidly turning yesterday's snow to a heavy slush, which would make driving easier if it didn't re-freeze again in the night and create huge icy ruts. He got in, started the car, and began to pull into the road before he noticed the snowplow making its way steadily and with surprising speed up the Hill. Before he could change direction to avoid it, the huge plow blade deposited hefty amount of slush and sand and mud onto the hood and windshield of Strauss' own personal vehicle. He could almost hear the green-and-yellow Vermont state paint job crack under the grit. He followed Junior's progress up the road and saw a huge arm waving merrily from the driver's-side window. Not much he could do, he thought, if the citizens of the state didn't want to take care of their cars. He started down the hill.

When he was a mile from Fairview, the radio crackled and the dispatcher called him.

"Strauss here."

"I've got Trooper Shubert on the phone, Detective. He says it's important that he get in touch with you concerning the Benton Harbor case."

"Where is he?" Wasn't the man supposed to be sleeping? Just when Strauss was starting to see some value in the man, he goes off on his own.

"Rutland."

"What's he doing there?"

"I'm just the dispatcher, Detective. I don't know anything."

"I'm almost to Fairview. Tell him I'll call him in five minutes."

Strauss considered the possibility of recommending the day dispatcher for a big-city position for which she was well qualified in terms of charm, and promoting his friend from the graveyard shift

An Investigation of Local Color

onto days. The charmer handed him Shubert's Rutland number without comment or even looking up from her *People* magazine as he passed by her desk.

"Holiday Inn, Rutland," came the response to his dial.

"Trooper Shubert, please."

"That you, Strauss?" The younger man sounded excited. That could only mean one of two things: He had either solved the case, which seemed unlikely, or he had reunited with Gwen, which seemed more probable since he was at her place of business.

"Of course it's me. Who else would be calling you there? What's up?"

"Gwen got a threatening note in her mail here at the Holiday Inn. She called me right away," he added proudly. "I told her she should call me at home if anything came up."

"What did the note say."

"I'm quoting now, Okay?"

"I assumed you would be. Could you just get on with it?" Strauss could keep neither the impatience nor the sarcasm out of his voice.

"'I'll try again. You won't escape next time.' Sounds pretty threatening to me. Gwen is quite upset."

"I can imagine," Strauss replied. "Why don't you stay right there with her. I'm going to make a couple of phone calls, and I'll be there in a short while."

"Will do," Shubert replied happily. More guard duty.

Strauss hung up, then dialed the phone company. He asked for long-distance phone records for late Thursday night and early Friday morning for both Dunfield residences and the New England Tampon Company.

"As soon as possible," he added.

ASAP still meant a couple of hours on the unsophisticated computer systems of the local phone company that handled the Benton Harbor lines, but they did have a fax machine, he was told with a certain amount of pride, and they would fax him his information as soon as they could get it. That would have to be good enough. He told the dispatcher he was expecting it and needed to be informed as soon as the information came across the wire. She nodded non-committally.

Maybe his multi-ticketed gum-chewing friend from the *Rutland County Enquirer* could use a new job.

Strauss found Gwenivere Dunfield happily doing her job as the front desk receptionist at the Holiday Inn while her bodyguard, Gary Shubert, lounged on one of the lobby couches protecting her. She didn't look in any way rattled by her brush with death the night before or by her more recent encounter with her would-be killer via the postal service. As soon as she had serviced her two customers, a pair of middle-aged business men in suits, and sent them off with a cheerful little wave and room keys, she immediately lapsed into the dramatic. With a hand to her massive bosom, she immediately appeared undone and on the verge of tears. Strauss decided, after several confrontations with her, that this was something that Gwen needed to work on a bit more. She wasn't terribly good at conjuring up tears in spite of her best efforts. Lack of tears did rather destroy the effect she was striving so hard for.

"Oh, Detective! I'm so happy to see you. I was so dreadfully frightened!"

"I'm sorry for that, Ms. Dunfield," Strauss replied in a voice that sounded considerably less than sorry, even to himself.

Ms. Dunfield, in her terror, managed not to notice. She continued on. "Of course, I called Gary right away, as he said I should."

Gary beamed happily at her while his partner raised his eyebrows at her use of his first name.

"He has been SUCH a comfort to me," she added, rewarding him with a smile. "I just don't know how I could have gone on without him."

"Well, that is what the Vermont State Police are here for, Ms. Dunfield, to serve our taxpayers." *That, and to guard the taxpayers' patrol cars*, he added to himself. "Could I see the note, please?"

Gwen handed over a plain white piece of paper.

"I'll try again. You won't escape next time."

An Investigation of Local Color

Just as Shubert had quoted to him over the phone. It was written in large, plain printing as if someone either hadn't mastered his handwriting skills or was making an attempt to disguise them.

"Where's the envelope?"

"The envelope?" Shubert repeated mindlessly. His face suddenly got very red. He exchanged glances with Gwen.

"The envelope this came in. Where is it?"

"Gwen?" Shubert passed the buck.

She waved her hands around uselessly, her massive jowls jiggling in irritation. "I don't know. I can't recall what I did with it. How can I keep track of everything when I've been so terrified?" Her voice rose in a manner that was becoming both familiar and increasingly annoying to Strauss.

"How about the rest of the mail. What did you do with that? Did you throw anything away or take it to other people here at the hotel?"

"I don't know! I just can't think!"

Shubert stepped around the desk and put a comforting arm around her shoulders. "Now, now. Just calm down, Gwen. We can work this out."

"Did you see an envelope, Shubert?" Strauss persisted.

"No, I did not," the younger trooper shot back angrily. "Would you stop with the envelope for a minute? There is no sense in harassing the victim, is there?"

Not if we're sure she's the victim, Strauss thought.

"Let's check the rubbish," Shubert suggested to Gwen.

It was a vain suggestion, however, for the trash had been emptied by the cleaning lady before Strauss' arrival. Dispatching Shubert to track her down proved equally futile, as all the trash from the entire facility had been trucked off earlier and was probably at this very minute being incinerated. Gwen, naturally, could remember no return address or postmark.

Anything mailed in Rutland last night after the shooting attempt would have reached the Holiday Inn that morning. It probably wouldn't have been too difficult for someone to have slipped the message into the Holiday Inn's daily mail either. For that matter, it would have also been possible for Gwen to have written the note herself to turn possible suspicion for Bill's murder away from herself. Someone had certainly been shooting at her last night, though. Unless she had an accomplice who was just trying to make it appear that Gwen was being threatened. Lee Stout, perhaps?

"Ms. Dunfield, do you have a safe place you can go after work this evening? A friend, maybe some family?"

She thought a moment. "I guess I could go to my mother's. She lives in Connecticut. It would mean taking some time off work." She stopped suddenly, then wailed, "Oh, no, but my horse, my Beauty. Who would feed him?"

"Now Gwen. Your own safety is much more important than a horse," Shubert soothed.

He really is very good at this, Strauss thought.

"He's right, Ms. Dunfield. I'm sure we can make some arrangements for the horse. Trooper Shubert can also speak with your boss and explain the necessity of a brief vacation for you."

The grateful Ms. Dunfield gazed at her champion, and Strauss could have sworn she actually batted her eyes at him. The champion, for his part, gazed back happily.

Good God, groaned Strauss inwardly. He put the threatening note into his pocket and motioned for Shubert to walk out with him.

"What are we going to do now?" the younger man asked.

"You are going to stay with Gwen until she's off work. Then you and I are going to spend the night at her house in hopes that our shooter carries out his threat to return."

Shubert's eyes widened. "You mean a stakeout?"

Strauss marveled that anyone actually got excited by a stakeout. After numerous excruciatingly boring, sleepless nights that yielded up nothing more often than not, he couldn't believe that anyone could possibly be intrigued by the notion of a stakeout. Even if Strauss managed to collar a suspect, he invariably gained an acid stomach from smoking too many cigarettes and drinking too much coffee. He could rid himself of the stomach by drinking a bottle of Maalox, but it

An Investigation of Local Color

usually returned as soon as he found out that some clever lawyer had gotten the suspect back out on the street within six hours of arrest.

"Listen, Shubert, this is to be kept very quiet. Don't tell Gwen we are staking out her house. Put her in her car at the end of her shift, and make sure she heads for Connecticut. We need a break on this case, and we aren't going to get it if the whole world is in on our plans."

"But it's Gwen's life that is in danger. Shouldn't she be kept apprised of the situation?"

"No, Shubert, she shouldn't. And if she finds out somehow, I will make sure you are driving Route 4 for the rest of your career." The Vermont equivalent of walking a beat in Boston, an effective threat where a state patrolman was concerned. "I hope you understand."

"Perfectly, Detective. You are still considering Gwen a suspect, in spite of the fact that the real suspect is staring you right in the face, and you refuse to admit it. I'd like to know how you think Gwen could shoot at herself."

"I don't have time for this, Shubert. While you're here, see if you can find anyone who might have seen someone suspicious hanging around here this morning, particularly in whatever area the mail is delivered in. Neither of us ever saw an envelope, you know," Strauss said with a pointed look.

"Gwen wouldn't lie," Shubert said.

"That seems to be what everybody says about Les Blake."

Shubert had no comeback for that, so Strauss got into his cruiser with the order to meet back at the barracks in the early evening.

Just as he was returning to the station himself, Strauss heard the sound of a bell alerting anyone who cared to hear, not the day dispatcher, certainly, that a fax was on the way. It was the information from the local phone company. The information from the Rutland company was already in his box. He took both copies and a phone book to his desk.

No calls had been placed from Dunfield's phone on the night of the murder. One had been placed from Gwen's phone at 11:45.

Strauss looked it up in the book. Lee Stout. They had talked for under two minutes. About what? he wondered.

He reached for the NET phone records. Even a company as large as NET didn't make many long-distance phone calls at that time of night, but Strauss had expected at least one to the Benton Harbor exchange. There were none. He checked the Glenns' number in the book, but it didn't match anything NET employees had made on the night of Dunfield's murder.

Strauss picked up the phone and asked for Lee Stout's phone records for the same time period to be faxed. While he waited, he tried to sort out the tangle that the case had become. Earlier in the day, he had thought Jack Glenn had helped narrow it down. Now he wasn't so sure. Had anyone ever really called the Glenns? Sally's story had changed course, he reminded himself again. Was she covering for an adored husband while he went off to stab an annoying neighbor? Or had he covered for her when she came home with blood on her hands? Sally wasn't a large woman, but she certainly had built up a significant amount of muscle through her obsession with exercise.

And what about Gwen? Talk about motive and opportunity. But she would need help. Was she getting it from Lee Stout? Of all the possible suspects, he had always seemed the least likely to Strauss based solely on the fragility of his arms. How could such skeletal arms drive a knife through one while a struggle ensued? Gwen could have managed, however.

Or was he simply guilty of ignoring what was right in front of his face, as Shubert said? Les Blake had done the stabbing. But if that was true he, too, would have needed help to get a note so quickly to Gwen this morning in Rutland. Strauss hated how quickly his brain reminded him that Adrian had left early this morning for Rutland. There was the matter of last night's weapon, though. He had seen for himself that it wasn't one of Adrian's. Or was it? He had no idea how many guns she owned, and he only had her word, as well, that Les himself didn't own a gun. By Adrian's own description, life in her much-loved hometown wasn't always pretty. Had that been an admission of sorts?

An Investigation of Local Color

The fax bell rang again. Lee Stout's phone records revealed no long-distance calls made the night of the murder. If anyone had called the Glenns that night, it had to have been locally.

Strauss groaned. He had the same list of suspects he had had from the beginning, i.e. anyone in Benton Harbor. He prayed the culprit would show tonight. More than one night on stakeout with Shubert would probably make him as crazy as they said he was already.

Across the room the phone on the dispatcher's desk rang.

"Phone, Detective," she called.

It was Adrian. *Careful,* Strauss cautioned himself. *Do good policework.* But even though he had had some time to think about it, he couldn't decide whether to tell Adrian about the stakeout. If she was involved and told Les, they would be left with the same blank they had seemed unable to fill in all along, and he would have the same nagging suspicion he had been unable and unwilling to prove.

"Did you talk to Les this morning?" he asked to stall for time. He knew what her answer would be.

"Yes. He says he didn't do it." Now there was a surprise.

"He said the same thing to me."

"What about the Glenns?"

"The only L. they could come up with is either Les—Sally says he wouldn't kill anyone, incidentally—or one Lily Stout, wife of Gwen's Witness friend who worked on second shift in the same area as Dunfield. Glenn says they got along fine, as far as he knows. While I was busy doing that, someone was busy delivering a threatening message to Gwen at the Holiday Inn that in effect said he wasn't done trying to do her in."

There was a long silence while Adrian either waited for him to say more or tried to come up with a suitable reply. Strauss didn't bother asking her if Blake had given her anything to mail. She would have said no even as Strauss revealed to her what she had mailed for her friend.

"Any idea where it came from?" she asked finally.

"I got plenty of ideas."

"Is there any chance that Gwen wrote it herself, you know, for attention or to throw us off track?"

"The thought crossed my mind. At any rate, she is leaving for her mother's in Connecticut as soon as she gets off work this afternoon, and we are staking out her house in hopes that the shooter will put in the repeat performance he is threatening. Want to join us?" Strauss asked before he could stop himself.

"And the us would be...?"

"Trooper Shubert and me."

"Strauss, the man nearly fainted last night when the shooting started. Are you sure you want him backing you up?"

"I don't have any choice, Constable. A stakeout takes two people. The man is my partner."

"You need a new partner."

"I know that. But as far as I'm concerned there is only one way of getting rid of one, and they told me I had to stop doing that if I wanted to continue being a cop. So are you coming?"

"I guess I'd better."

"Good. Bring coffee. We'll pick you up at five. Oh, and Adrian?"

"Yes?"

"No one knows about this. Okay?"

"I understand that, Strauss. But Les didn't do it." And Adrian firmly hung up.

God, the woman was stubborn! Strauss smiled.

"Why are we turning here? This isn't the way to Gwen's house," Shubert said in an annoyed voice.

He was dressed head to foot in camouflage hunting clothes, complete with a camouflage cap. He even had dark green and black greasepaint on his face so that his pasty complexion couldn't be seen in the dark. Strauss was uncertain if this disguise was the result of watching too many police dramas or if Shubert had hung out too much with the often fanatical, even by Vermont standards, bow hunters who crept through the woods in search of deer before the rifle hunters were turned loose.

An Investigation of Local Color

"We're picking up Constable Thibault," Strauss informed him for the first time.

"You've got to be kidding!"

"Actually, I'm perfectly serious. Do I look like I'm kidding?"

Strauss touched the brakes of his battered Skylark and felt that soggy feeling that called attention to the need for new brakes. How irritating. How long had he been ignoring them? he wondered, barely listening to his partner.

"Now that you've told her what we're doing, she's probably had the chance to warn Blake. The whole damn night's going to be a waste of time. I don't know about you, but I've got better things to do than sit around an empty house all night waiting for a killer who knows we're waiting for him."

Strauss looked at the younger man. He looked petulant, an expression that didn't especially go well with camouflage face paint.

"Is there something good on TV tonight, Shubert?"

"Very funny."

"Like it or not, Shubert, Adrian is working on this case with us. The murder took place in her town, after all, and I'm sure she is as interested in finding the killer as we are."

"Not if it's Les Blake, she isn't," Shubert snapped.

"You know, you're never going to become a serious cop if you insist on constantly focusing in on one suspect to the exclusion of all the rest. Blake isn't our only suspect here."

"He's a killer, Strauss. I know it. He's a murderer, and Constable Thibault is covering for him. I can't explain it to you, but I just FEEL it. I felt it the first time I met the man after the Borden murder, and I feel it now. It's an instinct. And if we don't catch someone tonight, it will be because you warned Adrian. I almost think that you don't want to catch the killer."

"Yeah. I just thought I'd spend a relaxing evening in a strange house with you and Constable Thibault for company." Strauss lit a cigarette and rolled down his window before Shubert could complain.

Adrian was watching for them. She came out of the house wearing dark, but not camouflage clothes, and carrying a thermos, and got into the back seat of the Skylark.

"Evening, Constable," Strauss said cheerfully.

"Detective."

She said nothing to Shubert. He scowled over his shoulder.

"Hello, Adrian. What's your hired hand doing this evening?"

"I wouldn't know, Trooper. I didn't ask him."

"Right." And because he couldn't think of any other way of drawing her out, Shubert was forced to remain silent.

In the mirror, Strauss saw Adrian settled back in the seat, obviously not in the mood to bait or be baited.

It was dark in Gwen's house when they arrived. The clear weather that had produced the sun and snowmelt earlier in the day now brought a sparkling cold night. They left the car in front of the house to give the appearance of someone being home. As they got out, a forlorn whinny greeted them. The horse! Damn, he had forgotten.

"Someone has to feed the horse," he said in a low voice.

"Don't look at me," Shubert returned. "You're the one who volunteered."

The man was afraid of animals, too. Strauss was disgusted. He cast a look at Adrian. She looked back.

"You volunteered."

"Come on, Adrian. At this point I know more about cows than about horses. Help me out here."

She shrugged and started for the barn.

"Go on in the house and turn on a few lights, Shubert, but stay away from the windows."

Any shooter in his right mind would run if he peered through the window and saw this imitation survivalist. Strauss followed Adrian, careful to watch for any strange movement. A quick trip up Frampton Hill had revealed no strange vehicles, but perhaps if the shooter showed tonight he would use a different tactic. Then again, came the unwelcome thought, maybe Shubert was right.

An Investigation of Local Color

He went into the barn before Adrian and looked around. It was a small building with no real place to hide, except in the hayloft, which this time of year was stuffed full with hay. The horse nickered softly. Adrian showed him how to feed it some grain in a bucket, though it was a skill Strauss had no intention of following up on. He had to admit, though, that the little barn with its single horse and warm hay smell was a significant improvement over the dairy barns he had been in. They switched off the light and waited for their eyes to reaccustom to the dark before going out into the cold.

Inside the house Shubert had turned on too many lights. Strauss switched off all but a couple of table lamps in the living room and a bedside lamp in Gwen's bedroom. He had no trouble identifying her touch there since the bed and its overhead canopy were all dressed in the pink ruffles she seemed to favor all her furniture with. That done, Strauss herded his partners into the dark kitchen to wait.

What was left of Shubert's enthusiasm for the stakeout after he discovered Adrian was coming along disappeared with his enormous ham grinder and 16-ounce Coke. At that point he learned what Strauss had known all along—that stakeouts were an exercise in excruciating boredom that was little relieved by sitting on hard kitchen chairs in the dark waiting for something to happen. When Strauss lit a cigarette, he jumped up angrily.

"You know, that's really rude! Gwen doesn't even smoke, and you're polluting her house."

"Well, now, I'm truly sorry about that, Shubert. I'm sure Gwen would consider it a small price to pay to have the State Police defend her."

"How would you know what Gwen thinks?"

Strauss didn't bother with an answer. Adrian handed him a cup of coffee and poured one for herself. In the dark he examined it as best as he could for signs of cream.

"Do you think it could be one of the Glenns?" she asked in a low voice.

"It crossed my mind," Strauss admitted. "I checked some phone records today, and the numbers called from NET on the night Dunfield was killed don't include the Glenns'. Something keeps bothering me about that problem on second and third shift. But Sally didn't like Bill. Why go after Gwen last night?"

"How sure are we that someone was after her last night?"

"Of course someone was after her!" Shubert jumped in angrily. "She wasn't shooting through her own front window, Constable."

Adrian ignored his outburst and turned to Strauss. "What about Lee? Did you check up on his whereabouts last night?"

Strauss shook his head.

"Who is Lee?" Shubert asked.

"Gwen's former lover," Adrian informed him. "At least they say they are former lovers."

Shubert jumped to his feet. He was so angry, he sputtered when he spoke, spraying both Adrian and Strauss.

"You are really a piece of work, you know that, Mrs. Borden," he said nastily. His scornful use of Adrian's married name didn't escape her. "You sit there casting the blame on everyone but the one person it should be placed on. I want to know why you are protecting Les Blake."

"I'm not protecting Les," Adrian snapped back. "He didn't do anything."

"Maybe you were in on it with him. Maybe it wasn't just once either."

"Don't be ridiculous." She looked up at Shubert, who used his considerable size to tower above her in what appeared to be an intimidating manner.

Strauss thought he should put a stop to the argument, especially as Shubert's voice was becoming loud, but in the back of his mind he knew that if Adrian was truly involved in any of this she couldn't go on forever without slipping up. Shubert wasn't smart enough to intentionally draw her out, but he might accidently do it.

"I don't have any reason to want either of the Dunfields dead."

"No. One of them was just sleeping with your husband, and the other couldn't keep his hands off any woman in town. If he makes a play for the town constable, well, just have the hired hand knock him off. It's been done before."

Without bothering to get to her feet, Adrian tossed what was left of her coffee in Shubert's face. Cool coffee combined with green

An Investigation of Local Color

greasepaint to smear all over that man's face when he tried to wipe it off. He would have looked more than a little amusing if he hadn't had such a dangerous expression. Adrian stared back in the expressionless manner she often adopted. Strauss stopped the younger man by placing a firm hand against his wet shirt when he made a move toward Adrian.

"That's enough," he said. He pushed Shubert roughly into one of the chairs. "Sit. Stay there and be quiet, for God's sake." Then he grabbed Adrian, though more gently, by the arm and pulled her to her feet. "You come with me. And they wonder why I can't work with partners," he muttered.

He went down the dark hallway to what was a spare bedroom, though there was no furniture in it.

"Have a seat," he said, indicating the floor since there was no place else. Then he went back to the kitchen and got the thermos and a saucer for his cigarette ashes. On his way out he turned to Shubert. "Get some sleep. I'll wake you if anyone managed not to hear you and shows up. Either that, or I'll just let them shoot you."

Shubert sneered at him, his face a slimy mess. "You can be sure that the chief will hear about this, Strauss."

"I've no doubt."

He returned to the empty room where he'd left Adrian and handed her the thermos.

"Shubert is definitely not a man who does well when he misses his nap," he commented mildly.

Adrian didn't reply. Strauss smoked a cigarette in silence. He glanced over at her. Her jaw was set stubbornly.

"You're a mean woman with a cup of coffee."

Adrian almost smiled. "Yeah, well, he's been asking for it for years. Coffee's pretty harmless, but it makes the point."

Strauss finished his cigarette and started another. His stomach would surely be shrieking in the morning, but the waiting was hard for him to bear. Maybe it was the same for Adrian because she was working on her third cup of coffee. Or maybe she wasn't really waiting for something the way he was. But sitting on the floor, their backs against the wall, their shoulders nearly touching, it wasn't an idea he wanted to spend too much time on.

"This Frampton Hill is probably the strangest place I've ever come across. There's Gwen building a house across the road from her ex; the Boyces saving all their money to come to this beautiful country spot only to find a nightmarish boredom; the Glenns building their dreamhouse, which Sally is afraid to be alone in; the Kinneys, who come here to relax but can't seem to get the job done in twenty-four hours or less. I thought there were a lot of quirky things in the city, but I never saw as strange a group as this."

Adrian rubbed her eyes. She looked tired after a full day's work on a nearly sleepless night. "It's hard to know whether to feel sorry for any of them or whether to think it serves them right."

"Why is that?" Strauss reached for the coffee.

"Tourists come up here to Vermont when they're on vacation, and they see this quaint little place with its easygoing, slow-moving lifestyle, and they think it's just the solution for their stress or their bad marriages or whatever else ails them. Once here they miss what they left, they want to change everything when they discover that cows are less than picturesque and all the pretty green hillsides turn to muck after the spring rains."

"I must not qualify as a tourist, then, because I never thought cows were even remotely picturesque, and after having gotten up close and personal with them they have done nothing to alter that opinion. And personally, I was hoping to miss the spring rains altogether, but my supervisor tells me there is little chance of that if I hope to remain a cop."

"You don't like the cows?"

"They stink, Adrian."

"They do?"

He nodded. She laughed.

"Well, at least you're honest. It's better than aspiring to be a farmer when you can't stand the hard work or the stink. So you're stuck here through the spring?"

An Investigation of Local Color

"Unfortunately, the Boston PD has the same idea about Vermont as the tourists do. I'm supposed to come back to the city a changed man after my slow-moving, easygoing, picturesque assignment here is up. I have my doubts about my very survival, though, if I have to go on many stakeouts with Shubert and you."

"You outsiders always expect too much." But she didn't say it with any malice in her voice.

They lapsed into a companionable silence in which Strauss entertained thoughts of kissing the woman beside him. He wondered if she just might be thinking the same thing. It certainly would turn this into the most wonderful stakeout of his life.

"The answer is right in front of us, if we could just think what it is," Adrian said softly, thereby bursting the bubble of her partner's imaginings.

As if in reply, there was a heavy clunk from the direction of the closet across from where they sat. Adrian and Strauss looked questioningly first at each other, then at the door, but before either of them could react it burst open to reveal a large woman dressed completely in camouflage. What was it about these people that they felt they had to dress like that for a night out? Strauss wondered. Then he noticed that she had a very large deer rifle. As she stepped out of the closet to give herself more room, she lifted it and aimed it with badly shaking hands at the law enforcers sitting on the floor.

"I couldn't stay in there a minute more. I was about to suffocate," she said, as if an explanation were required.

"Who the hell are you?" Adrian asked. She seemed more perturbed than alarmed.

"Adrian, meet Mrs. Lee Stout. Lily, isn't it?"

The woman nodded, looking extremely unhappy. The rifle waggled dangerously in their direction. Strauss couldn't help thinking that this was about the most unlikely looking Lily he had ever seen. Stout must have a thing for enormous blonde-haired women, because the one in front of him now very nearly matched the dimensions of the woman he had taken for a lover.

Adrian must have been thinking the same thing, for she leaned over and whispered, "Skinny Lee! Who'd have thought?"

"Why were you in the closet, Lily?" Strauss asked gently. He kept his eyes on her trigger finger.

"I was waiting for the sleaze that stole my husband. I've been waiting for hours. I didn't expect no cops. That's what you are, ain't it? Ain't you that cop who came snooping around the plant?"

Strauss nodded. In the dark he wasn't certain if Lily's eyes had the crazed look of one who could suddenly fly off the handle with a misplaced word or thought, but he could hear without any doubt the harsh anger in her deep voice. The fact that she wore hunting fatigues and appeared to know what a rifle was for was similarly bothersome.

"So what now, Lily?" he asked calmly. He wondered where Shubert was. Could the man possibly have done what he told him for a change and gone to sleep? Hell of a time to opt for obedience.

"I'll have to kill you now. God, I wish everyone would stop getting in the way so I could kill the right person!" Her voice rose in much the same manner as Gwen's did.

Stout really did know how to choose a woman. Unlike Gwen, though, Lily's hysteria seemed to be the real thing.

"I left my rifle in the kitchen," Adrian whispered.

"What?!"

"In the kitchen. I couldn't...."

"Stop that! Stop whispering!" Lily screamed. "It's skinny little bitches like you that wreck perfectly good marriages!"

Even in the dark Strauss saw the hatred in the woman's eyes, and he thought he saw her finger twitch. Without waiting to see, he threw himself on top of Adrian at the same time he heard the ear-shattering gunshot. Adrian yelped softly. Ah, the woman could be frightened. Strauss didn't think she had been hurt, though, because he felt a burning pain shoot through his own left thigh and felt the blood stream down his leg.

"Why'd you do that?" Adrian asked in a fierce whisper.

"I didn't want you to get hit," he replied. It seemed pretty obvious to him.

An Investigation of Local Color

"She'd have missed, Nick."

"I wouldn't have! I'd have hit you!" Lily roared and promptly put another bullet through Gwen's pink wall, not far from Adrian's head, showering them with sheetrock dust.

"Whoa there, Lily," he said in a voice he hoped sounded calmer than he felt.

Keep her talking, he told himself while he gritted his teeth. Surely Shubert was awake now. He felt Adrian's hand on the back of his neck. She knew he was hit and tried to help them both keep cool.

"Before you shoot us," Adrian's hand nearly strangled him then, "maybe you could just help us with this problem that has really been bothering us for the last few days. Can you do that?"

"I guess so," she replied meekly enough.

"If you were after Gwen all along, how come you killed Bill?"

"It was sort of an accident," Lily answered in the same way one might say "Oops, I spilled milk on the floor."

"Lily, the man had a hunting knife sticking out of his chest."

"I know. It was messy, too. And I really, really liked Bill." Lily's voice wavered for a moment. Then she went on in a stronger tone. "But I got the wrong house. I thought Gwenivere lived in the farmhouse. When I got home from work early that night and Lee wasn't there, I came here to kill her. She wasn't home either, so I figured the two of them were out together and I hid in the closet. I heard her come in, only it wasn't her, it was Bill. When I jumped out of the closet with the knife and he recognized me, I really had no choice, did I?"

"You were going to kill Gwen with a knife?" Adrian asked.

"Shut up!" Lily screamed at her.

Where in the hell is Shubert? Strauss wondered.

But Lily continued calmly. "Then I called Mr. Glenn and said there was a problem at work. I figured he'd go there, and his wife would be at home, and Gwenivere would be with my husband, and a lot of folks wouldn't have no alibis. Pretty clever, huh? Who would ever come looking for me?"

"Pretty clever, Lily," Strauss agreed. His leg was really beginning to ache, and he worried about the amount of blood gushing down his leg. "How about last night? How did you get away?"

She seemed surprised by the question. "I just drove over the hill in my Jeep."

"Yes, but how did you know you could do that?"

He felt a bit lightheaded. Adrian rubbed the back of his neck to keep him going.

"Easy. I went deer hunting with everyone else. I scouted the whole area and found out where I'd gone wrong with the houses. Then I made a plan. It was a good one, too, until that skinny bitch there turned up."

Strauss guessed she meant Adrian since Gwen didn't really qualify. Since skinny bitches seemed to set the woman off, he asked, "Lily, did you ever actually see Gwenivere?"

"No, but Bill talked all about her when he told me about her and Lee having an affair. He said she was tall and skinny with long legs like a model. I knew Lee would never look at me again while he could have her." There was an insane sadness in her voice.

"Bill lied to you. Gwen doesn't look at all like that."

"No?"

"No. She is quite overweight and not at all glamorous, I'm afraid."

"Liar! Liar!" she screamed. "Why would Lee leave me for someone who looks just like me?"

"That's what I'd like to know," Adrian whispered.

"You're just saying that to throw me off. Well, I ain't letting you go! I have to kill you. You know about me now."

"What good would killing us do, Lily?"

"Ha, you think I'm stupid, but I'm not. You didn't know it was me until I stepped out of the closet, so no one else knows either. I don't got nothing against you two, but I don't want to go to prison just for the sake of leaving you alive. 'Course, it was really Gwenivere I wanted to kill all along, and I guess I'll kind have to leave off that idea, at least for the time being. It never looked like it would be so

An Investigation of Local Color

hard to kill someone when you watch the TV." Her voice rose again to a scream. "But it ain't my fault that everyone got in the way!"

"There's another man in the kitchen, you know," Strauss informed her. "It might be hard to kill us all."

"There ain't no one else here." But Lily looked uncertainly toward the door.

"There really is. Didn't you hear him earlier?"

"I just heard you and her."

"Honestly, Lily. Let me call him."

"Go ahead. You just be careful, though. No tricks."

Strauss shifted to what he hoped would be a more comfortable position with no luck.

Lily waved the rifle at him in warning. "I said, no tricks."

"Shubert! Shubert! Answer me!"

Silence.

"Shubert!"

Lily gave him a smug look. "I knew it. Thought I'd be stupid enough to go have a look, didn't you?"

"Damn him!" Adrian whispered.

"Come on, Shubert, we need some help!" Strauss tried one last time.

"Do you think I'm stupid enough to give my position away, Strauss?" Shubert finally replied, then followed with a softer "Oh, shit!"

Lily flew for the door and fired her rifle in the general direction of the kitchen. Strauss struggled to his feet and pulled his service revolver.

"Stay there!" he ordered Adrian and ran after Lily.

Of course, Adrian didn't stay. When would he ever get a partner who listened to him? he wondered.

Another blast rang out from Lily's rifle, and the light from the living room disappeared. Now the only light in the house came from a bedroom lamp, which was too far to lend much glow in the kitchen. He crept slowly down the hall with Adrian right behind.

Suddenly the silence was pierced by a yell that could only have come from Shubert, followed by another shot and the sound of someone scrambling out the back door. Hoping it was Lily making a run for it, Strauss moved quickly to the kitchen. A hasty peek around the corner told him that someone had gone out into the night, leaving the door open.

"Shubert! Shubert!" he called.

"Over here," came the whispered reply.

Following the sound of his voice, Strauss found that Shubert had squeezed himself into the gap between the cupboards and the sink. Strauss wouldn't have thought it possible for a man of Shubert's bulk to force himself into such a small space, but he supposed when the flesh yellowed and cringed anything was possible.

"Great hideout, Shubert. Are you hit?"

"I don't know."

"You don't know!"

"I don't feel so hot."

"Believe me, you'd know," Strauss assured him as he hobbled to the door.

"Good God," Adrian muttered. She had collected her rifle on her way through the kitchen and now followed Strauss out into the night.

Even though there was no moon, yesterday's snowfall illuminated the night so that they could see fairly well, much better than they had inside the house.

"Where's the damn car?" Adrian asked. "We looked for the car."

Strauss scanned the edge of the property, waiting for movement. "There!"

He pointed to the massive figure hurtling herself through the snow toward the Dunfield farmhouse. He started to follow before he realized that he would never make it with his leg dragging. When he glanced down, he saw that he was leaving a trail in the snow.

Great, he thought.

Adrian followed the direction of his gaze and sized up the situation. "I'll go," she said.

Strauss grabbed her just in time to stop her. "No. The car. Help me."

Adrian wasn't as skinny as Lily had accused her of being, and she was strong. She put an arm around his waist and together they half ran, half hobbled to the Skylark and climbed in just as they heard another engine cranking. The one thing Strauss had always credited

An Investigation of Local Color

the car with was a never-fail starting ability, and it didn't let him down now. He threw it into gear and gunned it, causing it to fishtail badly in the snow. Up ahead, he saw the lights of Lily's Jeep come on as it started to roll out from its hiding place behind the farmhouse. Strauss floored the Skylark. The rearend swung out on its balding tires, then grabbed hold and headed for its fateful but heroic end.

Lily saw him coming and tried to speed up, but she wasn't fast enough. She had a choice of either of the two maples that stood on opposite sides of the drive, or the more forgiving option of broadsiding the oncoming car. She chose the latter and plowed headlong into the driver's door of the Skylark, pushing the door rest into Strauss' wounded leg and sending him flying across the seat into Adrian, though he couldn't have said whether it was the force of the impact or the pain that sent him sprawling. He was pretty sure, though, that it was the pain that caused him to momentarily black out so that Adrian had to push him roughly aside in order to go after their suspect. While Strauss' head spun, she dashed to the driver's door of the Jeep, which had been opened, though the driver had a similarly spinning head from an encounter with her steering wheel.

Unfortunately, the sight of a woman one-third her size, hauling on her arm, trying to yank her out of the Jeep, caused Lily to become lucid again. She climbed out, shoving Adrian to the ground on her way. But the constable was as game as all the rest of the Thibaults. She got to her feet, avoiding the kicks aimed in her direction, and fastened herself the larger woman's upper arm.

"You skinny bitch! Let me go!" Lily howled.

Through his haze Strauss heard her, but couldn't respond.

"I'll kill you!"

"Strauss, I need some help! Nick! Nick!" Adrian's voice still sounded fairly calm as it cracked through the blur in his brain.

He hauled himself out of the car, taking his revolver with him. The sight that greeted him would have been amusing at another time, when he didn't hurt so badly. Adrian was glued to Lily's arm, and in her fury Lily had lifted the smaller woman right off her feet. Stubborn as she was, Adrian wasn't about to let go, so Lily was starting off through the snow, dragging her along right toward Strauss. The fat woman was so angry she failed to see the detective standing in the way, gun in hand.

"Let me go, you skinny bitch. Women like you deserve to be shot!" She aimed a furious blow, which landed on Adrian's head but not firmly enough for her to let go. "Let me go! Bitch! Bitch!"

It was all too reminiscent of Gwenivere's tirades, in Strauss' opinion. Where in the world did Lee Stout get his taste in women? He walked the remaining two steps toward the struggling women and thunked Lily over the head with the butt of his service revolver. She fell to the ground with a thud that caused it to shudder, taking Adrian with her.

"You know, fat women really hate you, Adrian." And he passed out on the ground beside her.

Strauss awoke to two sets of flashing red lights and a group of people hovering over him. He raised his head enough to see a handcuffed Lily Stout sitting in the backseat of a State Police cruiser while an EMT held an icepack to her head. Shubert was talking to two officers from the barracks whose names Strauss couldn't immediately recall.

Judging from Shubert's manner, he had retrieved both his courage and his swagger from beneath the cupboards, where they had apparently fled when he had needed them most.

Then a hand pushed him back down, none too gently either, and Franklyn Birch's face came into his line of vision. He stared at Strauss a moment, then he smiled.

"I knew you'd get her in the end," he said with a greater show of faith than Strauss believed he had ever truly possessed. "'Course, I didn't know we was necessarily talking about a woman, less it was the ex. You were pretty smart to crack this one."

"Good job, Detective!" Donnie Thibault grinned, pushing Birch aside.

"Hey, is he awake?" One of the Chandlers came into his sights. He was dressed in firefighting garb. "Hey, boys, he's woke up!"

An Investigation of Local Color

And two more Chandlers in fire gear joined their brother, grinning madly.

"You got her, Detective. Good job!"

"Never had a doubt in you! Nope, not for a moment."

"How come all the equipment?" Strauss asked wearily. Two ambulances and a firetruck and two state cars? It was a virtual parade for one collared suspect and a cop who'd been shot in the leg.

"The way it works is that when the Benton Harbor ambulance gets called, like Adrian done tonight, the Fairview ambulance gets called to transport to the hospital. The state boys come along to watch and get in the way. And us firemen go along just in case."

"In case of what?"

Birch shrugged as if it had never occurred to him why he got called out at night when there was no fire. "You know. Just in case."

Adrian shoved her way into the circle of men. "Are you guys helping him or just chewing the fat?"

"We were just explaining the way things get done around here, Adrian," Donnie told her.

"Couldn't you have cleaned and bandaged and got him up off the snow while you did it?"

"Naw, he's a tough guy. He'd rather have the nurse, anyway. Wouldn't you, Strauss?"

"Yeah, she's prettier than you guys."

Adrian blushed furiously. "Go away, all of you. You're all worthless pieces of garbage," she said gruffly.

"You won't be so quick to say that when you need to get him in the back of one of these here wagons," Birch reminded her.

The men laughed at her, but she didn't look very annoyed.

She helped him to sit up, which caused him to feel bleary and distinctly untough. "Are you warm enough?" She laid a cool hand on his forehead in her best nurse impersonation, and he felt instantly warm, at least inside.

"I'd be warmer if I wasn't sitting in the snow."

"Damn! You guys bring a stretcher from the squad."

"Come on, you worthless pieces of garbage, get a stretcher!" Birch repeated.

He had no sooner done that than his wife, Madge, wearing a Benton Harbor Emergency Squad jacket, came over and pulled off the bloodied bandage on his leg and replaced it with a new sterile sponge.

"How're you doing, Mr. Strauss?" Madge's eyes sparkled. She was having as much fun as everyone else, excluding Strauss, of course.

"Not too badly, Madge. How about you?"

"A little excitement is good for warming up a cold winter night," she said. She patted his shoulder gently. "Fairview wants to get going, Adrian. They said they'll take it from here."

"They're just being heavy-handed shitheads, like usual, dear," Franklyn told his wife. "They can wait while we take care of our own. Won't get done right if we don't do it ourselves."

Madge smiled first at her husband, then at Strauss, then got to work on a proper dressing for his leg for the trip to Rutland. When she was done, Franklyn and Adrian helped Strauss onto a stretcher and into the Fairview ambulance.

But as she started to climb in after him, one of the Fairview EMTs placed an arm across the door, barring her way. From his limited vantage point, Strauss saw the Benton Harbor team bristle in response. Good God, he could only thunk so many heads in one night!

"Let her come along, son, she's my wife."

"There's only room for two attendants as it is. Besides, that's Constable Thibault. She's not your wife."

Small towns were such a nuisance. Wasn't there anybody who didn't know everybody, besides him?

"Okay, she's not my wife. But I'm pretty sure I'm going to puke all over your nice ambulance here if she doesn't get to come along."

The EMT wisely stepped aside, and Adrian climbed in. The last thing Strauss saw before the door shut was a hearty thumbs-up from Birch.

"Ick, where did you come up with that?" Adrian asked, settling onto a seat beside him.

An Investigation of Local Color

"I don't know. It was the only thing I could think of with all the blood rushing out my leg."

In the bright light inside the ambulance, Adrian looked strangely pale. She sat close to him, probably more because the quarters demanded it than by choice, but her nearness made him feel happy. It was almost worth the hole in his leg, but maybe not quite worth enduring the siren that the driver had seen fit to turn on as though anyone would be making his way up Frampton Hill that time of night. Besides, anyone who was anyone had heard about the incident on their scanners and was already up on Frampton Hill following them down. The squad bumped and pounded its way down, jarring his leg and causing it to bleed again.

Adrian put a hand on his forehead again. He thought she might have left it there just a little longer than necessary, but he wasn't one to complain.

"You don't look so great. Does it hurt much?"

"No, not much." It did, but macho big-city cops were supposed to say it didn't. They didn't exactly teach that at the academy, but they wanted to.

"Thanks for saving my life."

"It was nothing." Another of those supposed-to phrases. "You were right. She would have missed. Lily wasn't a terrific shot. She missed Shubert, after all. How could anyone have missed him all neatly tucked up under the cupboards like that?"

Adrian smiled, but she looked whiter than ever. She clutched her hands tightly in front of her.

"That reminds me, next time you go after a suspect, take your gun with you. It's a little easier to make an arrest if you have a gun."

At that moment the ambulance driver, drunk on speed and full of purpose, hit the only curb between Benton Harbor and Rutland as he rounded the corner onto the Route 4 bypass. Strauss cringed as he felt a stabbing pain shoot down his leg. Instinctively, he reached for his wound and felt the warm ooze of fresh blood on his hand. Adrian quickly replaced the bandage Madge had applied with a tighter-pressure bandage. She worked quickly with the skills of one who did the job often. But when she turned again toward him, Strauss saw that her face was now frighteningly pale. The only people he had ever seen that white had been dead for a few days.

He reached for her clutched hands. They were cold, even though she had just been working with them. "You don't look so great yourself. Are you okay?"

She nodded.

"Adrian?"

"I can't stand the sight of blood," she whispered so the Fairview EMT couldn't hear her.

"But you're a nurse!" This wasn't so good.

"Well...I...." And she fainted dead away with her head slumped over on his chest facing him.

The remaining EMT who had braved Strauss' puke threats to ride along moved to help Adrian to a less bothersome position for Strauss.

"No, she's alright here. We're almost there, anyway."

The attendant settled back down, with a look that implied they were both a little looney.

Strauss smiled. The woman of his dreams—at least his dreams of the past five days— asleep on his chest. Maybe...if he just...could pick his head up far enough.... He kissed her sleeping lips. Finally. And she didn't even seem to mind.

Then, because he felt a little tired himself, Strauss dozed off, with his arms around the slumped-over Adrian.

9

When he woke much later, he was in a hospital bed. His leg beneath the sheet was bandaged neatly, and he had that woozy feeling one gets with too many painkillers. He wondered how long he had been asleep, but there was no clock in the room and a quick glimpse of his surroundings showed that his personal effects were nowhere in sight. Since he seemed unable to go back to sleep, he began to wish someone would come along and fill him in on the past few hours. He couldn't exactly go looking for anyone since he had been dressed in one of those hospital garments that didn't encourage strolling the halls unless a man had no modesty and/or a truly fabulous butt. So he waited. He waited such a long time that he began to wish for a roommate until he remembered that the last time he had been shot, his roommate smelled of urine and moaned obscenities about someone called Sister Mary Margaret, which called up some interesting visual images that became significantly less interesting in the middle of the night. So Strauss wished instead that Adrian would come along. It worked, too, because within five minutes she walked through the door. She wore the pale-colored scrubs that ER nurses wore these days and a nametag.

"Hi, there." She smiled.

"You look like a nurse. Are you my nurse?" he asked hopefully.

"No. I'm on my lunch break. I came up to see how you're doing."

"I'd be better if they gave me clothes with a backside to them so I could get up and go home."

"You're probably not quite ready for that. You were in the OR earlier this morning having the bullet dug out of your leg."

Adrian stood beside the bed with her hands resting on the rail meant to keep him from falling out. Why did they put those rails there, anyway? If a man didn't fall out of his bed at home, what were the chances he would adopt the habit while visiting the hospital?

Casually, Adrian picked up a chart at the end of the bed and read it, or pretended to. She looked and spoke very briskly, very nurse-like.

"I don't suppose you assisted with the surgery, what with you hating the sight of blood and all."

The nurse-like manner disappeared instantly, replaced by embarrassment. "Look, Strauss, that has to stay our little secret. Okay?" she insisted in a lowered voice.

He grinned. It was fun seeing her off guard for a change. "You mean no one knows but me?"

"Well, I never actually passed out before," she replied in an irritated voice.

Strauss laughed. "Maybe it's just my blood that particularly sickens you."

"No, it's everyone's. Yours just makes me pass out. You can stop laughing anytime now."

He wanted to, truly he did, but didn't seem to be able to. Was this part of his craziness or just the remnants of the anesthesia?

"I'll go get your nurse to give you another shot of painkiller," Adrian said bluntly, the nurse again.

"No, wait." He grabbed her hand and held it until she finally asked what he wanted.

What did he want? She returned his gaze with eyes that were neither friendly nor unfriendly. She was granting him one wish, and he couldn't think of what it should be. He let go of her hand.

"Could you just tell me when I can get out of here?" He felt very tired again.

"They'll let you go tomorrow morning, barring any sort of complication."

"Good." He closed his eyes, not really caring anymore.

"They couldn't save your car, Nick."

"That's okay. It needed new brakes and tires, anyway. Besides, it always kind of reminded me of my ex-wife."

An Investigation of Local Color

Strauss didn't bother to open his eyes, but he could sense Adrian still hovering in the doorway. He peeked one eye open.

"I'll have someone give you a ride back to Fairview."

"That's alright, Adrian. The chief will send someone for me. Probably my partner."

"That's what I'm afraid of. He's a hero, you know. You both are."

Strauss had to smile at that. So Adrian didn't tell about Shubert cringing under the cupboards, and such a good story it was, too. But she was a smart woman. She would make sure Shubert forever trod softly in her presence and never again came looking for Les Blake.

"So Shubert's a hero. Now I really need a new partner."

"Maybe not. Maybe they will let you go back to Boston now."

"Oh." He had become so accustomed to the idea of forced labor in Vermont that he didn't exactly know what to say. "Maybe they will."

"Yes, well, get some sleep. I'll send a nurse in."

Couldn't you just stay? he wanted to ask, but she didn't seem to encourage it, so he didn't. When he opened his eyes again, she was gone.

In the end it was Chief Peterman who sent a car to take Strauss back to Fairview. Fortunately, he was either smart enough not to send Shubert or Shubert was smart enough to decline the assignment, and the trooper who drove him was merely on Route 4 traffic duty that day.

The doctor who dug the bullet out gave him a cane fresh out of some medical supply house and told him not to put undue stress on his leg, and it would be good as new in a few weeks. Unfortunately, he also told him he couldn't work for at least two weeks and then only on desk or traffic duty. Strauss thought the idea of pulling over a BMW from New Jersey, and then limping over to the driver with his cane, would present an interesting set of circumstances. Probably the driver would speed away before he could hobble up to the window. The doctor also gave him some painkillers, which he had thoroughly enjoyed during his brief hospital stay, but thought he'd better stay away from at home.

He hadn't seen or talked to Adrian since her visit to his room.

Mrs. Hutchins had, in fact, read about the arrest of Lily Stout in the *Rutland Herald* and was basking in the glow of having a real-life hero living in her upstairs apartment. Her phone, she said, had been ringing off the hook, but she nevertheless wanted to hear the details right from the horse's mouth. Was he supposed to be the horse? But Strauss told her that his doctor had recommended rest for a few days and had suggested to him that he not relive the details for a while anyway. And he limped upstairs to his dingy apartment and slept for two days straight, dreaming at times of screaming fat women and other times of kissing unconscious nurses. When he finally woke up for good, he couldn't have said if he felt better, or merely more rested.

What Strauss did find for certain was that he was a hero to the townsfolk of Benton Harbor. He wasn't a hero so much for discovering the murderer in their midst—or, more aptly, stumbling onto the murderer in their midst—but for saving the life of their much-loved constable. He received more flower arrangements than most macho big-city cops are comfortable with and numerous cards with personal notes on them, including a batch from the Benton Harbor Village School, whose students numbered all of thirty-eight, none of whom he had ever met. The flowers he gave to a delighted Mrs. Hutchins, who picked up her phone immediately on receiving them. The cards he read with amusement. He didn't bother to tell anyone that if he hadn't heroically dived in front of "the bullet meant for our dear Adrian," it would have sunk harmlessly into the floor of Gwenivere's spare bedroom. It was easier to be a hero. Apparently Adrian wasn't telling either. As she had in the matter of Shubert cowering under the cupboard, Adrian, it seemed, was trading Strauss' secret for hers.

He had some visitors, too. Franklyn and Donnie came one afternoon and relieved his boredom with some rousing tales of firefighting in Benton Harbor as well as an offer to let him join the department.

"We have a Hell of a good time. Even fight some fires now and again."

Franklyn came back twice more, once alone and once with Madge, who fussed over his bandage like someone's mother and brought him a casserole. Sally and Jack stopped by with some paper-

An Investigation of Local Color

backs for him to read during his convalescence. Sally told him how grateful she was that he had believed Jack's story, and Strauss had the feeling he had gained unflagging devotion from her forever. He couldn't, however, eat the food she brought. Apparently her culinary skills were limited to a great cup of coffee and anything that could be done with tofu and vegetables. No wonder Jack was so thin.

Finally, toward the end of his required resting period, when Strauss thought he would go out of his mind with boredom, the phone rang. He still walked with the aid of a cane and hobbled over to pick it up.

"You're developing a better phone manner, Nick."

"Petrosky? How are you?"

"The question is, how are you?"

"I'm fine. Bored with sitting around, but too crippled to do much else. Besides, I got a landlady who's got me literally held hostage in her upstairs and a car that died suddenly in the night."

"The leg's going to be all right?"

"Eventually. It's just going a lot slower than I thought it would. Last time I got shot, it wasn't this slow in healing."

"Last time you got shot, it was in your ass," Petrosky reminded him. "You couldn't sit around."

"Yeah, well, I'm bound to get some desk duty out of this. Even that sounds pretty good right now."

"How does coming back to Boston sound?"

"What?" Strauss nearly gasped.

"You heard me. Come on back to town." Petrosky laughed at Strauss' disbelief.

"You'd better not be jerking me around, Lowell. Two weeks ago you were telling me I'd be lucky to have a job when I get sprung from this place next August. Now you're telling me I can come home?" To himself Strauss wondered if disbelief was all he was feeling.

"And in time for Christmas, no less. You've been given a reprieve."

"Why?"

"According to the reports out of Vermont, your performance in your latest investigation was exemplary. You were reported to have been professional and clear-thinking throughout. In addition, you showed courage by protecting your partner and, though wounded in the process, still managed to arrest the suspect."

Strauss heard the sound of papers being shuffled over the line. "Are you quoting, Lowell?"

"Yes, I am. I don't think you've ever acted professionally in your life. Furthermore, it is reported that an arrest of the correct suspect could not have been made without the expertise of Nick Strauss."

Strauss thought a moment. But Lowell Petrosky was one of his best friends.

"I gotta be honest here, Lowell. I kind of stumbled accidently onto the suspect. I stupidly threw myself in front of a bullet that otherwise would have hit nothing more important than a floorboard, and the arrest was made while I was unconscious."

"This isn't the time to be questioning providence, Strauss. If someone says you were a hero and it gets you back here, be a hero, for God's sake. You said you wanted to come home. Either someone up there wants to help you out or you've made yourself so repulsive that they want to give you back. I'd have assumed it was the latter but for this flattering account of your skills. Reading it almost makes me want to come up there and get you."

Why wasn't he jumping up and down?

"Why aren't you jumping up and down?"

"Who filed that report?" Strauss asked.

More paper shuffling. "Report filed by A. Thigh-bait."

"Thibault," Strauss corrected him absently.

"Whatever. As soon as it came across the wire, I ran to Internal Affairs. Even Dr. Brown agreed to give you another shot."

"That's big of her. Look, I owe you. This is really great."

"Something is sounding not-so-great in your voice."

"No, really, this is great, thanks, Lowell."

"So, we'll see you back just as soon as you get things wrapped up there in Vermont?"

"I'll give you a call next week."

An Investigation of Local Color

Strauss replaced the receiver and dropped back into his chair. Was Adrian trying to help him out, or now that her town was in order was she trying to give him back? It might have been easier to guess if he had seen her since her visit to his hospital room. But she hadn't come to see him, she hadn't called or sent a card, and she most certainly hadn't sent flowers.

He felt himself working into a funk, which puzzled him. He had just been told he could get out of this miserable place, he thought, as he looked around the dark, shabby apartment, which had very few luxuries or signs of home. Of course, his apartment in the city didn't have any more homey effects. But at least it was in Boston. In his irritation he threw a stack of unread magazines against the door, only to have someone knock on it.

"Come in!" he shouted in no less irritated a voice.

To his surprise and horror, Adrian poked her head around the door and eyed the stack of magazines splattered against it.

"Is this a bad time?" she asked.

"It is if you're appalled by poor housekeeping."

Strauss wished he had bothered to pick up the place the way he had when his convalescence had begun and he had hoped she would stop by. After a while he had stopped hoping in direct proportion to the frustration he suffered from being confined. Now it occurred to him, as it often did, but not with sufficient impact to cause him to do anything about it, that he really did live like a pig.

But Adrian merely shrugged. She didn't say one way or another what she thought, but she did come in and sit down. In her hands she carried a walking stick of heavily sanded and polished wood. The top of it had been shaped into a handle the perfect shape for grasping. She ran her hands over it as if she were proud of the smooth feel of it before she handed it to Strauss.

"I brought this because Franklyn said you still weren't getting around too well."

He took the stick and pretended to examine the wood to cover his awkwardness. He wasn't accustomed to receiving gifts. And this gift appeared to be handmade, a work of skill that would have made the Kinneys, with their designer-crafted walking sticks, envious.

"Much nicer than the hospital variety," he said. "Did you make it?"

Adrian shook her head. "Les did. He likes to work with wood, and he wanted to thank you for believing him when he said he didn't kill Dunfield."

"I don't know if I believed him, Adrian. I just looked into every possibility."

"I know that. But he doesn't. Let him believe what he wants."

"What did you believe?"

Adrian looked him right in the eye. "I thought it was someone else. And I'm glad you found the right person."

Even though he truly believed Adrian was honest beyond question, he thought she was lying at the moment. He thought she had been scared to death that her lifelong friend had killed Bill Dunfield and then gone after Dunfield's ex-wife. He wondered what she had really thought five years ago, when it was her husband who was dead.

"I think we did a good job of finding the right person. Or at least letting her stumble onto us. We make a pretty good team, don't you think?"

She shrugged noncommittally.

"I got a call this morning telling me I could come back to the city," Strauss said.

Adrian nodded like she already knew. "That's great, Nick."

"I take it I have you to thank for that."

"No. I just filled out the report."

Strauss nodded. The awkwardness between them grew.

"So when are you leaving?"

"I've got to get something to drive first. And it seems best to give some sort of notice to the chief here."

"Yes, I can't imagine you would be very easy to find a replacement for," Adrian commented.

He couldn't tell if she was joking.

"Besides, it seems silly to go back to the city until I can walk a little better or they will make me sit behind a desk. At least here they

An Investigation of Local Color

will let me drive around in a car and look important. Maybe I'll be gone in about two weeks."

Adrian nodded, unsurprised, unflinching. Uncaring? She stood up abruptly.

"That's really great," she said again. "I'm happy for you, Nick. I'd better get going."

Strauss got to his feet too and made use of his new walking stick to follow her to the door. "Thanks for coming by."

"I'm just glad everything is in order again. Thanks for your help."

She stepped over his magazines and was out the door before he could think of anything else to say.

This was definitely not good, he thought. And neither was the dark mood that had descended on him. It was a mood to rival any he had had since coming to this horrible place. In order to give himself something else to think about he changed his clothes, donned his parka and boots for the first time in days, and set out to buy himself a car.

Unless he wanted to bum a ride to Rutland, which he didn't, he was limited to Fairview's only car dealer, Bernie Hazzard, a salesman of the sort that movies stereotyped. Bernie made every make and model his specialty, or he said he did. Strauss was suspicious by nature of anybody who sold things for a living. He doubted if his job as a cop would give him much status in a used car salesman's eyes even if he was the living legend of Benton Harbor at the moment, so he avoided saying what exactly he did. His no-frills lifestyle made him able to pay cash for his cars and he drove them until they died or, as in the present case, were killed, and by then he had usually saved enough to buy another. His beat-up, though fully owned, vehicles had always been one of his ex-wife's loudest complaints, but that certainly didn't matter anymore.

Hazzard Motors had a surprisingly large variety of vehicles to choose from. The entire back row looked just the way the Skylark had looked the last time he saw it. In the middle were rows of the type he usually bought, less than gently used, no-frills cars. The front row had newer luxury and sport models. As he looked around the line of cars most like his former purchases, tuning out Bernie's sales pitch—the man had a good reason why each car would be just perfect for Strauss—his eyes kept straying to a sporty black four-wheel drive pickup with a red stripe sitting in the front row. It was the last vehicle he needed to buy and, in a city where fender benders and parking accidents were the norm, the least practical thing he could think of. In the end it was the only vehicle he test drove.

He sat up as high as the snowbanks. He even took it down to the Grand Union parking lot and backed it into a bank left by the plow and put the four-wheel drive to the test. It made him feel powerful. It must have made him look powerful, too, because as he pulled out of the snow a youngster in a similarly equipped truck rolled down his window and asked if he would like to meet out at the slate pits, wherever that was, for a little contest of trucks. The other truck sat about ten feet higher than the one Strauss was testing. It had big tires and as the engine idled the driver pressed on the accelerator, causing it to rumble deep in its holey muffler. Strauss casually flipped his badge at the kid, who blanched.

"Go on back to school, son," he said.

Sometimes being a big-city cop was fun, though in truth, cruising the streets of Fairview in the black truck, he felt more like a hick cop. He went back to the car lot and bought the truck, which Bernie said was perfect for him. Then he went back to the Grand Union and bought himself some groceries and sneaked past Mrs. Hutchins' window up to his apartment and set about a cleanup.

It wasn't an easy job for a man hobbling around, especially since it had been so long since he had bothered to even tidy up. He was relieved when there was a second knock on his door and he had an excuse to stop.

"Come in!" he shouted.

As there were no magazines in front of the door this time, Ira Thibault came in unimpeded. He looked around him and Strauss could see that his cleaning efforts weren't impressive in that man's eyes. Well, he was a vet, after all, and that was something like being a doctor in terms of cleanliness, Strauss thought. He would have to

An Investigation of Local Color

remember that in the unlikely event that he ever had an animal in need of treatment.

"How are you, Nick?" Ira asked. He came across the room and put out a hand. "We've missed seeing you down at the Hook in the morning."

"I don't get around too well," Strauss replied, though in truth it hadn't occurred to him to go to the Hook for morning coffee now that he didn't have a case.

"That's what Franklyn said," Ira told him. Franklyn sure was getting around with his information. "But a man does have to have his coffee, too, you know. Say, that's a pretty fancy stick you've got there."

"Thanks." Strauss held it up so Ira could better admire it. "Les made it for me. Adrian brought it over this morning."

"Oh? Adrian stopped by? How are things with her?" Ira sounded as if he didn't live just right down the road from her, as if she wasn't his cousin or whatever relation they were, and as if she didn't come by at least once a week for cow injections or whatever it was she needed from the local veterinarian.

"What things do you mean?" Strauss asked suspiciously.

Ira's eyes behind their wire frames looked puzzled. "Just wondered how she was, is all," he answered with a shrug.

"Oh. Fine, I guess."

"I take it that means you two didn't exactly engage in witty repartee?"

"You've got to talk like a normal person, Ira. I don't know what you mean otherwise."

"Sorry. It just sounded like you didn't have a good chat with Adrian."

Strauss frowned. "That's about right. It was 'Here's a walking stick for you. Thanks for your help. See you around.' She was the same way at the hospital."

"That could only mean one thing, Nick."

"What's that?"

"Adrian has completely fallen for you."

Strauss laughed, although he didn't really see any humor in the revelation. "You know, I might just be an ignorant city cop to you folks around here, but I think when a woman doesn't speak to a man and goes out of her way to avoid him it means pretty much the same thing everywhere. Unless, of course, I've gotten it wrong all this time."

"You've probably got it right. Adrian's different, is all. Adrian is the quintessential perfectionist. She hates to make a mistake, hates to do anything less than the best. Why do you think she's such a good shot? Why do you think we want her to be our constable and the head of the rescue squad? The only really big mistake she ever made was getting involved with Brian Borden. It turned out to be such a disaster and brought so much trouble to everyone she really loved that I thought for the longest time she might never forgive herself, and I think the only reason she did is because she demanded it of herself in order to get on with life. A lot of folks thought the whole problem was brought on by Borden's being from out of town. Ultimately, I think Adrian herself believed that. So, if she keeps you at arm's length, there is most likely your answer. Maybe you should give it more time."

"What good would that do?" Strauss asked. "I'm an outsider myself. Time won't change that."

"You seem like a nice guy, Nick. Borden was never a nice guy, not even in the beginning. No one, myself included, ever knew what Adrian saw in him, and she never told. Maybe it was just that she'd always been so damned sensible, she wanted to do something totally insane. The thing about a small town like Benton Harbor is that if you are despicable but you were born here, you'll still be accepted. If you're depraved in some way but you're from out of town, then you should go home where you belong and not inflict your depravity on others. It's not a perfect place, it's just our place."

Strauss thought about the people on Frampton Hill with their big dreams and their even bigger disappointments.

"It's not like you can't join in, Nick. It just takes more time."

"I haven't got more time. I'm going back to the city in two weeks."

Ira didn't even seemed mildly surprised by the news. "You have to?"

An Investigation of Local Color

"No. My supervisor said that I could if I chose. It seems that Adrian recommended that my department grant me a stay on my sentence here and I can return when I want."

"And you want to?"

For some reason unknown to him, Strauss shrugged with indifference. He didn't know if he wanted to stay or go. "Why shouldn't I? I'm really not much of a country guy, Ira."

Ira nodded his understanding, though it was certainly more comprehension than Strauss felt.

"Well, that's that, then." He looked around at the clutter in the room. "You know, if you change your mind, decide to stay a little longer, a week or whatever, let me know. My wife and I have an apartment over our garage that we would like to rent out. It would be perfect for you. Much brighter than this place, much less closed in."

"Thanks, Ira. I'll keep it in mind," Strauss replied, puzzled.

Ira got up to leave and Strauss hobbled after him. As he turned to say goodbye, Ira's eyes fell on the walking stick.

"I know the town is grateful to you for saving Adrian's life and finding Dunfield's murderer," he said.

"Mostly, though, everyone is glad it wasn't one of their own," Strauss added.

Ira smiled. "Yeah, there is some of that thinking as well."

"Tell me, Ira. Do you think Les killed Borden?"

The Thibaults were an honest lot, Strauss had learned, but this was one subject where Adrian might lie. Ira would answer truthfully.

"I think that Les said he didn't and Adrian believes him. She has to because if she doesn't, who does she really have left after her mistake? Sometimes we have to believe the person we love no matter what he—or she—is saying." Ira stuck out his hand again. "Good luck, if you decide to go back to the city, Nick."

"Yeah, thanks," Strauss replied vaguely, his mind on something else Ira had just said.

"And stop by for coffee and news in the morning."

"I will."

The following morning Strauss drove his new truck over to the barracks to give his notice to Chief Peterman. He had spent a nearly sleepless night and figured it was time to stop lying around all day and get back to work.

The chief accepted his notice, and though he offered congratulations for his work on the Dunfield case Strauss had the distinct impression that the man wouldn't be disappointed to see the last of him on his roster. His impression was further enhanced by his very light assignment to Route 4 traffic duty, without a partner, to finish out his time.

Strauss hoped that the state of Vermont would see fit to reimburse him for his car. It had been killed in the line of duty, after all. But maybe they were just considering themselves even for the damage done to Shubert's cruiser, and he decided to let it go before that was pointed out to him. The Skylark wasn't worth much, anyway.

Next he drove his new truck to the Hook, Line, and Sinker, where he entered to *oohs, ahhs,* and healthy smattering of *holy shits.* The entire clientele of the eating establishment emptied into the parking lot as he came in to admire his new wheels. Strauss remained standing in the doorway, where no one had even bothered admiring him, mostly because it was too much trouble for him to negotiate the Hook's hazardous handicap ramp even when both legs were working properly.

"You sure as Hell'd better hope they all get back in here and pay their tabs or you're in deep shit," Harvey growled at him from the kitchen doorway. Obviously, he was in one of his better moods.

"I'm sure they will," Strauss said. He pulled up a chair and lit a cigarette.

"Don't be so sure. Wouldn't be the first time everybody up and left on some pretense. Like the fire whistle goes off, and everyone gets up and goes, like the food was free."

But the door flew open on a gust of cold air, and the men of Benton Harbor's coffee club filed back in. Harvey muttered and went back into the kitchen and threw a pan, the return of paying customers having greatly improved his humor.

"A very fine set of wheels, Nick," Franklyn informed him. "Very fine."

An Investigation of Local Color

"Now you can get around as good as the rest of us." Donnie grinned.

"Even got room for a deer or two," one of the Chandlers added. One of his brothers elbowed him in the ribs.

"He'd only shoot one, Leo. He's the law."

"Well, he might hunt with a friend. Or maybe the constable."

Strauss thought they could shut up on that subject just about any time. And they did, if only to light fresh cigarettes.

"How's it feel to be a hero, Mr. Strauss?" Junior asked.

"I think 'hero' might be stretching it just a bit, Junior," he said but offered no further explanation.

"Sure you're a hero," Franklyn argued. "You got shot saving Adrian. That makes you a hero in anyone's book."

"Yeah," added one of the Chandlers. "Hey, can we see your gunshot wound?"

Strauss looked at him in disbelief. Whichever Chandler he was looking at looked back hopefully. Did the man really expect him to drop his pants and show him the wound in his thigh? His question was answered immediately by one of the man's brothers.

"Do you guys remember the time one of the Howe sons got shot in the ass, and he came in here, and we asked him to see it?"

There were nods and laughter all around. Obviously, everyone except Strauss remembered, so the speaker filled him in.

"Sure enough, that young buck dropped his overalls and leaned over to show us his bullet hole, right in the middle of the dinner hour, like it was something he done all the time. And a really worthwhile bullet hole it were, too."

The story made Strauss more than a little glad that no one in Benton Harbor knew that he, too, had been shot in the ass. It was a fact he mostly liked to keep to himself, anyway. Besides, though he had never exactly checked, he wasn't sure the wound could be classified as "really worthwhile." He looked around the table at the expectant faces of his coffee mates.

"My bullet hole still has a lot of bandaging on it," he told them, although it didn't.

"Maybe another time."

Hopefully by the time they remembered it he would be on his way back to Boston.

"Say, now that you've got that fancy new truck, you can get around most anywhere. You'll be able to drive out on the lake for the Fishing Derby," Birch pointed out, drawing the conversation back to more important matters. "Maybe you'll be wanting to enter it in the ice race."

"Yeah, and you won't have to worry about driving off the road anymore," Junior added with what Strauss thought looked like a suspicious grin.

"Want to join the fire department now that you can get around town?" Donnie repeated his request of a week ago.

"That would be a Hell of a lot of fun," one of the Chandlers threw in.

"I'm sure it would be," Strauss said, though he wasn't at all sure. "But unfortunately, I'm going back to Boston in two weeks."

His announcement met with silence and questioning stares from all the men at the table except for Ira, who had apparently not had a chance to fill his buddies in before Strauss' arrival.

"You mean just for a visit?" Birch asked finally.

"No. I'm going back to work at my old job."

"What the Hell for?" Birch had apparently resumed his old job of group spokesman.

Strauss looked to Ira for help, but that man only sipped his coffee and looked out the window.

"I was always planning to return to the city, guys. It was just a question of when." He didn't add that the when depended on when the Boston Police Department either thought he had recovered his sanity or when a helpful constable from Vermont recommended that he return to the city.

"Huh," Junior grunted for no particular reason.

It appeared to speak volumes for the rest because no one else had anything else to add. Cigarettes started to go out on the edges of breakfast plates, usually a prelude to the coffee club breaking up and going back to the cows.

An Investigation of Local Color

"Two weeks, you say?" Franklyn asked.

"That's right."

"Why don't you stay on a couple of extra days and come out to Remembrance Night? You wouldn't want to miss that."

"What's Remembrance Night?"

"It's a party the town has to start the Christmas Season and remember our loved ones. There's a tree lighting and the school kids do a live Nativity scene. They even clean up the animals, Strauss, so they don't stink."

"Then there's food and dancing in here afterward," Donnie added. "You don't want to miss it after working so hard here in Benton Harbor, Nick. It'd be a good way to end your time in Vermont."

"I guess it doesn't matter a few days either way," Strauss agreed. There wasn't much else he could have said. He glanced again at Ira, but his eyes were as puzzled and innocent as they perpetually were. "I'd be glad to come."

10

Strauss spent the next two weeks arresting speeders on Route 4 and packing the few belongings he had carried with him to Vermont into grocery boxes to make the return trip back to the city. Mrs. Hutchins, in her eagerness to rent his apartment quickly so as not to lose a month's rent, ran what seemed to be an endless stream of potential tenants through his lodgings whether he was home or not. If he was there she introduced him as the brave law enforcer who had single-handedly subdued the dangerous Benton Harbor murderer. It seemed as though she thought his celebrity would make his former rooms more valuable. She always neglected to tell renters that the dangerous murderer was a crazy fat lady who mostly subdued herself by bashing her head on her own steering wheel. He merely finished off the job and then passed out.

Early mornings he spent drinking black coffee at the Hook, Line, and Sinker. Because the Dunfield case had been solved, he found that he was less of the center of attention, which suited him just fine. Cow doings and hunting and whose kid had just piled up the family pickup were much more the topic of conversation. To his surprise, no one said anything more about his return to the city. He was included in the gossip as though he would always be as much a fixture as the other coffee drinkers and cigarette smokers.

He would have almost felt happy with the newfound camaraderie, but for Adrian. After giving Ira's advice much thought and one or two fitful nights of sleep, Strauss picked up the phone and asked her to dinner. She refused, saying only, by way of explanation, that it would be better if they didn't. Strauss took this to mean that Ira's advice was worth about as much as the byproducts from the village cows and gave up. He forced himself to look forward to Remembrance Night the way everyone else in Benton Harbor seemed to be doing and, more importantly, his return to the city the following day, which no one else seemed to be doing.

Strauss had never been anything, though, if not stubborn. It made him a good cop, but in the scheme of human nature it just made him a stubborn man. So on his last day of work he turned in his cruiser, signed out, and went back to his apartment and called Adrian at work.

"Hi, Constable, Strauss here."

"Hi." She sounded reserved, but it was hard to tell with only one word, and a short one at that.

"Ride with me to Remembrance Night tonight?" he asked, feeling rather adolescent in his request.

She didn't answer right away.

"It's really very safe, Constable. I'm leaving for the big city of Boston tomorrow morning early. My soon-to-be ex-landlady wants me out so she can start collecting rent on the new guy. Besides, I want to show you my new wheels." Now there was just about the smoothest line he had ever used.

"I heard about your new truck."

"Of course you have, and probably before I even got it off the lot, too. But let me tell you, words can't even begin to describe this truck."

Adrian heaved a sigh that was surely meant to be heard. "Then I guess I'd better have a look. Around 6 o'clock."

"Six it is."

"And only because it would be rude not to say goodbye after all your help."

"Right. See you at 6." Well, he had asked for it, after all.

He got cleaned up, glad to see the last of his shower, though in truth his shower in the city wasn't an improvement. It merely clattered where this one clanked. But at least he could count on city-treated water, whereas Strauss had always suspected that his Fairview water might come from the grimier end of Lake Champlain or the nearby brackish Poultney River.

An Investigation of Local Color

It was a cold night, so he bundled into a heavy chamois shirt with a sweater and jeans to go under his Vermont parka. He wouldn't be needing that anymore either, but if only for the use he got out of it on Frampton Hill, he was glad that he had bought it. And because it made him feel less like he stuck out, he thought as he pulled into Adrian's drive. She came out the back door dressed in a similar coat before he could get out of his truck.

"Nice truck," she commented. She walked around and ran her hands over it and peered underneath and behind in her best imitation of the boys at the Hook. "This ought to help you get around in the city."

If she meant to be sarcastic, he ignored it. "I thought so. Some young puppy even asked to take me on out at the slate pits," he added as if he actually knew what that meant.

Adrian gave him an amused look. "And you did it, of course?"

He smiled knowingly but figured she knew he hadn't. "The heater works, too, in case I ever have to go on another stakeout."

"And I bet you'd never be noticed sitting in this truck in the back streets and alleys of Boston."

If he had been forced to say it aloud, Strauss would have had to admit that he had never thought of that. To Adrian he said, "Good point, but it gives me a reason not to take my personal vehicle on stakeout again. Last time I did that, it didn't turn out so well."

"I remember. You just missed the turn."

How could he possibly have missed the turn for the Hook after all the times he had come down this road? He groaned, though wisely not out loud. He backed up, turned around, and turned onto the road to the center of town.

The village green, not a big one even by Vermont standards, was already seething with activity, none of it organized in any way. School kids dressed like Christmas shepherds and Wise Men—did he see a Wise Woman?—were running around with a lack of dignity that belied their costumes. One Wise Man had a shepherd pinned on the ground and was in the process of bloodying his nose. A girl dressed in street clothes pulled on the hair of another little girl whom Strauss assumed must be Mary since she was costumed and carrying a swaddled doll. Mary screamed mightily, and Baby Jesus went flying beneath the feet of a donkey brought by one of the farmers for the live Nativity scene. Mothers grabbed elbows and scolded. Adrian went to retrieve the doll before it became unfit for its intended purpose, and Strauss was left to wonder if he had been abandoned for the rest of the evening.

"It's a bit hectic until things get underway," said a voice beside him.

"Hi, Martha," Strauss said. He supposed he should have remembered the name of the pig she held in her arms since he knew it would be important to her, but he simply didn't have the powers of recall. "And is this one of the cast?"

"Yes, he is. Do you know that I've already had three calls for Esmeralda's piglets? By the time they're ready to wean, I may have them all sold." Martha grinned.

Esmeralda! How could he have forgotten?

"That's great, Martha."

"It sure is. None of my other ventures have started out so well. I think it bodes well, don't you?"

"I sure do."

"You ought to stick around and see how it all turns out," Martha said. Her eyes roamed over the fray on the green so that Strauss was uncertain whether she was talking about the outcome of the pig business or something else. "Oh, oh, they're calling for Boris. I'm off for the manger." Martha started across the green, but she turned around and called. "Think about it, Mr. Strauss. It might be fun!"

"What are you supposed to be thinking about?" Adrian asked.

"You know, I'm not really sure," Strauss said honestly.

"That's okay. Martha probably wasn't either. Oh, look, Nick, there's our friend and former partner."

Adrian was looking at a spot over his shoulder, but he didn't need to look to know that she was talking about Shubert. Strauss hadn't seen Shubert since he himself had been lying on a stretcher in the middle of Dunfield's driveway except to catch a glimpse of the younger man ducking into the men's room or behind a cruiser in the parking

An Investigation of Local Color

lot in an obvious effort to avoid Strauss. He didn't look thrilled to see his former partner now either, but he was being dragged along, almost literally, in their direction by the irrepressible Gwenivere Dunfield. When the big woman came to a stop near them, she linked her arm possessively through the arm of the man who could only be her new beau. The beau avoided looking directly at them, but Gwen, never the mistress of subtlety, didn't have a problem gushing.

"Oh, Detective Strauss! I'm so grateful to have caught up with you at long last," she said in a dramatic voice that suggested she had been relentlessly pursuing him across the countryside. He really hoped not. "I'm just so...so...well, listen to me, I can't find the words!"

Strauss was fairly sure she would eventually.

Gwen wore a pink parka with a fur-trimmed hood, which she had pulled up to frame her fleshy cheeks. It would have been a jacket better suited to a little girl, but for the amount a fabric required. She laid a pink-mittened hand on her massive bosom in a now-familiar gesture.

"I just have so many reasons to be grateful to you, Detective Strauss, so sincerely grateful!"

"That's okay, Gwen. I was just doing my job."

"Oh, but you just went so far BEYOND. I mean, I would be DEAD if not for you!"

"Actually, it was Constable Thibault who made the arrest." Strauss couldn't resist giving credit where it was due.

He was rewarded with a firm boot planted directly over his instep. Gwen ignored Adrian's contribution completely.

"And you brought Gary and I together," she continued, gazing lovingly at Shubert, who returned the look with equal emotion but still seemed unable to meet the eyes of his former superior.

"It most certainly was my pleasure," Strauss told her sincerely.

"Thank you, thank you so much!"

Gwen reached out a hand and gave what she must have thought was an affectionate little squeeze but, in fact, gave Strauss a bruise that was sure to last well into the following week. And snuggling closer still, the two moved off to view the festivities.

"Shubert isn't exactly the stuff of romance novel covers, is he?" Adrian asked, watching them go.

"Well, maybe he is to her." It wasn't a vision Strauss wanted to devote a great deal of thought to.

"At least he doesn't have a wife," Adrian pointed out. "He doesn't, does he?"

"God, I hope not!"

Something wet slurped at his hand, and he jerked it away quickly. A dog! His entire body, limp and all, moved three feet sideways, taking Adrian with him.

"Sorry, Detective. No licking, Tor. Hi, Adrian," Sally Glenn said with a cheerful smile. She, too, held on to the arm of her beloved, though she didn't have to work hard at appearing natural in that position.

"Hi, Sally, Jack." Strauss smiled but kept his eye on the slurping canine.

"He's all right, Detective Strauss. This is Tor. He's just a youngster. He's been asked to be in the Nativity scene," Sally said proudly.

"Great, Sally." Strauss tried to muster some enthusiasm because he knew it was important. He really hadn't known that there were German Shepherds back in biblical times.

Tor grinned at him.

"Tell them about your job, Sally," Jack urged.

"You got a job?" Adrian asked.

Sally beamed. "Mrs. Billings, the principal at the school, came to see me to ask about using one of the dogs tonight, and we got to talking and one thing led to another, and she asked me if I would be interested in setting up an exercise program for the school kids. It's three afternoons a week. Games for the little ones up to more important calisthenics for the older kids. I'm so excited. I can't believe she asked me. I've always wanted to do something like this, but I didn't know quite how to go about it. I've already met the teachers, and they were all really nice. They said maybe they'd be interested in doing a group exercise after the kids leave for the day."

"Congratulations, Sally. That's wonderful," Adrian told her.

An Investigation of Local Color

"I think my wife will have every woman in Benton Harbor in an exercise leotard before she's done," Jack said.

Personally, Strauss couldn't appreciate the picture, but he smiled anyway.

"Yes, and then we'll start working on you men." Sally poked her husband through his parka in the direction of his thin stomach.

"Excuse me, Mrs. Glenn," a very serious-looking female shepherd pulled at Sally's parka. "I'm holding your dog for the Nativity scene."

"You are? Well, here he is. This is Tor."

Strauss admired the child's courage as she patted the dog's head and received a lick on her cheek. Sally showed her how to hold the leash to tell the dog to sit quietly at her side, then they went off in the direction of the manger, with Tor walking obediently at the child's heel. Adrian gave him a pointed look, which he was sure was meant to remind him that at even small children weren't afraid of dogs. But she was nice enough not to say it. She must be getting into the holiday spirit.

"Come on, we can go over and get our remembrance light while we wait for things to get started."

She led the way over to Madge Birch and Jean Thibault, who were dressed in their rescue squad jackets and wearing money-changing aprons filled with money and Christmas tree lightbulbs. For a dollar that went to sponsor the fire department and rescue squad, the women gave out a bulb and a thick candle with a cardboard holder reminiscent of a long-ago candlelight church service in Strauss' childhood. It had been years since he had been in a church on Christmas, but that particular service had always stuck in his mind.

"What you do, Detective, is buy a bulb to put on the tree on the green in memory of a loved one," Madge explained. "The candle is for the procession to the manger and for the singing of carols afterward."

"How are you doing?" Adrian asked. She peeked into Jean's apron.

"We're doing well because of the delay," Jean replied. "People are coming over to buy bulbs for something to do."

"What's the problem, anyway?" Madge asked. "We're going to have a lot of cold and dirty shepherds if they don't get this show on the road soon."

"I'm not sure. There's Les, though. I'll run over and ask him."

Les stood near the floodlit manger scene holding on to one of his prize Guernseys. A young boy stood near him waiting to take over as soon as the other members of the cast were ready. All three looked contented even in the midst of the chaos surrounding them, though only the cow was contented enough to chew her cud.

"We're waiting for Mr. Howe's Holstein," the youngster informed them in response to Adrian's question.

"It's something of a privilege to have an animal in the Nativity," Adrian explained to Strauss. "Since there are so many cows in town, they draw lots."

"We always have to wait a little when it's B. B.'s turn," Les added.

Somehow the news didn't surprise Strauss much, even though the elder Howe had four strapping boys to clean up the cow.

"I didn't have a chance to thank you for the walking stick," Strauss said. "I don't know that I ever had a nicer gift made for me."

"You don't need it no more, I see," Les said, eyeing Strauss' limp.

"No, but in my line of work it never hurts to have the extra walking stick around the place. I'm sure I'll be using it again."

The only time Strauss had ever seen as much of a smile from Blake was when he had snatched the howling Elizabeth from the top of Strauss' head. He took it to be a good sign. He felt so cheered for some reason that he patted the cow.

At that moment, with the roar of a faulty muffler, followed by an equally loud human roar, the B. B. Howe and Sons (etc.) truck, now equipped with sideboards for hauling its privileged cargo, pulled up alongside the green. B. B. and one son, looking pretty much the same as they had the day of the shooting match, jumped out of the front. The other three boys emerged from the back of the truck when the tailgate was lowered for the cow. A hearty round of applause burst out as the cow made her way out of the truck, and no wonder. She was one of the black-and-white models that tourists made so popular

An Investigation of Local Color

in Vermont, and she had been scrubbed to spotless perfection, making her by far the cleanest of the Howes. B. B. himself proudly led her around for a moment to show her off before handing her off to the youngster assigned to her for the Nativity scene. That done, teachers and parents hustled their charges into their places, the Howes bought their bulbs, and procession was ready to begin.

On the far side of the green a more subdued Mary made an effort to climb aboard the donkey, who shied away from her costume despite the best efforts of a very youthful Joseph, who was dressed in what could only have been his mother's best striped bedsheet over his overalls and boots. A decidedly unbiblical-looking farmer stepped from the audience to loan a firm grownup hand to the donkey's halter, and the four made their way around the green to the manger, where the other animals and assorted shepherds and Wise Men waited. There was total silence except for the wind in the still-dark Christmas tree and the hoofbeats of the donkey. When they arrived at the manger Joseph, taking his job very seriously, helped Mary to the ground. The swaddled doll appeared from somewhere in the hay, and the scene was complete. After a few minutes of quiet, the school children sang "Away in a Manger" while a light was passed from candle to candle until they were all lit.

Strauss had always considered himself to be immune to sentiment, but he felt a chill go down his spine. The voices of the children, probably not totally in tune, nonetheless sounded like angels. He realized it had been a very long time since he had thought of Christmas in terms other than what it would cost him, either in overtime hours or in money. While more carols were sung, a line formed as the townsfolk made their way to the Remembrance Tree to screw in the lights that would remind them of their loved ones. Strauss watched as Adrian and Les lit their bulbs, he assumed in memory of their parents. Afterward, Les patted Adrian awkwardly on the shoulder before going back to watch over his cow. She, surprisingly, came back to stand near Strauss.

As soon as the tree was lit and everyone had had a moment to admire it, chaos broke loose again. The children, so angelic only seconds before, whipped off their bedsheets and headed into the Hook for hotdogs. Animals were packed back into their assorted conveyances. One of the firemen hauled a keg out the back door of the kitchen and tapped it. A line formed immediately. Someone else hauled a speaker from the jukebox inside out into the parking lot and some very un-Christmas-like music boomed forth.

"Here's some hot cider, you two." Franklyn Birch, with his wife in tow, handed over two steaming mugs.

Strauss took his, glad of something warm to drink. It was warmer than he imagined, though, and the burning had very little to do with the temperature.

"Oooh, you raided the adult punchbowl, didn't you?" Adrian asked after a gulp.

"You looked cold."

"Not anymore." She laughed and her cheeks flushed.

"What did you think of our Remembrance Ceremony?" Donnie asked as he joined them.

"Very nice," Strauss answered honestly.

Donnie's grin was full of mischief as usual. "We used to put candles on the tree, but one year we burned the thing down and damned near lit up the Hook as well. The only thing worse than having Hell freeze over would be having the Hook go up in smoke."

"If you think this was good, wait until you see the Fishing Derby," Jean told him.

Several glances were exchanged before Strauss felt he had to reply.

"Uh, I'm going back to Boston tomorrow, Jean."

"For good?"

"I told you that. Remember, the other night when you were making dinner?" Donnie reminded her.

"I'm afraid so," Strauss confirmed.

"Well, why in the world would you want to do that?"

Even though Strauss felt the reason to be fairly self-explanatory, and he had spent a bit of time explaining it already, all eyes were fixed on him awaiting yet another, more valid explanation..

An Investigation of Local Color

"Uh...," Strauss said, sounding like he had breakfasted once too often with Junior Thibault.

"Oh, put it off a few days, Detective," Madge said as if it were that easily done.

"A few days?"

"Just until after the Fishing Derby."

"And when's that?"

"A short time away. End of January. It would be foolish to miss it, Mr. Strauss."

Strauss felt very much on the spot. Beside him Adrian said nothing.

"She's right, Strauss," Franklyn agreed in his growling voice, his eyebrows lowered in his fiercest glower.

"I can't really. I need to get back."

"Hell, what's the hurry? What's so great about the city?" Donnie asked. "It's dirty, it's smelly, it's got crime."

Strauss thought it would be rude to point out that Benton Harbor had all of the above, so he merely said, "Besides, I don't have a place to live anymore."

"Sure you do. You can take Ira's apartment." Donnie grinned, having solved the problem.

"Donnie!" hissed his wife. Then she turned and smiled sweetly at Strauss.

So they were all in on it together.

"Well, he can!" Donnie said, protesting his scolding. "Come on, Nick. Just stay until the Fishing Derby, then go back to the city. Those criminal types will wait for you."

"Eeewww!" Jean said.

Strauss assumed her wrinkled-nose expression to be the result of her vision of criminal types as opposed to his own picture of dead fish bleeding on the ice while the people of Benton Harbor celebrated. It would be deer hunting season all over again.

"I guess I could do that," he agreed, "but only until the Fishing Derby. Then it's back to the city for me."

For the first time since the beginning of the conversation, Adrian turned toward him and smiled slightly.

"All right!" Franklyn growled. "Glad to see you have some sense, Strauss. Donnie, this calls for more cider."

So Strauss raised his mug with the rest of the citizens of Benton Harbor and drank enough to keep himself warm while he ate hotdogs and homemade baked beans and pie outside in the December cold. Afterward, he danced with what he thought must be every woman in town, including Gwenivere Dunfield, though that was a feat that required longer arms than he was ever going to possess. When he finally had a chance to ask Adrian, she smiled.

"Only because it's Christmas," she said.

Strauss found himself doing something he never would have imagined—dancing with a farm girl in a parking lot on a freezing December night with a lot of people who mostly milked cows for a living. And having a great time.